W9-AFC-944

SARAH MORGAN

Maybe This Christmas

HARLEQUIN® HQN™

If you purchased this book without a cover you should be aware that this book is stolen property. It was reported as "unsold and destroyed" to the publisher, and neither the author nor the publisher has received any payment for this "stripped book."

Recycling programs
for this product may
not exist in your area.

ISBN-13: 978-0-373-77898-0

Maybe This Christmas

Copyright © 2014 by Sarah Morgan

All rights reserved. Except for use in any review, the reproduction or utilization of this work in whole or in part in any form by any electronic, mechanical or other means, now known or hereinafter invented, including xerography, photocopying and recording, or in any information storage or retrieval system, is forbidden without the written permission of the publisher, Harlequin HQN, 225 Duncan Mill Road, Don Mills, Ontario M3B 3K9, Canada.

This is a work of fiction. Names, characters, places and incidents are either the product of the author's imagination or are used fictitiously, and any resemblance to actual persons, living or dead, business establishments, events or locales is entirely coincidental.

This edition published by arrangement with Harlequin Books S.A.

For questions and comments about the quality of this book, please contact us at CustomerService@Harlequin.com.

® and TM are trademarks of Harlequin Enterprises Limited or its corporate affiliates. Trademarks indicated with ® are registered in the United States Patent and Trademark Office, the Canadian Intellectual Property Office and in other countries.

Printed in U.S.A.

Praise for Sarah Morgan's acclaimed O'NEIL BROTHERS series

"Uplifting, sexy and warm,
Sarah Morgan's O'Neil Brothers series is perfection."
—Jill Shalvis, *New York Times* bestselling author

"This touching Christmas tale will draw
tears of sorrow and joy, remaining a reader favorite
for years to come."
—*Publishers Weekly,* starred review
on *Sleigh Bells in the Snow*

"No one does the double-edged sword of the holidays
like Sarah Morgan."
—*Dear Author* on *Sleigh Bells in the Snow*

"Morgan's foray into full-length romance
is a holiday hit. Her visual narrative epitomizes
rustic Vermont in full winter finery while
showcasing her witty humor and inherent understanding
of the human condition."
—*RT Book Reviews* on *Sleigh Bells in the Snow*

"Sarah Morgan puts the magic in Christmas."
—*NOW Magazine*

"Morgan's romantic page-turner will thrill readers.
The well-paced narrative is humorous [and] poignant…
The chemistry between the misunderstood hero
and the victimized heroine is combustible
[and] her storytelling rocks. Brava!"
—*RT Book Reviews* TOP PICK!
on *Suddenly Last Summer*

"Morgan charms readers with her second visit to
Snow Crystal, Vermont. Poignant and heartfelt, this
paradoxically warm contemporary will leave readers
eager for another visit."
—*Publishers Weekly* on *Suddenly Last Summer*

"Each book of hers that I discover is a treat."
—Sarah Wendell of *Smart Bitches, Trashy Books*

DEC 19 2014 ⑭ 12-2019 09-2017

**Also available from
Sarah Morgan
and Harlequin HQN**

The O'Neil Brothers
SUDDENLY LAST SUMMER
SLEIGH BELLS IN THE SNOW

And watch for the first book in Sarah's brand-new series
FIRST TIME IN FOREVER
Coming soon!

Maybe This Christmas

Dear Reader,

From the moment I first introduced Tyler O'Neil in *Sleigh Bells in the Snow*, I was looking forward to telling his story. I know from my emails that lots of readers are eagerly waiting to read about him, mostly because we all love a reformed bad boy!

Since the injury that ended his career as a medal-winning downhill skier, Tyler has been helping with the family business at Snow Crystal, Vermont. He is a single father raising his teenage daughter, Jess, a situation that brings challenges for a man used to putting himself first. He's had plenty of relationships, but the only woman who has been a constant in his life is Brenna, whom he has known since childhood. Brenna's feelings go way beyond friendship, but she knows Tyler doesn't see her that way. Or does he?

Tyler's story is a romance, but it also explores love in its widest sense and what it means to be a father, a son, a brother, a lover and a friend. Sometimes when I'm writing a story it takes me a while to work out the exact details of the final chapter, but with *Maybe This Christmas* I knew right away how I wanted this book to end, and writing it felt wonderful.

If you ask a writer to pick their favorite book they will usually tell you they love them all equally, and that's exactly what I'd say if you asked me that question—but if I *did* have a favorite then *Maybe This Christmas* would be right up there at the top of my list. I hope you love it, too.

Sarah
xx

PS Don't forget to visit my website and sign up to my mailing list to be sure to never miss a new book release!

www.sarahmorgan.com
Twitter: @SarahMorgan_
Facebook.com/AuthorSarahMorgan

To my parents, who taught me the importance of family.

3 1326 00499 4713

CHAPTER ONE

TYLER O'NEIL STOMPED the snow off his boots, pushed open the door of his lakeside home and tripped over a pair of boots and a jacket abandoned in the hallway.

Slamming his hand against the wall, he regained his balance and cursed. "Jess?" There was no response from his daughter, but Ash and Luna, his two Siberian huskies, bounded out of the living room. Cursing under his breath, he watched in exasperation as both dogs cannoned toward him. "*Jess?* You left the door to the living room open again. The dogs aren't supposed to be in there. Come down here right now and pick up your coat and boots! Do not jump up—*I'm warning you*—" He braced himself as Ash sprang. "Why does no one listen to me around here?"

Luna, the more gentle of the two dogs, put her paws on his chest and tried to lick his face.

"Nice to know my word is law." But Tyler rubbed her ears gently, burying his fingers in her thick fur as Jess emerged from the kitchen, a piece of toast in one hand and her phone in the other, head nodding in time to music as she pushed headphones away from her ears. She was wearing one of his sweaters, and the gold medal he'd won for the downhill dangled around her neck.

"Hi, Dad. How was your day?"

"I made it through alive until I stepped through my

own front door. I've skied off cliffs safer than our hall-way." Glowering at her, Tyler pushed the ecstatic dogs away and nudged the abandoned snow boots to one side with his foot. "Pick those up. And leave your boots on the porch from now on. You shouldn't be wearing them indoors."

Still chewing, Jess stared at his feet. "You're wearing your boots indoors."

Not for the first time, Tyler reflected on the challenges of parenting. "New rule. I'll leave mine outside, too. That way we don't get snow in the house. And hang your coat up instead of dropping it over any convenient surface."

"You drop yours."

Holy hell. "I'm hanging it up. Watch me." He shrugged out of his jacket and hung it up with exaggerated pur-pose. "And turn the music down. That way you'll be able to hear me when I'm yelling at you."

She grinned, unabashed. "I turn it up so I can't hear you yelling at me. Grandma just sent me a text all in capitals. You need to teach her how to use her phone."

"You're the teenager. You teach her."

"She texted me in capitals all last week, and the week before that she kept dialing Uncle Jackson by accident."

Tyler, entertained by the thought of his business-focused brother being driven insane by calls from their mother in the middle of his working day, grinned back. "I bet he loved that. So what did she want?"

"She was inviting me to come over when you're at the team meeting at the Outdoor Center. I'm going to help her cook." She took another bite of toast. "It's fam-ily night tonight. Everyone is coming, even Uncle Sean. Had you forgotten?"

Tyler groaned. "Team meeting and Fright Night? Whose idea was that?"

"Grandma's. She worries about me, because I live with you, and the only thing that never runs out in our fridge is beer. And you're not supposed to call it Fright Night. Can I come to the team meeting?"

"You would hate every moment."

"I wouldn't! I love being part of a family business. The way you feel about meetings is the way I feel about school. Being trapped indoors is a waste of time when there's all that snow out there. But at least you get to ski all day. I'm stuck to a hard chair trying to understand math. Pity me." She finished the toast, and Tyler frowned as crumbs fell on the floor.

Ash pounced on them with enthusiasm.

"You're the reason the fridge is empty. You're always eating. If I'd known you were going to eat this much, I never would have let you live with me. You're costing me a fortune."

The fact his joke made her laugh told him how far they'd come in the year they'd been living together.

"Grandma says if I wasn't living with you, you'd drown in your own mess."

"You're the one dropping the crumbs. You should use a plate."

"You never use a plate. You're always dropping crumbs on the floor."

"You don't have to do everything I do."

"You're the grown-up. I'm following your example."

The thought was enough to bring him out in a cold sweat. "Don't. You should do the opposite of everything I have ever done." He watched as Jess bent to make a fuss of Luna, and the medal around her neck swung forward, almost hitting the dog on the nose. "Why are you wearing that?"

"It motivates me. And I like the example you set. You're the coolest dad on the planet. And you're fun to live with. Especially when you're trying to behave."

"Trying to—" Tyler dragged his gaze from the medal that was a painful reminder of his old life. "What's that supposed to mean?"

"I mean I like living here. You don't worry about the same stuff as most grown-ups."

"I'm probably supposed to." Tyler ran his hand over the back of his neck. "I have a new respect for your grandmother. How did Mom raise three boys without strangling us?"

"Grandma would never strangle anyone. She's patient and kind."

"Yeah, right. Unfortunately for you, I'm not, and I'm the one raising you now." The reality of that still terrified him more than anything he'd faced on the downhill ski circuit. If he messed this up, the consequences would be worse than a damaged leg and a shattered career. "So have you finished your assignment?"

"No. I started, but I got distracted watching the recording of your downhill in Beaver Creek. Come and watch it with me."

He'd rather poke himself in the eye with a ski pole.

"Maybe later. I had a call from your teacher." Casually, he changed the subject. "You didn't hand in your assignment on Monday."

"Luna ate it."

"Sure she did. You are allowed one late assignment in each trimester. You've already had two."

"Weren't you ever late handing in assignments?"

All the time.

Wondering why anyone would choose to have more than one kid when being a parent was this hard, Tyler tried a different approach. "If you have five late assignments, you'll be staying late at homework club. That cuts into your skiing time."

That wiped the smile from her face. "I'll get it done."

"Good decision. And next time, finish your homework before you watch TV."

"I wasn't watching TV. I was watching you. I want to understand your technique. You were the best. I'm going to ski every spare minute this winter." She closed her hand around the medal, making it sound like a vow. "Will you be at race training tomorrow? You said you'd try to be there."

Floored by that undiluted adoration, Tyler looked into his daughter's eyes and saw the same passion that burned in his own.

He thought of all the jobs that were piling up at Snow Crystal. Jobs that needed his attention. Then he thought about the years he'd missed out on being with his daughter. "I'll be there." He strolled through to his recently renovated kitchen, cursing under his breath as cold seeped through his socks. "Jess, you've been dripping snow through the whole house. It's like wading through a river."

"That was Luna. She rolled in a snowdrift and then shook herself."

"Next time she can shake herself outside our house."

"I didn't want her to get cold." Watching him, Jess pushed her hair behind her ear. "You called it *our* house."

"She's a dog, Jess! She has thick fur. She doesn't get cold. And of course I called it *our* house. What else would

I call it? We both live here, and right now there's no chance of me forgetting that!" He stepped over another patch of water. "I've spent the past couple of years renovating this place, and I still feel as if I need to wear my boots indoors."

"I love Ash and Luna. They're family. I never had a dog in Chicago. Mom hated mess. We never had a real Christmas tree, either. She hated those because she had to pick up the needles."

Tension and irritation fled. The mention of Jess's mother made Tyler feel as if someone had stuffed snow down his neck. Suddenly, it wasn't only his feet that were cold.

He clamped his mouth down on the comment that wanted to leave his lips. The truth was that Janet Carpenter had hated just about everything. She'd hated Vermont, she'd hated living so far from a city, she'd hated skiing. Most of all, she'd hated him. But his family had made it a rule not to say a bad word about Janet in front of Jess, and he stuck to that rule even when the strain of it brought him close to bursting. "We'll have a real tree this year. We'll take a trip into the forest and choose one together." Aware that he might be overcompensating, he reverted back to his normal self. "And I'm glad you love the dogs, but that doesn't change the fact you should keep the damn living room door closed when they're in the house. This place is no longer a construction site. The new rule is no dogs on sofas or on beds."

"I think Luna prefers the old rules." Her eyes sparkled with mischief. "And you're not supposed to say damn. Grams hates it when you swear."

Tyler kept his jaw tightened. "Well, Grams isn't here, is she?" His grandmother and grandfather still lived at the resort, in the converted sugarhouse that had once been the hub of Snow Crystal's maple syrup production. "And if you tell her, I'll throw you on your butt in the snow, and you'll be wetter than Luna. Now go and finish your assignment or I'll get the bad parent award, and I'm not prepared to climb onto the podium to collect that one."

Jess beamed. "If I promise to hand in my assignment and not tell anyone you swear, can we watch skiing together in your den later?"

"You should ask Brenna. She's a gifted teacher." He was about to reach for a beer when he remembered he was supposed to be setting an example, so poured himself a glass of milk instead. Since Jess had moved in, he'd disciplined himself not to drink from the carton. "She'll tell you what everyone is doing wrong."

"She's already promised to help me now I've made the school ski team. Have you seen her in the gym? She has sick abs."

"Yeah, I've seen her." And he didn't let himself think about her abs.

He didn't let himself think about any part of her.

She was his best friend, and she was staying that way.

To take his mind off the thought of Brenna's abs, he stuck his head back in the fridge. "This fridge is empty."

"Kayla's giving me a lift into the village later so I'll pick something up." Her phone beeped, and she dug it out of her pocket. "Oh—"

Tyler pushed the door shut with his shoulder and then caught sight of her expression. "What's wrong?"

"Kayla texted to say she's tied up with work, that's all."

"Sounds painful. Never mind. I'll go to the store tomorrow."

Jess stared at her phone. "I need to go now."

"Why? We both hate shopping. It can wait."

"This can't wait." Her head was down, but he saw color streak across her cheekbones.

"Is this about Christmas? Because it's not for another couple of weeks. We still have plenty of time. Most of my shopping gets done at three o'clock on Christmas Eve."

"It's not about Christmas! Dad, I need—" she broke off, her face scarlet "—some things from the store, that's all."

"What can you possibly need that can't wait until tomorrow?"

"Girl stuff, okay? I need girl stuff!" Snapping at him, she spun on her heel and stalked out of the room leaving Tyler staring after her, trying to understand the reason for the sudden mood explosion.

Girl stuff?

It took him a moment, and then he closed his eyes briefly and swore under his breath.

Girl stuff.

Comprehension came along with a moment of pure panic. Nothing in his past life had prepared him to raise a teenager. Especially not a teenage girl.

When had she—?

He glanced toward the door, knowing he had to say something, but clueless as to the most sensitive way to broach a topic that embarrassed the hell out of both of them.

Could he ignore it?

Tell her to search the internet?

He ran his hand over his face and cursed under his breath, knowing he couldn't ignore it or leave something that important to a search engine.

It wasn't as if she had her mother to ask. He was the only parent in her life. And right now she was probably thinking that was a raw deal.

"Jess!" He yelled after her, and when there was no response, he strode out of the kitchen and found her tugging her boots on in the hall. "Get in the car. I'll take you to the store."

"Forget it." Her voice was muffled, her hair falling forward over her face. "I'm going to walk over to the house and ask Grandma to drive me."

"Grandma hates driving in the snow and the dark. I'll take you." His voice was rougher than he intended, and he stretched out a hand to touch her shoulder and then pulled it back. To hug or not to hug? He had no idea. "I was going to the store anyway."

"You were going tomorrow, not today."

"Well, now I'm going today." He grabbed his coat. "Come on. We'll pick up some of that chocolate you like."

Still not looking at him, she fiddled with her boots, and he sighed, wishing for the hundredth time that teenage girls came with an operating manual.

"Jess, it's all good."

"It's not good," she muttered in a strangled tone, "it's like a *massive* avalanche of awkward! You're thinking this is your worst nightmare."

"I'm not thinking that." He gripped the door handle. "I'm thinking I'm messing it up. I'm saying the wrong things and making you feel uncomfortable, which is not my intention."

She peeped at him through her hair. "You're wishing I'd never come to live here."

He'd thought they'd got past that. The insecurity.

Those creeping, confidence-eroding doubts that had eaten away at her happiness. "I'm not wishing that."

"Mom told me she wished I'd never been born."

Tyler zipped up his jacket viciously, almost removing a finger in the process. "She didn't mean that." He dragged open the door, grateful for the blast of freezing air to cool his temper.

"Yes, she did." Jess mumbled the words. "She told me I was the worst thing that ever happened to her."

"Well, I've never thought that. Not once. Not even when my socks are wet because you've let the dogs drag snow into the house."

"You didn't sign up for any of this." Her voice faltered, and the uncertainty in her eyes made him want to punch a hole through something.

"I tried to. I asked your mom to marry me."

"I know. She said no because she thought you'd be a useless father. I heard her telling my stepdad. She said you were irresponsible."

Tyler felt the emotion rush at him. "Yeah, well, that may be true, but it doesn't change the fact I wanted you, Jess, right from the start. And when your mother wouldn't agree to marry me, I tried other ways of having you live here with us. Why the hell are we talking about this now?"

"Because it's the truth. I *was* a mistake." Jess gave a tiny shrug as if it didn't matter, and because he knew how much it mattered, he hesitated, knowing that the way he responded was vitally important to the way she felt about this whole situation.

"We didn't exactly plan to have you, that's true. I'm not going to lie about that, but you can't plan every single thing that happens in life. People think they can.

They think they can control things and then whoosh—something happens that proves you're not as in control as you think. And sometimes it's the things you don't plan that turn out best."

"I wasn't one of those things. Mom told me I was the biggest mistake of her life."

His hands clenched into fists and he had to force himself to stay calm. "She was probably upset or tired."

"It was the time I snowboarded down the stairs."

Tyler managed a smile. "Right, well, there you go. That's why." He dragged her against him and hugged her, feeling her skinny body and the familiar scent of her hair. His daughter. *His child.* "You're the best thing that happened to me. You're an O'Neil all the way, and sometimes that drives your mom a little crazy, that's all. She doesn't have that much love for us O'Neils. But she loves you. I know she does." He didn't know that, but he reined in his natural urge to speak the truth.

"Her family isn't close like ours, and that makes her jealous." Her voice was muffled against his chest, and he felt her arms tighten around him.

"You may skip classes, but you're not stupid."

Jess pulled away, her cheeks streaked pink. "Is that why you don't want to ever get married? Because of what happened with Mom?"

How was he supposed to answer that?

He'd learned that with Jess, the questions came with no warning. She bottled stuff up and held it inside until she burst with trying to contain it.

"Some people aren't the marrying type, and I'm one of those."

"Why?"

Tyler decided he'd rather ski a vertical slope in the

dark with his eyes closed than have this conversation. "All people are good at some things and bad at others. I'm bad at relationships. I don't make women happy." *Just ask your mother.* "Women who care about me often end up being hurt."

"So you're never going to get involved with anyone again? Dad, that's really dumb."

"You're telling me I'm dumb? What happened to respect?"

"All I'm saying is it's okay to make mistakes when you're young. Everyone messes up sometimes. It shouldn't stop you trying again when you're older."

"Jess—"

"Maybe you'll be better at it now you've got me. If you want to know how the female mind works, you can ask," she said generously, and Tyler opened his mouth and closed it again.

"Thanks, sweetheart. I appreciate that." Deciding that the conversation was getting more awkward, not less, he dug out his car keys. "Now get in the car before both of us freeze in the doorway. We need to get to the store before it closes."

"It would have been easier for you if I'd been a boy. Then we wouldn't have to have embarrassing conversations."

"Don't you believe it. Teenage boys are the worst. I know. I was one. And I'm not embarrassed." Tyler's tongue felt thick in his mouth. "Why would I be embarrassed by something that's a normal part of growing up? If there's anything you want to ask—" *please, God, don't let there be anything she wanted to ask* "—you come straight out and say it."

She tugged on her boots. "I'm good. But I need to get to the store."

He grabbed her coat and thrust it at her. "Wrap up. It's freezing out there."

"Can Ash and Luna come?"

"On a trip to the store?" He was about to ask why he would want to take two hyperactive dogs on a trip to the village, but then saw her hopeful expression and decided the dogs might be the best cure for awkward. And hopefully, they'd take her mind off her mom and the complexity of human relationships. "Sure. Great idea. Nothing I love more than two panting animals while I'm driving. But you'll have to keep them under control."

Jess whistled for Ash and Luna, who came bounding out, ecstatic at the promise of a trip.

Tyler drove out of Snow Crystal, slowing down for the guests who were returning from a day on the slopes.

The resort was half-empty, but it was still early in the season, and he knew visitor numbers would double once the Christmas break arrived.

And across the Atlantic in Europe, the Alpine Ski World Cup was underway.

He tightened his grip on the wheel, grateful that Jess was chattering away. Grateful for the distraction.

"Uncle Jackson told me the snowmaking is going really well. Loads of runs are open. Do you think we might have a big fall of snow? Uncle Sean is here." She talked nonstop as she stroked Luna. "I saw his car earlier. Gramps said he was here for the meeting, but I don't get why. He's a surgeon. He doesn't get involved in running the business. Or is he going to be here to fix broken legs?"

"Uncle Sean is working up a preconditioning program

with Christy at the spa. They're trying to reduce ski-ing injuries. It was Brenna's idea." Tyler slowed as they reached the main highway and turned toward the village. The snow was falling steadily, coating the windshield and the road ahead.

"How come Brenna is the one in charge of the outdoor program when you're the one with the gold medal?"

"Because Uncle Jackson had already given her the job before I came home, and because I hate organization almost as much as I hate shopping and cooking. I'm only interested in the skiing part. And Brenna is a great teacher. She's patient and kind, whereas I want to dump people in a snowdrift if they don't get it right the first time." He glanced briefly in his rearview mirror. "Are you going to sleep over with Grandma tonight?"

"Do you want me to? Are you planning on having sex or something?"

Tyler almost swerved into the ditch. "Jess—"

"What? You said I could talk to you about anything."

He steadied the car. Focused on the road. "You can't ask me if I'm planning on having sex."

"Why? I don't want to get in the way, that's all."

"You don't get in the way." He wondered why this conversation had to come up while he was driving in difficult conditions. "You never get in the way."

"Dad, I'm not stupid. You used to have a lot of sex. I know. I read about it on the internet. This one article said you could get a woman in bed faster than you could make it to the bottom of the slope in the downhill."

Feeling as if he'd been hit by another avalanche of awkward, Tyler slowed right down as he approached the village. Lights twinkled in store windows, and a large Christmas tree stood proudly at the end of Main Street.

"You don't want to believe everything you read on the internet."

"All I'm saying is, you don't have to give up sex just because I'm living with you. You need to get out there again."

Speechless, he pulled into a parking space by the village store. "I'm not having this conversation with my thirteen-year-old daughter."

"I'm nearly fourteen. You need to keep up."

"Whatever. My sex life is off-limits."

"Did you ever have sex with Brenna? Was she one of the ones you had a relationship with?"

How was it possible to sweat when the air temperature was below freezing? "That is personal, Jess."

"So you *did* have sex with her?"

"No! I never had sex with Brenna." Sex with Brenna was something he didn't allow himself to think about. Ever. He didn't think about those abs. He didn't think about those legs. "And this conversation is over and done."

"Because it would be fine with me. I think she really likes you. Do you like her?"

Realizing he'd just been given permission to have sex by his teenage daughter, Tyler raked his fingers through his hair. "Yeah, of course I do. I've known her since we were kids. We've hung around together for most of our lives. She's a good friend."

And he wasn't going to do anything to damage that. Nothing. Not a damn thing.

He'd messed up every relationship he'd ever had. His friendship with Brenna was the one thing that was still intact, and he intended to keep it that way.

Jess unclipped her seat belt. "I like Brenna. She's not

all gooey eyed about you like some women are. And she talks to me like a grown-up. If you could give me some money, I'll go and buy what I need. I'll buy some stuff for the fridge, too, so if Grandma drops by she'll be impressed by your housekeeping."

"Gooey eyed?" Tyler pulled his wallet out of his pocket. "What is that supposed to mean?"

Jess shrugged. "Like some of the moms at school. They all wear makeup and tight clothes, in case you're picking me up. The other day when Kayla picked me up, there was almost a riot. Sometimes the other girls want to know if you're coming or not. I guess their moms don't want to bother with the whole lipstick thing if you're not going to show up."

Tyler stared at her. "Are you serious?"

"Yeah, but it's okay." Jess tugged her coat around her skinny frame. "I'm cool with the fact my dad is a national sex symbol. But if you're going to pick someone I have to live with and call Mom, I'd like you to pick someone like Brenna, that's all. She doesn't flick her hair all the time and look at you with a dopey smile."

"No one is coming to live with us, you won't be calling anyone *Mom* and, for the final time, I'm not going to have sex with Brenna." Tyler spoke through clenched teeth. "Now go buy whatever it is you need."

Jess slid down in her seat. "I can't." Her voice was strangled. "Mr. Turner has just gone in there with his son, who is in my class. I want to die."

Tyler breathed deeply and then rummaged in the mess in his car until he found an old restaurant bill and a pen. "Make me a list."

"I'll wait until they've gone." It was dark in the car, but he could see she was scarlet again.

"Jess, we need to do this before we both die of hypothermia."

She hesitated and then snatched the pen and scribbled.

"Wait here." Tyler took the bill from her and walked into the store. If he could ski Austria's notorious *Hahnenkamm* at a speed of 90 mph, he could buy *girl stuff*.

TEN MINUTES LATER, Brenna Daniels walked into the store, relieved to be out of the bitter cold.

Ellen Kelly came out from the room behind the counter, carrying three large boxes. "Brenna! Your mother was in here earlier today. Told me she hadn't seen you for a month."

"I've been busy. Can I help you with those, Ellen?" Brenna took the boxes from her and stacked them on the floor. "You shouldn't carry so many at once. The doctor told you to be careful lifting."

"I'm careful. Storm's coming, and people like to stock up in case they're snowed in for a month. We're all hoping it's not going to be as bad as 2007. Remember Valentine's Day?"

"I was in Europe, Ellen."

"That's right, you were. I forgot. No snow at all in January, and then three feet in twenty-four hours. Ned Morris lost some of his cows when the barn roof fell in." Ellen rubbed her back. "By the way, you just missed him."

"Ned Morris?"

"Tyler." Ellen bent and opened one of the boxes. "And he had Jess with him. I swear she's grown a foot over the summer."

"Tyler was here?" Brenna's heart pounded a little harder. "We have a meeting back at the resort in an hour."

"I'm guessing they had an emergency. Jess stayed

in the car, and he came in and bought everything she needed. And I do mean everything." Ellen Kelly winked knowingly and started unpacking the boxes and transferring the contents to the shelves. "I never thought I'd see Tyler O'Neil in here shopping for a teenage girl. I remember people had nothing but bad to say about him when Janet Carpenter announced she was pregnant, but he's proved them all wrong. That Janet is as cold as a Vermont winter, but Tyler—" she arranged cans on the shelf "—he may be a bad boy with the women, but no one can say he hasn't done right by that child."

"She's almost fourteen."

"And looking like a different person from the one who arrived here last winter, all skinny and pale. Can you imagine? What sort of mother sends a child away like that?" Ellen clucked her disapproval and bent to open another box, this one packed with Christmas decorations. "Disgraceful."

Brenna was careful to keep her opinion on that to herself. "Janet had a new baby."

"So she gave up the old one? All the more reason to keep Jess close, in my opinion." Ellen hung long garlands of tinsel on hooks. "She could have been scarred for life. Lucky she has Tyler and the rest of the O'Neils. Would you like decorations, honey? I have a big selection this year."

"No thanks, Ellen. I don't decorate. And Jess isn't scarred. She's a lovely girl." Loyal and discreet, Brenna tried to steer the conversation in a different direction. She didn't mention the insecurities or any of the problems she knew Jess had suffered settling in. "Did you know she made the school ski team? She has real talent."

"She's her father's daughter all right. I still remember

that winter when Tyler skied down old Mitch Sommer-ville's roof." Smiling, Ellen sat an oversize smiling Santa on a shelf. "He was arrested of course, but my George always said he'd never seen a person so fearless on the mountain. Except you, perhaps. The two of you were inseparable. Used to watch you sneaking out when you should have been in class."

"Me? You've got the wrong person, Ellen." Brenna grinned at her. "I never sneaked out of school in my life."

"Must be a real blow for Tyler, losing his career like that. Especially when he was right at the top."

Brenna, who would rather jump naked into a freezing lake than talk about another person's private business, made a desperate attempt to change the subject. "There's plenty to keep him busy up at Snow Crystal. Bookings are up. Looks like it might be a busy winter."

"That's good to hear. That family deserves it. No one was more shocked than me to hear the place was in trou-ble. The O'Neils have lived at Snow Crystal since before I was born. Still, Jackson seems to have turned it around. There were people around here who thought he'd made a mistake when he spent all that money building fancy log cabins with hot tubs, but turns out he knew what he was doing."

"Yes." Brenna picked up the few things she needed, wondering if there was such a thing as private business living in a small town. "He's a clever businessman."

"He's always known his own mind. And that girl of his—"

"Kayla?"

"Her heart is in the right place even if she does walk in here with those shiny shoes looking all New York City."

Brenna added milk to her basket. "She's British."

"You wouldn't know it until she opens her mouth. Take some of those chocolate cookies while you're there. They're delicious. Not that you're short of good things to eat at Snow Crystal, with Élise in charge of the kitchen. Now that Jackson and Sean are settled, it will be Tyler's turn next."

Brenna dropped the jar she was holding, and it smashed, spreading the contents across the floor. *Crap.* "Oh, Ellen, I'm so sorry. I'll clean it up. Do you have a mop?" Annoyed with herself, she stooped to pick up the pieces, but Ellen waved her aside.

"Leave it. I don't want you cutting your fingers. There was a time when I thought the two of you might end up together. You couldn't be separated."

Double crap.

"We were friends, Ellen." This conversation was the last thing she needed. "And we're still friends."

By the time she left the store, she was exhausted from dodging gossip and thinking about Tyler.

She drove straight back to Snow Crystal and parked outside the Outdoor Center next to Sean's flashy red sports car. The snow was falling steadily, the path already covered with half a foot of white powder. The temperature had dropped, and there was the promise of more snow in the air, which was good news for Snow Crystal because snow cover was directly related to the number of Christmas bookings.

And they needed those bookings.

Despite what she'd said to Ellen, she knew the resort was still struggling to stay afloat. The log cabins, each with its own hot tub and private view of the lake and forest, had been expensive to build. For the past two years they'd had more cabins empty than occupied. Things were slowly improving, but they still had too many vacancies.

Brenna stamped the snow off her boots, pushed open the door and was enveloped by a welcome rush of warm air. She walked through to the peace and tranquility of the spa. The lighting was muted, the walls a soothing shade of ocean-blue. Soft music played in the background, and the air was filled with the scent of aromatherapy oils. It tickled her nose, but then she'd never been one to lie around and let someone she didn't know rub oil into her skin. It seemed intimate to her. Something a lover might do, not a stranger.

Not that lovers played much of a part in her life.

Christy, who had joined them in the summer to run the spa, glanced up from behind the desk. A mini Christmas tree twinkled from the corner of her desk. "Still snowing out there?" She was a cool blonde, a qualified physiotherapist who had added massage and aromatherapy to her already impressive list of qualifications. "You've had a long day. Is it always as crazy as this at the beginning of a winter season?"

"There's a lot of planning and preparation, that's for sure." Brenna pulled her hat off her head, sending another flurry of snowflakes to the floor. "Is everyone here already?"

"We're still waiting for Élise, and—"

"*Merde,* I am late." Élise, the head chef, sped past her like a whirlwind. "We are full in the restaurant tonight and also there is a party of thirty who booked out the Boathouse for an anniversary dinner. I don't have time for this. And I know already my plan for the winter season, which is to give people the best food they 'ave ever tasted. I will see you in the gym first thing tomorrow,

Brenna. I'm sorry I missed this morning. It is the first time for months but we were crazy in the kitchen."

"It's Christmas, and your restaurant is the one part of this resort that has never been in trouble." Brenna pushed her hat into her pocket. "You're stressed. You only ever drop the *h* when you're stressed."

"Of course I am stressed. I am doing the work of eight people, and now I am expected to sit in a meeting." Disgusted, Élise strode off, as light on her feet as a dancer, her shiny cap of dark hair swinging around her jaw.

Christy raised her eyebrows. "Is she caffeinated?"

"No, she's French." Brenna glanced out the window. "I saw Sean's car, so I guess that means everyone is here?"

"Everyone but Tyler. He's late. I texted him but he hasn't replied."

"He's probably turned the ringer off on his phone. He does that a lot. He used to have to change his number once a month because women kept calling him."

"I'm not surprised. The man is so insanely hot, I disconnect the smoke alarm whenever he walks through that door. I saw him in the gym this morning, which was a special treat given he usually uses the one in his house. The guy can bench press the weight of a car." Christy fanned herself with her fingers. "I'm thinking of adding his name to the list of attractions at Snow Crystal."

"He's already on the list. Kayla has talked him into doing a few motivational talks, and he occasionally acts as a guide for experienced skiers who are willing to pay a price to ski with Tyler O'Neil." And she knew he hated it. He wasn't interested in fame or adulation, just in skiing down a mountain as fast as possible. He didn't want to talk about what he did; he just wanted to do it. Other people didn't seem to understand that, but she did. She understood the love of the snow and the speed. "He'll turn up when he's ready, as he always does. He operates in his own way, in his own time."

"I love that about him. It's a very sexy trait. I guess you don't notice. You've known the O'Neils your whole life. They're probably like brothers to you."

How was she supposed to answer that? Two out of the three O'Neils were like brothers, that was true. As for the third—she'd long since reconciled herself to the fact Tyler O'Neil didn't return her feelings, and she'd learned the hard way that dreaming made things worse. As children they'd been inseparable. As adults—well, things hadn't turned out the way she'd once hoped they might, but she'd learned to live with it. She knew better than to wish for something that was never going to happen. She had her feet firmly on the ground, and if her brain ever wandered in that direction then she pulled it back fast.

"You're lucky—" Christy fed a fresh stack of paper into the printer "—you get to work with the guy every day."

And that probably should have been hard. When she'd accepted Jackson's offer of a job running the outdoor program for Snow Crystal Resort, she hadn't known she'd be working with Tyler.

But it wasn't hard.

Working with Tyler was one of the things she loved most about her job. She got to spend most days with the man of her dreams.

She'd tried curing herself. She'd tried dating other men; she'd even worked abroad, but Tyler was wedged in her heart, and she'd long since accepted that wasn't going to change.

And if over the years it had hurt her to see him with

women, she consoled herself with the fact that the women in his life came and went, whereas their friendship had lasted forever.

"How is the spa doing? Are you going to be busy over Christmas?"

"It's looking that way." Christy keyed something into the computer, her perfectly manicured nails tapping the keyboard, her shiny blond hair curving around her smooth cheeks. "I'm fully booked for the Christmas week."

"You're doing a good job, Christy." Brenna wondered how many hours it took to look as polished as Christy. As a child, she'd barely sat still long enough for her mother to drag a brush through her hair. She'd hated ribbons and bows and shiny shoes, which had come as a disappointment to a woman who had longed for a little girl who would wear pink and play quietly with dolls. All Brenna had wanted to do was climb trees and play in the dirt along with the three O'Neil boys. She'd envied them the freedom of their lives and envied their close family, so accepting and supportive.

The O'Neil boys weren't expected to be a certain way or satisfy a set of rules before they were loved.

She'd wanted to do everything they did, whether it was climbing trees or skiing steep slopes. She didn't care how messy or dirty she was; she didn't care if she came home with scraped knees and torn clothes. With them, she'd felt accepted in a way she never was at home or at school.

"So is Tyler seeing anyone at the moment?" Christy's voice was casual. "I guess there's a line."

"He's not known for long-term relationships."

"Sounds like my type of guy." Christy inputted some

figures into the spreadsheet. "I love them wild. All the more fun when you tame them."

"I'm not sure Tyler can be tamed." And she didn't want Tyler tamed. She didn't want a different version of him. She wanted him the way he was.

"So what's a guy like him doing here? I mean, Snow Crystal is lovely, but it's more of a family resort than a hive for the rich and famous."

"Tyler loves Snow Crystal. He grew up here. And this is a family business. He does what he can to help." And she knew it half killed him to no longer be competing. "If we get another fall of snow in the next few days, it might tempt a few more people to book. I know Kayla is putting together some packages."

"Yes, I've been working on a nonskier program with her. And talking of Kayla—" Christy rummaged in the drawer of her desk "—can you give this to her? It came in this morning, and I forgot to tell her. It's nail polish. The shade is Ice Crystal. She's going to use it in a promotion she's doing. Has she mentioned her plans for an ice party to you?"

"No."

"She's planning a pre-Christmas event here for locals as well as guests. An ice party. Fire pit, ice sculpture, sled dogs, hot food, fireworks—it sounds fabulous."

"I can't wait to hear more. Aren't you joining us for the meeting?"

"No. There are only two of us in today. Angie has the flu so I'm covering the phones, and anyway I'm not sure I can cope with all that O'Neil testosterone in one room. What do you think of the nail polish? It's pretty, don't you think? Perfect for the holiday party season."

Brenna turned the bottle over in her hand, watching

it sparkle in the light. "I spend most of my day with my hands in thick mittens, or else I'm chipping my nails hauling skis all over the resort, so I can't honestly say Ice Crystal is going to have much of a place in my life, but yes, it's very sparkly."

It was the sort of thing her mother would have liked her to wear.

"You should come in and have a spa morning before we get busy. My treat. I could massage away all those skiing aches. And you must tell me what you do to your hair. It's so shiny. I want a bottle of whatever you're using." Christy's expression changed from friendly to feline as the door opened, letting in a blast of cold air. She smoothed her already smooth sheet of blond hair and smiled. "Hi!"

Brenna didn't need to turn her head to see who had walked in. Any one of the three O'Neil brothers might have caused a woman to sit up straighter and moisten her lips, but given that two out of the three were already in the meeting room, she knew exactly who was standing behind her.

Her heart lifted along with her mood as it always did when Tyler walked into a room.

"Hi, Bren." Tyler slapped her on the shoulders with the same casual affection he showed his brothers, his attention focused on Christy, whose eyelashes were working overtime.

"You're late, Tyler. Everyone else is here."

"Saving the best until last." He winked at her. "So how's it going here in Beauty Central?"

Brenna watched as Christy's cheeks turned a little pinker. The same thing happened every time Tyler O'Neil smiled at a woman. He radiated energy, and the combination of dark good looks, masculine vitality and casual charm proved an irresistible combination.

"It's going great." Christy leaned forward, giving him the full benefit of her green eyes and cleavage. "We're busier than last year, and Kayla and I have been working out some great ski/spa promotions. Anytime you fancy a massage, let me know." She flirted easily, naturally, as most women did when they were around Tyler.

Brenna was hopeless at flirting. She didn't have that way of looking, that way of smiling—but most of all, she didn't have the clever words.

Christy used words like a rope, throwing them out, using them to draw him in like a wild horse being broken.

Watching the show, Brenna felt as if her heart were being squeezed in someone's hands.

She was about to melt away quietly to the meeting room when Tyler caught her arm.

"Did you hear the forecast?" His eyes gleamed with anticipation and she nodded, reading his mind.

"Heavy snow. Good for business."

"Powder day. Good for us. What about it? Deep snow, backcountry and just the two of us making tracks the way we used to when we were kids." His voice was a soft, sexy purr and she felt her knees weaken as they always did when she was this close to him.

She consoled herself with the fact that this was something she shared with him that Christy couldn't. She might not be able to flirt, but she could ski. And she skied well. She was one of the few people who could almost keep up with him.

Ellen was right that they'd skipped classes.

On one occasion, her mother had been called down to the school, but the tense atmosphere at home in the aftermath of that confrontation had been worth it for those few blissful hours spent alone with Tyler doing what they both loved best.

But there was no skipping anything now.

They both had responsibilities. "I'll have to get in line. We have a waiting list of people willing to pay good money to ski powder with you."

His smile faded. "Lucky me." He let his hand drop and turned back to Christy, who had somehow managed to apply another layer of gloss to her lips in the short time Tyler's head had been turned.

She smiled, giving him the full effect. "I expect you're looking forward to skiing the hell out of those slopes. I watched a replay of your medal-winning run the other day on TV. You were unbelievably fast."

Knowing it was a sensitive subject, Brenna glanced quickly at Tyler, but his expression didn't change. There was nothing in that wickedly handsome face to suggest this situation was difficult for him.

But she knew it was. It had to be, because Tyler O'Neil had lived to race.

From the moment he'd strapped on his first set of skis, he'd been addicted to the speed and adrenaline of downhill. It had been a passion. Some might have said an addiction.

And then he'd fallen.

Thinking about that day made her stomach turn. She could still remember the gut-wrenching terror of waiting to hear if he was dead or alive.

The whole family had been there to support him while he raced, and because she'd been working for Jackson in Europe, she'd been there, too. They'd stood in the grandstand, watching skiers hurtle down at brutal speeds, wait-

ing for Tyler. Instead of beating them all and ending the
season triumphant, he'd fallen and ended his downhill
career for good. He'd spun, twisted and crashed heavily
before sliding down the near vertical run and slamming
into the netting. Like all skiers, he'd had falls before, but
this one was different.

There had been screams from the crowd and then the
murmur of anticipation followed by the dreaded stillness
and the breathless agony of waiting.

Trapped in the crowd, Brenna had been unable to do
anything but watch helplessly as he'd been lifted, seriously injured, into the helicopter. There had been blood
on the snow, and she'd closed her eyes, breathed in the
freezing air and begged whoever might be listening,
please let him live. And she'd promised herself that as
long as he survived, she'd stop wanting the impossible.

She'd stop wanting what she couldn't have.

She'd stop hoping he'd return her feelings.

She'd stop hoping he'd fall in love with her.

She'd never complain about anything ever again.

As she'd waited for news along with the rest of his
family, she'd told herself she didn't care who he was with,
as long as he was alive.

But of course that promise, made in the scalding heat
of fear, hadn't been easy to keep. Even less so now, when
they worked alongside each other every day.

She'd witnessed his frustration at being forced to give
up the racing career he loved. He hid his feelings under
layers of bad-boy attitude, but she knew it hurt him. She
knew he ached to be back racing.

He was a gifted athlete, and it made her sad to see him
standing on the sidelines or coaching a group of kids. It
was like watching an injured racehorse trapped in a rid-

ing school when the only place he wanted to be was on the track, winning.

She hadn't made a sound, but he turned his head and looked at her.

He had the O'Neil eyes, that vivid, intense blue that reminded her of the sky on the most perfect skiing day. A knot of tension formed in her stomach. A dangerous lethargy spread through her body. Neither Jackson nor Sean had this effect on her. Only Tyler. For a moment she thought she saw something flicker in those blue depths, and then he gave her a slow, lazy smile.

"You ready, Bren? If I'm going to die of boredom, I don't want to do it alone."

No matter how bad the day, Tyler always made her laugh. She loved his wicked sense of humor and his indifference to authority. If he did something, then it was because it made sense to him, because he believed in it, not because it was laid out in a rulebook.

As someone who had grown up with the rulebook stuck in her face, she envied his cool determination to live life on his terms. He had a wild streak, but his downhill skiing career had fed his desire to duel with danger and provided an outlet for that excess energy. How he would have used that wild streak had he not been a skier had been the subject of endless speculation both in the village and on the world-cup circuit.

He threw a final smile in Christy's direction and strolled toward the meeting room, six foot three inches of raw sex appeal and lethal charm.

Brenna followed more slowly, giving herself a lecture.

It was the beginning of the season. She had to start as she meant to go on—being realistic about her relationship with Tyler.

He saw her as "one of the boys." A ski buddy. Even on the rare occasion she dressed up and wore heels and a tight dress, he didn't look in her direction. Which might not have been quite so galling had it not been for the fact he looked at almost every other female who crossed his path.

She had the distinction of being the one girl in Vermont Tyler O'Neil hadn't kissed.

In the background she heard the phone ring. Heard Christy pick it up and answer in her pitch-perfect professional voice. "Snow Crystal Spa, Christy speaking, how may I help you?"

You can't, Brenna thought miserably. *No one can help me.*

She'd been in love with Tyler her whole life, and nothing she did, or he did, had ever changed that. Not even when he'd got Janet Carpenter pregnant, and she'd felt as if her heart had been sliced in two.

She'd taken a job on another continent in the hope of curing herself. She'd dated other men in the hope that one of them would do the job, before coming to the conclusion there was no cure. Her feelings were deep and permanent.

She was doomed to love Tyler O'Neil forever.

CHAPTER TWO

TYLER SPRAWLED IN A chair at the edge of the room, only half listening as Jackson and Kayla gave a presentation on plans for the winter season. It was his least favorite way to spend an evening, and he had to force himself to concentrate as they flicked through slide after slide showing projected figures, visitor numbers, repeat business versus new business until after a while everything blurred, and he stopped listening, bored out of his skull.

If he never heard the words *cash flow* again, it would be too soon.

He should have been in Europe, studying videos with his team or discussing plans with Chas, his ski technician, whose expertise and magic with edges, overlays, wax and finishes had sliced seconds from Tyler's time. They'd been a winning team, but it wasn't just the winning he missed. It was the anticipation, the rush of speed, the one hundred seconds when you were right on the edge between control and out of control hurtling down the slope at speeds most people wouldn't even reach in a car.

It had been his life, and that life had changed in an instant.

Fortunately, the news that his leg wouldn't be able to withstand the forces placed on it by competitive skiing had coincided with the news that Jess was coming to live with him, so he had something else to focus on at least.

His thoughts drifted to his daughter and the conversation they'd had earlier.

There was no escaping the fact she wasn't a kid anymore.

She was a teenager.

Everything was changing. Exactly how much did she know about his sex life? How much did she know about sex in general?

Sweat broke out on the back of his neck, and he shifted in his chair, the discomfort almost physical.

At what age were you supposed to have that talk? He had no idea. He had no idea about any of it.

And what was going on with school? He didn't know, but it was obvious that something wasn't right.

He needed to spend more time with her, and the easiest way to do that was to focus on her skiing.

Thinking about skiing helped him to relax. With that, at least, he was in his comfort zone.

She was good, but having grown up in Chicago with a mother who hated everything about skiing, she lacked experience. Somehow he had to cram that experience in while still fulfilling his obligations to the family business. What she needed was more hours on the mountain with someone who had the ability to coach her.

He knew he had the ability, if not the patience.

Still, the prospect of training her lifted his mood. He might not be able to ski competitively anymore, but he could ski with his daughter. He saw a lot of himself in her, which was probably why her mother had all but kicked her out the winter before. Janet had tried everything in an attempt to stamp the O'Neil out of Jess, but nothing had worked.

Pride mingled with the slow simmer of anger.

The Carpenter family had paid a fortune to slick law-yers to make sure Janet had custody of Jess. For twelve years he'd had to put up with only seeing her in the sum-mer and at Christmas, but then Janet had become preg-nant again. The combination of a new baby and Jess hitting her teenage years had culminated in her sending Jess to live with him.

Tyler had vacillated between relief and happiness that his daughter was finally where he'd wanted her all along, and fury and disbelief that Janet had sent the child away.

As far as he was concerned, family was family, and they stayed that way even when the going got tough. You couldn't sign off or resign. Walking away wasn't an op-tion. He'd been eighteen when Janet had told him that their single encounter had left her pregnant, and no mat-ter what emotions had rippled through the O'Neil family at the time, he'd never doubted that he'd had their support.

The Carpenter family had been less accepting, and Janet had never forgiven him for making her pregnant. She blamed him for the whole thing, as if she hadn't been the one who had walked into the barn that day wearing nothing but a smile. And that blame had permeated her relationship with her daughter. It was no wonder Jess had arrived at Snow Crystal feeling insecure, unwanted and vulnerable.

"What do you think, Tyler?"

Realizing he'd been asked a question he hadn't heard, Tyler woke up and looked at his brother. "Yeah, go for it. Great idea."

"You have no idea what I said." Jackson folded his arms and narrowed his eyes. "This is important. You could try paying attention."

Tyler suppressed a yawn. "You could try being less boring."

"The high school ski team is a coach down. The team is losing more than they're winning. They want our help."

"I said *less* boring."

His brother ignored him. "I said we'd help out at the school for a couple of sessions. We can talk theory and give a waxing demonstration."

"Waxing?" Kayla's eyebrows rose. "We're still talking skiing, yes? Not grooming?"

Tyler gave her a look. "How long have you lived here?"

"Long enough to know exactly how to wind you up." Smiling, Kayla made a note on her phone. "Helping the high school team will be good publicity. I can do something with that locally."

Tyler stared moodily at his feet and waited for them to ask him to do it.

Once, he'd skied alongside the best in the world.

Now he was going to be coaching a losing high school ski team.

Regret ripped through him along with sick disappointment and a yearning that made no sense. What was done was done.

He was about to make a flippant comment about how he'd finally made it to the top, when Jackson said, "We thought Brenna might do it."

Brenna was the obvious person. She was a PSIA level three coach and a gifted teacher. She was patient with kids and adventurous with expert skiers.

Glancing at her, Tyler noticed the change in her expression and the stiffness of her shoulders. You didn't have to be an expert in body language to see she didn't want to do it.

And he knew why.

He waited for her to refuse, but instead she gave a tense smile.

"Of course. Kayla's right. It will be good publicity and good for our reputation." She gave the answer Jackson wanted and listened while he outlined details, but there was no sign of the smile that had been evident a few moments earlier. Instead she stared hard out the window and across the snow-dusted forest to the peaks beyond.

Tyler wondered why his brother hadn't noticed the lack of enthusiasm in her response and decided Jackson was too caught up with the pressures of keeping the family business afloat to notice small things. *Like the rigid set of her shoulders.*

He felt a rush of exasperation.

Why didn't she speak up and say how she felt?

He knew she didn't want to do it. Unlike most of the women he'd met, he found Brenna easy to read. The expression on her face matched her mood. He knew when she was happy; he knew when she was excited about something; he knew when she was tired and cranky. And he knew when she was unhappy. And she was unhappy now, at the news she'd be coaching the high school team.

And he knew why.

She'd hated school. Like him, she'd considered the whole thing a waste of time. All she'd wanted to do was get out on the mountains and ski as fast as she could. Lessons had got in the way of that. Tyler had felt the same, which was why he sympathized with Jess. He knew exactly how it had felt to be trapped indoors in a classroom, sweating over books that made no sense and were as heavy and dull as old bricks.

But in Brenna's case, it hadn't been a love of the mountains or a dislike of algebra that had driven her loathing of school, but something far more insidious and ugly.

She'd been bullied.

On more than one occasion, he and his brothers had tried to find out which kids were making Brenna's life a misery, but she'd refused to talk about it, and none of them had witnessed anything that had given them clues. It hadn't helped that she was younger, which meant that they rarely saw her during the school day.

Tyler had wanted to fix it, and it had driven him crazy that she wouldn't let him.

If it had been one of his brothers, he would have sorted the problem, so he couldn't see why she wouldn't let him help.

On one occasion, she'd walked back from school with grazed knees and a cut on her face, her schoolbooks damaged from her encounter with whoever had pushed her in the ditch.

"I don't need you to fight my battles, Tyler O'Neil." She'd dragged her filthy, muddy schoolbag onto her skinny shoulder, and he remembered thinking that if he ever found out who was doing this to her, he was going to push them off the top of Scream, one of the most dangerous runs in the area.

He never had found out.

And presumably the person, or persons, responsible were now long gone from Snow Crystal, leaving only the memory.

Was she thinking of it now?

He ran his hand over his jaw and cursed under his breath. He didn't want to think of Brenna as vulnerable. He wanted to think of her as one of the boys. He'd disciplined himself not to notice those sleek curves under the fitted ski pants. He'd trained himself not to notice the sweet curve of her mouth when she laughed. She was a colleague. A friend.

His best friend. He was never, ever going to do anything to jeopardize that.

Shit.

"I'll go into school. I'll coach the race training camp and whatever else needs doing." Even as he said the words, part of his brain was yelling at him to shut up. "Brenna has enough to do around here."

Jackson's eyebrows rose in surprise. "You?"

"Yeah, me. Why not?"

"The question is more 'why would you?'"

He waited for Brenna to admit how she felt, and when she didn't, he searched his brain for an explanation. "They are the stars of tomorrow." He regurgitated something he'd read at the top of Jess's school report and then decided he needed something more plausible. "And there's no feeling quite like basking in the adulation of teenage girls. I don't get anywhere near enough adulation around here, so I'll do it."

"No." Brenna finally found her voice. "We all know it's not your thing. I'll do it."

"I'm making it my *thing*. I'm doing it, and that's final."

Kayla gave a delighted chortle. "I can see the headline now—downhill champion coaches losing high school team. Great story." She started to pace, her enthusiasm and excitement visible in every tap of her heels. "I could see if it would interest someone as a documentary. Could I do that?"

Tyler, who loathed the press after a particularly nasty piece about his alleged involvement with a stunning Austrian snowboarder, felt the hairs on the back of his neck lift. "Not if you want me to do the coaching."

Jackson was frowning. "Are you sure you want to do it?"

"I'm sure." Tyler thought of what he'd just committed himself to and decided Friday was now officially his worst day of the week. "Are we about done? Because staring at all those lines on the spreadsheet is making me feel as if I'm behind bars. I have work to do on some of the equipment. Proper work, I mean, not the sort that means giving presentations."

It was fun to wind his brother up, and it took his mind off the fact Brenna was hurting, a thought that made him restless and uncomfortable.

"We're nearly done." Jackson refused to be rushed. "As you know, they're predicting a big statewide snowstorm. A winter storm watch is up. According to the forecast, the storm will be right down the New England coast, which puts us in the sweet spot for snow, good news given that the snow pack is twenty percent down on the average for this time of year."

"Hey, it's winter in Vermont. One minute you're skiing on grass, then you're slithering on ice, and if you get really lucky, you're up to your neck in powder." But the mention of snow roused Tyler from his state of boredom. "How much snow, exactly?"

"Between twelve and fourteen inches. Possibly more."

"That is the best news I've had in a long time. I love a good powder day."

"So do our guests, and they'll pay for a guide so you'll be busy."

"Trust you to ruin good news. Do you ever think of anything other than work?"

"Not with our busiest time of the year approaching, no. We're a winter sports resort."

Kayla glanced up from her laptop. "And you're our USP."

"I'm your *what?*"

"Our unique selling point. No other resort has a gold-medal-winning downhill skier available for hire."

"I'm not for hire."

Ignoring his dangerous tone, Kayla smiled. "You are for a price. A good price, I might add. You're not cheap. Have you taken a look at our new website? There is a whole page devoted to you. *Ski with the best in the world.*"

Tyler suppressed a yawn. "Can't I give them a map and let them find their own way?"

Jackson ignored that. "People will pay good money to lay down tracks in fresh snow and enjoy the silence."

"And with all those people enjoying it, there won't be any silence," Tyler pointed out, but Jackson wasn't listening.

"The snow will be fun on the slopes, less fun on the roads." As usual, his brother focused on the implications for the business. "If it happens, we'll need to find rooms for as many staff as possible because the snowplows will have trouble keeping up."

Deciding that logistics weren't his problem, Tyler rose to his feet. "My bed is big enough for two. Three if they're blonde." He kept his eyes away from Brenna's shiny dark hair. "I'm going now before I die of boredom and you have to remove my rotting corpse. Not that I know anything about marketing, but I'm guessing that wouldn't be good for business."

TRYING TO ERASE an image of Tyler sharing his bed with two blondes, Brenna zipped up her jacket and stepped out into the freezing night. Tyler was already striding ahead, and she looked at those broad, powerful shoulders, thinking that meetings never lasted long when he was involved. He drove things forward, impatient to be out in the fresh air, incapable of sitting still for any length of time.

Trapping Tyler O'Neil in a meeting room was like trying to cage a tiger.

Her feet brushed through a light dusting of fresh snow, and she knew without any help from the weather forecast that they were going to have more before the week was out. She could smell it in the air. The temperature had plummeted, and the sky was heavy with it.

As far as she was concerned, there was no place on earth more perfect than Snow Crystal. She loved the stillness and peace of the lake in the summer, the burst of fall color that turned the dense leaves of the forest to flame, but most of all she loved the frozen beauty of winter.

"Brenna, wait." Kayla hurried across to her, her laptop bag banging against her hip, her blond hair sliding over her stylish berry-red coat. Like Christy, her hair was smooth and perfect. Like Christy, she could have walked into any boardroom in New York and not looked out of place.

"Everything all right?"

"Yes, but I haven't seen you for a couple of days. It's been crazy. Are you using the gym tomorrow?" Kayla's phone beeped, and she checked it quickly. "Text from my ex-boss in New York, offering me a promotion if I go back. Hilarious. He's sending me one a week at the moment. They've won a big account, and they're desperate for staff."

"Would you go back?"

"Not in a million years. Manhattan at Christmas is my nightmare. Give me fir trees and forest every time. I'd rather hug a moose than visit Santa."

"And most of all, you'd rather hug Jackson."

Kayla gave a wicked smile. "True enough. That man makes it hard to get up in the morning, that's for sure." She slipped her phone back into her pocket. "I love it here. And this winter I'm determined to get better at skiing so I'm not left behind. I'm done with Tyler's derogatory comments about my lack of ability." She followed Brenna's gaze and saw him striding away. "He doesn't hang around, does he? I wanted to persuade him to run a master class for advanced skiers, but he ran off before we'd finished."

"I suspect the prospect of coaching the high school team and guiding was enough of a challenge for one meeting."

"I don't get the problem. He loves skiing. He finds it fun. What's wrong with skiing with guests?"

"Because he's the best. And fun for him is skiing places that would give any other person a heart attack."

"All of it gives me a heart attack. The idea of launching myself down a vertical slope is terrifying."

"That's because this is only your second season."

"I'm pretty sure I'm always going to find it terrifying. I'm a coward, and it isn't natural to put myself in a position where I could kill myself. How do you do it? I mean, you hurl yourself down slopes that would make me cry. Jackson said the other day he thought you could have made the U.S. ski team if you'd had more encouragement from your parents."

It was something Brenna didn't let herself think about. "They wanted me to get a proper job."

"You run the Outdoor Center. That isn't a proper job?"

"Not to them." Brenna tilted her face and felt flakes of snow flutter onto her cheeks. "I guess I'm a disappointment."

"How can you be a disappointment? You're such a talented teacher, equally good with wimps and daredevils." Kayla's eyes gleamed. "Hey, that is a great idea. We should name a class *daredevils*."

"Not if you want me to take it. Kids don't need any encouragement to act crazy on the slopes." Brenna pulled her hat out of her pocket. "I'll catch him up. See if I can persuade him to do your master class."

"Perfect. Then he can kill you and not me. All we need now is snow." Kayla turned as Jackson joined them. "Ready for dinner? Your mom texted. She's made pot roast. Although what her text *actually* said was *pit rot*, so you might want to order takeout."

"I'm not sure I'm in the mood for a family gathering. How does pizza in bed sound?" Jackson slid his arm around her shoulder. "Are you joining us, Brenna?"

"For pizza in bed? I don't think so." She pulled her hat onto her head and smoothed her hair away from her face. "I have to finish working on plans for the race series."

"We can't have pizza in bed," Kayla murmured. "I promised Elizabeth we'd be there. It's family night. Sean and Élise are coming, too, and Jess is already there."

"I love my family, but there are days when I could happily move to California." Jackson lowered his head, kissed her and then gave Brenna an apologetic look. "Everything all right in Forest Lodge? You're comfortable?"

"It's perfect. I love it. Forest Lodge is my dream home.

And it's convenient. Thanks for letting me stay again this season."

"It helps us out having you here on-site, and we have empty cabins so it makes sense. Good night, Brenna."

"Good night." She watched as the two of them walked toward the main house, their arms looped around each other as they picked their way over the snow. She felt a pang of envy and stood for a moment, her emotions tangled. She was pleased for them. Happy they were happy, but somehow their happiness and what they shared made her conscious of what was missing in her own life.

Feeling tired and cross with herself, she made her way down the snowy path that led from the Outdoor Center to the lakeside trail and Forest Lodge. It was one of the first log cabins Jackson had built when he'd taken over the running of Snow Crystal, and Brenna loved it. All the cabins were beautiful, but Forest was special.

The resort had been in the O'Neil family for four generations, but it wasn't until Jackson's father had died that the truth had emerged. The business had been at risk, and it was Jackson who had walked away from a successful ski business in Europe to come home and run the family business, helped by Tyler, whose own career had crashed and burned in spectacular fashion.

She walked along the path, breathing in the smell of pine and the crisp night air. The sounds of the forest calmed her. The snow cover was still thin, but they were all hoping that was about to change.

She was so deep in thought, she almost walked straight into Tyler, who was waiting for her.

In her flat snow boots she barely reached his shoulder. "I thought you were long gone."

"There is only so much corporate boredom I can take at a time."

"So why are you still here?"

"You were upset in that meeting. Why do you never speak up?" He reached out and pulled her hat farther down over her ears. "You should have told my brother no when he asked you to coach the high school team."

He'd always been able to read her, which made his apparent lack of awareness about her feelings for him all the more surprising. Over the years she'd come to the conclusion that the fact he knew her so well was the very reason he hadn't guessed the truth. They'd been best friends for so long it hadn't ever occurred to him to question that relationship or see her in any way other than the girl he'd grown up with.

And she preferred it that way.

It was easier for both of them if he didn't know.

She didn't want the awkwardness that would inevitably come should such an imbalance in the relationship be revealed.

"I was going to do it, until you volunteered."

The silence of the forest wrapped itself around them. They stood on the intersection between the path that led to the Outdoor Center and the path that led through the forest to the lake.

"Someone had to do it, and I didn't want it to be you." The collar of his jacket brushed against the dark shadow of his jaw, and his eyes glittered impatiently. "You should have said no."

"This is my job. Jackson asked me to do it."

"And he shouldn't have, but when it comes to Snow Crystal, my brother has tunnel vision."

"I guess that happens when you're fighting to save

a business. You didn't have to volunteer. I would have done it."

"But only because doing it was preferable to having a difficult conversation."

"Excuse me?"

"You do anything to avoid confrontation."

"That isn't true." She looked away, embarrassed and frustrated because she knew it *was* true. "What did you expect me to do? Tell my boss no?"

"Why not? You hated everything about that school. You couldn't wait to leave. We both know you don't want to go back there."

Her stomach curled into a tight, uncomfortable knot.

There were so many things she wished she'd said and done differently. Things her grown-up self would have told her teenage self as well as her tormenters.

"I wasn't that interested in studying."

"We both know that wasn't why you hated the place."

She flushed, unsettled that he knew her so well. Her school days had been a miserable time. That whole period of her life would have been miserable had it not been for the O'Neil brothers, Tyler in particular.

"Why are we talking about this? It's long since over and done with."

"There you go again—avoidance. When it's something difficult, you duck. Hide. Who was it? I want to know."

"Who was what?"

"Who gave you a hard time?"

He'd asked her the same question repeatedly over the years, and she'd never given him an answer. "Why are you bringing that up now? It was a long time ago."

"Exactly. So you might as well tell me."

His persistence exasperated her. "It was no one."

"You fell in the ditch by yourself?" He put his fingers under her chin and tilted her face to him. "Jackson and I had a few suspicions. Was it Mark Webster? Tina Robson? Those two caused most of the trouble in your grade."

"It wasn't them." She tried to ignore the way his hand felt against her skin. "I was clumsy, that's all."

"Honey, you skied with me, and most of the time you kept up. There were moments when you were almost better on that hill than I was."

"Almost? Arrogance isn't attractive, Tyler." But she'd seen the gleam in his eyes and knew he was playing with her.

"Neither is evasion." A smile that was altogether too attractive flickered at the corner of his mouth. "You're never going to tell me, are you?"

"No. It's behind me and anyway, I don't need you protecting me."

"Cameron Foster?"

"Tyler, stop!"

"If you'd told me who it was, I would have pushed them in the ditch."

She knew that was the truth. Tyler O'Neil had spent more time in the principal's office than he had in the classroom. "That's why I didn't tell you. You were in enough trouble without me being responsible for more. Look, I appreciate you volunteering to take that class, but you don't need to. I can do it. We both know you'd hate it. Why would you want to put yourself through that?"

"Because it's you."

Her heart pumped a little faster. Hope, that thing she kept ruthlessly suppressed, flickered to life inside her. "What's that supposed to mean? Why would you do it for me?"

He frowned, as if he thought it was a strange question. "Because I care about you. Because we've been friends since you could walk."

Friends.

She felt a thud of something inside her and recognized it as disappointment.

How could she possibly be disappointed about something that had been her reality forever? She should be grateful for his friendship. It was greedy of her to want more, but still she *did* want more. She wanted it all. She wanted the whole fantasy.

But that was all it was ever going to be, of course.

A fantasy.

Tyler gave her a friendly pat on the shoulder. "Stop looking so sick. I'm taking that class and that's final. If it makes you feel better, you can buy me a bottle of whiskey for Christmas to numb the agony."

"I already bought your Christmas present."

"You did? What is it?"

"A box set of chick flicks for you to watch with Jess. I thought it would help you bond."

He groaned. "You had better be joking. But talking of Jess, I need your help. She is desperate to ski."

Like father, like daughter.

It was bittersweet, because she'd longed for that very thing—the man and the child. Home. Family. Snow Crystal. Officially being an O'Neil. She didn't know if it was because she was old-fashioned, or because she'd known right from the start that the only man she wanted in her life was Tyler. She hadn't needed to meet hundreds of other men to know he was the one.

But he didn't want that. And he certainly didn't want it with her.

She forced herself to focus on the topic of Jess. "She skis with you. There is no better training than that."

"It's all she wants to do. She's falling behind with her schoolwork. Not concentrating in class." He dragged his hand over his jaw. "How am I supposed to handle that? I try and tell her to do her homework, but I never did mine, so does that make me a hypocrite? Do I tell her to do as I say or do as I did? I don't know. I can't stop thinking about last winter when I tried holding her back. Look how that turned out."

"She was pushing you. Testing you. You worked through it."

"She ran away!"

"You found her almost right away."

"But not before she'd given us all a heart attack."

Brenna thought about the night Jess had gone missing. "I suppose you have to set boundaries."

"You ignored the boundaries. So did I. How do I enforce them with my daughter?"

Seeing him question himself was a novel experience. Tyler was fearless and confident. Both qualities were an essential part of a sport that demanded total precision. He'd never had any doubts about what he wanted out of life, and she found his attempts to adapt to living with a teenage daughter endearing. Suspecting that *endearing* wasn't an adjective he'd thank her for, she kept it to herself.

"Why would you be messing it up? You made it clear from the moment Janet sent her here that she was loved and wanted. That's the most important thing."

Jess hadn't revealed much about the years she'd spent with her mother in Chicago, but she'd said enough to make Brenna, who had always considered herself to be even-tempered, hope she never came face-to-face with Janet ever again.

"Loving her isn't enough though, is it? I'm worried I'm a lousy father. That's the truth." He took a deep breath and pressed his fingers to the bridge of his nose. "I haven't admitted that to anyone but you."

Her heart felt as if it were being squeezed. "You're a good father. How can you doubt that?"

"I didn't manage to keep her when she was born, did I?"

"Not because you didn't try." She knew how hard the O'Neils had fought to keep baby Jess. Knew what losing had done to them. "Why are you thinking about that now when it was all so long ago?"

"Because she mentioned it earlier."

"The custody battle?"

"The fact she was an *accident*. Janet obviously said something to her. I'm worried we've screwed her up."

"For what it's worth, I don't think she's screwed up, but if she's been affected by her childhood then you're not responsible for that. You weren't the one telling her those things."

"I'm responsible for what happens from now on though, and that responsibility scares me."

"I can't imagine you feeling scared." Of all the words people might have applied to Tyler O'Neil, *fear* definitely wasn't one of them. "You're not scared of anything or anyone."

"I'm scared of this." He stopped walking and turned to look at her. For once there was no hint of humor in those blue eyes. "I don't want to mess this up, Bren."

His sincerity brought a lump to her throat, and she reached out and put her hand on his arm, her fingers closing around brutally hard biceps. Tyler O'Neil was everything male, but she tried not to think of him that way. Tried not to notice the wide shoulders, the thickness of muscle under his jacket or the telltale shadow on his jaw. She tried to think of him as a friend first and a man second. Today, for some reason, that wasn't working out so well, and the jolt to her senses woke her up.

For her own sanity, she normally made a point of not touching him, but today she'd broken that rule.

She was hyperaware of him. Shivers ran up and down her spine. Her nerve endings buzzed. The impulsive urge to stand on tiptoe and kiss the sensual curve of his mouth was almost overpowering.

If she did that, how would he react?

He'd die of shock.

And then he'd make some stammered excuse about how he didn't think it was a good idea because they worked together, whereas what he'd really be thinking was that she wasn't his type, and he didn't find her attractive.

She was careful never to cross the line between friendship and something more intimate because she knew once they'd crossed it, they could never go back. Her feelings were her problem. She didn't want to make him uncomfortable or do anything to risk damaging their friendship.

She removed her hand, turned her head and studied the tall trees of the forest, trying to block out the image of that mouth, those sexy blue eyes and that gorgeous hair ruffled by the wind.

He seemed tense, too, but she knew that was because he was thinking about Jess, not her.

He thought of her as a friend first and second. She doubted he was even aware of her as a woman. She was genderless, one of the few people he could trust in a life filled with sycophants, hangers-on and people who wanted something from him, greedy for crumbs of secondhand fame. The downhill circuit had been crazy, she knew that. And through it all, they'd maintained their friendship.

"I think you need to relax. Follow your instincts and do what feels right. There's no one right way to be a parent."

"There are plenty of wrong ways."

Don't I know it. "You love who she is, and that's the most important thing for any child. You don't wish she were someone different."

"Are we talking about you here?" His gaze sympathetic, he lifted a hand and brushed snow out of her hair. "How is your mom? Have you entered the dragon's lair lately?"

The fact he knew instantly what was going through her head was another indication of how well they knew each other.

"I haven't seen her in a month. I'm due a visit, but I keep putting it off." Brenna forced a smile. "I have to brace myself to get through an hour of being scolded about how I'm wasting my life here."

"They're lucky to have you, Bren."

No, they weren't. "I don't think they'd agree. I'm a disappointment to them. I'm not the way they wanted me to be." She'd given up trying to change the facts. Some families, like the O'Neils, were a team, and others stumbled along like a band of misfits, as if they'd been thrown together by an unhappy accident.

"You're you." He frowned. "They should want you to be you."

He had a way of simplifying things.

She knew that many people saw Tyler as a sports-obsessed, superficial bad boy. But that was the surface. Beneath the veneer of carelessness, he was astute and perceptive. "It's because you understand that, and believe that, I know you're a great dad. You accept Jess as she is. That's the best thing a parent can do."

"She's crazy about skiing. I'm trying to encourage a little balance in her life."

She smiled. "Did we have balance at that age?"

"No. We spent every moment outdoors."

Brenna stooped and picked up a pinecone. "So let her do the same. If you're caught in a strong current, you don't try and swim against it. Let her ski in every spare moment, and perhaps if you don't hold her back, she'll be more willing to spend a little time on other things. Steer her gradually."

"That sounds reasonable."

"By the way, you ran off before Kayla could ask if you'd consider running a ski master class."

"Offering to help out with ski school was enough of a shock to my system for one day." He checked the time on his phone. "What are you doing now? Are you busy?"

"I was going back to my lodge, and you have family night." The O'Neils tried to be together one night a month for a meal. It was something she both envied and admired. She had no idea how a family achieved that level of closeness. Hers certainly hadn't.

"You're welcome to join us, you know that. I wish you would. I need moral support to face the sight of my two brothers slobbering over their women."

"They're in love."

Tyler shuddered. "That's why I need you there. We're the only sane people left."

"Not tonight." She pushed the pinecone into her pocket and started to walk again, her feet crunching on the thin layer of snow. If the forecasters were right, she'd be knee deep soon enough. "I have paperwork." And she needed some space from Tyler to pull herself together.

"Your life is so exciting. It must be hard to sleep at night."

She breathed in the scent of snow and forest. "I happen to like my life, although I prefer the outdoor part to the indoor part."

"Do you fancy a quick drink? I need to talk about sex."

"You—what?" She stumbled, and he shot out a hand and steadied her, his grip hard and strong.

"Careful. I take it back. Maybe you are a little clumsy when you're not concentrating." He let go of her arm. "I realized I have no idea how to talk to Jess about sex, and I want to work out what I'm going to say before I have to say it. I don't want to fumble like I did tonight over the other stuff."

Jess.

He wanted to talk about Jess.

Her knees felt as if she'd downed a bottle of vodka. "What other stuff?"

"It doesn't matter, but it got me thinking."

She was thinking, too, and she wished she wasn't because those thoughts revolved around him naked. "Thinking about what?"

"For a start, at what age are you supposed to talk to a kid about sex? What age were you when you talked to your mom?"

I still don't talk to my mom.

"We didn't talk about stuff like that."

"Never? So how did you—?"

"I can't remember!" Feeling as if she was being strangled, she unzipped her jacket. She and Tyler had talked about everything over the years, but never this. As far as she was concerned, he couldn't have picked a more uncomfortable subject. "Other kids? Books?"

"But other kids say all sorts of stuff that's wrong. I don't want to tell her more than she needs to know, but I have no idea how to find out what she already knows. This is what I mean about parenting being a nightmare. I need a book or something. I'd use the internet, but I'm afraid to type *sex and teenagers* into a search engine in case I'm arrested."

It was impossible not to laugh, but she was grateful for the dark and the biting cold of the winter air because she knew her face was burning. Emotions churned inside her; feelings she'd tried to ignore rose to the surface. She wished she were more like Élise, who viewed sex as a physical act as simple and straightforward as eating or drinking.

Élise would have simply told Tyler how she felt, stripped him naked, had sex with him and then moved on as if all they'd done was enjoy a meal together.

"Tyler, you don't need a book. You know plenty about sex." More than plenty, if rumor was to be believed. There had been times when she'd wished she could walk around wearing noise-reducing headphones to block out the gossip.

"Doing it, yes, but not talking about it with teenagers. And to make it worse, she keeps finding all this stuff that's been written about me, and most of it's crap. I already have parental control on her laptop, but that's not going to stop her reading all sorts of stuff that isn't true."

Brenna thought about all the *stuff* she'd read about him and wondered which bits weren't true.

The night after he'd won a World Cup downhill in Lake Louise when it had been rumored he'd spent several hours in a hot tub with four members of the French women's team? Or the night he supposedly skied seminaked on part of the *Hahnenkamm,* one of the most notorious runs in Europe, with a whiskey bottle in his hand instead of a ski pole?

Oblivious to her train of thought, he ran his hand over his jaw. "Any ideas? Can you remember being thirteen? What did you think about when you were that age?"

Him. She'd thought about him. Tyler O'Neil had played a starring role in every dream and adolescent fantasy.

"She probably already knows everything. They teach them pretty young at school."

"Yeah, but how much do they teach them? I want her to be fully informed, that's all. I don't want some guy with a libido on overdrive taking advantage of her."

"She's not even fourteen, and all she thinks about is skiing. I don't think you need to worry about that quite yet."

"I want to be ahead of the game." He glanced up at the sky. "It's snowing again. You'll freeze standing here. Have a drink with me, and you can tell me what sounds right and what doesn't."

She wasn't freezing. She was boiling hot. She was pretty sure her face was scarlet. "You want to talk about sex?"

"You were a teenage girl once. Help me out here, Bren."

Should she confess that sex wasn't exactly her specialist subject? "You're supposed to be at family night."

"All the more reason to have a drink. A meeting followed by an evening of O'Neil family togetherness is too much for any man."

He took it for granted, the closeness of his family, the fact that they were always there in the background supporting each other.

He'd never known anything different.

"If we go to the bar, you'll be accosted by guests."

"Which is why we're going to drink the beer from your fridge. I promise to replenish it tomorrow."

"My fridge?" Her heart bumped a little harder. "You want to come back to my lodge?"

"Why not? You do have beer?" He slipped his arm around her shoulders, and she was conscious of the weight of his arm, of the power of his body as it brushed against hers.

His touch was casual.

The way she was feeling was anything but. It would have been safer for her pulse rate and her blood pressure if she pulled away, but that would have raised questions she didn't want to answer, so she decided her cardiovascular system was going to have to take the hit.

"Jess has talent," she croaked. "You're too busy to ski with her all the time, so I was thinking that maybe she should join the under-14 class. I'm focusing on mountain free-skiing, bumps, gate training, gate drills and free-ski skills. We'll mix up the fun with the work. She might enjoy it, and it would be good for building confidence. What do you think?"

"I think she'll be bored out of her mind. That's fine for most of the kids, but not Jess. She needs to be stretched."

"Are you saying my lessons are boring?"

"No. You're a gifted teacher, but Jess is different. She has something."

"She's her father's daughter."

Tyler gave a grim smile. "Which is probably why Janet kicked her out."

They'd reached the steps to her lodge. A single light glowed in the window. "I agree she needs to be stretched, but if you're going to make the most of that something, it's important to get the basics right. To focus on style."

"Style is irrelevant. Speed is what's important."

Brenna rolled her eyes and delved for her keys. It was an argument they'd had more times than she could count. "Good style comes before speed."

"Nothing comes before speed. You want to be the fastest, not the prettiest." He tugged her hat down over her eyes. Then he stooped and scooped up a handful of snow from the steps and she backed away, her keys still in her hand.

"Don't you *dare!* Tyler O'Neil if you so much as—*crap.*" She ducked too late as snow hit her on the chest and exploded into her face. "I am soaking!"

"You shouldn't have unzipped your jacket."

"I hate you, you know that, don't you?"

"No, you don't. You love me, really." He was smiling as he scooped up more snow, but this time she was quicker, and the snow in her hand hit him full in the face.

She did love him. That was the problem.

She really loved him, but there was no way she was going to let him know that.

She made the most of her temporary advantage and let herself into the lodge, reasoning that even Tyler wouldn't dare throw snow indoors.

The lodges were the pride of Snow Crystal. Set in the forest and overlooking the lake, each one felt private and intimate, but Forest was her favorite. "I'd forgotten what good aim you have. I have snow blindness." Still laughing, Tyler wiped snow out of his eyes, tugged off his boots and coat and left them by the door.

"You're neat and tidy all of a sudden."

"I'm trying to set a good example. I'm working on being a responsible parent. It's exhausting." He sprawled on one of the sofas, his powerful frame dominating even this large, spacious room. The fabric of his jeans clung to hard, muscular thighs, a legacy of years of downhill skiing.

Brenna pulled off her hat and hung up her coat. It was only when she noticed Tyler taking a leisurely look at her body that she realized her soaked, roll-neck sweater was clinging to her breasts.

Alternatively freezing and then burning, she turned away, but it was impossible to ignore his presence or the fact they were alone.

It felt strangely intimate. The lodge was at the far end of the lake, wrapped by the forest that showed itself as dark shapes through acres of glass.

The only other property partially visible through the trees was his.

If she knelt on her bed high on the sleeping shelf, she could just glimpse his bedroom.

Trying not to think about his bedroom, she pulled open the fridge and took out two beers. She opened them both and handed him one.

"I'll be back in a second. Thanks to you, I need to change my sweater."

His gaze collided with hers briefly, and then she backed away and took refuge in the bedroom.

When had he ever looked at her before?

She pulled on a dry sweater, took a deep breath and rejoined him in the living room.

"About that thing you were asking me—"

"What thing?"

She curled up in the chair opposite him. "Sex. Jess."

"Are you blushing?" His eyes narrowed on her face. "You're cute when you're embarrassed, do you know that?"

"You're never cute. You're a pain in the ass the whole time."

"I love it when you talk dirty to me." He winked at her. "Go on. How do I deal with it?"

"Honestly? I think you should wait for her to bring it up. I would have died of embarrassment if my parents had tried to talk to me about sex."

"What if she doesn't like to ask? What if she turns around in a few years and tells me she's pregnant?"

"I think you need to chill." Brenna sipped her beer. "Make sure she knows she can talk to you about anything. Create an atmosphere where she is comfortable to say whatever she wants."

"Judging from the conversation earlier, I think we've already got that atmosphere. Can you believe she was actually trying to fix me up?"

Brenna almost choked on her beer. "Who with?"

Christy. It had to be Christy with the smooth blond hair. Or maybe pretty, bubbly Poppy, who worked closely with Élise in the restaurant.

There was a brief pause. His eyes met hers and then

slid away again. "No one in particular, but she thinks I should have a sex life."

Definitely Christy.

She was always flirting with Tyler.

Brenna wasn't good at flirting. And anyway, how did you flirt with someone you'd known all your life? Tyler had seen her soaked to the skin and exhausted after a day in the mountains. He'd dragged her out of ditches and picked her up when she'd wiped out on her skis. He knew everything about her. They had no secrets. She could imagine his reaction if she'd fluttered her eyelashes or made a sexual comment. He'd either laugh or run for the hills.

The reason they were able to be friends was because he didn't think of her like that.

Women came and went from his life, but their friendship was constant.

And Brenna realized the reason the past year had been so blissful, the reason she'd been able to enjoy his company and his friendship, was because he'd been focusing on Jess. For once in his life he'd mastered his short attention span and put aside his urge to sample the charms of every female who crossed his path. The only woman who'd had his attention was his daughter. He'd put his own needs on hold.

Knowing what he was like, how physical and sexual he was, Brenna had often wondered if he was seeing someone discreetly, but she'd never asked. Instead she'd made the most of her time with him and occasionally, when they'd been out on the mountain guiding or teaching, it had almost felt like being kids again.

Their friendship was stronger than ever.

Was that about to change?

If Jess was actively encouraging him to date then no doubt it would.

And Brenna knew it would take Tyler O'Neil less than thirty seconds in the company of a woman to resurrect his sex life.

How was she going to feel about that?

CHAPTER THREE

TRYING TO DELETE the image of Brenna with her snow-soaked sweater plastered to her breasts from his memory, Tyler strolled up the snowy path to the main house.

In no hurry to face the overwhelming reality of family night, he paused and breathed in the freezing air, watching the forest transform before his eyes. Snow layered on snow until all traces of green vanished and the trees were draped in a mantle of white. As a child it had been his favorite sight. He'd kneel in his bedroom window and watch the first of the flakes fall, hoping it would continue until the snow was up to his waist. The first winter snowfall had been the cause of great excitement in the O'Neil household.

The mountains had been his playground; the adrenaline rush of downhill skiing his drug of choice.

Now he greeted snow with mixed feelings.

It was good for business, and he knew how badly Snow Crystal needed that.

He was enjoying the silence when his phone rang.

Irritated by the disturbance, he dragged it out of his pocket intending to switch the ringer off and then saw the name.

Burying his emotions deep, he lifted the phone to his ear. "Chas? How's it going?"

He didn't ask where his friend was. He didn't have to.

Chas was one of the finest ski techs in the racing world. The fact that Tyler was no longer racing meant that Chas was available for another member of the U.S. Ski Team, which meant right now he had to be in Val Gardena, Italy, on the World Cup circuit.

If it hadn't been for the accident, Tyler would have been there, too.

They would have been discussing strategy, the course, the snow conditions, in an effort to come up with the perfect plan. Chas's job had been to use his skill and experience to make Tyler the fastest skier down the mountain. Over the years they'd shared beers, hotel rooms, victory and defeat. Chas had been more than just another member of the machine behind the ski team. He'd been Tyler's wingman and close friend.

Along with his brother Sean, Chas had been the first person he'd seen after his accident.

Tyler tightened his hand on the phone and stared blindly at the trees and mountains.

"How was today?"

"Didn't you watch?"

"Things are busy around here." He didn't say that he hadn't watched skiing since his accident. Instead he listened while Chas outlined the U.S. triumph in the giant slalom.

"He clinched his fourth World Cup GS title."

"That's great. Buy him a beer from me."

"Why don't you come out? The team would love to see you."

And sit in the bar or the stands watching others do what he used to do himself?

It would be like twisting a knife in a raw wound.

The season stretched ahead. There would be a short

break over Christmas before it all started again in Bormio, Italy, and then on to Wengen, Switzerland, and Kitzbuhel and the notorious Lauberhorn. Beaver Creek, Lake Louise, another day, another country, another mountain, another race. That had been his life.

Until the race that had ended it all.

"I'm not going to be able to make it. We're busy here."

"Great! From what you told me, this time last year busy didn't exist so I'm pleased to hear things are going well. Has Jackson tied you to the resort? What are you doing?"

Coaching the high school ski team.

Trying not to think about my old life.

Tyler looked up at the sky. Snow was still falling steadily, big fat flakes that rested on his shoulders and dampened his hair.

"I'm helping Brenna run the outdoor program."

"Right. Well, that sounds—" there was a pause "—that sounds great."

They both knew that what he really meant was *that sounds like a pile of crap.*

Tyler agreed.

Not that he didn't love Snow Crystal, but they both knew he'd rather be racing.

He realized now how much he'd taken it for granted. He'd treated it as a right rather than a gift.

He half listened while Chas updated him on the individuals and their performances on the slopes, made the right noises and a vague commitment to watch the next race if he had the opportunity, then hung up feeling worse than he had before.

The conversation had left him keenly aware of what he'd lost.

It didn't help that the one person who would have understood, his father, had been dead for almost two and a half years.

Shaking off his black mood, he paced to the door of the main house where he and his brothers had grown up and where his mother still lived.

It still gave him a pang to know that when he walked into the kitchen that had been the hub of the household growing up, his father wouldn't be there.

His mother loved to decorate for Christmas, and the evidence of that love was everywhere. Tiny lights were strung across the windows, and decorations sparkled through the glass. A festive wreath hung on the door, as it had every year for as long as he could remember. As a child he'd sat on the kitchen floor waxing his skis while his mother had worked magic from the tangle of forest greenery spread over the kitchen table. She'd snipped, weaved and pulled it all together into a wreath.

Tyler pushed open the door. Sleigh bells jangled, announcing his arrival, and he blinked as he saw the number of people already seated around the table. Those numbers had increased over the past year. First Jess had joined them, then Kayla and finally Élise. She was often too busy running the successful restaurants at the resort to join them for family nights but tonight, perhaps because it was close to Christmas, she'd found the time.

There were at least three different conversations going on around the table and Maple, Jackson and Kayla's miniature poodle, greeted Tyler ecstatically, leaping up and down on the spot as if she had springs in her paws.

Tyler stooped to make a fuss of her and then hung up his coat.

His mother was busy at the stove while Jess was

seated at the large scrubbed table, listening, rapt, while his grandfather, Walter, told a story about how he'd once met a moose when he was skiing. It was a story Tyler had heard a hundred times but it was new to Jess.

"And did it move, Gramps, or did you have to ski around it?"

"It stood there and glared at me, and I glared right back. I'm telling you, that animal was as big as a house."

Jess laughed, and Tyler noticed how her eyes sparkled as she listened to her great-grandfather. She soaked up every story about Snow Crystal, every morsel of information, as if trying to fill in the gaps and make up for the parts she'd missed by living so far away.

His mood lifted slightly.

If he'd still been skiing the World Cup circuit, he wouldn't have been here when Jess had needed him.

"You're exaggerating, Walter." Alice, his grandmother, slipped her glasses into her purse. "He always exaggerates. Ignore him, Jess."

"I am not exaggerating! Were you there?" Walter grunted. "This was in the days before ski runs and grooming machines. There were no chair lifts."

Jess leaned closer, her long hair sliding forward over her shoulder. "How did you get to the top of the slopes, Gramps?"

"We walked! We attached skins to our skis, and we walked. We didn't need machines to haul us to the top like you wimps do today. We used muscle."

Tyler saw his mother lift a large blue casserole out of the oven. "Let me get that for you. Apparently, I need to build muscle." He crossed the room in a couple of strides, but she shook her head and placed the casserole in the center of the large table.

"I lift heavier things than that in the restaurant every day, and if you build any more muscle, I'll be sewing up your jeans even more frequently than I do already."

Kayla reached for her wine. "What happens to your jeans?"

"Occupational hazard of being a downhill skier. I have muscles like Thor." Tyler pulled out a chair and winked at her. "Starting to think you've picked the wrong brother?"

"No." Kayla looked him in the eye. "Muscles or not, I'd kill you."

"Only if I hadn't killed you first." The normality of the exchange lifted his dark mood, and Tyler took a beer from his brother. "Thanks."

"What took you so long?" His mother removed the lid, and delicious smells of cooking mingled with the scent of cinnamon and pine. "I was about to send out a search party! The others said you'd gone on ahead and then you never appeared." She handed him a stack of plates, and soon the food and the conversation were flowing and the question of where he'd been vanished in the chaos.

"I just spoke to Chas." He didn't mention the twenty minutes he'd stood in the forest, watching the snow fall and trying to pull himself together. He didn't mention the sick feeling that came from knowing that the Ski World Cup was underway. He should have been traveling the world, skiing in a different country every week in his pursuit of the coveted crystal ball that came with winning what many believed to be the most prestigious title of all.

He felt as if he'd been forced off a moving train and was watching while it carried on without him, leaving him stranded on a deserted platform.

Except it wasn't deserted.

He had the business to think of. Responsibility. His family. *Jess*.

His grandfather's eyes brightened. "Chas is still the best tech on the circuit."

"Yeah." Tyler sat down and moved a bowl of pinecones out of the way so he could reach the food.

The house was always the same at Christmas. Vases were filled with branches of forest greenery, candles flickered on shelves next to handmade decorations. It was a home. Lived in and loved.

Boots lay abandoned near the doorway, magazines stacked in an untidy heap on the table under the window. Since his mother had started working in the restaurant with Élise, she'd been spending less and less time in the house, something that Tyler and both his brothers had greeted with relief.

Over the past year, she'd regained some of her old energy and enthusiasm for life.

It also hadn't escaped his notice that Tom Anderson, who owned a farm a couple of miles away, was a more frequent visitor than his role as a local supplier to the restaurant warranted.

Tyler wondered if he was the only one who had noticed Tom's visits were becoming increasingly regular.

Jackson was seated across from him, his arm across the back of Kayla's chair. "So where's Chas right now?"

"Italy. Val Gardena."

"Molto bene." His older brother grinned. "You must be missing all the—er—pizza."

Tyler ignored the innuendo and pushed the bowl of fluffy mashed potatoes toward his grandfather. "The food is pretty good here."

"So what were you talking about for over an hour?"

"I wasn't talking to Chas the whole time. I encountered a moose the size of a house."

"Seriously?" Kayla put her glass down. "Because if that's the truth, I want to know exactly where so I don't walk that way."

"The moose would be more scared of you than you would be of him." Jackson reached across the table for the salt. "You've lived here a year. You know that."

"I do not know that. The only moose I feel safe with is the chocolate variety Élise serves in the restaurant."

Jess giggled. "That's a different spelling. Was there really a moose?"

"Sure." Tyler never missed an opportunity to tease Kayla. "It was hoping for an encounter with a city-loving Brit so I gave it directions to Kayla's barn. It should be snuggled up waiting for her when she gets home. I might have mentioned that Jackson wants antlers for the wall. He looked pretty annoyed."

"You're not funny. Carry on like that and I'll move back to New York." Kayla glowered at him, and Jackson curved his arm round her shoulders in a protective gesture.

"I've got your back, sweetheart."

"What about the rest of me?"

Jackson dropped his eyes, and a smile flickered in the corner of his mouth. "I've got that, too. I promise to come between you and the moose from this day forward, for better for worse…"

"Stop it! You're freaking me out." But Kayla leaned across to kiss him, and Tyler shuddered.

"You're freaking me out, too. I can only take so much romance on an empty stomach and anyway, we have children present. Keep it clean, people."

Jess straightened defensively. "I'm not a child."

"I know, but I'm using you as an excuse to stop this disgusting public display of affection, so if you could look shocked, that would be great."

Jess helped herself to potatoes. "I'm not shocked. They're always kissing. You should be used to it by now."

"I'll never get used to it. I'd rather watch ice dancing on TV."

"You hate watching ice dancing. Dad, can I have new skis?"

He opened his mouth, caught his mother's eye and remembered that he had to suppress the overwhelming urge to overcompensate for a less than perfect childhood and give Jess everything she wanted. "You already have skis."

"One pair."

"So? You have one pair of legs."

"How many pairs of skis did you have when you were racing?"

"Sixty."

"*Sixty?*" Jess's eyes were round. "No wonder you needed Chas."

His mother shook her head. "I remember days when I couldn't move around this place for skis. Between your father and you three boys, we could have supplied the whole village."

The conversation turned to skiing as it so often did, and from skiing it moved on to the business.

"Brenna should have joined us tonight. That girl is working too hard." Elizabeth O'Neil checked that everyone's plates were full. "I hate to think of her all alone in that cabin. You should have invited her."

"I saw you talking to her." Across the table, Kayla

sent him a look. "Did she mention my idea for offering a master class?"

"She might have done."

"Great. So will you do it?"

"Go easy on him." Jackson picked up his fork. "He's agreed to coach the high school ski team. There's only so much bad news he can take in one day."

"I invited Brenna," Tyler said, deliberately switching the subject as he heaped vegetables onto his plate. "She said she had things to do."

"You should have insisted." His grandmother passed him a napkin. "She probably wanted to join us but was worried she might be intruding."

"That's nonsense." Walter gave a grunt. "That girl virtually grew up here. Why would she think she's intruding? You can't intrude when you've known someone for a lifetime."

"Then why isn't she here?" Alice picked at the food on her plate. "Are you going to let her use Forest Lodge for the whole season, Jackson?"

"Providing we don't suddenly have a flood of bookings. And I invited her to join us, too, by the way. She said she was busy."

Distracted by images of Brenna in a wet, clinging sweater, Tyler turned his attention to his plate. "And if we do have a flood of bookings? You can't kick her out."

"No. But we'd have to find somewhere else for her to sleep. Don't worry. I doubt it will happen."

Kayla looked at him thoughtfully and then exchanged glances with Élise. "Don't her parents live in the village? Couldn't Brenna stay with them in an emergency?"

"No way! She'd hate that," Jess blurted out. "Her mom

is a total neat freak. She wouldn't let her have a dog or anything, because of the mess."

Tyler looked up from his food. "She told you that?"

"We talk." Jess fiddled with the food on her plate. "What? So she doesn't treat me as if I'm six. Why is this news to everyone?"

"I don't treat you as if you're six. And you're right that Brenna wouldn't want to live at home." Brenna's mother liked everything pristine. Maura Daniels would be out polishing windows while there was a foot of ice on the ground and most other folk were sheltering indoors.

He used to joke with his brothers that she didn't need a home-security system because her house was surrounded by an impenetrable wall of disapproval.

"She's not close to her parents." Tyler wondered if he was the only one who really knew her. "Staying with them would drive her nuts."

"I bumped into her mother in the store last week," Elizabeth murmured. "She barely acknowledged me. I swear you'd think we'd known each other three minutes, not thirty years."

"Cold as fish is Maura Daniels, and the husband's almost as bad, although living with her, it's not surprising. She's frozen enough there are days a person could skate on her without risk of falling through the ice on the surface." Walter slipped Maple some food under the table. "Don't know how the pair of them produced someone as warm as Brenna."

"Is that why she spent all her time over here when she was young?" Jess asked, and Tyler saw his mother exchange looks with his grandmother.

"She was an only child, and I expect she liked the company." Closing down that line of conversation, Elizabeth started talking about plans for Christmas. "When will you be able to fetch me a tree, Jackson? I want one exactly like the one you found me last year."

Tyler pushed his chair away from the table and stretched out his legs. "I'm taking a trip into the forest tomorrow to look at one of the trails. I'll pick one up for you."

"We need a tree, too." Jess sat up straighter. "Can I come? Please? I want to help choose it."

"You'll be at school."

"You could wait until I'm home."

"Then it will be dark, and I'll risk chopping off vital parts of my anatomy along with the tree." He saw her expression change from excitement to disappointment. "We'll go on Saturday, after skiing. We have a vaulted ceiling. We can have a bigger one than Grandma."

His mother smiled, and Jackson picked up his beer.

"If you're picking up a tree for Mom, can you choose one for Moose Lodge, too? It's booked from this weekend for a week and then the Stephens family is having it after that."

Tyler raised his eyebrows. "They're back?"

"Well, of course they're back." His grandfather gave a grunt. "That's what Snow Crystal is about. Families returning over and over again. Making memories. The Stephenses have been coming here summer and winter for the past five years. Or is it six?"

Jackson glanced up. "It's six. And they've booked two weeks. Good to know what happened in the summer didn't put them off."

Kayla shuddered. "Can we not talk about it? I still get flashbacks."

"*You* have flashbacks?" Cool and calm, Sean reached

across the table for a knife. "You weren't the one covered in the kid's blood."

Catching sight of his mother's white face, Tyler decided it was time to change the subject. "You may have fixed the boy, but I fixed the bike. I deserve some of the hero worship."

"Last time I talked to his dad, everything was fine." Sean helped himself to more food. "No ill effects and the kid's still riding that red bike of his, so I guess the whole incident scared us more than it scared him."

Tyler doubted his brother had been scared. Even as a child, Sean hadn't been bothered by the sight of blood or bone. On the contrary, it had fascinated him, a factor that had no doubt influenced his decision to become a surgeon.

"You called him?" Jackson reached for his beer. "That was nice of you."

"All part of the service."

Walter glanced at his grandson. "How is the new job working out? Are you missing Boston?"

"I'm not missing the traffic. And it's good to be closer to here."

"We love having you close by." Elizabeth sneaked more potatoes onto Jess's plate. "You need to keep your strength up. We have a lot of baking to do on Sunday, sweetheart. You'll need to come over early. And if you want to spend the night on Saturday, that's fine."

"I'm skiing. It's race training. Dad's coming." Jess's whole face lit up like a Christmas tree, and Tyler put his fork down.

"Wouldn't miss it."

"Will Brenna be there, too?"

"Yeah, she should be."

"That's good. She's a good teacher."

Jackson lifted his beer. "Which is why I suggested she coach the high school team. But you had to interfere."

"That's right. I did."

"Mind telling me why?"

"Because it's Brenna's idea of a nightmare. You shouldn't have put her in that position."

"What position?"

"Asking her to do something that's hard for her when she already does so much for you."

"Why is it hard?" Jackson looked blank. "She's the obvious choice. She teaches that age all the time."

His temper started to simmer. "But not the high school team. You're asking her to go into the school. That place doesn't have good memories for her." He wondered how Jackson could possibly have forgotten, and then realized his brother had barely come up for air since the shocking discovery that Snow Crystal Resort was in serious trouble.

As if to confirm that, Jackson stared at him for a moment, eyes blank and unfocused as if he'd suddenly walked into the light after a decade underground. "That was a long time ago." He thought for a moment and then cursed under his breath, earning himself a reproving look from his grandmother. "It was thoughtless of me. So why didn't she refuse?"

"Because she hates confrontation, you know that. And she wants to please you. You're her boss."

"I've known her since kindergarten."

"Doesn't change the fact you're her boss."

"So how did you know?"

"I took a look at her face."

Jackson raised an eyebrow. "Since when have you been Mr. Sensitive?"

"You don't have to be sensitive to read Brenna." Tyler finished his beer. "Everything she's feeling is written right there on her face. All you have to do is look. Brenna is an open book. Always has been. She doesn't have secrets."

Kayla gave him a long look. "Every woman has secrets."

"Not Brenna. I've known her all my life. There is nothing she thinks that I don't know about."

The conversation moved on, and by the time he and Jess finally left, the snow had increased in intensity.

Jess zipped up her jacket and pulled her hood over her hair. "You should invite Brenna over for dinner or something one night."

"Why would I want to do that?" Tyler strode through the snow. "It's enough trouble cooking for you without adding another person. And no woman in her right mind would want to set foot over the threshold of our house. If they didn't break a limb in the hall, they'd drown or be attacked by dogs."

"We could tidy up, and Brenna loves Ash and Luna. She's always saying she'd love a dog, but she's too busy working to have one." She jogged alongside him to keep up with his long stride.

"Seems like the two of you have talked about more than school."

"She's cool."

He scooped up snow and threw it at her, and she squealed and ducked. "Dad! Behave."

"I've been cooped up with family night. I need to have a little fun."

"You should start dating. It's not natural for you to spend your evenings with me."

Tyler thought of all the years he hadn't had his daughter with him and looped his arm around her shoulder. "I like spending evenings with you when you're not being a pain in the a—neck."

"You were going to say *ass*."

"I was not. And I don't need to be fixed up by a—a—how old are you again?"

"Thirteen!"

"I don't need to be fixed up by a thirteen-year-old."

CHAPTER FOUR

THE ANTICIPATED SNOWSTORM hit during the early hours of the morning, bringing the worst weather locals had seen for years. Across the state there were power outages and havoc on the roads. Branches snapped and windshield wipers struggled to keep up with the intensity of the snowfall. The Highways Department plowed and sanded, and schools were closed.

Snow Crystal escaped all but the much longed for snowfall, which coated the mountains, the forest and the trails in a deep, thick layer of white.

The resort's efficient snow-clearing operation had been underway for a few hours by the time Brenna left her lodge. The path that led through the forest to the Outdoor Center had already been cleared, and she trudged through the winter-white, her feet sinking into the snow, grateful for her warm clothing as she felt the sting of cold on her cheeks. She breathed in the smell of pine and paused for a moment, savoring the muffled silence that always followed a heavy fall of snow.

It wasn't even seven o'clock but Élise was already in the gym, pounding on the treadmill while music shook the walls of the room that had been built as part of Jackson's development of the spa. Glass walls overlooked the forest, and the trees loomed, ghostly white, out of the darkness.

Brenna winced at the throbbing beat and dropped her bag on the door. "Is this French? I don't know what she's singing about, but I'm really sorry it happened to her, and I think she needs therapy."

Élise didn't slow her pace. "She is angry because a man has treated her badly. Me, if a man did that to me I would—" She made a throat-slitting gesture, and Brenna shook her head as she peeled off her jacket.

"How does Sean sleep at night with you next to him? Does he hide all the sharp knives?"

"He is a surgeon. He is very skilled with a knife. If I chose to kill him, that would not be my way."

"Good to know." Brenna stepped onto the elliptical machine. "Did he make it to the hospital this morning? The roads must be in chaos with all this snow."

"He stayed last night. He had a full operating list today and didn't want to risk being snowed in. I slept alone."

"Ah—" Brenna hit start "—so that explains your mood and the pounding music."

"There is nothing wrong with my mood. My mood is as good as it ever is before the sun rises." Élise ran as if she were being chased by a bear. "And you know I hate the gym. Me, I would always rather be running outdoors. I feel like a rodent on this treadmill. When I lived in Paris, always I ran outdoors."

"I can't imagine running in a city." Brenna scooped her hair into a ponytail. "You'd be breathing in fumes and dodging traffic."

"Who is breathing in fumes?" A sleepy-looking Kayla walked into the gym, her gaze fixed on her phone as she scrolled through her emails. Her blond hair was bunched untidily on top of her head, and her oversize sweater slid off her shoulder. "Who decided this was a good time to exercise? It's barbaric."

Brenna adjusted the controls. "It's the same time we met every day in the summer to run around the lake."

"But it was daylight. Now it's dark, and I hate the dark. Any chance we could start this an hour later?"

Élise glanced across at her. "What time did you start work when you were working for that fancy company in New York?"

"5:00 a.m., but I was in my own apartment at the time. Back then I worked with reasonable people. No one expected me to show up at a gym and exhaust myself physically before my day started."

Élise lifted her eyebrows. "As if you haven't been exhausting yourself physically all night with Jackson."

Kayla gave a smug smile. "That's different."

"Isn't that his sweater?"

"It might be." Her phone rang, and she checked the number. "It's Lissa in Reception. Excuse me, fellow morning masochists, I need to take this. Hi, Liss, how's it going?" Still listening, she dropped her bag on the floor. "Wow—that's great news. Yes, I know it's a lot—don't worry, I'll handle it. Leave it to me." She hung up, and Brenna increased her pace.

"What's great news? What are you handling now?"

"A run of bookings!" Kayla did a pirouette. "We've had another twenty since last night. The snow is bringing them in like wasps to a honeypot." She typed an email quickly. "This storm is exactly what we needed. I'm starting to think there's a possibility we could even be full."

Élise wiped her brow with her forearm. "And this news is enough to make you dance? I will never understand you."

"That's fine, because I don't understand you, either. Or *je ne comprends pas vous,* as you would say."

Élise winced. "That is not what I would say. Your French is truly terrible. I beg you, please speak only English."

"I have to tell Jackson. God, I love my job." Grinning, Kayla dialed, tapped her foot impatiently and then pulled a face. "His phone is switching to voice mail. Where is he?"

"Probably looking for his sweater."

Brenna intervened. "Knowing Jackson, he's already somewhere in the resort sorting out a problem." She thought about the year before, when they'd all been worried that the business might go under. Jackson had been gray and exhausted with the pressure of keeping the family business going and handling sensitive family issues. "What you've done is an incredible achievement, Kayla. Great job."

"Team effort. I get them here, Élise gives them food they'll never forget and you show them the best time on the slopes so they want to come back. We should do a staff gathering, open champagne or something. Make a fuss. Get some excitement going. It would be motivational for everyone after all the uncertainty. I'll suggest it to Jackson." Kayla pressed Send on her email. "I need to talk to him because if we're full, that puts pressure on the whole resort. Not only accommodation, but ski rental, classes, snowmobile hire—all the usual stuff."

"If you're accommodating extra people then they need to eat!" Scowling, Élise increased the speed on the treadmill. "Which means thanks to you, I am going to be working twice as hard this Christmas. I don't know why

I even bother with this treadmill when I spend so much time running around the kitchen."

"You love being busy." Kayla stepped onto the machine next to her, her phone still in her other hand.

Brenna exchanged a glance with Élise, who simply raised her eyes to the ceiling and gave a Gallic shrug.

"She was born with the phone attached to her hand. Sometimes I think for Kayla, her phone is more important than her heart. It keeps the blood flowing. If she puts it down, part of her dies."

"Put the phone away, Kayla," Brenna said mildly, "or you'll have a horrible accident."

"And then blood would truly be flowing." Élise slowed her pace and reached for her water. "And my Sean, he is very busy today already, so he will not have time to put your bones back together if they are crunched by a treadmill."

Kayla shuddered. "That is disgusting."

"It is his job."

"I know what his job is. I don't need details."

"Sometimes I think our jobs have many similarities." Élise put the water bottle down. "We both spend our day dealing with bones and raw meat."

"Oh, *please*." Kayla turned green, and Brenna smiled.

"She's doing it on purpose to wind you up. She's laughing at you."

"She won't be laughing when I lose my breakfast over her feet. I am so glad I don't live in your house, Élise. I wouldn't want to be present for your end of workday conversations."

"You think we waste our time together talking about work? We are both passionate about what we do, but when we finish, that is it. Sometimes we don't talk at all. We just have sex."

"Too much information." Kayla grabbed the remote and turned up the music then realized it was French and turned it down with a disgusted sound.

Élise turned it up again. "You are so uptight. What is wrong with sex?"

"I never said there was anything wrong with it. I just don't understand your need to talk about it all the time."

"Why not? Sex is a perfectly normal, healthy thing. And the O'Neil men are all very physical, sexual men. The moment Sean walks through that door, he stops thinking about his day." Élise gave a naughty smile. "Last night we—"

"No!" Kayla covered her ears with her hands. "Brenna, stop her! She listens to you."

Brenna glanced at Élise, envying the ease with which she talked about sex, and envying her relationship with Sean. How would it feel to come home to someone you loved at night instead of an empty house? How must it feel to know that the person you loved, loved you back? You wouldn't have to hide it, or hold it in. You wouldn't have to dig your nails into your palms to stop you from reaching out and touching.

Kayla was clearly still in work mode. "Élise, I know you were thinking of closing the Boathouse for Christmas Eve and Christmas Day, but if we're full, I think you might need to keep it open."

Élise was running fast again, her dark hair brushing her jaw. "Are you telling me how to manage my restaurants?"

"I'm telling you our guest numbers have doubled." Strolling on the treadmill, Kayla was still checking emails on her phone. "They're going to need to be fed. I see an opportunity."

"I see a nervous breakdown." Out of breath, Élise stabbed a button on the machine and slowed down. "I will need to hire extra staff for the Christmas week."

"Tell me what you need, and I'll make it happen." Kayla scanned an email. "I'll mention it to Jackson. Can't Poppy take over the running of the Boathouse for the holidays?"

"She is busy in the restaurant with me. I will work something out. And now that is enough! What happened to our rule never to talk about work while we exercise? Not that what you are doing could be called exercise. The only part of you moving is your fingers. You haven't burned any calories at all."

"This isn't work, exactly. It's exciting! And I burned plenty of calories before I left the house this morning."

Brenna reflected on the changes that could happen in a few months.

This time last year the three of them had been single. Now she was the only one not in a relationship, and while she loved the fact her friends were so happy, it made her feel lonelier than ever.

How would she cope when Tyler started dating again?

"Are you all right, Brenna?" Élise stepped off the treadmill and looped a towel around her neck. "You're very quiet."

"I'm fine." But she wasn't fine, was she? She wasn't fine at all. Not wanting to draw attention to the way she was feeling, she tried to change the subject. "Great news about the bookings, Kayla. Anything that guarantees the future of Snow Crystal is a reason to celebrate as far as I'm concerned. For a start, it means I keep my job."

Which meant she'd carry on working with Tyler.

She'd witness every date. It would be like working on the gates at Disneyland, watching everyone else indulging in a once-in-a-lifetime experience while she was stuck as a spectator.

Élise wiped her forehead with the towel. "If you are *fine* then why are you looking sick?"

Brenna hit the pause button and breathed deeply. "It's nothing."

Élise exchanged looks with Kayla. "You will tell us what this *nothing* is and together we will solve it."

"You can't solve it."

"I am very good with a knife. Is it a person? Give me a name. I will fillet them for you."

Kayla winced, and Brenna stared at the machine in misery, unable to pretend any longer. They were her friends. The first close female friendships she'd had. She remembered how Kayla had confided in them after her first night with Jackson. "It's Tyler."

Élise's eyes narrowed. "He has hurt you? I will definitely fillet him."

"No, he hasn't done anything." Brenna stepped off the machine. "It's me. And it's complicated." It was something she'd never talked about before. Not to anyone. She'd never been one to share her feelings about things. A lump formed in her throat, and she swallowed hard, knocked off balance by the sudden rush of emotion. It was because she was tired. The conversation with Tyler had unsettled her more than she'd wanted to admit. She hadn't been able to shake it off, not even on the slopes, and that was unusual for her.

Kayla stepped off the machine, too. "How is it complicated?"

"I really—well, I like him." She stumbled over the words and decided that for once she was going to tell the truth. "I love him."

Élise raised her eyebrows. "You think this is news to us?"

They *knew?* "You suspected? How? Is it obvious? Oh, that's terrible."

Élise opened her mouth, but Kayla got there first.

"We had a suspicion," she said tactfully. "Why is it complicated? What has changed?"

She wasn't used to talking about her feelings for Tyler. "Jess wants him to start dating."

Kayla put her phone down. "She told you that?"

"He told me that."

"He talked to you about dating other women?" Élise scowled. "I'm going to fillet him *and* sauté him in hot oil. How can he be so insensitive?"

Their loyalty was touching, but she knew it wasn't fair to let them blame Tyler. "It wasn't insensitive. He was talking to me as a friend. He has no idea how I feel about him."

Kayla gave her a long look. "Are you sure about that?"

"Of course!" But *they* knew, didn't they? And if they knew then— "Do you think he's guessed?"

"No, of course not," Kayla soothed, "it's only that we've known you a long time, and we think you'd be perfect together."

"Tyler has known me a long time, too. He's known me forever. He's very good at reading my feelings. He did it the other night when Jackson asked me to take the high school class. He knew I'd hate it. That's why he offered to step in." Brenna lifted her hand to her mouth. "If he knew, that would be awful. I don't want him feeling sorry for me. This is my problem, not his. I don't want things to change."

Élise glanced across with exasperation. "*Merde,* of course you want things to change! And for once instead of putting your head in the snow—"

"Sand," Kayla murmured and earned herself a glare.

"Snow, sand, mud—whatever you do when you don't want to face something. You could tell him the truth. You want to have sex with him. You want him to go from clothed to naked faster than his sports car goes from zero to sixty. You want him to be as in love with you as you are with him."

"But that isn't what would happen. That isn't what he wants. If he found out, it would be hideously awkward."

"Unless you're wrong about the way he feels about you."

"I'm not wrong. I know him as well as he knows me, and I know I'm not his type." There were things that they didn't understand. Things she'd never shared with anyone. "I think he'll be dating Christy by next week."

"Christy?" Kayla looked astonished at the suggestion. "No way. For a start, Tyler is a true outdoorsman, and Christy is most definitely an indoor girl. She's worse than I am! If she breaks a nail, she needs therapy. She'd drive Tyler mad in under sixty seconds. You have *totally* got that wrong."

"She's the sort of girl he hung out with all the time on the ski circuit."

"Maybe. But that was after the skiing had finished, and none of those relationships lasted."

"He flirts with her all the time."

"Tyler flirts with everyone under the age of fifty. It is how he communicates."

"Not with me."

Élise selected a pair of hand weights. "That is interesting, no? That tells you something."

"Yes, it tells me he doesn't see me that way. I'm someone to ski and climb trees with, not flirt with."

Élise pushed the weights up from her shoulders. "Kayla is right. You two are perfect together." The way she rolled her *r*s made her sound like a contented cat. "You may need to do something drastic and take control of the situation."

"I'm already in control of the situation. I'm working very hard to make sure he doesn't know how I feel."

"*Je ne comprends pas.* This I don't get." Élise looked bemused. "Why would you not want him to know?"

"Because it would damage our friendship."

Kayla leaned against the wall. "Perhaps it's time to turn what you have into something more than friendship."

Élise lowered the hand weights. "You should ask him straight-out and then there can be no mistake. With Sean, I made it clear I was interested."

"It's different." Brenna reached for her water bottle. "You and Sean have crazy chemistry. You've always shared something special. I already know how Tyler feels, and it isn't the same way I do," she said quietly. "I've learned to live with that. I learned to live with all those photos and rumors when he was on the ski circuit. I suppose that's one of the reasons the past year has been really special for me. With Jess living with him, the whole thing's been easier. And because of work we've been spending more time together, and it's been great."

Élise looked perplexed. "So if you are really happy with the situation, then carry on."

"That's just it. I've been pretending that we can, but

we can't. It's inevitable he is going to meet someone. I'm not sure how easy it's going to be to live with that. What woman is going to want him being friends with me?" She sat down on the machine. "I'm wondering if the whole thing would be easier if I moved away."

"You did that before." Élise put the weights down. "Did it work?"

"No." Suddenly, it felt difficult to speak. "He's in my heart so wherever I go, he comes with me."

"Oh, Bren, don't say things like that." Kayla's eyes filled, and she lifted her hand to her mouth. "You're making me cry, and I never cry. You are *not* moving away. You can't! Don't even think of it. You're an essential part of the team."

"Yes, without you, Kayla would turn into a lazy sloth." Élise's eyes were a little brighter than usual. "She needs you to help her keep that tight butt of hers. Without you, she'd sit at a desk all day."

"Crap." Kayla brushed her cheeks with the palm of her hand and sniffed. "Promise me you won't do anything rash. Somehow we'll fix this."

Knowing Kayla's formidable abilities to make things happen, Brenna came close to a smile. "Thanks, but even you can't fix this."

"Tyler hasn't started seeing anyone yet. It might not happen."

"It's going to happen. He's been putting his own needs second because of Jess, but if she's encouraging him, then it's going to happen. He's gorgeous. Women are all over him." She'd had to watch it her whole life. The way they looked at him. The lengths they went to get his attention. "I'm being stupid and pathetic. Ignore me. I'm tired. In fact, I think I'm going to skip the rest of our workout this morning." She stooped and picked up her bag as Kayla exchanged looks with Élise.

"But you never skip our workouts. Never. You always say there isn't a single thing in life that exercise can't help with."

"It can't help with this. I need to get going and organize today's lessons. I'll see you later."

There was no solution; she knew that.

She could move away, she could take another job on the other side of the world, but how did she get Tyler out of her heart?

KAYLA WAITED UNTIL the door closed behind Brenna and then breathed out heavily. "Look at me! I'm a mess."

Élise looked. "*C'est vrai.* You are a mess. I thought you were a cool Brit who never cried. Your eyes are the color of tomato salsa. Or maybe purée."

"Why does everything in your life have to have a culinary reference?" Kayla selected the camera app on her phone and checked her reflection. "Crap, you're right. I'm never wearing makeup to have a conversation with Brenna again."

"I have never seen her this emotional. She is a very calm, controlled person. It is the first time she has ever admitted her feelings."

Kayla slid her phone in her bag. "It must be hell being in love with a man who isn't interested. And when she said that bit about him being in her heart—" Her eyes filled again, and Élise glared at her in frustration.

"*Merde, j'en ai assez,* enough! What use is all this howling and sobbing? We need a plan." She muttered something in French and spread out a yoga mat. "And he's interested."

Kayla sniffed. "I must admit I thought so, too. Did you see the way he took over in that meeting when Jackson suggested she go and teach in the school? I almost melted on the spot. The man would slay a dragon for her, and she can't see it."

"Mmm." Élise looked thoughtful. "Fillet of dragon, dragon burger—"

"Stop thinking about food for five minutes! What I'm saying is that he is *so* protective, and he isn't like that with anyone else. When I fell over on the ice the other day, he laughed and stepped over me, so why doesn't he do something? Why hasn't he made a move? He isn't shy with women."

"I don't know why." Élise twisted her body into a shape that could have been yoga or Pilates. "I don't claim to understand the way a man's brain works. Other parts, yes. But not the brain."

"Maybe he doesn't see her like that. He grew up with her. She's like a guy to him."

"No one could see Brenna as a guy." Élise changed her position and stretched her limbs. "Perhaps it is lack of opportunity."

"They see each other all the time. They have plenty of opportunity." Kayla tilted her head to one side as she watched her friend. "Am I going to have to call the fire service to get you out of that position? How can you even do that?"

"I did ballet for a while. And they see each other at work, not at any other time."

"That isn't true. They had a drink together the other night."

"How do you know?"

"Because I saw them walking toward Forest Lodge.

He had his arm around her shoulder and they were laughing." She raised her eyebrows as Élise sank elegantly into the splits. "I am not winching you out of that position."

"He had his arm around her?"

"Yes. But it was more friendly than loverlike."

"It must be very hard for Brenna." Élise leaned forward, elegant and supple. "You're right. That would have been the perfect opportunity to make a move."

"Which suggests you're wrong and she's right. He isn't interested."

"Or that he is holding back."

Kayla pondered. "If that's the case, then he needs to be pushed outside his comfort zone. They need time together. At least then we'd find out one way or another."

"*D'accord.* I'm so over this will-they-won't-they crap. It's blowing my brain."

"But how do we engineer that at the beginning of the busiest season we've had for years? They'll be lucky to meet in passing on the ski slope."

"I am a chef, not Cupid. And I am not good with the indirect approach you all seem to use. If I were Brenna, I would simply say, 'Tyler, all my life I find you very hot and now I'd like to have sex with you. Yes or no?'"

Kayla grinned. "Is that what you did with Sean?"

"No, with Sean I didn't ask. I took what I wanted." She stretched her arms above her head. "I ripped his clothes off, and he ripped mine right back."

"There is no way Brenna would ever do that. Nor would she tell Tyler she finds him hot and wants to have sex. She's pretty shy about that sort of thing. And traditional. If anything is ever going to happen between them, he needs to make the first move." She watched in fascination as Élise raised her legs up slowly and lowered them again. "We need a plan."

"Brenna will not thank you if you interfere."

"I don't want thanks, and I will interfere gently. She won't know."

Élise stood up in a graceful movement. "Me, I still prefer the direct approach, but we'll try it your way first. Now stop watching me and do some exercise yourself."

BRENNA SAT IN BED high on the shelf of Forest Lodge, her hands curved around a mug of herbal tea. Her alarm wasn't due to go off for another hour, but she'd lain awake for half the night, thinking about Tyler.

Forest Lodge had a luxurious bedroom on the floor below, complete with bathroom and a private hot tub outside the door, but she chose to sleep up on the mezzanine floor because she loved the view. She lay snug in the bed, looking through acres of glass to the forest beyond. It was like living in a tree house, the view more breathtaking than anything an artist could produce with oils and canvas.

It was still dark outside, but the snow was luminous in the moonlight and she could see the forest smothered in another deep coating of winter-white. It draped itself over the trees in extravagant folds, blunting sharp lines, the weight of it causing branches to droop.

Who needed a Christmas tree when every day at Snow Crystal during the winter was like Christmas?

Kneeling on the bed, she peered through the gaps in the trees. She was just able to see Lake House, where Tyler lived with Jess.

She'd spent so many happy summers and winters in these woods along with three generations of O'Neil men—Sean, Jackson and Tyler, their father Michael and their grandfather, Walter—exploring the outdoors, transforming rambling, tumble-down structures into something habitable. She'd hauled bricks, sanded wood and stood knee-deep in the lake while they'd built a deck. Somewhere out there was a tree where she'd carved his name.

It wasn't that she didn't love her parents, but sometimes it felt as if she'd been born into the wrong family. They didn't understand her love of the mountains and the outdoors, and they certainly didn't share it. When her parents had thought to dampen her love of the mountains and skiing by refusing to fund her equipment needs, Michael had given her Tyler's old skis and let her keep them at Snow Crystal.

Brenna had never understood her mother's hostility toward the O'Neils, who were well liked and respected by everyone else in the county. She'd decided it was just that Maura Daniels was violently opposed to anything to do with skiing and winter sports. She shut the snow out of her small, pristine house and complained endlessly about the long, cold Vermont winters until it sometimes seemed to Brenna that the mountains must have offended her personally in some way.

And so she'd lived her life growing up in one house but spending all her time in another until the day she'd found out Janet Carpenter was pregnant.

It had been the worst day of her life.

She'd vanished into the mountains for two days without telling anyone where she was going.

It had been Jackson, home from college for the summer, who had found her.

Strong, steady Jackson, who had ignored the orders of

her parents, his parents and the mountain rescue team and trekked on foot to the ridge where they'd often camped out as children, following a hunch.

He'd wanted her to talk about it, but she'd kept her mouth clamped tightly shut because she always found it easier to keep things inside than let them out.

Strangely enough, that had been the one time in her life when her mother had been a comfort. It was as if finally she knew what her daughter, alien to her in every other way, needed.

It had been her mother who had urged her to get up in the morning, wash her hair, get dressed and keep going through another year of school. It had been her mother who had fed her homemade soup, spoonful by spoonful, and held her when she'd cried.

They'd never talked about the details, but for once her mother had stopped nagging her and shown a kindness and empathy Brenna hadn't witnessed before or since. It was a painful irony that the worst time of her life had also been the best.

Then Tyler had been given his place on the U.S. ski team. From that moment on he'd been away, traveling from one place to another and not coming home in between, so there were months when the only time she saw him was on TV.

She'd trained as a ski instructor and worked for four years with Jackson in Europe, in the hope that distance might kill those feelings, but Tyler was skiing in Europe, too, and she'd frequently joined the family to watch him race.

She'd watched as his star had risen and he'd won medal after medal, skiing faster, harder than anyone else, his sheer talent and aggression on the mountain setting him apart from the others. The media described him as ferocious and fearless on the slopes, but she just saw him as the boy she'd skied with since she was a toddler.

She understood him.

She understood it wasn't ambition that drove him, but a love of speed. The media accused him of being ruthlessly competitive and he was, but she knew the person he was competing against was himself. She'd spent hours alone on the mountain with him, watching him tackle new routes, seemingly impossible angles and slopes. As he'd pushed himself to the limit, she'd been the only witness.

Pulling a warm fleece over her pajamas, she walked down the curving staircase that led to the ground floor and was about to make herself another cup of tea when she saw him standing in the door.

For a moment she wondered whether her mind had conjured him, but then she saw him smiling and pointing to the snow.

Wishing she were wearing something other than pajamas, she walked across and opened the door. A blast of ice-cold air almost knocked her off her feet, and she snuggled deeper into the fleece. "Is something wrong? It's the middle of the night!"

"Nearly dawn, and we need an early start if we're going to get first chair."

First chair? "You want to ski?"

"Have you seen the snow? Take a look over my shoulder."

"I already did."

Later the air would be filled with the shrieks of happy, excited children but for now Snow Crystal was enveloped in that strange, eerie silence that always followed a heavy snowfall.

"It's a perfect powder day."

"Yeah, and before we devote it to other people, I thought we should take time for ourselves. An early Christmas present. Time to head to the office, Ms. Daniels, before the rest of the world arrives. Get dressed and let's go ride some powder." His eyes were a lazy, sleepy blue, the only color in a world that had turned white overnight, and she stood for a moment, mesmerized.

"Now?"

He gestured with his head. "There is three feet of untracked snow out there waiting for us. You should already have your feet in your boots."

She knew plenty of locals, civilized people at all other times, who would kill each other to be first on the four-person chairlift up the mountain on a day like today. "There will be a line for first tracks."

"All the more reason not to hang around. I'll give you two minutes to get dressed." He was wearing a hat pulled down low over his forehead, and his hands were thrust into the pockets of his coat. Judging from the stubble shadowing his jaw, he hadn't wasted time shaving. His smile was sure and confident and she wondered if any woman had ever said no to him.

Awareness dragged low in her stomach. "We have a full day of work ahead."

"All the more reason to make the most of the next few hours. Or you could go back to bed and have another hour of sleep if that's what you prefer." The gleam in his eyes told her he knew the answer to that.

"I wasn't asleep."

"I never had to work this hard to persuade you when

we were teenagers. I smuggled you out of your window more than once."

"That was a long time ago!" A lifetime. Before Janet. "We're adults now. Responsible."

"Too much responsibility is bad for a person. I'll be responsible after 8:30 a.m. The whole mountain will have been messed up by then anyway, but for now I'm on my own time. Come on." His voice was deep and persuasive. "If I have to spend my day skiing with people who don't know a ski pole from the North Pole, the least you can do is let me have some fun with you first."

Élise would have used that as an opening. Élise would have flirted, or maybe even dragged him over the threshold and back to the bed that was still warm from her body.

Maybe she should try.

"You could come in for a while," she said casually, and he frowned.

"What would be the point in that? You haven't turned into one of those women who takes ages to get dressed in the morning, have you? I remember you once pulling your ski pants on over your pajamas. I'll wait here while you change."

She felt the color rush into her cheeks. *How were you supposed to flirt with a man when he didn't even know you were flirting?*

"Why me?" Her voice was a croak. "You could have skied with your brothers."

"Too complicated and anyway," his tone was ultra casual, "I enjoy skiing with you."

It was the one thing they shared. The one thing she had that other women didn't.

The ability to keep up with him.

"I'll be out in two minutes."

He gave a slow, sexy smile. "Make it one minute. We need to make the most of the quiet time. God knows there's little enough of it round here with visitor numbers increasing."

She understood, because she felt the same way. Like Tyler, she'd always rather be outdoors than indoors. "Where's Jess?"

"She slept overnight at my mother's. They were stocking the freezer for Christmas. There's a strong chance school will be canceled this morning, and if it is, I'll ski with her later. If not, Mom will take her to school. Now hurry up and get dressed before the rest of the village beats us to it."

Trying not to read anything into the invitation, Brenna dressed quickly in her ski gear, grabbed what she needed for the day and joined him outside.

He drove to the base of the quad lift that carried four people at a time up the mountain. It had been replaced a few years previously, and the new lift had fewer problems with the ice and cold weather.

It was still dark and, despite her predictions, they were the first skiers on the lift.

Tyler brushed the snow from the seat, and Brenna settled next to him on the chair, her thigh pressing against his. They sat in silence, enjoying the slow glide of the lift as it carried them smoothly up the mountain. From here she had an aerial view of winter perfection. She looked down at the trees and narrow trails, mentally plotting a route, trying not to think about the pressure of his leg against hers.

It was bitterly cold, and she snuggled deeper inside her jacket, her shoulder resting against his.

How many times had they done this? Sat side by side

watching the sun rise over the ridge, the light dazzling and dancing over the untouched surface of new snow, the ice crystals sparkling under the warm blue of the winter sky.

As they skied off the lift and paused at the top, Tyler turned to her. "Glad you didn't stay in bed?"

"Yes. I love the way the forest feels after snow." No possession, nothing she'd ever owned, could be this beautiful or give her the same kick of excitement as nature did when she shone light down on the mountains and forest. "This is perfect." And being with him made it all the more perfect.

It was because she was thinking about him and not concentrating that she caught an edge and landed flat on her back.

"Oh, crap."

Laughing, he skied over to her. "I can't remember the last time I saw you fall." As she struggled to sit up, he reached into his pocket for his phone.

"What are you doing?"

"Savoring the moment. And gathering photographic evidence."

"Don't you *dare*."

"I'm kidding." Still laughing, he slipped the phone back into his pocket, reached out and hauled her to her feet.

Her ski tangled with his, and he slid slightly and clamped her hard against him to stop them both falling.

She rested her hand on his shoulder to steady herself, looking first at his jaw, then at his mouth and finally his eyes.

Serious eyes, all suggestion of laughter gone. "All right?"

"I'm good."

His gaze held hers for a moment, and then he released her, disentangled their skis and turned toward the trees.

For him, the moment had passed but her mind, her memory, was full of moments like this. His name wasn't just carved on a tree somewhere, it was carved in her heart.

She stood still, watching him move fluidly through the deep snow. He made it look effortless and easy as only an expert could.

It didn't matter whether he was bombing from the top to the bottom in a World Cup downhill, floating through deep snow or arcing on groomers, he was the best. A supreme athlete, in tune with his surroundings. In a sport where the difference between winning and coming in second was the matter of a hundredth of a second, he had been right at the top of the game.

She followed as he took a route through three feet of perfectly layered snow, instinct and local knowledge helping him find the perfect path through the deep powder. He was a skilled, aggressive skier, attacking the slopes with no visible signs of fear, regardless of the conditions. She heard him whoop as he executed a run of smooth, perfect turns, gliding through the snow with fluidity and rhythm. She followed as he swooped down into the glades, and they weaved through snow-sculpted trees, their branches misshapen and heavy from the weight of their winter load. The only sound was the whisper of skis and the soft thud of snow falling on snow as they wound their way through hardwood forest toward the main part of the resort.

Eventually, he paused, and she stopped next to him

in the clearing, her cheeks stinging from the cold, her breath clouding the air.

"That was incredible." The early morning sun danced across the surface of the new snow, and ice crystals sparkled like spilled sugar. High in the trees a pair of chickadees were singing, and the sky behind them was an unblemished blue.

"It's the best time of day." He tugged off a glove and lifted his ski goggles. "It's going to be a good one."

It had already started in the best possible way.

"Thanks for asking me to join you. Most people would kill their neighbor for first tracks."

"Hey—" he turned his head and gave her a smile that connected straight to her knees "—I still made first tracks. You were behind me."

She pushed him but he didn't budge, rock solid on his skis. "Next time, I'm going first."

"If you can catch me, you're welcome to go first."

"Remember when we used to skip school and come up here?" She leaned on her ski pole. "We felt as if we owned the mountain."

"We did."

"And then they called my mom, and both our parents were hauled up to the school. Mom grounded me for the weekend. As we walked out of the school, she was telling me how I'd embarrassed her and all I heard was your dad asking you what the snow was like."

"I still remember the look your mom gave my dad. If she could, she would have buried him in a snowdrift. The O'Neils were never her favorite people. She thought Dad was irresponsible." He stared straight ahead. "I guess a lot of people thought that. Still think that."

She felt the change in his mood. "He was a good man."

"He was a lousy businessman. He was trapped in a life he didn't want, and instead of dealing with it he let a lot of people down. Hurt them."

"Does your mom ever talk about it?"

"Never. She's nothing but loyal. She loved him, faults and all."

"Isn't that what love really is? Loving someone as they are. If you want someone to be different, how can that be love?" Brenna watched as a bird swooped between the branches, showering snow across the forest floor.

They were alone in this wintery wilderness, wrapped by the cold and the endless white, with only the breathtaking beauty of the forest for company.

"Without Jackson, she would have lost her home. So would Grams and Gramps. Sometimes it's hard not to let the bad memories overtake the good." His rough confession, his unusual admission of inner struggle, made Brenna catch her breath.

Why was it that whenever he hurt, she hurt, too?

It was his pain, and yet it felt like hers.

It had been the same after his accident. The same after his father had died.

Whatever he felt, she felt, as if they were connected by an invisible wire that transmitted his emotions straight into her with no filter.

"I always think of your father when I'm skiing in the glades." She chose her words carefully, hoping to heal not hurt. "We skied here so often. I can still hear his voice telling me to look at the gap between the trees, not the trees themselves."

"I think of him here, too."

Breaking her own rule, she put her hand on his arm. "There was so much good. He was fun. Adventurous, and he encouraged you to be adventurous. There wasn't a single day when he wasn't proud of you, when he didn't encourage you. He was a skilled outdoorsman, and he saw those same skills in you. It was your dad who taught me to ski, and he was brilliant."

"His idea of teaching was to stand at the top of a vertical slope and say 'follow me.'"

"Exactly. My parents never let me do anything remotely risky. He encouraged you to pursue your dreams."

"And he pursued his own. A little too enthusiastically." He drew breath. "I don't usually talk about this. I guess because you knew him—"

"I loved him," Brenna said simply, and Tyler turned his head.

His blue eyes fixed on hers, and she caught her breath because what they shared in that moment was intimate and deeply personal.

"And he loved you. He thought you were the coolest girl on the slopes."

"I envied you so much because you had a dad who really understood your passion. Shared it." Shaken by the strength of her feelings, she let go of his arm. "I tried to talk to my mother about it. I tried to explain how it felt to surf down soft powdery snow while the sun turns the forest and mountains from snowy-white to burned-orange. I tried to explain how when I'm skiing, all my problems vanish, how I can't think of anything else but my skis and the mountain, how it clears my head and makes my heart feel free."

"She didn't understand?"

"She delivered a lecture on how education would be my ticket out of this place." She'd never understood that Brenna would have been happy to ski the mountains around Snow Crystal for the rest of her life. That she hadn't wanted that ticket. "Everything I ever wanted is right here, and she never understood that."

His gaze was fixed on her face. "What is it you want?"

"The mountains. This life." *Tyler O'Neil.*

Careful not to reveal that part, she dipped her head and poked her ski pole in the deep snow. "I guess I'm lucky. Most people don't get this close to living their dream. But I envied you that day. I imagined you going back and sitting round your kitchen table telling everyone about it. I bet Elizabeth made you hot chocolate."

"Probably. I'm guessing you didn't get hot chocolate?"

"I got a lecture on being responsible and how easy it was to sabotage a life by making bad choices."

He gave her a slow, wicked smile. "And let me guess, I was one of those bad choices she was warning you about."

Brenna's heart skipped and bounced like skis on rough ground.

"Only because she never understood that I would have done all those things even if you hadn't been there."

"She didn't approve of our friendship."

"My mother didn't approve of anything I did. It wasn't personal." She frowned, because sometimes it had *felt* personal even though she knew it couldn't be. The O'Neil family had never been anything other than warm and civil to Maura Daniels, so there was nothing to explain the frozen atmosphere except that she resented their lifestyle and their easy relationship with her daughter. "She didn't like me spending time at your house, and I've never understood that."

Tyler reached out and brushed snow from her shoulder. "She was worried we were a bad influence. Three boys and her baby girl."

"Are you patronizing me?" Brenna raised an eyebrow. "I did everything you did. And most of the time, I did it better."

"I guess that's why she was worried. Did your mother ever know you climbed out through your bedroom window?"

"No. If she'd known, I would have been grounded for a month."

"If she'd known half the things we did together, she would have grounded you until you were eighteen." There was laughter in his eyes, and she thought about how many times in her life she'd been ready to kill him for something he'd said or done, only to be cut off at the knees by that smile. All the anger, the irritation, the frustration, would leave her in a rush, leaving only one emotion. The most powerful emotion of all.

Her heart fluttered as if trying to remind her of its existence. Awareness washed over her, warming her skin and stealing her breath. To him, she was a friend, but to her, he was always a man.

She loved his strength and his unapologetic determination to live the life he wanted to live. He broke hearts but not promises, mostly because he never made any. To his friends and family, he was fiercely loyal and protective.

What would it feel like to be kissed by him? For a fleeting moment she wished she were one of those women who flirted and enjoyed his attentions. Maybe their time with him was fleeting, but she was willing to bet they enjoyed every minute.

His eyes held hers for a moment, and then he turned away. "We should go."

"Yes." Her voice was croaky, but it didn't matter because he was already skiing away from her, picking a route through the trees while she stood for a moment hoping that, on this occasion at least, he hadn't been able to read her mind.

When it came to her feelings, he was uncannily perceptive, which was why she'd learned to hide what she felt.

She followed more slowly. This time she didn't try to keep up, not only because the trees were closer together as they neared the bottom of the slope, but also because she didn't trust her legs.

They were shaky. Unstable.

Deciding that thinking about kissing Tyler was a quick way to a serious accident in this terrain, she tried to focus on her skiing. She'd already fallen once. She wasn't going to do it again.

She reached the lift to find him already waiting for her, and as she removed her skis, her phone chimed.

"Back to reality."

"You shouldn't have had that switched on." He sounded impatient. "Ignore it."

"I can't. I'm supposed to be working." Pulling her phone out of her pocket, she read the text. "I didn't bother switching it off because there's no reception in the trees anyway."

"Who is it?"

"Kayla." She texted back. "Emergency staff meeting at 7:45 a.m."

"Emergency?" Tyler dragged off his gloves. "My future sister-in-law has a strange definition of an *emergency*. For us it's an avalanche. For Kayla it's a journalist with a deadline."

Brenna smiled because it was true. "She has helped transform this place. She has a lot to do with the fact

Snow Crystal has a future. And she and Jackson are so cute together. I never thought I'd see him so crazy about a woman."

Tyler bent to unfasten his boot. "Does it bother you?"

"Why would it bother me?"

"You had dinner with him a few times." His voice was casual. "You've worked together for years. I wondered, that's all."

"There's never been anything between Jackson and me except friendship." Whereas her feelings for Tyler were something different entirely. Not wanting to dwell on it, she slid her phone back into her pocket and bent to pick up her skis. "We'd better go back before they send out a search party."

CHAPTER FIVE

"So THERE'S GOOD NEWS, and there's bad news." Kayla paced across the room as she always did when she was thinking. "The good news is that all the snow has brought another flurry of bookings. It's incredible. I never thought we'd be this busy, this soon."

"Me, I am always this busy, and right now I should be in the kitchen preparing for lunchtime service." Impatient to be back in the restaurant, Élise tapped her foot on the floor. "What is the bad news?"

"The extra bookings mean that we're right at capacity." Kayla sent Brenna a guilty look. "I've had to book Forest Lodge. I'm *so* sorry. I feel terrible about it, but I had no choice."

Brenna's stomach swooped. It hadn't occurred to her that she wouldn't be able to stay in Forest Lodge over the winter. Dismay was followed by disappointment and concern about where she'd live in the short-term.

Jackson frowned. "Forest isn't for rent. Put them in one of the other lodges."

"The others are booked. And they specifically requested Forest."

"It's fine," Brenna said quickly, but Jackson shook his head.

"Brenna has stayed in that lodge since it was built. Why would they request it? It isn't on the website."

"They must have seen it on the resort map and liked the position. They offered full brochure price for it, Jackson. What was I supposed to do? We're running a business, and they wanted Forest Lodge." Visibly stressed, Kayla rubbed her fingers over her forehead. "Maybe I made the wrong decision. I should have told them we were full. I'm sorry. Look, I'll call them back. Tell them I made a mistake."

"No, you can't do that!" Brenna told herself it was ridiculous to be hurt when Kayla was doing her job, and doing it well. "You're right. We're running a business. Not only that, we're trying to save a business."

Kayla gave her a grateful look. "The numbers are looking healthy, but maybe I'm getting carried away. Jackson always says that one day he's going to find people sleeping in the stable."

"Well it *is* Christmas," Elizabeth murmured, and Brenna forced a smile.

"You did the right thing. Don't worry. When do I need to be out?"

"They're arriving Saturday because they wanted the week before Christmas. It's always quieter on the slopes. Then I've booked out the full two weeks around Christmas and New Year's after that."

"This coming Saturday?"

"Yes. It doesn't give us much time to get the lodge ready. They've made lots of special requests. Tree, extra logs—" Waving her hand, Kayla recounted a vague list, and Brenna realized that someone else would be spending Christmas in Forest Lodge.

"I'll work something out." She spoke firmly, as much to convince herself as Kayla.

"You can have a room in the hotel," Jackson said, but

Kayla shook her head as she checked something on her phone.

"Lissa booked the last room this morning. It's free tonight, but Brenna doesn't want to be moving her things around."

Brenna felt a flash of anxiety. She didn't have the time to hunt for somewhere new to live with less than two weeks to go until Christmas. "I don't have many things to move. I'm not a possessions person."

"You need somewhere you can treat as home, and a soulless hotel room isn't the answer even if we did have one available, which we don't."

Jackson intervened. "Firstly, our hotel rooms aren't soulless, and secondly you're babbling."

Kayla looked flustered. "I have a lot on my mind. I'm sorry, Brenna. I know how much you love Forest Lodge, and it's conveniently close to the ski lift. You could stay with Jackson and me, but we're farther away so—wait a minute!" Her face brightened, and she turned to Tyler. "You have four bedrooms, right?"

Tyler had been glowering through the entire exchange. "You know I do."

"So why doesn't Brenna stay at Lake House with you? It's stunning since you finished the renovations, and you're even closer to the ski lift than Forest Lodge, so the position couldn't be better." She clapped her hands. "I'm a genius!"

Jackson frowned. "Kayla, you can't just—"

"I wish I'd thought of it before, then I could have presented the solution with the problem and saved all the anxiety." Ignoring Jackson, Kayla beamed and paced the length of the room like a general marshalling troops. "Brenna can stay on at the resort, and we can rent Forest Lodge for top rate. This is all turning out brilliantly. Champagne is called for."

"At eight-thirty in the morning?" Jackson's tone was mild, and he was looking at Kayla with a mixture of exasperation and amusement.

Brenna wasn't amused. She was appalled.

Move in with Tyler?

She couldn't think of anything worse. "I can't live with Tyler!" She didn't dare contemplate his reaction. She couldn't look at him. She didn't need to because she knew exactly what he was thinking. Because of Jess, he'd been forced to curtail his wild lifestyle, but now he was on the verge of getting back out there again. The last thing he needed was his childhood friend moving in with him. "That's not a solution. I'll rent an apartment. I was always going to have to do that once Snow Crystal started to recover, but there was no reason to do it when the place was half-empty."

"You won't be able to rent an apartment before Christmas." Kayla was still pacing. "And even if you found one in the New Year, it wouldn't be practical for you to be driving backward and forward. That's why you started living in the resort in the first place."

Brenna didn't know which option was worse—the thought of renting somewhere away from Snow Crystal, or the idea of moving in with Tyler.

"I can stay with my parents as a short-term solution."

"No, you can't." Tyler's voice held none of its usual humor. "Visiting drives you insane, so living there is not an option. You can live with me. Jess and I have loads of room. It makes sense." Those blue eyes locked on hers, and everyone else in the room faded into the background. It was just the two of them and her feelings, which were so huge, so out of control, she thought surely he'd see them.

He read her so well, but for some reason he was blind to this one thing.

She should tell him. She should stop avoiding the issue and be honest about how hard it was for her. That's what he would do.

But she wasn't going to do that in public, so instead she gave a shake of her head. "It wouldn't feel right."

"If it makes you feel better, we can share the cooking."

"You'll come off worse from that deal. I'm a terrible cook."

"You can cook bacon, so we'll put you in charge of breakfast." Tyler stretched out his legs, those powerful thighs pushing against the fabric of his ski pants. "Bacon is a perfect way to start the day. And Jess would love having you around. She'll drive you mad talking about skiing. That will ease the load on me, and we need extra hands to keep the dogs off the sofas."

"I will fill your fridge," Élise offered. "That will be my contribution to make up for the inconvenience you must suffer, Brenna."

Food was going to be the least of her problems.

They were asking her to live with Tyler.

She'd have to watch him dress up and go out with some other woman. Maybe even bring one home. And it wasn't only Tyler, was it? There was Jess to think about. She was relishing the time alone with her father after all those years apart.

How would she feel about having another person intruding?

It was Christmas. A time for families.

She'd be in the way.

"Perhaps I could stay with Elizabeth." Desperate, she scrabbled for an alternative. "Until I can work something else out." She looked at the woman who had been more of a mother to her than her own. "Elizabeth, would it inconvenience you hugely?"

"Stay with Elizabeth?" Kayla's face fell, and she looked thrown, as if that option hadn't crossed her mind. "Well, I er—"

Elizabeth stirred. "I'm so sorry, dear, at any other time of course you could, I'd love having you, but I'm expecting hordes of relatives over from England."

"Relatives?" Jackson raised an eyebrow. "Which relatives?"

"Very distant," his mother murmured, "second cousins. You've never met them. They're on my mother's side. British. You know I have relatives you've never met."

"*Hordes* of them?"

"I don't exactly know how many," Elizabeth said vaguely. "I issued an open invitation, which probably wasn't very sensible now I think about it. They wanted to come to Vermont, and it's always a little lonely in the house at Christmas, so I suggested they visit. Oh, what a nuisance. Such bad timing. I'm so sorry, Brenna."

"Lonely?" Tyler looked incredulous. "I would pay money to be lonely around here. The place is teeming with people night and day, and it sounds as if it's going to get worse if Kayla keeps this up. We can offer many things at Snow Crystal but *lonely* isn't on the list. Brenna, you can move in with Jess and me. You'd be doing me a favor. Otherwise, I'm going to turn round one day and discover Kayla has rented my empty rooms to tourists."

Kayla's face brightened. "That's a—"

"Don't even think about it," Tyler growled. "Are we

about done here? If there's one guaranteed way of ruining a perfect powder day, it's filling it with meetings."

"I'm done! I'm so glad it's settled." Kayla threw them
all a look of relief. "Now I don't feel so guilty. Oh, my
goodness, is that really the time?" She glanced at her
phone in a panic. "I have a press interview scheduled
for nine. And, Tyler, one other thing. I have a reporter
coming to ski powder with you this morning. Hope that's
okay."

"It's one piece of good news after another," Tyler
drawled. "Which publication does he work for? *Car-
toon Weekly?*"

"He's freelance, and his work is published everywhere
from *The New York Times* to *Outside* magazine, but this
is a piece for a ski blog. They've got half a million followers. He's doing a piece on undiscovered ski resorts
and happened to be in the area, so he called me first
thing. Fantastic coincidence that you're free. He's going
to live tweet it."

Tyler's expression turned from menacing to stormy.
"He's going to *what?*"

"Live tweet skiing with you." Kayla avoided his eye as
she typed an email on her phone. "He wants to give his
followers a feel for what it's like to ski with Tyler O'Neil."

"I hope his followers enjoy the part where he skis off
a cliff." Tyler rose to his feet, and Jackson sighed.

"Sit down, Ty. They guy only has two hours to spare
and it will be good publicity."

Tyler shrugged on his jacket, his powerful frame sim-
mering with suppressed volatility. "I will take your stupid master class, I will help coach the high school team
if I have to, but I am *not* pausing in the middle of a run
so that some guy I've never met and don't care about can

share the experience of making first tracks in powder with another half a million people I've never met and don't care about."

Kayla froze. Slowly, she let her hand drop. "I'm sorry. I can see I've overstepped." She sounded contrite. "I thought it was a good idea."

Jackson smiled. "It was a good idea. Ignore him. He's been indoors for a full five minutes. That always puts him in a filthy mood."

Tyler scowled. "If it's such a great idea, you can do it."

"I would do it," Jackson said calmly, "but no one is interested in skiing with me. You're the one with the crowd-pulling power, although I've never been able to understand why, given that you're such a moody son of a—"

"Jackson!" Elizabeth gave her son a reproving look, and Jackson closed his mouth and shook his head.

"We're all doing what we can to get publicity for the place, that's all."

Sensing that Tyler was about to combust and knowing that if that happened, they wouldn't see him for the rest of the day, Brenna decided her own problems could wait. "The reporter can't live tweet it. That isn't possible." Everyone turned to look at her and she shrugged, wondering why she was the only one who could see the problem. "If he only has two hours then that restricts where on the mountain he can ski. If he wants powder, then he'll have to ski the runs above the resort and down into the glades, but he won't be able to use his phone. There is no reception there. It cuts out constantly."

Jackson pulled a face. "She's right. I hadn't thought of that."

"And if he really wants to get a feel for what it's like to ski with Tyler O'Neil," Brenna continued, "then he'll be skiing fast, hard and probably way out of his comfort zone. That is expert terrain. I'm assuming he's an expert, but either way, he needs to concentrate or be killed. I suggest instead of live tweeting, which could easily become dead tweeting, he writes a piece afterward about how it felt. Maybe add a few quotes from Tyler."

Tyler's eyes gleamed. "Great idea. Here's a quote. 'Get the hell off my mountain.'"

Brenna suppressed the desire to laugh and a flash of envy that he was never afraid to speak his mind. "Give him my number, and I'll give him some quotes on what it's like to ski powder here."

Kayla bit her lip. "He thought if the world knew Tyler skied here, it would draw the crowds."

"I hate crowds." Tyler's tone was dangerous, but Jackson laughed.

"I love crowds. Crowds mean business. It's fine. Tyler will do it. If he doesn't, I'll kick his butt."

Tyler sent him a glance. "Can we live tweet that?"

Now that the crisis was averted, Brenna's mind drifted back to her own problem. They'd moved on. They were already talking about other things. This didn't matter to them; it wasn't significant. But to her it was hugely significant.

Not just because she would no longer be living in Forest Lodge, which she adored, but that they expected her to move in with Tyler.

She didn't know which part upset her most—the fact that Kayla could have put her in this awkward position when she knew how Brenna felt, or the fact that Tyler clearly wasn't bothered.

If she needed further evidence of his lack of feeling toward her, she had it now.

He didn't see the situation as awkward because it wasn't.

To him, she was a lodger, nothing more.

He wasn't worried that he might bump into her in her underwear.

Kayla was talking details. "The journalist will be here at 9:30 a.m. Will you do it, Tyler?" She looked anxiously at him, and he sighed.

"Yeah, I'll do it. But you owe me."

Kayla beamed, strode across the room and kissed him on the cheek. "I love you, have I told you that lately? You're going to be a perfect brother-in-law."

"Going to be? I'm already perfect." He glanced between Kayla and Jackson. "So have you two finally set a date to get this thing over and done with?"

"*This thing* is called a wedding," Jackson said mildly, "and *over and done with* isn't the phrase I would have picked."

Kayla rubbed the lipstick from Tyler's cheek. "The answer is no, we haven't set a date, but it's on my to-do list."

"June." Jackson spoke firmly. "I've blocked out the whole place. We're going to get married at Snow Crystal, in the orchard behind the house."

"Oh!" Thrown, Kayla's eyes flew wide, and she pressed her hand to her chest. "Seriously? That's— well—" she breathed "—married?"

"You're wearing my ring," Jackson said softly. "I'm ready to make it official."

She glanced down at the diamond sparkling on her finger, and when she spoke her voice sounded strange. "I'll check my schedule for June."

"I've already blocked it out in your calendar. It's the only way I'll get priority over your job."

"That's not true! But June—" Breathless, visibly flustered, Kayla started to pace again. "It's not long. I'm not sure I can organize everything by then. There's a lot to do."

"Not for you. You're not organizing your own wedding."

"But—"

"You're not organizing your own wedding, Kayla."

"Then who will?"

"We will. Gramps, Grams, Mom, Élise, Sean—your family." He spoke the words with quiet emphasis, and Kayla stopped in midstride, her eyes shining. She met his gaze, and something passed between them.

Elizabeth gave a soft sigh of satisfaction, and Jackson stood up and pulled Kayla into his arms.

"Get a room." Tyler zipped his jacket. "And do it fast before Kayla books them all out because you're sure as hell not staying with me. I'd better go and find your reporter." He walked out, and Brenna stood up, too.

"Congratulations." She walked across the room and hugged Jackson and Kayla, happy for them and envious at the same time. They didn't share only friendship, they shared everything.

She'd never had that closeness with anyone, and it wasn't because she hadn't tried.

She knew that Élise treated sex as little more than an athletic workout. If rumor was correct then Tyler was the same. She didn't know if she was different, more old-fashioned, or whether it was simply that she'd been in love all her life, and that had affected the way she related to other men.

The few physical relationships she'd experienced had

been fun at the time, but there had been no deeper connection.

For her, love wasn't fleeting or temporary. It wasn't something that could be cured by absence or willpower. It couldn't be found in a glance or a single night. It was deep and permanent. Loving Tyler was as much a part of her as her limbs and her hair color. She couldn't switch it on or off.

"I have a class to teach." She kept the smile on her face as she stepped out of the door and made sure it didn't slip until she was safely clear of everyone.

"So now tell me the truth." Waiting for the room to empty, Jackson blocked the door as Kayla tried to walk past him.

"The truth about what? How I feel about the wedding? I'm thrilled. Nervous, of course, and a little overwhelmed because I have a million things to do and—"

"Not the wedding. Why did you book Forest Lodge?"

"Oh, that—" She didn't meet his gaze. "I already told you, I had a flurry of bookings and—"

He slid his fingers under her chin and forced her to look at him. "Honey, do you think I'm stupid?"

"You think I'm inventing guests?"

"No, but I think you could have chosen to put them somewhere other than Forest Lodge. You know how much Brenna loves that place. She was hurt that you're making her move, and on the surface it's a mean thing to do, especially this close to Christmas—"

Kayla winced. "Jackson—"

"—but I know you're not a mean person, so there has to be something else behind it and given your 'brilliant idea' that she moves in with Tyler, I'm assuming the two are linked."

"It *is* a brilliant idea. I'm so glad I thought of it."

"Yeah, but you didn't think of it two minutes ago. That isn't how your brain works. You are a master problem solver. You analyze every possible solution. You started that meeting knowing exactly how you wanted it to end. So my question is, why are you trying to throw Tyler and Brenna together?"

Kayla opened her mouth to refute that accusation and then caught his eye. "Because Brenna has been in love with him her whole life, and nothing ever happens. It's *infuriating.*"

"You can't interfere, sweetheart."

Her face fell. "I feel guilty. We're so happy. I have you, and Élise has Sean, and Brenna loves Tyler *so much,* and he's blind and stupid."

Jackson closed his hands over her shoulders. "He is neither blind nor stupid. Emotions aren't as easy to control as you wish they were. You can't force feelings. They're either there or they're not."

"You're a man. You don't understand."

"I understand more than you think. I grew up consoling women who were in love with Sean." He smoothed her hair with his hand. "You can't make one person fall in love with another. That isn't how it works."

"I know that!" She scowled at him. "Do you think I wanted to fall in love with you? I didn't! It derailed all my plans."

"Yeah, that turned out really badly." Smiling, he lowered his head and kissed her. When he finally lifted his head, she blinked dizzily and locked her hand in the front of his shirt.

"You always do that when you're losing an argument."

"I wasn't losing anything."

"What were you saying?"

"I was saying that a person can't interfere with other people's love lives. What happens between two people is a personal thing."

"What if two people are perfect for each other and nothing ever happens?"

"Then maybe it's not meant to happen. They've known each other since Brenna was four years old. If something was going to happen, surely it would have happened by now."

"It would have done if your brother wasn't so blind."

Jackson gathered her against him. "He isn't blind."

"Don't defend him."

"I'm not defending him. I'm just saying he's not blind."

"Then why hasn't he made a move?"

"It isn't a conversation I've had because I figure it's his business, not mine." He eased away from her and gave her a pointed look. "But I'm sure he has his reasons."

"Are you telling me you've never thought they'd be perfect together?"

Jackson hesitated. "They have plenty in common, that's true, but Brenna is the settled type. I wouldn't exactly describe Tyler as settled, and I wouldn't want either of them to be hurt."

She wrapped her arms around his neck. "But you think they are good together."

"They're best friends. But there is a difference between being friends and being lovers. You can't make it happen because you'd like it to."

"Maybe not, but I can help things along by at least

putting them in the same place. Sometimes people need a little help to see what's right in front of them."

"Presumably my mother is also in on this, given that we are about to be visited by 'hordes of relatives from England,' none of whom we've heard of before?"

Kayla pulled away from him and picked up her purse. "She wasn't *in* on anything, but maybe she thinks Brenna and Tyler need encouragement, too."

"All right, what's done is done—" Jackson pulled her back to him and this time his eyes were serious "—but promise me you'll leave it alone now."

"I really do need Forest Lodge. I thought you'd be pleased that we're so busy."

"You haven't promised."

"Heads on beds. That was my brief when you gave me the job last Christmas."

"We've come a long way since then." He stroked his thumb over her cheek. "You're not going to promise, are you?"

"I'm going to try really hard, but if I hang extra bunches of mistletoe around the place, you're not to blame me."

He shook his head. "What you've achieved here is beyond impressive. I still can't believe that last Christmas I was awake at night wondering if we'd even have a business left in a year's time."

She slid her arms around his neck. "I love you."

"I love you, too. But the only relationship I want you invested in is ours. Got that?"

"Mmm." She pressed her mouth to his. "Maybe. But what about all the mistletoe? Shame to waste it."

"I'm sure we can put it to good use."

CHAPTER SIX

TYLER FINISHED THE run, delivered the reporter back to the main house for a debrief with Kayla, took a bumps-and-trees class he'd committed to in a weak moment and ended his day rescuing a toddler who had face-planted in a snowdrift.

By the time he arrived home, he felt like a bear with a thorn in its paw.

"Dad!" Jess shot out of the den, Ash and Luna at her heels. "Is it true?"

"Is what true? That I'm never skiing with a reporter again? Yeah, that's true. They ask me stuff I wouldn't tell my mother, and then wonder why I want to bury them in a snowdrift." He shoved the dogs down. "How many times do I have to tell you not to let the dogs into my den?"

"Grandma says Brenna is coming to live with us?"

"Not live, exactly." He dropped his gloves on the table. "But how would you feel about her staying awhile? I should have checked with you first, but she was in a bit of trouble so I wanted to help out."

"Dad, you don't need to ask! I love Brenna. It will be so cool having her here. Especially over Christmas. Christmas is always more fun when there are lots of people around. It will be great, hanging around the Christmas tree in our pajamas."

Thinking of Brenna in her pajamas, Tyler unzipped his

jacket. He hadn't dared think about what it would be like to have Brenna living here. "Maybe it's not a great idea."

"It's a great idea. It will be like being a family."

Which presented him with a whole new problem. "Do you mind it being the two of us normally? Do you miss your mom and half sister?"

Jess shrugged, and her sweater slid off her skinny shoulder.

Tyler felt a rush of frustration. "Is that a yes or a no? Whatever you're thinking, say it straight-out. I can take anything, but don't give me door slamming, hormones or one of your shrugs. You know I don't speak teenager."

"I'm not giving you hormones! And I don't miss Mom." Jess pulled Luna into her arms and buried her face in her fur. "Living with her was too stressy. And if I'm honest, Carly doesn't feel like my sister. I mean, she was only weeks old when Mom sent me away, so it's not like we know each other. I wasn't even allowed to hold her in case I dropped her. I don't hate her or anything, I just don't feel anything much. I guess you think I'm a bad person now."

Tyler, who had been judged by people for most of his life, heard the insecurity in her voice and frowned. "I think you're a great person."

Jess looked up at him. "I guess I worry about what other people think about me having a half sister I never see. Mrs. Kelly in the store asked how the baby was doing. When I said I didn't know, she looked all disapproving."

He was willing to bet the disapproval had been aimed at Janet, not Jess, but he hunkered down next to her and made a fuss of Luna. "I've had more practice ignoring advice than giving it, but I'm going to give it anyway.

Don't live your life worrying about what someone else is thinking about you. Firstly because most of the time people are thinking about themselves, not you, and secondly and most importantly, because how you choose to live your life is no one else's business. You get on with your life and let them get on with theirs."

"What if they're all judgy?"

"Then that's their problem."

"I guess I don't want people thinking bad things about me."

"The people who matter are those closest to you, and the person who matters most is you. As long as what you're doing feels right to you, and you're not hurting anyone, I don't see that there's anything to worry about." He stroked his fingers over her cheek and stood up. "Let's go help Brenna move her stuff. Friends. Family. They're the people who count, Jess. Keep them close."

"Do you think there's something wrong with me that I don't feel anything?" She blurted the words out. "Because I've kind of wondered about that. Like maybe I'm cold and unfeeling or something?"

He cursed under his breath and dragged her into his arms. "There's nothing wrong with you, honey. Carly arrived, and you were sent away. That's going to make things complicated. No one would blame you for resenting her a little bit."

"That's not it." Her voice was muffled against his chest. "I don't resent her. If anything, I'm grateful. She's the reason I'm here, and I'd rather be living with you than with Mom. And I guess I feel guilty because maybe I'm supposed to be sad or something."

"Right." Tyler's throat felt scratchy and raw. "Well, then, that's good because everyone is happy. You don't have to feel guilty about that. Now let's stop talking about deep stuff because it's making my head ache. Tell me about your day."

"Mine was good. Better than yours." She sniffed and pulled away. "Tell me about the reporter. Grandma was worried you might kill him."

"I tried. He got away."

Jess laughed. "He was a good skier?"

"He was lucky." Aware that she hadn't really answered the question about her day, he made a note to tackle it later. "Let's go pick up Brenna."

"Both of us?"

"Sure. She looked pretty sick about having to move out of Forest Lodge, and seeing you might cheer her up." Reasoning that a third person in the mix would be better for all concerned, Tyler scooped up his keys. "Let's go before she trudges all the way over here with her cases. We can help her pack up the lodge if she hasn't already done it. Zip your coat up because it's freezing out there."

"I'm not three years old, Dad."

"Good. Because there is no way I'd be changing your diaper and mashing up your food."

"I stopped wearing diapers when I was two years old." Jess grinned. "You don't know a thing about babies, do you? Can we take Ash and Luna? I don't like leaving them."

"Jess, we're driving two minutes down the track. They're not going to die of neglect in two minutes."

"Yes, but it's snowing, and anything could happen. They might worry about us, especially Luna. Huskies are a social breed. She likes to know where I am at all times. They're family, and you said family is important." She grabbed the dogs, and Tyler resigned himself to another drive with panting dogs.

"Come on, then, although where Brenna's luggage is going to fit, I have no idea, and if Ash howls or scratches my car, I'm taking him to the pound."

"I know you don't mean that because you and Uncle Jackson were the ones who rescued Maple."

"Yeah, well, Maple was cute and vulnerable. Ash is a bruiser."

Jess buried her head in Ash's fur. "Ignore him, sweetie, he loves you, really."

"I do not love him." Relieved to see her smiling again, Tyler walked to the door. "He's a smelly, rabid apology for a dog."

"He is not rabid!" She followed him to the car. "I saw Dana today. She's going to help me train him."

"That is the first piece of good news I've had today. That animal is in dire need of training, that's for sure, and no one has more experience with Siberian huskies than my cousin. Fasten your seat belt."

"She said if I go over there she'll teach me about sledding. That would be so cool. I'd love to take the team out in the forest. Have you done it before?"

"Yeah, but it's too slow for me. When they breed a turbo-charged husky, I'll try it again."

"But a whole team of dogs pulling you through the forest—that's so cool. Tourists pay a fortune for it. If Dana's your cousin, and she's your grandfather's sister's granddaughter, what relationship is she to me?" Jess sprang into the seat next to him, and the dogs piled in after her, smacking Tyler in the face with wagging tails.

"Probably second cousin or—I have no idea. Don't ask difficult questions. Save them for Grandma. And get those dogs in the back. Last time I checked, neither of them could drive a car." Shaking his head, Tyler reversed out of the space and drove down the track. The snow had accumulated during the day, but the roads that ran through the resort had been plowed and the snow was piled thick and deep at the side of the road.

Jess whooped with delight. "So much snow. Will I still be able to race tomorrow?"

"Yes, providing the visibility is good." He pulled up outside Forest Lodge.

Through the huge glass windows, he could see a lone suitcase sitting in the middle of the floor.

"Brenna obviously hasn't finished packing, so let's get inside and help her." He sprang from the car and the dogs followed, sending snow flying as they bounded up the steps of the lodge.

Opening the door without knocking, Tyler walked in, and the dogs pushed past him.

"Sit. *Sit.*" He grabbed Ash by the collar and pushed the dog's rump down onto the wooden floor. "Stay. If you mess this place up my brother will kill me, and then I'll kill you."

Jess unwound her scarf from her neck, sending snow flying. "If Uncle Jackson killed you first, you wouldn't be able to kill Ash."

"Then you'd have to kill him for me. Stay with them and make sure they don't jump on the sofa."

"It says on the website that well-behaved dogs are allowed in the lodges."

"Exactly. Ash and Luna are the worst-behaved dogs on the planet. That's why they're living with me and not Grandma."

"Because they played rough with Maple?"

"Yeah, well a miniature poodle and two bruiser huskies aren't a good mix. They treated every game like football, and Maple was the ball. *Brenna?*" Where the hell was she?

He knew she was upset, which was why he hadn't fought against Kayla's all too obvious manipulation of the sleeping arrangements. He didn't want Brenna upset.

"I'm up here." She finally appeared above him on the sleeping shelf. "What are you doing here?" Her face was partially in shadow, but he thought her eyes looked a little red.

Had she been crying?

No. He'd never seen Brenna cry. Not once. Not when she'd fallen and broken her ankle skiing, nor when those idiots who she refused to name had pushed her into a ditch.

But he knew how much she loved living in this particular lodge.

He remembered how excited she'd been when she'd first moved in. She'd chosen to sleep on the shelf, rather than in the master bedroom, and that decision hadn't surprised him. Brenna would have slept on the forest floor if that had been a practical option.

"Thought you might need some help packing up the rest of your things."

"It's done."

"Great! So tell me where the cases are, and I'll get them loaded up. Room's all ready for you." He'd given her the room that was farthest from his, and he'd put Jess in charge of making up the bed and making the place welcoming.

"That's it. That's the case. You're looking at it."

Tyler stared at the single small suitcase standing forlornly on the hardwood floor. "Everything you own is in that?"

"Well, not *everything*. Not my sporting equipment obviously. I keep that in the Outdoor Center."

He thought of the Canadian ice skater he'd been dating at the time of his accident. Her makeup case had been bigger and heavier than this suitcase. When they'd traveled, they'd needed a separate car for her luggage.

Thinking of it reminded him why he and Brenna were such good friends.

"I love a woman who travels light."

Something flickered in her eyes, and then she looked away. "Stay there, I'm coming down." Her voice didn't sound like her own, and Tyler dragged his hand over the back of his neck and glanced at Jess, but she was making a fuss of Ash and didn't seem to have noticed a problem.

Panic knotted in his chest.

Please don't let her be crying.

It seemed like ages before she appeared. Then she walked to the kitchen area, checked the fridge was empty and smoothed her hand over the granite work surface while Tyler watched, trying to find something to say that wasn't clumsy or tactless.

"I know you love this place." Now it was his voice that sounded strange. Rough, a little husky, as if he'd been up all night drinking in a smoke-filled room. "I know it's important to you."

"The things that are important to me are outside, not inside. Blue sky, snow, powder, the smell of the lake in the summer. I can't frame those things or put them in a vase. But it's true, I love this lodge." She glanced up at the soaring ceiling. "Jackson did so well when he built these."

"Gramps nearly killed him for spending so much

money. They didn't stop arguing. We had fireworks every day for months."

"But Jackson was right." With a last look around the living room with its cathedral ceiling and huge stone fireplace, she walked toward the door and noticed Jess for the first time. "Hi, Jess. I have to stay with you for a couple of nights, until I find somewhere for myself. I hope that's all right. I promise not to get in the way."

"You won't be in the way. And you're going to stay for more than a couple of nights. Can we watch skiing together?"

"Sure." Obviously finding the situation a little awkward, Brenna stooped to hug Luna, who licked her ecstatically. "You'll have to tell me the rules of your house. I've lived alone for so long I haven't had to think about other people."

Tyler clenched his jaw. The look on her face made him feel as if he'd put his boot on a basket of kittens.

"There aren't any rules." Jess gave a wicked grin. "Dad pretends there are, but then we both break them."

"That sounds like your dad." Brenna smoothed Luna's fur. "He's never been too good with rules."

"Hey! I'm pretty house-trained since Jess moved in, isn't that right, sweetheart?"

"It's not right. You still put your feet on the table when no one is looking, and you drink milk from the carton." Jess was trying to stop Ash leaping on the sofa. "But he's trying, Brenna. Sometimes there's even food in the fridge along with the beer."

Some of the tension in his shoulders eased.

"Forest Lodge has a great view, but my place is better. You're going to love it. I've put you in the back bedroom. It faces the forest. Jess made the room up for you while I was teaching my final class."

He glanced at Jess for confirmation, but she wasn't looking at him.

Had she forgotten?

"Jess?"

"Mmm?"

"You made up the room, right? Because if you forgot, I am selling your skis and enrolling you in after-school history club."

"I made up the room! Come on, Luna, let's take Brenna to her new home."

Brenna picked up her jacket and slid her feet into her boots. "This must be so inconvenient for you so close to Christmas. Don't let me stop you doing any of the stuff you'd normally do."

"Last year was my first proper, permanent Christmas here so we're still making stuff up. I want lots of decorations but Dad says the house is already a mess, so I'm still working on that." Jess dragged a wriggling, writhing Ash toward the door. "We're having a real tree, though. We're going to choose it soon. You can come. We could go after race training."

"If there's enough light." Tyler opened the door and pushed the dogs out into the cold. Jess followed, and he was about to step after her when Brenna put a hand on his arm.

"Are you sure this is all right? Would you be honest?"

"I'm always honest." But that wasn't true, was it? Right now, staring down into those soft dark eyes, he wanted to say things that he knew would change their relationship forever. Because of that, he stepped back. "What are friends for? Maybe we'll watch a movie tonight or something." He knew he had to do something to take her mind off the way she was feeling, because seeing her this upset was killing him. "After you've cooked me dinner." He chose his words to goad her, and was relieved to see misery replaced by a dangerous gleam.

"You think I'm cooking you dinner?"

"Of course. You're the girl. I'm the boy. I get to sit down and watch football with a beer. You get to cook. You and Jess can decide between you who cleans up the kitchen." His words had the desired effect. Roused from her state of inertia, she stooped and scooped up snow.

"I have one thing to say to that, Tyler O'Neil."

He told himself that a snowball in the face was worth it to hear her laughing. But of course it didn't stop at that because both dogs decided to join in as well as Jess, and before he could put a stop to it they were all soaking wet and covered in snow.

Ash hurled himself at Brenna, and she went down on her back, pushing the dog as he tried to lick her face. "Get him off me!"

"Sorry about that." Tyler hauled the dog off by his collar and then dragged her to her feet. "Dana is going to help Jess train Ash."

"I wish her luck with that." But Brenna was still laughing as she brushed away clumps of snow from her jacket. "I might need a shower before dinner which, by the way, I'm not cooking unless you want to be poisoned."

"I was kidding. Élise promised to send food over, although her exact words were something like 'don't get used to it.'" The scent of Brenna's hair reminded him of summer flowers, and he had to work extra hard not to look at the soft curve of her mouth. Fighting a tug of lust, he stowed her case in the trunk.

She was his friend. He was going to help her out, and helping out didn't involve pushing their relationship into something he'd been careful to avoid. This was one relationship he was determined not to mess up, and the only way he could be sure of not messing it up was to leave it alone.

"THIS IS YOUR BEDROOM." Jess pushed open the door. "It looks over the forest and the lake, and it's next to Dad's."

Something in the way she said that made Brenna turn her head, but Jess was trying to stop Luna from scrambling onto the bed. "The dogs aren't supposed to be upstairs so we have to be quiet about it."

Brenna put her case down. "I thought your dad said I was having a room at the back."

"Did he?" Jess sounded vague. "I'm sure he said this one. It has the best view."

Brenna looked at the wall of the bedroom and imagined Tyler sleeping on the other side. Ideally, she would have preferred a little more distance, but she wasn't in a position to complain, was she?

"This bedroom is lovely."

Huge windows stretched up to the vaulted ceiling, and ahead of her stretched the lake, the forest and beyond that the mountains. The large bed was draped in warm green and cool cream, and a rug covered part of the hardwood floor. Not masculine, exactly, but unfussy. The way she preferred things.

Lake House had stood abandoned and uninhabited on the Snow Crystal land for decades until Tyler had decided one day that despite his nomadic lifestyle, he needed a permanent base of his own.

Secluded and set on the most remote part of the resort, Lake House had been the obvious choice and he'd set about restoring it whenever he was home, with occasional help from his family.

Never one to deprive himself, Tyler had installed a large wraparound deck, the same outdoor hot tub as the lodges and added a private dock where he kept a couple of kayaks in the summer.

Downstairs, the living room had the same soaring ceilings and stone fireplace as the lodges, but the floor space was considerably bigger. He'd taken advantage of that space to build a state-of-the-art media room and he'd converted the basement into a well-equipped gym.

"How was school today?" Brenna opened her case and transferred the contents to the drawers by the bed. The exception was a dress, her only dress, which she hung up carefully in the wardrobe.

It was black and made of a stretchy fabric she knew flattered her shape. She wore it every time she needed something smarter than ski pants or sweats, which fortunately wasn't very often.

"I like that dress, but black is for a funeral." Jess forced Ash to sit. "You should wear blue. The same blue as your hat. You look pretty in blue."

"I hardly ever wear the black dress, so I can't justify a blue one and anyway, I don't want to accumulate more luggage. It's easier this way." Easier to move on when she had to, and she was fairly sure now that she was going to have to. This idyll couldn't last for long, especially now she was living in such close quarters with Tyler. She sensed it was going to get awkward pretty quickly. "So which is your room?"

"I'm at the back of the house. I look over the forest." As Luna lay down on the floor, Jess sprang onto the bed and crossed her legs. "I like it. There's a tree right outside my window. I can climb out if I want to."

Like father, like daughter.

Brenna, who had climbed out of her bedroom window at home more times than she cared to remember, decided that a lecture would be hypocritical. Beginning to understand Tyler's dilemma, she tried a different approach. "Your dad is pretty easygoing. If you want to leave the house, you could use the front door. He's not going to stop you, and you're less likely to break a bone that way."

"I like climbing trees. Mom would never let me do anything like that because she thought it wasn't ladylike."

Brenna pushed ski socks into a drawer. Talking about Janet Carpenter was one way of turning a bright day dark. "Do you speak to your mom often?"

"Every few weeks. It's a pretty awkward conversation." Jess wrapped her arms around her legs. "She isn't interested in hearing about my skiing, and she hates everything to do with Snow Crystal so I can't talk about that. If I mention Dad she almost hangs up, so I spend the whole time trying to find things to say that don't involve him or skiing, which is pretty tough when you live in a place like this." She scraped her hair back from her face in a universally teenage gesture. "I guess I'm a major disappointment. I've never been what she wants."

"I'm sure that's not true." Brenna's mouth was dry. She didn't want to talk about this. She couldn't. It made her heart race and her stomach churn. She wanted desperately to change the subject, but that wasn't fair to Jess.

"According to my mom, I'm too much like Dad. You don't know her, but—" Jess frowned "—*do* you know her? It isn't like Snow Crystal is that big a place, and you must have been at school at the same time."

Brenna pulled a couple of T-shirts from her suitcase. "I knew her a little."

"I wonder why she's never mentioned you? She was older, so I guess your name never came up."

Her hands were shaking. "That's probably it."

"You're going to love this room. After twelve years living in Chicago, it's like heaven to look out on the forest." Jess picked at a thread in her sock. "Sometimes I sleep with the window open so that I can breathe the air. At school I try and sit by the window, too."

Brenna slid the T-shirts into a drawer. "Are things any better?"

"At school? No. It's like being in a cage. Was that how you felt?"

"Some of the time." *All of the time.* Brenna opened another drawer. "How are the other kids?"

"Annoying, mostly." Jess avoided her gaze. "Are you nearly done? Because we should go help Dad cook. He can make a real mess if he's left on his own. Even the dogs won't touch his food."

"One more minute." Brenna pulled out the last of her clothes and thought back to a conversation she'd had a few weeks earlier. She'd picked Jess up from school, and the teenager had been visibly upset. On the drive home she'd been unusually silent. It was that miserable silence that had induced Brenna to tell her a little of her own experiences at school in the hope of encouraging Jess to open up.

It hadn't worked, but the way she'd listened and the questions she'd asked had convinced Brenna that something similar might be happening to Jess. If that was true then she wanted to help.

"Now I'm staying here for a while we should be able to ski together a bit more often, if you'd like to."

"I'd love that! Thanks. I want to win everything this season. I want to make Dad proud."

"He's already proud, Jess. He loves you."

"I know he loves me, but you know Dad. With him you either win or you lose."

"There were plenty of times when he lost as well as won. It isn't all about winning."

"He says that's the whole point. No one competes to come second. Can we watch skiing together tonight? I want to watch some of the World Cup runs and analyze technique."

"You should ask your dad to do that with you. He's good at seeing what people are doing wrong."

"He won't." Jess's voice was flat. "He never watches skiing."

"Well, he's busy and—"

"It's not because he's busy. He watches football, baseball, basketball, ice hockey—any sport that happens to be on TV. But not skiing."

Brenna paused, a sweater in her hand. "Never?"

"Never." Jess gave an awkward shrug. "I guess it's hard for him. I shouldn't have told you. He probably doesn't want either of us to know."

"I— You were right to tell me." Aching for him, Brenna stuffed the sweater in the drawer and pushed it closed. "Does he ever give you a reason?"

"Yes, but after a year of excuses you realize there has to be something else going on. I want to ask him, but I don't want to make it worse and anyway, I'm just a kid. I guess he wouldn't want to talk to me."

"You're a great kid. He loves you," Brenna said softly,

"but he's not the type of guy who finds it easy to talk about the way he feels."

"I know. Macho man and all that."

"Not only that." Brenna wondered how much Jess knew about Tyler's life. "When he was on the ski team, it was hard for him to be private. There was always someone taking photos or pushing a microphone in his face. People printed things whether he'd said them or not, so he learned not to say anything." It had made her mad— *furious*—to read some of the lies they'd printed.

"He might talk to you, especially now you're here all the time. He trusts you. You understand him, and you guys have been friends forever." Jess slid off the bed. "I hope he does. He should talk to someone. I think it's driving him nuts. That's why he nearly murdered that reporter this morning. The guy was stupid enough to ask him how it felt to not be able to ski competitively anymore."

"He asked that? How do you know?"

"Kayla told me. She was furious because apparently she told the guy 'not to ask anything about his career or his family' and he did both. He was lucky Dad didn't bury him in an avalanche." Jess winced as a crash came from the kitchen beneath them. Ash whimpered and slid under the bed for cover. "We should go, before he breaks everything or poisons himself."

Brenna followed the teenager downstairs.

They were all so busy, so stretched trying to save the resort, that none of them had given enough attention to how being here and not being able to ski was affecting Tyler.

They walked into the kitchen to find him crashing and cursing as he pulled out pans. Food was spread out over the counter, and Brenna raised her eyebrows.

"I thought Élise was providing dinner."

"She was—" he sent her a look that would have started a fire without a match "—but apparently I not only have to cook it, I have to reheat parts of it, too. It would have been easier to call for takeout."

"But not as healthy." Jess took the frying pan from his hand. "I've got this, Dad. You sit down and enjoy a nice, relaxing drink with Brenna."

She made it sound as if they were on a date, and Brenna's heart gave an extra bump.

Why did this feel so *awkward?*

Tyler waved a hand. "There's steak—"

"I know." Jess was patient. "You fry it. It's not hard."

"You're vegetarian."

"That was last year."

"Right." He lifted the same hand and dragged his fingers through his hair. "There's a sauce."

"...Which needs to be heated, but not boiled or it will curdle."

Tyler stared at her. "Since when did you turn into a chef?"

"Since Élise gave me a few lessons." Looking pleased with herself, Jess tipped oil into the pan and waited for it to heat. "She said that basic cookery is a survival skill, and as I'm living with you I'm going to need all the survival skills I can get."

"She said that? Charming. That's the last time I help Élise with her skis." Tyler tipped salad onto plates. "Brenna, there's beer in the fridge. Help yourself. It will numb your taste buds for whatever is about to exit that frying pan."

He was treating her the way he always treated her. The same way he treated his brothers.

There was no reason to feel uncomfortable.

"It's going to be delicious." Jess flipped one of the steaks awkwardly and it landed on the kitchen floor. Ash crossed the room in a single bound and devoured it.

"Obviously it *was* delicious," Tyler said drily. "That was yours, right?"

Jess was giggling helplessly. "Bad boy. Bad Ash."

Ash wagged his tail happily, and Tyler sighed.

"You've got some way to go learning how to discipline that dog. If you say 'bad boy' you don't laugh at the same time."

"He's adorable, especially when he knows he's been naughty. He has this cute, guilty look. It's fine. Élise sent more than we'd need. I guess she knew we might mess it up."

Tyler scowled at Ash. "You are out of control. And notice I'm not smiling when I say those words. And I don't think you're adorable. I think you're a pain in the—"

"Language, Dad." Jess tipped another steak into the pan, and Ash wagged his tail, his eyes fixed hopefully on her.

A delicious smell of cooking wafted through the kitchen, and this time when Jess turned the steak, she did it with exaggerated caution.

Ash whined and settled down on the floor, hoping for another culinary error in his favor. Luna, the better behaved of the two dogs, lay quietly under the table watching Jess.

Tyler shared salad between the plates and pulled a couple of beers out of the fridge. "Why have you never cooked for me before?"

"Because I'm still learning. Élise has been teaching me at Grandma's. I wanted to surprise you." Jess added steaks and a baked potato to the plates and put them on the table.

"It's a surprise." Tyler handed Brenna a beer. "A good one. Does this mean you're also going to stop dropping your clothes around the house and do the laundry?"

Brenna twisted the cap off the beer. She'd been in this kitchen more times than she could count. So why did everything suddenly feel different? Her response wasn't logical. "You shouldn't have cooked for him, Jess. You're reinforcing gender stereotypes."

"I'm not. I'm making sure I eat well." Jess sat down and picked up her knife and fork. "It's his turn to cook tomorrow. Dad, you can't put ketchup on that delicious steak. It will ruin the flavor."

Ignoring her, Tyler added a huge dollop of ketchup to his plate. "If tomorrow is my night then we're having takeout food."

Jess glanced at Brenna. "What's your favorite?"

"Mexican." Tyler sliced into his steak. "Her favorite is Mexican."

Jess gave him a long look. "You guys know everything about each other."

"Not everything." Brenna focused on her plate. The things she didn't know about Tyler were the little things. Personal things. *Did he sleep naked?*

"You can cook Mexican from scratch, Dad. All you need is beans, tortillas—I don't know, but I bet it's not that hard. I'll text Élise and ask her, and then we can go shopping tomorrow." Jess fed a slice of steak to Luna under the table. "Brenna will be impressed."

"Or she might be poisoned. I'm not trying to impress Brenna. She's known me forever so she's past being impressed. This steak is good. For this, I'll tidy the house, but you can do your own laundry. And stop feeding that dog under the table. So how's your room, Bren? Great view of the forest?"

He knew more about her than anyone, and yet he didn't know the most important thing of all. The way she felt about him. "It's beautiful, thank you, and I love being able to see the lake."

He paused with his fork halfway to his mouth. "You can see the lake?"

"Yes. Jess put me in the room next to yours." And she was wondering how she was going to sleep at night, knowing that all that separated them was a thin wall.

Tyler put his fork down slowly. "Next to mine?"

"Is that a problem?" Brenna tried to sound casual. "I can easily move if you'd rather I used a different room."

His gaze locked on hers, blue and disturbingly intense. "No." His voice was slightly thickened. "It's a nice room." His gaze flickered to Jess but she was absorbed in her food.

"Sorry," she said brightly. "My mistake. I thought you said the front room. No point in moving now. It makes no difference, and Brenna liked the room. There's more steak if anyone is still hungry."

Hungry?

Brenna could barely force food down her throat.

She never would have thought being with Tyler could have felt this uncomfortable.

CHAPTER SEVEN

OVER IN THE main house that had been home to the
O'Neils for four generations, Walter O'Neil settled himself at the scrubbed kitchen table and watched as Alice,
his wife of sixty years, helped Elizabeth arrange cookie
dough on large baking sheets.

"So Brenna has moved in with Tyler."

"She needed somewhere to go." Elizabeth removed
two trays of cinnamon stars from the oven, replacing
them with the next batch. "We're so lucky Tyler has
room."

Walter grunted. "Last time I counted, you had five
spare rooms."

"I invited relatives from England." Elizabeth transferred the cookies onto a cooling tray.

Walter glanced at the empty chairs around the table.
"I don't see any relatives from England."

"I'm not sure what's happening yet, but it didn't seem
fair to invite Brenna and then risk having to ask her to
move. She needs somewhere permanent."

"Permanent?" Walter's gaze sharpened. His face was
weathered and lined from a life spent outdoors, but he
still had a full head of hair and looked at least a decade
younger than his eighty years. "Exactly how long were
you thinking she'd stay with Tyler?"

"I don't know." Elizabeth broke one of the cookies

in half to check it. "At least until Christmas. Jess loves Christmas so much, and it will be good for Brenna to be part of that."

"You're throwing the two of them together, aren't you?"

"I am doing no such thing." Elizabeth nibbled a cookie. "But those two virtually grew up together, and Jess loves Brenna. It makes sense for her to move in with him."

"I'm old, not stupid. You're interfering."

"You're not old." Alice reached across and patted his hand. "And I seem to remember you interfering plenty with Sean and Élise."

"You're imagining things." But there was a gleam in Walter's eyes. "All I did was point out what the rest of the world knew. Those two were both too stubborn to see what the rest of us saw."

"It's the same with Tyler. It's obvious how Brenna feels about him." Elizabeth picked up a bowl of icing, and Walter looked at her thoughtfully.

"But how does he feel about her? She's not his usual type. Nothing like the others."

"He wasn't serious about the others. They were just part of that life he led. And I don't remember fielding phone calls from any of those women when he was lying in the hospital with his career in ruins. Where were they then?" Elizabeth wiped her hands on her apron. "It was Brenna who sat by him. She was there night and day, and there was no getting her to leave. She was the one who coaxed him out of his bad temper when the rest of us were almost afraid to walk into that room. She's been there for him through thick and thin."

"And in all that time, nothing has ever happened. I remember the party in the summer. He didn't even look at her. What they have is friendship, and it's never going to be anything else." Walter reached out to steal a cookie, and Alice rapped his knuckles.

"They're for the Boathouse Café."

"They won't miss one, and I don't want to give the guests what I haven't tried myself."

"You've eaten enough of those in your life, Walter O'Neil. Remember what the doctor said."

"He said moderation." He caught Alice's eye. "One cookie is moderation, and I was shoveling snow all morning."

"He cares about her." Elizabeth dusted the cookies with icing sugar. "I sometimes think being here is slowly killing him, but he offered to coach the high school team because he knew she didn't want to walk into that school again. He wouldn't have done that for anyone else. It's the most romantic thing I ever heard."

Walter sighed. "That boy has been tearing after women since he hit puberty. I've never seen him show the slightest interest in Brenna that wasn't to do with friendship."

"He didn't object when Kayla suggested she move in with him."

"How could he? You were all squashing him like an ant under a log pile. Likely he'll rebel, as he always does when you try and cage him."

"No one is trying to cage him, Walter."

"Maybe your plan will backfire. Maybe she's not what he needs."

"I think she's exactly what he needs, and hopefully he'll discover that himself." Calm, Elizabeth poured the tea.

TYLER TOOK THE DOGS outside and waited, his breath clouding the freezing air.

He wasn't in any hurry to go back inside knowing that

Brenna was curled up in his den. She and Jess had picked a movie, and between the two of them they'd sentenced him to an evening of romance and sugar he was unlikely to survive without the support of a bottle of whiskey.

The choice didn't surprise him.

He already knew Brenna was romantic. It was a side of her that would have surprised some people given her tomboy ways, but not him.

She believed in love and happy ever after, which was another reason he'd stayed the hell away from anything more than friendship with her.

Unfortunately, that plan had become more complicated since Jess had put her in the room next to him.

He breathed deeply and tried to banish what could only be described as inappropriate thoughts.

Brenna had been in his house a million times, and not once had it felt awkward.

Until tonight.

Not for one moment did he think his daughter had made up the room next to his by accident. Nor did he think relatives from England were likely to show up anytime soon, but he hadn't wanted to embarrass Brenna by telling his infuriating, interfering family what they could do with their plans, especially as she already seemed embarrassed enough.

How was he supposed to sleep knowing she was on the other side of the wall?

Did she sleep naked?

From what he'd seen, there wasn't much room in that suitcase for clothes.

He heard the front door open, and Jess came out to join him.

"Brenna is making hot chocolates. She does the whole thing, with whipped cream and marshmallows."

"We don't have any marshmallows."

"She had them left over in her cupboard and packed them in her case."

Which left even less room for clothes.

"Great." He unzipped his coat to let the air cool his skin. "So if I wasn't already going to die of a sugar overdose watching that movie you've both picked, I will now."

Jess stamped her feet to stay warm. "I like having another woman around the house. I hope she stays forever."

"You need to stop what you're doing, Jess."

"What? What am I doing?"

He preferred straight talking and saw no reason to change that approach with his daughter. "You need to stop trying to fix me up with Brenna."

"Are you suggesting—?" Her mouth fell open, and he enjoyed her exaggerated display of surprise and offense for a moment before shaking his head.

"My advice? Don't join the drama club. You're not convincing. Stick to the ski team."

Her mouth closed. "I made a mistake with the rooms, that's all."

"Yeah, right. I suppose I should be grateful you didn't put her in mine. Now stop meddling, or I'll have to find somewhere else for Brenna to stay because it isn't fair to her." And it wasn't fair to him, either. He'd gone from never allowing himself to think about sex and Brenna at the same time, to not being able to separate them.

Sweating under his jacket, Tyler hoped the movie they'd picked didn't have any sex scenes.

"Dad, can I ask you something?"

"Sure." Wrenched from a disturbing daydream that

featured Brenna naked in the shower, he forced himself
to pay attention.

"Even if it's something we've never talked about before?"

Now she had all his attention. *Was this going to be
the sex question?* After his conversation with Brenna,
he'd made up his mind to buy a book on how to talk to
teenagers about sex, but he hadn't got around to it. He
had no idea where to start. "You can ask me anything."
His voice came out as a croak, and he cleared his throat.
"We made that deal when you came to live with me last
winter. You're still very young but we can talk about the
details if you want to—" *please don't let her want to*
"—but the first thing to know is that it's best if you're
in a relationship."

"What is?" Jess stared at him. "What are you talking about?"

Why the hell hadn't he bought that book? "All I'm
saying is that it's fine to talk about the mechanics, but
it should mean something, that's all." He reasoned that
as the expert on meaningless sex, that qualified him to
talk about it.

"What should?"

"Sex." His mouth was dry. "That is what you were
asking me, isn't it?"

"No! Dad, that's gross." She turned scarlet and kicked
the snow with the toe of her boot. "I don't want to talk to
you about sex! Ugh—this is *so* awkward."

"It isn't awkward." *It was up there with the most awkward moment of his life.* "You can ask me about that stuff.
It's important that you know the facts, not pick up a load
of false information from your friends."

"I don't want to talk about sex! I know everything already, okay?"

"Everything?" Suddenly, he had a new worry. "How can you know everything? You're thirteen years old."

"Nearly fourteen, and we're taught all that at school and—" she lifted her hands to her face and then shook her head "—never mind! That wasn't what I wanted to ask you!"

Tyler felt as uncomfortable as she did. "Good. It doesn't really matter anyway, because I'm not letting you out of the house until you're forty."

"Chill, Dad. I'm more interested in skiing than boys."

That was good news, but not enough to make him chill.

He was going to order the damn book right away so next time the subject came up, he'd be able to tackle it without feeling as if his tongue were knotted in three places. "So what did you want to ask me? Don't turn into one of those women who expects a man to play guessing games. If there's something on your mind then come right out and say it."

"I was going to ask if you missed it."

"Sex?"

"No!" Jess gave a snort of laughter. "Dad, is sex *all* you think about?"

Yes, since you've put Brenna in the room next to me. "Let's start this conversation again," he breathed. "Do I miss what?"

"Skiing," Jess blurted the word out, and he frowned.

"Why would I miss it? I still ski."

"But not competitively. You can't race anymore since the accident—" she looked at him anxiously "—I wondered if it was hard, that's all. I mean, you never watch skiing on TV. Ever. Do you hate that you can't race any-more?"

"If I was racing, I wouldn't be able to teach you. I love teaching you."

"Seriously?" Her face brightened. "It doesn't bore you?"

"No." He realized that was the truth. "I get a real kick out of it. You're good. And you're going to get better."

"Cool. I love skiing together."

He looped his arm around her shoulders and pulled her close. "I love that, too."

"And you love skiing with Brenna."

He let his hand drop and gave her a look. "Unless you want snow stuffed down your jacket, you can stop that right now."

"I was just saying."

"Well, don't say. And don't think, either."

"YOU GET DOWN SAFE." Brenna checked Jess's helmet and zipped the top of her jacket against the biting wind. "It's not the winning that counts, it's the taking part."

"Of course it's the winning that counts." Tyler stood relaxed and easy on his skis, oblivious to the attention he was getting from the other kids and their mothers. "Otherwise, what's the point of risking your neck hurtling downhill at inhuman speeds? You might as well stay home."

Brenna sighed. "All I'm saying is that it doesn't mat-ter if she doesn't win."

"And I'm saying it does matter. She's going to win, and if she doesn't, we're going to work out why." Tyler put his hands on Jess's shoulders and turned her to face him. "Listen to me because I'm going to give you more advice since I'm getting so good at it. Forget everything except your skis and the way they feel on the hill. Trust yourself. Focus. You can beat the crap out of all of them."

Jess grinned, delighted. "You're not supposed to say crap. Major parent fail."

Brenna didn't know whether to laugh or bash her head against a tree. "And you can't tell her she has to beat them. You're supposed to be a coach. If you talk like that at Friday night sessions the high school will be swamped with complaints by parents."

"Good. Then they'll fire me, and I can go back to doing something interesting with my evenings. I've no patience with people who don't want to hear the truth."

"If they fire you, I'll have to do it."

"Fine." He gritted his teeth. "I can give coachlike advice if I have to." He turned back to Jess. "You need the apex of the turn to be at the gate. Watch the transition, and try to keep a constant rhythm."

Jess bobbed her head up and down. "Are you going to be watching?"

"The whole time."

"I'm going to make you proud, Dad."

There was a pause and Tyler cleared his throat. "You shouldn't be talking to us. You should be focusing. Don't let anything or anyone distract you." He stooped and checked her bindings, knocked snow off her skis and then nodded. "We need Chas."

Jess tightened her boots. "He's with the U.S. ski team."

"The man clearly has his priorities wrong. But if he won't come to you, you'll have to go to him."

"Dad, I'll never make the U.S. ski team."

"*Never* is a banned word in the O'Neil family. Now go out there and kick butt."

Brenna stood listening, wondering if helping Jess made it worse for him.

She wanted to say something, but Tyler O'Neil wasn't the sort to share his feelings and she didn't want to be the one to make him do it.

Had he talked to anyone about it? His brothers? Probably not. The three brothers were close, but she doubted they ever sat down and exchanged thoughts on their feelings. They talked about skiing, about anything with an engine and, inevitably, the business.

She stood, conscious of his powerful bulk next to her as they watched Jess position herself.

Brenna could almost feel her nerves. "She's anxious."

"That's not a bad thing."

"She's thinking about pleasing you, not about skiing the course. You expect too much of her."

Tyler gave a grunt. "It's the small things that can make the difference between winning and losing. And I don't expect anything she isn't capable of achieving."

Brenna glanced at him in exasperation. His eyes were fixed on his daughter. She'd seen the same look on his face a thousand times in the past. Complete focus. But now that focus was directed toward his daughter. It was something she hadn't noticed before. "There's more to life than winning a race, Tyler."

"So I'm told."

"She isn't you."

A frown touched his brows. "What are you suggesting?"

"I'm worried you're putting too much pressure on her."

"Pressure is part of racing. She can take it."

"It's not all about the winning, Tyler! If you make

her think that then she's going to be crushed when she doesn't win."

"What sort of crazy liberal shit is that? It's a competition. Of course it's about the winning. What's the point, otherwise?" He dragged his eyes from Jess long enough to give Brenna an incredulous look. "You want her to slow down and be polite so that the girl behind her can win?"

She wanted to laugh because in that moment, he reminded her of the boy he'd once been, tearing down the slopes as if he'd had rocket boosters attached to his skis. "All I'm saying is that she wants to please you so badly, she might put herself at risk."

"Skiing downhill is always a risk."

"But there is a fine line between breaking speed records and breaking your neck!"

"She's good."

"But she was brought up in Chicago by a mother who hated skiing!"

"All the more reason to catch up now. She's an O'Neil. Not just her hair and her blue eyes, but the way she feels the snow. Or haven't you noticed?"

"Yes, I've noticed." Brenna gave up. Instead she focused on Jess, willing her to do well and not fall.

"She wants to ski. I don't push her to do anything she isn't already desperate to do. I tried holding her back last winter, and look where that got us."

Brenna thought back to the night when Jess had disappeared, determined to impress her father by skiing the most difficult run in the resort. "That was a horrible night."

"She's next." Tyler watched as Jess pushed through the start wand, gaining speed immediately.

"Her style is good."

"Her hand is going back. She's rotating her body and losing seconds at every gate."

"She's doing well." Brenna winced as one of the gates, the poles that marked the course, swung back and hit Jess in the face. "It's her first real winter season here, Tyler, and the season only started a few weeks ago."

"Which means we have a lot of time to make up. She's concentrating on the gates and not her turns."

"Tyler." A woman stepped up to him, her glossy red mouth curving into a smile. "I'm Anna. Patty Clarke's mother."

She couldn't have picked a worse time to try and catch his attention.

Tyler didn't spare her a glance. His eyes were on Jess. "She's sliding into her turns. She's putting too much weight on the inside ski early in the turn, and she needs a tighter line as she approaches the gate."

"We can work on that. She's a junior, Tyler, she doesn't have the physical strength of a World Cup skier!"

"She's losing time."

Seeing that he wasn't going to respond to Anna Clarke, Brenna intervened. "Patty is showing real promise, Anna."

Patty's mother ignored her and moved closer to Tyler.

Brenna's face burned and for a moment she was fifteen again, on her own in school corridors that echoed with the laughter of other kids. Whenever she thought of school, the dominant memory was of being alone while all the other kids traveled in packs. Some days she'd been invisible, others she'd felt like a lone gazelle surrounded by a pack of hyenas. She'd preferred the invisible days, days when her tormentors left her alone, even though that loneliness had been a miserable state. Skipping school to meet Tyler had been the only bright spot in an otherwise gray period of her life.

She glanced briefly at Anna, wondering what it must be like to be that socially confident. To be so sure of a positive response to your overtures. Brenna had been knocked back so many times it had left her wary of putting herself out there.

She'd left school with her self-esteem shredded and even though she'd gradually woven it back together, she was aware of its intrinsic fragility. On the ski slope she was confident. With the people she knew and loved, she was confident. But when it came to people like Patty's mother, she reverted to being an awkward teenager.

Anna showed no signs of awkwardness. If she'd experienced rejection in her life then it had left no scars. "I wondered if you'd be prepared to give her private lessons. I'd be there, too."

Tyler watched as Jess finished the course and then turned his head, his handsome face blank of expression. If he noticed the smile Anna Clarke gave him, he didn't respond. "If she's on the school team, she'll be at training sessions on Fridays. I'll be coaching some of those."

"I saw the new brochure online, and it said that you were available for one-to-ones." The husky tone of her voice implied she was interested in more than Tyler's expertise on the snow.

"Expert skiers only, and then only on a case-by-case basis."

"Who decides who you take?"

Tyler stared down into those eyes, apparently unaffected by the liberal application of mascara. "Brenna." His voice was silk over layers of steel. "If she thinks a skier shows exceptional talent, then I'll coach them. You'll have to talk to her."

Anna Clarke said nothing, but her color rose, and she said something to him in a low voice before skiing away.

Brenna's heart was pounding. "You shouldn't have done that."

"You're right. You should have done it." There was an edge to his tone. "She was rude, and you let her get away with it."

Her heart was bumping. "It doesn't matter."

"It matters, Brenna. You need to speak up. If you let a person step on you, they'll do it again and again."

"We're surrounded by kids and parents. I didn't want to get into a fight. It's unprofessional."

"We both know you wouldn't fight even if your back was against the wall."

Did he think she was pathetic? "You think I have no backbone."

His gaze locked on hers. "Honey, I've seen you ski. You have more backbone than anyone I've met. You'll ski a vertical slope without hesitation, but when it comes to people, especially people like Anna, when there's a social situation that makes you uncomfortable, you shut down."

"You're saying I'm a coward."

"No." He frowned. "You're not good at handling those sorts of people. But we're going to change that."

He'd never said anything like that before, and Brenna gave a breathless laugh. "You want me to get into a girl fight with Anna?"

"No. I'm going to teach you to be assertive." He adjusted his glove. "Next time, instead of letting her snub you, you will say a few quiet words that demand she treat you with respect."

"I'm not so great with words. I usually think of the right thing to say a week after the chance to say it has passed."

"So we'll think of it in advance. I have the perfect string of words to say to a woman like that." He leaned closer, whispered in her ear and she gasped and glanced over her shoulder to make sure no one could have overheard.

"No *way* would I ever say that."

"I guarantee she'd never do it to you again if you did."

Half laughing, half shocked, Brenna shook her head. "I don't think she's ever going to talk to me again anyway. You were pretty rude to her."

"She was mean to you." He said it simply. Then he tugged off his glove and curved his hand behind her head, forcing her to look at him. He was big. Protective. The strength in those fingers a direct contrast to the gentleness in his eyes.

No one had ever pushed this man into a ditch or made him feel less than he was.

Her heart was pumping so hard it felt as if it might burst out of her chest. "I can look after myself. I always have. I always will."

"You walked away from it, which is one way of handling it. Now we're trying my way." He let his hand drop, but not before he'd stroked those fingers over her cheek.

The gesture was as unexpected as it was intimate, and it turned her stomach inside out.

For a fleeting moment she thought she saw something in his eyes and then it was gone, and he was tugging his glove back on and focusing on the racing.

"I've learned to be brutally direct with some people

or the next time I open my bedroom door, one of them could be lying there naked."

"Naked?" She felt as if she'd stepped off a cliff into a bottomless void. Not for the first time she felt out of step with the life he'd led. Never in her life would she have lain on a bed naked, waiting for a man she didn't know. "That happened?"

"More often than you'd imagine. Apparently, there are a bunch of women out there who think that lying down in a man's bed guarantees them personal attention."

Misery mingled with fascination. "How did you handle it?" And then she caught his wicked grin and blushed. "Sorry. Forget I asked."

"I told them to get in line behind the others." He was teasing her, and she didn't know how to respond because over the years of their long friendship, they'd talked about everything but this. She knew there had been women, of course. The media had had a field day with his passion for speed and women. At one point in his career, it had been difficult to work out which was his priority.

That was the point when Brenna had stopped reading the news.

"I can't imagine what sort of woman would climb into the bed of a man she doesn't know." She spoke without thinking and then realized how unworldly she sounded. How unsophisticated. And he was used to women who were neither of those things.

"Want me to describe her?" He was laughing, turning tension to humor as he always did. "The first time it happened was after my first world championship win. I walked out and demanded a different room. The hotel was so terrified I was going to sue them for a breach of security, they gave me the President's Suite. The second time Jackson was there. He dealt with it."

She could imagine Jackson, calm and tactful, extracting naked women from Tyler's bed. "He used to deal with all the women sobbing over Sean, too."

"He was a busy guy. And that's enough talk of my past because we have company." He smiled over her shoulder as Jess skied down to them. "You're leaning toward the gate to clear it and because of that, you're over rotating your body and losing balance. Your line of descent needs to be tighter. Ow! What?" Rubbing his arm, he turned to look at Brenna. "Why are you digging your elbow into me?"

Brenna didn't know whether to laugh or hit him over the head with her ski pole. "Because she did loads of things right, and all you're doing is pointing out the stuff she did wrong. It was a great first run, Jess. Well done."

Tyler looked bewildered. "She doesn't need me to tell her what she did right. She already knows what she did right. My job as a coach is to tell her what she did wrong so she can fix it next time."

Brenna took a deep breath. "She's young, Tyler. She's not a professional athlete. Your job is to encourage as well as coach. Otherwise, people will lose heart and give up."

"You're saying that if I don't tell people what they're doing right, they'll give up? That's fine with me. If they're that wimpy then they should go right ahead and give up."

Cheeks flushed, Jess laughed. "I'm not that wimpy."

"Of course you're not." Disgusted, Tyler leaned forward and unclipped her helmet.

"Sorry I didn't win, Dad." The words were said casually, and Tyler opened his mouth and then caught Brenna's eye.

"You're doing great. And we're going to work on the bits that aren't so great. You'll be beating them all by the end of the season. Now let's go home and Brenna can make you one of her hot chocolates. If I get lucky she might make me one, too."

TYLER TILTED HIS CHAIR back and put his feet on the table, watching as Brenna fried bacon. Since she'd moved in, he hadn't been able to relax in his own home. He was used to feeling comfortable around her. That feeling was long gone, replaced by tension, sexual awareness and an overwhelming desire to flatten her to the table and discover the parts of her he didn't know.

"We're eating breakfast for dinner?"

She flipped the bacon expertly and threw him a look. "Add tomatoes and chili and breakfast becomes a perfect pasta sauce." Her sweater was a bright shade of blue and clung to her curves.

Curves he didn't want to notice.

"You could write a book. *A Thousand and One Things to Do with Bacon*."

"Are you complaining?"

"As long as I'm not the one cooking, I never complain." It had been over a year since anyone had stayed here apart from him and Jess, and even before Jess had arrived to live with him, he hadn't encouraged overnight guests. In his experience they were too difficult to eject.

He wished Jess would join them, but he could hear sounds of the TV coming from his den and knew he was on his own with this.

"If it carries on snowing like this it would be worth getting up early tomorrow to ski."

"I can't tomorrow." She stirred the pot. "I'm having breakfast with my parents."

"Why? They drive you crazy. Whenever you see them, you come back upset. Why put yourself through that?"

"Because they're still my parents." She poked at the sauce with the spoon. "And because I feel guilty."

"Why would you feel guilty?"

"I disappointed them. This isn't what they wanted me to do with my life."

"But it's what you wanted to do with your life, so that has to mean something, surely?"

"Maybe. Doesn't change the fact that I haven't been home for a month, and I'm living down the road."

"You have a full-time job." He locked his hands behind his head and grinned. "And now you're cooking for me, too."

"I'm not planning on revealing that part." She turned the heat down under the pan and let it simmer. "And I'm going for breakfast because that way I have an excuse to leave for my ten o'clock class."

"Just make sure you don't let them walk all over you. Want me to run you over there?"

"You're offering to stand between me and my mother?" A smile tugged at the corner of her mouth. "I always thought you were brave, Tyler O'Neil, now I know it for sure."

"I'm not scared of your mother."

"You should be. You're not her favorite person."

"She thinks I'm bad news." *She was probably right.* "How's she going to react to the fact you're living with me?"

"I'm not living with you. I'm staying in your house. It's not the same thing." Her gaze slid to his and away again. "I'm still living at Snow Crystal. She doesn't need to know more than that."

He thought about her walking barefoot around the house and sleeping next door to him. "Probably a good decision."

CHAPTER EIGHT

IT WAS STILL DARK when Brenna slid into her car the following morning.

The drive to her parents' house took around twenty minutes, and there wasn't a single second of that time when she didn't feel like turning around and driving back to Snow Crystal. It had been snowing steadily for days, but not enough to make the journey treacherous, and the road had been cleared so she had no reason to postpone her visit.

Her mood plummeted along with the temperature.

Visiting her parents was a duty, not a pleasure, and it was a duty that always left her feeling flat, depressed and more than a little guilty.

Compared to Kayla and Élise she was lucky, wasn't she? She had two parents still married and living together.

She pulled up outside the vintage brick colonial that was her mother's pride and joy. To Brenna, a house was somewhere to be indoors when you couldn't be outdoors. She'd as soon live in a tent. Occasionally in the summer, she'd done just that, erecting her little tent in the backyard until her mother had forced her back inside, worried about what the neighbors would say.

To Maura Daniels, the opinion of the neighbors came second only to God's.

Brenna sat for a moment, bracing herself for what

lay ahead, promising herself that she wasn't going to get upset.

She had a key in her pocket, but she rang the bell and then waited, tense as a deer scenting the wind. She would have walked straight in to any one of the O'Neil properties and been sure of a warm welcome. Here, in the house where she'd grown up, she hesitated to cross the threshold without permission. Nothing annoyed her order-obsessed mother more than people dropping in without warning or invitation.

To Brenna, it had been like growing up in a strait-jacket.

She heard the rhythmic tap of her mother's low heels on the cherrywood floor and then the door opened.

"Hi, Mom."

"You're wet!"

"It's snowing."

"Leave your boots outside."

She would have done it without being told, but her mother left nothing to chance when it came to her home.

Brenna had learned at an early age that snow was to be kept outside the house. Her mother couldn't control the weather, but she worked every hour of every day to control its less welcome effects, from shining the windows to removing imaginary marks from her lovingly polished floor.

"How are you, Mom?" She stepped inside, careful not to slip. The last thing she needed at the start of the season was a broken ankle, especially as a result of her mother's overzealous cleaning habit.

"Good. Things have been busy at work." Her mother eyed her black ski pants, and Brenna intercepted that look as she pulled off her boots and left them on the step.

"I'm teaching at ten o'clock. I thought I'd have more time if I didn't have to go back and change first."

"If you visited more often, you wouldn't have to cram so much into each visit."

Brenna knew better than to respond to that one. Conversations with her mother were like a game of tennis. Whenever she returned the ball, it came back at her harder, but even she had to admit that her mother seemed more tense than usual.

She wondered what had happened.

She stepped into the house and immediately felt as if the walls were closing around her, trapping her inside. She wanted to push back at them, wanted to free herself. It didn't help that they were painted a dark shade of red and hung with paintings and photographs. Her mother was a collector of things. Paintings, ornaments, vases, figurines—the house was crammed with them and no doubt Christmas would bring another flurry of objects to add clutter to the already cluttered walls and surfaces. Brenna couldn't see the point of filling a house with objects, but her mother enjoyed adding things to the home.

It was the house she'd grown up in but it had never felt like home to Brenna. The place suffocated her. She missed the soaring cathedral ceiling of Lake House and the acres of glass that captured the sunlight and framed the trees. Winter or summer, it was like looking at a postcard, and she never tired of it. It scared her how quickly it had begun to feel like home.

She followed her mother through to the kitchen.

Her father sat at the breakfast bar, his eyes glued to the TV.

"Hi, Dad." She leaned forward and kissed him, and

he gave her a quick hug, briefly taking his eyes off the football game.

"You should turn that off when your daughter is home. Lord knows, it's not something that happens often." Her mother reached for a mug and filled it with coffee. "I hope those O'Neils are paying you well for all the hours you put into that place."

There it was again, the friction, the tension. If her mother were an engine, Brenna would have checked the oil to see if she could get her working more smoothly.

"It's my choice to work hard, Mom. I love my job. And Jackson O'Neil is a good employer. I love working with him."

"So you're set to work another season for the O'Neils." The set of her mother's mouth expressed her opinion on that decision.

"Yes." Brenna curved her hands around the mug, warming herself. Her mother could chill the atmosphere more effectively than any air-conditioning unit. "Bookings are up. It's pretty exciting after the past few years of struggling through."

"If Michael O'Neil had paid more attention to his responsibilities, they wouldn't have been struggling."

The bitterness shocked her. "He's dead, Mom. You shouldn't speak like that of the dead. And Jackson and Kayla have worked really hard over the past year. It's a really exciting time, and I'm enjoying my job." If she'd hoped that news might invite a positive response, she was once again disappointed.

"We both know it's not the job that keeps you here." Maura Daniels thumped her mug down on the shiny granite countertop, her emotions released in a cacophony of clattering and banging as she pulled bowls out of the cabinet and eggs out of the fridge. "You could have stayed in Europe. You had a chance to escape from these long, endless winters and the O'Neil family, but did you take it? No. You came back here first chance you got and threw away your life."

She'd barely been in the house five minutes and already it had started. Brenna looked out the windows toward the mountains she loved and tried to imagine being this happy somewhere else. When Jackson had started his business in Europe, she'd lived in Switzerland for a while. It was beautiful, but it wasn't Snow Crystal.

"I'm not throwing anything away. I'm happy."

"Are you?" Her mother paused with a box of eggs in her hands. "Don't you want more than this? What about a home? A family?"

Her mom made her feel as if she'd done something wrong.

Brenna looked at her father, but he'd obviously decided not to get involved and was staring hard at the TV.

"I'm settled. I came back because I wanted this job."

"You came back because of *him*."

"I came back because Jackson told me the family business was in trouble. They're my friends, Mom. Jackson offered me a job, and I took it."

"We both know why you took that job, Brenna Daniels. You thought if you were both in the same place, you'd have a chance with him. You've always been a fool about Tyler O'Neil."

Brenna felt her cheeks burning. "That isn't true."

"You can lie to yourself all you want, but you can't lie to me. He was a bad influence on you growing up, and he's a bad influence on you now. You're throwing your life away because of that boy."

"It's my life, and I don't consider I'm throwing anything away. I love Snow Crystal. It's where I want to be."
And he's not a boy. She thought of Tyler's broad, muscular shoulders, the athletic power of his body and the
dark stubble that grazed his jaw. Oh, no, not a boy. He
was all man.

"Would you want to be at Snow Crystal if he wasn't
there? You're making a fool of yourself, that's what you're
doing and embarrassing all of us."

Brenna gripped her mug. "How am I embarrassing
you?"

Tight-mouthed, her mother whisked eggs and tipped
them into the pan. "You weren't going to tell me, were
you?"

"Tell you what?"

"That you've moved in with him. I'm your mother,
and I have to be the last to know my daughter is living
with Tyler O'Neil."

She knew?

Brenna's stomach lurched, and she cursed herself for
not anticipating that possibility. "Mom—"

"Instead of hearing the news from my own daughter,
I had to hear it from Ellen in the store. How do you think
that made me feel?"

"How does Ellen know?"

"How does anyone around here know anything? Because people talk."

The thought of everyone gossiping made Brenna
squirm. It was like school all over again, everyone whis-
pering about her. "I'm not living with him, Mom! I'm
staying in his house, that's all, and it happened a few days
ago. Business is looking up. They needed to book out

the lodge and I needed somewhere to stay. I'm a grown woman, and I make my own decisions. Get off my back!"

"You could have stayed here. Your room is there for you, same as it has always been."

Heat pricked the back of her neck. "I start work early and finish late. With bad weather coming, I don't want to have to make the drive every day."

"We both know that's not the reason why." Her mother tilted the pan, adjusted the heat. "He was wild as a boy, and he's wild as a man. The Carpenters have never forgiven him for what he did to Janet."

"You make it sound like he assaulted her or something, and we both know that isn't what happened. Why does everyone blame Tyler? Janet was at least half responsible." In her head, more than half. But there were things Brenna knew that she hadn't shared and never intended to. *What was the point?* "And Jess is wonderful."

"I don't blame the child. It can't have been easy for her growing up as Tyler O'Neil's daughter."

"She's proud of him. She adores him. And he's a good father. He shows an interest in her. He accepts her as she is." She added as much emphasis as she dared and tried to ignore the fact that her own father hadn't once joined in the conversation. "The O'Neils fought to keep Jess. It was Janet who took the baby away."

"Don't think I have any sympathy for that woman, because I don't." Her mother tipped a perfect omelet onto a plate and placed it in front of Brenna. "You still haven't told him, have you?"

"Told him what?"

Her mother paused. Looked her straight in the eye. "You haven't told him that Janet Carpenter was the one who bullied you at school."

Sweat drenched her, and she started to shake.

How could it still affect her so badly after so many years?

"I don't want to talk about that."

"You never did." Her mother dragged open a drawer and removed a couple of forks. "That girl made your school life a misery, but you never told him."

"How could I? She's Jess's mother. If I told him what happened, everything would be even more complicated. It would be awkward for him and awful for poor Jess."

"I lost count of the number of new schoolbags and coats I had to buy you."

That hadn't been the worst part. No, the worst part had been the words that had carved chunks out of her confidence.

You're not his type, Brenna. Flat chest and brown hair isn't his thing. He'll ski with you but he will never, ever, want to have sex with you.

Coats and bags had been replaced, but she hadn't been able to erase those words from her brain. "Janet's parents were splitting up. I think she was having a hard time at home."

"That is no excuse for making another person's life a misery." Her mother passed her a fork. "I was relieved when she took the baby away from here. It was the right thing to do."

"Janet took Jess to Chicago, miles from the O'Neils! How was that the right thing?"

"It was right for you! How would you have felt bumping into Janet and Jess at the store every day? And Tyler O'Neil wasn't here anyway. He was traveling all over the world. Couldn't sit still for five minutes."

"He was on the ski team. Tyler is a world-class athlete."

"Was." Her mother turned another perfect omelet onto a plate and sat down next to Brenna. "Maybe he *was* a world-class athlete, but whatever talent he has isn't going to do him much good now, is it?"

"And that's hard for him." She knew, even though he never talked about it to anyone. And it broke her heart. "Don't you feel any sympathy?"

"Sympathy for what? That he's no longer living the high life with a different girl in every country?"

Brenna winced as if her mother had stabbed her. "You were the one who taught me not to believe everything I read and hear."

"Well, let's hope his daughter didn't read or hear it, either."

Brenna stared down at the food congealing on her plate. No good would come from speaking her mind. And no good would come from continuing this discussion.

"Jess is back now, and she's happy. You should see her ski. She has so much talent. Just like her father."

Her mother took a bite of food. "How long until he tires of having a teenager under his feet?"

"They have a great relationship. You should see them together, they—"

"Tyler O'Neil is never going to settle down. He will never be what you want him to be, and all the hoping in the world isn't going to change that. And moving in with him isn't going to change it, either."

"I don't want him to be anything other than he is." Brenna poked her eggs. Why had she come? "He's a good friend. My best friend."

"A man and a woman can't be best friends."

"I don't believe that."

"Then you really are a fool. One person always feels more than the other."

Brenna swallowed because she knew in this case, her mother was right. And she was the person who felt more than Tyler. "It doesn't matter."

"No?" Her mother put her fork down with a clatter. "What happens when he meets someone? You think she's going to be pleased he has you as a best friend? And he *will* meet someone."

It was impossible to talk to her. Impossible to have a conversation that went to and fro. Instead it was like being pelted by words, and those words hammered into her flesh and her bones like hailstones. They hurt flesh already sensitive following Tyler's confession that Jess had wanted him to have a love life.

"I'm friends with Sean and Jackson. Their relationships with Élise and Kayla haven't affected our friendship."

"That's different. You're not in love with Sean or Jackson. You'll be cut out of Tyler's life, and it will be as if your friendship had never happened." There was a bitterness in her tone that even Brenna hadn't heard before. And something else. A sadness.

Brenna felt a flash of guilt. Was her situation really so distressing for her mother?

"Tyler wouldn't cut me out. We've known each other forever."

"And if something was going to happen it would have happened by now. It's time you faced the fact Tyler O'Neil doesn't have those feelings for you."

He'll ski with you but he will never, ever, want to have sex with you.

"That's enough, Mom."

"You should walk away and build a new life somewhere else instead of humiliating yourself waiting around for a few crumbs from his table."

"Can we talk about something else?"

"You can't build a life on dreams, Brenna. You should date other men. See other people. Helen and Todd were in signing a license last week. Getting married first week in February. And Susan Carter was in last month. That wedding is going to be a big one. Visitors from out of town." As Town Clerk, her mother had all the information on who was marrying whom.

There were times when she wished her mother had a different job. "I do date other men."

"Who? When?"

Cornered, Brenna groped wildly in her brain. "I'm going out with Josh this week. Tuesday." The words left her mouth before she could stop them. She saw her mother's face brighten for the first time since she'd walked through the door and realized in a flood of panic that by trying to make things better, she'd made them worse. Her mother would probably tell Ellen Kelly in the store and before the snow had settled, everyone would know Brenna Daniels was dating Josh. Everyone, that was, except Josh himself. Somehow she had to retrieve the situation before Josh found out.

He was going to kill her.

"Mom—"

"Well—" Her mother breathed out slowly and her shoulders relaxed. "I'm pleased. Josh is well respected in this town. He's the youngest chief of police ever appointed, and he has a calm, steady head on his shoulders. He's not short of admirers."

Oh, *crap.*

Deciding to unravel that mess later, Brenna changed the subject. "So Helen and Todd are finally getting married. That's great." She talked about nothing, anything to pass the time and keep her mother from talking about Tyler.

Somehow she made it through breakfast but by the time she left, her head was throbbing and the small amount of egg she'd eaten had settled like a stone in her stomach.

She arrived at the Outdoor Center feeling emotionally exhausted and gave a groan when she recognized the four-wheel drive cruiser that belonged to the chief of police.

I'm going on a date with Josh.

Why did he have to be the first person she bumped into?

She pulled into the space next to him, closed her eyes and promised herself that if she untangled this mess she was never, ever telling a lie again.

The door opened, and she turned her head and saw him standing there.

"You look like you've had a hell of a day, and it's not even nine-thirty. Want to talk about it?" His voice was calm, his gaze steady, and she felt color whoosh into her cheeks.

Half the girls in her class had been in love with him. The half that hadn't been in love with one of the O'Neils. "I didn't expect to see you here. Is this a social visit, or are we in trouble with the law?"

Josh raised an eyebrow. "I don't know. Should you be?"

"I may have broken a rule or two in my time." And

told a lie. A big fat lie. Her tongue was stuck to the roof of her mouth.

"Been anywhere exciting?"

There was no reason not to tell him, especially as people would have seen her car outside her mother's house. "Visiting my parents."

"Ah." Those dark eyes were perceptive. "And how did that go?"

"It was—" Brenna bit her lip "—stressful."

"Want me to arrest them?" He gave a smile that was warm and sympathetic, and she wondered how long that smile would last once word spread and someone asked him about his "date."

She slid out of the car, her nerve failing her as she found herself facing those broad shoulders. "Look, Josh—" It was going to be embarrassing to confess, but it was going to be much more embarrassing if he found out from someone else. "I need to tell you something— and I need you to listen and not get mad."

He stood, legs spread, strong, dependable and thoroughly decent. "I'm listening."

How was she supposed to do this? "I—when I was with my mom, she was going on and on about how I was wasting my life, how I should have left Snow Crystal years ago instead of staying here. She was listing all the folks who are getting married—"

His eyes gleamed. "Ouch. Do you know what set her off?"

"Yes." Her heart was hammering, and her palms were damp. "She'd heard that I'd moved in with Tyler."

"You moved in with Tyler?"

She saw the change in him and wondered why everyone automatically assumed there was something going on. "Yes, because Kayla booked Forest Lodge and there was nowhere else to go! I'm staying with him until I can sort something else out."

There was a long, pulsing silence. "I'm starting to understand why your mom was stressed out."

"She wouldn't stop talking about it. She told me I should move away, that I should see other people—oh, she went on and on and the only way to shut her up was—I mean, I told her I was—" she shrugged awkwardly "—well, seeing someone."

Josh looked at her steadily. "Judging from your expression and the fact you haven't been able to look me in the eye since you climbed out of your car, I'm guessing I'm that someone."

"I'm sorry." Guilt mingled with mortification, and she covered her face with her hands. "I don't know why I said it. She wouldn't stop telling me I was wasting my life, that I should date other people, and it slipped out, and then I tried to undo it and I couldn't, and the whole thing is a mess, and I know she's going to tell people because she thinks you're the perfect catch—"

"Hey, calm down. That's a lot of words in a short space of time." Strong hands locked around her wrists, and he gently drew her hands away from her face. "You need to breathe, honey."

The *honey* made her guilt worse. "I'm so sorry, Josh. I don't know what I was thinking. And now you're going to go into the store and everyone will be asking you and—oh, you know what they're like. They gossip. I'm going to call her in a minute and tell her it was a lie. I'll tell her she has to back off."

"Don't call her. I have a better idea."

She forced herself to look at him, expecting anger and seeing amusement. "You do?"

"Yeah, we go on that date."

"We can't. Josh, there will be gossip."

"I handle drunks, car thieves and even the occasional armed robber. I think I can handle gossip."

"I can't let you do that. I wish I'd never said it. I should have been assertive and told her my love life was my business, but the wrong thing came out of my mouth. I wanted to stop her."

"Then let's stop her. When is this *date* of ours?"

Her face was as hot as a fire pit. "I told her Tuesday."

Josh considered. "It will take a bit of juggling, but I guess I can do Tuesday. I have a meeting with the mountain rescue team at six to talk about the winter season, but I'll be through by seven-thirty."

A skilled rock and ice climber, Josh was a training officer for the Snow Crystal Mountain Rescue Team.

"Are you sure?" She couldn't shake the embarrassment. "I'll pay. And I'll meet you somewhere."

"No." He was thoughtful. "I'll pick you up from Tyler's place. Eight o'clock suit you? We need to go somewhere public so that news of our date will be spread around the local population. That will keep your mother happy for a while and keep her off your back. And now I have to go. I'm late for a planning meeting about the next snowfall heading our way."

"You don't have time for this."

"It's the usual drill. We'll suspend parking, pre-treat the roads and keep the plows running through the storm. Whatever the weather brings, we still have to eat." Josh was calm. "I'll book somewhere in town."

"It's not fair to you."

"It's dinner, that's all," he said mildly. "Two friends sharing food and talking. It doesn't have to be more complicated than that."

"Doesn't it? What happens afterward?"

"We'll work that out when we get to the end of dinner. We can either have dinner again, or we can publicly declare we're not suited. You can say you have an aversion to dating a cop. I don't know—we'll think of something."

"I feel like I'm using you."

"You're not. You've been honest with me." He hesitated. "Maybe I'm out of line saying this, especially as I think you know the way I feel about you, but we've known each other a long time, and I don't want to see you hurt. In this case I think you should listen to your mom. Tyler isn't the settling-down type. Having his daughter living with him isn't going to change that."

It was the first time he'd put his feelings into words, and hearing it was somehow worse than suspecting. "Josh—" It was agony to think he might be hurting as she was hurting. "We've been friends a long time and— you've never said anything and—" she breathed "—and I have no idea what to say."

"You don't have to say anything. My feelings, my problem."

He was trying to make it easy for her, but it didn't feel easy. Probably because she was in the same situation. Everything he was feeling, she was feeling, but for a different person.

"We can't go out for dinner with you feeling the way you do. It would be wrong."

"Like you can't live with Tyler, feeling the way you do? I'm not about to read something into it that isn't there.

You don't have to worry about that. Would I like more? Yes, but I'll settle for friendship."

And no one understood that better than she did.

She'd done the same, hadn't she? All her life.

She felt a flash of envy for Élise and Kayla. Their love lives seemed so simple. Hers was a tangled mess.

"Why does everything have to be so complicated?"

Josh gave a soft laugh. "I think it's called life."

It should have been easy to love him. He was everything most women would look for in a man. But she knew love and logic weren't necessarily close relations. "Are you going to be okay?"

"Big tough guy like me? Sure. I'll go and arrest some folks to let off steam."

It was typical Josh. Strong, patient and steady. It was the reason people still sent him Christmas cards even after he'd locked them up for the night.

Why couldn't she have fallen in love with him?

Her mother was right. It would have been so much simpler.

"But I will say one thing." Josh put his hands on her arms, and his tone was deceptively mild. "If Tyler ever hurts you, I'll be the arresting officer."

"My feelings, my problem." She delivered his own words back to him, and Josh looked at her for a moment and then let go of her arms.

"Maybe. But if I see you with red eyes and I know you haven't been peeling onions, then it's going to be his problem, too."

Hoping the situation between Tyler and Josh wasn't about to deteriorate, she grabbed her backpack from the car, hurried toward the Outdoor Center and walked straight into Tyler.

"Hey—" he locked his hands on her shoulders, steadying her "—what are you running from? Fire or avalanche?"

Love.

She was running from love.

Seeing him unsettled her, coming so soon after the conversation with her mother and then Josh. Knowing that Josh was still outside, she decided it might be best to keep Tyler talking for a few minutes. She wouldn't put it past the chief of police to read Tyler his rights.

How had it all got so complicated?

How on earth had she got herself into this mess?

By not speaking up.

She should have told Tyler she couldn't move in with him, and she should have told her mother to mind her own business.

"Sorry. I haven't had the greatest morning so far."

"You had breakfast with your mom. From the look on your face, I'm guessing that went the way you were afraid it would."

"I came away with indigestion and I don't think it was because of the omelet."

"She gave you a hard time?" He stood, legs spread, arms folded. She felt his impatience, the restless energy that was so much a part of him. He was the polar opposite of Josh's quiet, steady calm.

He had none of Josh's gentle subtlety, but his offer to listen touched her more because she knew he probably wouldn't have made that offer to anyone but her. Tyler's response to a stressful situation wasn't to talk about it. He didn't analyze or deconstruct, and his idea of therapy was to hurl himself down a vertical slope as fast as humanly possible.

"Nothing to talk about. It was a duty visit, and it's done. But thank you."

"Come on, Bren," he sounded impatient, "tell me what upset you."

"She thinks I'm wasting my life." It was quicker to tell a half-truth than to argue or avoid the question. "She wants me to go and get a proper job."

"Don't do that. You belong here." He brushed his fingers over her cheek. "You're an honorary O'Neil."

Her breath lodged in her throat.

Brenna O'Neil.

How many times had she scribbled those words in the back of her schoolbook?

"The truth is I spend more time with your family than I do with my own."

"That tends to happen when your own gives you indigestion. Cheer up. You're going to be too busy to go home for the next few weeks anyway. I'm coaching Jess again later, and then if there's time we're going to get a Christmas tree. Want to join us?" He dismissed the problem, moved on and Brenna was relieved.

"Maybe, if Jess doesn't mind. I need to get my gear and then I'm teaching all day. You?"

"Jackson has asked me to join him for lunch with some visiting businessmen. I'm not looking forward to the conversation. It will be stocks, shares, bonds—" He looked so horrified, she couldn't help laughing.

"They live boring lives stuck behind a desk. They all envy and admire you. They want to rub shoulders with a gold-medal-winning downhill skier and try to absorb some of that adrenaline and thrill-seeking secondhand. Be yourself."

She wondered if that was bad advice. Telling Tyler

Peel off seal and place inside...

An Important Message from the Editors

Dear Reader,

Because you've chosen to read one of our fine novels, we'd like to say **"thank you!"** And, as a **special** way to thank you, we're offering to send you **two more** of the books you love so well plus **2 exciting Mystery Gifts** – absolutely FREE!

Please enjoy them with our compliments...

Pam Powers

For Your Reading Pleasure..

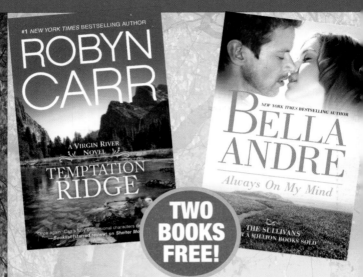

#1 NEW YORK TIMES BESTSELLING AUTHOR

ROBYN CARR

A VIRGIN RIVER NOVEL

TEMPTATION RIDGE

NEW YORK TIMES BESTSELLING AUTHOR

BELLA ANDRE

Always On My Mind

THE SULLIVANS
A MILLION BOOKS SOLD

TWO BOOKS FREE!

Each of your FREE books will fuel your imagination with intensely moving stories about life, love and relationships.

We'd like to send you **two free books** and two free gifts to introduce you to the Harlequin™ reader service. Your two books and two gifts have a combined price of over $20, but they are yours free! There's no catch. You're under no obligation to buy anything. We charge nothing – **ZERO** – for your first shipment.
You can't lose!

Visit us at
www.ReaderService.com

© 2014 HARLEQUIN ENTERPRISES LIMITED.
® and ™ are trademarks owned and used by the trademark owner and/or its licensee.
Printed in the U.S.A.

YOURS FREE!
and two free gifts

The Editor's "Thank You" Free Gifts include:
- *2 FREE books!*
- *2 exciting mystery gifts!*

Yes! I have placed my Editor's **"Free Gifts"** **seal** in the space provided at right. Please send me 2 free books and 2 fabulous mystery gifts. I understand I am under no obligation to purchase any books, as explained on the back of this card.

PLACE
FREE GIFTS
SEAL HERE

194/394 MDL GGGL

FIRST NAME	LAST NAME

ADDRESS

APT.#	CITY

STATE / PROV.	ZIP / POSTAL CODE

Thank You!

Offer limited to one per household and not applicable to series that subscriber is currently receiving.
Your Privacy—The Harlequin Reader Service is committed to protecting your privacy. Our Privacy Policy is available online at www.ReaderService.com or upon request from the Harlequin Reader Service. We make a portion of our mailing list available to reputable third parties that offer products we believe may interest you. If you prefer that we not exchange your name with third parties, or if you wish to clarify or modify your communication preferences, please visit us at www.ReaderService.com/consumerschoice or write to us at Harlequin Reader Service Preference Service, P.O. Box 9062, Buffalo, NY 14240-9062. Include your complete name and address.

◄ DETACH AND MAIL CARD TODAY ▼

⟨⟩ HARLEQUIN READER SERVICE — Here's How It Works:

Accepting your 2 free Romance books and 2 free gifts (gifts valued at approximately $10.00) places you under no obligation to buy anything. You may keep the books and gifts and return the shipping statement marked "cancel." If you do not cancel, about a month later we'll send you 4 additional books and bill you just $6.24 each in the U.S. or $6.74 each in Canada. That is a savings of at least 22% off the cover price. It's quite a bargain! Shipping and handling is just 50¢ per book in the U.S. and 75¢ per book in Canada.* You may cancel at any time, but if you choose to continue, every month we'll send you 4 more books, which you may either purchase at the discount price or return to us and cancel your subscription. *Terms and prices subject to change without notice. Prices do not include applicable taxes. Sales tax applicable in N.Y. Canadian residents will be charged applicable taxes. Offer not valid in Quebec. Books received may not be as shown. All orders subject to credit approval. Credit or debit balances in a customer's account(s) may be offset by any other outstanding balance owed by or to the customer. Please allow 4 to 6 weeks for delivery. Offer available while quantities last.

▲ If offer card is missing write to: Harlequin Reader Service, P.O. Box 1867, Buffalo, NY 14240-1867 or visit www.ReaderService.com ▲

BUSINESS REPLY MAIL
FIRST-CLASS MAIL   PERMIT NO. 717   BUFFALO, NY

POSTAGE WILL BE PAID BY ADDRESSEE

HARLEQUIN READER SERVICE
PO BOX 1867
BUFFALO NY 14240-9952

NO POSTAGE
NECESSARY
IF MAILED
IN THE
UNITED STATES

O'Neil to *be himself* was asking for trouble, and his next words confirmed she wasn't alone in thinking that.

"That's interesting, because Jackson told me to try hard *not* to be myself for an hour." His eyes were ocean-blue so that even in the depths of an icy winter, it made her think of summer. Looking at him sent warmth rushing across her skin and seeping into her bones. It weakened her limbs and melted her tension.

"I disagree. I think they're interested in the real you."

"Apparently, the real me is a loose cannon." His mouth tilted at the corners. "I'm wild and dangerous."

And she wanted wild and dangerous so badly she could almost taste it.

"Jackson is still mad at you for telling that group last week that they should probably pick a different activity."

"They were dangerous."

"You made them feel inadequate. They wanted to give up and go home!"

"They were inadequate. In my opinion, they should have given up and gone home! I don't understand how I'm to blame for that. They lied about their experience, which, I could point out, is dangerous not only for them but also for me. Apart from almost boring me to death, I nearly froze to death waiting for them to catch up."

No matter how down she was, he always made her laugh. "We'll make people do a test run before skiing with you. I'll see you later."

"Hey, Bren—" he caught her arm, his voice ultracasual "—I saw you talking to Josh. What did he want?"

How was she supposed to answer that? "He wanted to take me to dinner."

"Why?" A muscle flickered in his jaw. "Why would he take you to dinner?"

The fact that he would even ask that question hurt her already hurting heart.

You're not his type, Brenna. Flat chest and brown hair isn't his thing.

"I know it's not something you notice, Tyler, but underneath my ski gear, I'm a woman." The hurt made her snappier than she'd ever been with him before. "I go on dates. I have feelings." And those feelings were so raw, so close to the surface, it was beginning to scare her.

His fingers tightened on her arm. "I know you're a woman." He spoke through clenched teeth. "I notice."

"Do you?"

It was a question she'd never asked before. A topic neither of them had ever broached.

They stared at each other, and she knew that by speaking up, by saying those few words, she'd crossed an invisible line.

Their bodies were close but not quite touching, her awareness of him so acute she could hardly breathe. If she took one more step she'd be pressed against that hard, powerful body, and she wanted it more than anything. Wanted every sexy bad-boy inch of him. She wanted to breathe in the male scent of him, be crushed under his weight, be tangled up with him.

All she could think of was sex. Her head was filled with it, and her senses were on fire.

She turned her head and looked at his hand, still locked around her arm. They rarely, if ever, made physical contact, and she stared down at those strong fingers and imagined how they'd feel against her bare flesh. He'd be skilled, she knew that.

But she was never going to find out exactly how skilled, was she?

She waited for him to say something, but he didn't. Instead he stared at her, his breathing shallow.

He was obviously trying to work out why someone like Josh would want to date her.

She wished she could go back to bed and start the whole day again. "I need to go," she said wearily but instead of letting her go, Tyler tightened his grip.

"He asked you to dinner, but you told him no, right?"

Her heart pumped. "I told him yes." Suddenly, she was tired of it. Tired of being told what she should and shouldn't do. Tired of keeping her mouth shut when her mind was shouting out loud. "He's picking me up eight o'clock Tuesday."

CHAPTER NINE

"Tequila. Straight up." Brenna thumped her head down on the bar and missed the look Kayla sent Élise.

"You heard the woman." Kayla winked at Pete, the barman. "Give us the bottle and three glasses. This is girls' night. We're celebrating."

"I'm not celebrating. I'm commiserating."

"Who with?"

"Myself." Brenna lifted her head and dug her fingers in her hair. "Forget the glass. Pour it straight down my throat and do it fast. I want to be unconscious."

"That bad?" Kayla waited for Pete to fill the glass and pushed it toward Brenna. "So—are you going to tell us what's going on?"

"What makes you think something is going on?"

"Er—apart from the fact you don't usually drink spirits?"

Brenna picked up the glass, knocked it back in one mouthful and then choked as it set fire to her throat. "That's disgusting."

"It's an acquired taste, and you obviously haven't acquired it. As a matter of interest, why did you order tequila?"

"Because it's Saturday night, I've had a totally crap week and a beer wasn't going to do it. When I see people drink tequila in the movies, they always look as if they're having fun. I deserve to have fun, and as I'm obviously not going to have any naked-between-the-sheets sort of fun anytime soon, I thought I'd go with empty-the-bottle sort of fun."

"How can you have had a crap week?" Élise ignored the tequila and ordered a glass of wine. "It's almost Christmas, business is booming and you've moved in with Tyler. This is your dream, no?"

"If I didn't love you, I'd kill you. Both of you. For interfering. For putting me in this position. And for the record, it isn't my dream to have the man of my fantasies sleeping in a different bed with a wall between us." Brenna pushed her glass toward Kayla. "Fill it up. Don't hold back."

"If I don't hold back, you won't be able to walk tomorrow."

"I'll worry about that tomorrow. Don't you dare ever interfere again." She drank and felt the warmth spread from her throat down to her knees. "My life has been a nonstop disaster since you made me move in with him."

"Bren, you've only been living with him for a couple of days. Disaster can't happen that fast."

"It can in my life. I've crammed a lot into those couple of days." Brenna pushed her glass toward Kayla. "More."

"No." Kayla pushed the bottle back toward Pete with a meaningful look. "What happened?"

"I visited my parents. And because this place has a communication system more sophisticated than anything developed by NASA, they had already heard the happy news about my new living arrangements."

Kayla winced. "Oops."

"*Oops* doesn't cover it. I had a lecture on all the reasons I'm stupid to move in with Tyler. I've given my mother your phone number. From now on the two of you can talk about it together and cut out the middle man." She picked up Kayla's drink and knocked it back. "That's me, by the way. I'm the middle man. I'm the person everyone ignores."

"*Merde,* what have you done to her?" Élise leaned across and peeled the glass away from Brenna's fingers. "Enough, or you will fall on your face in the snow."

"At least she only does that when she drinks. I do it sober." Kayla gestured to Pete. "Can we have a couple of sodas?"

Brenna lifted her head. "I don't want soda. I want tequila."

Concerned, Pete handed her a soda. "Everything all right, Brenna?"

"No." She slouched on the bar with her chin on her palm. "My life sucks."

"That's the tequila talking," Kayla said hastily. "She drank it too fast. We're fine here, Pete. You have a ton of people waiting for you down the other end of the bar. Don't let us keep you."

"I've known Brenna since she was a little girl. I've never seen her like this."

"Everyone has known me since I was a little girl," Brenna said gloomily. "Everyone has an opinion about how I should live my life, and everyone expresses it apart from me. Go right ahead, Pete. Tell me what I'm doing wrong. Then call my mother and commiserate. Or maybe call Ellen Kelly, and you can bypass the phone altogether. Beam it across the nation. Houston, Brenna has a problem."

"I don't think you're doing anything wrong, Bren."

Looking nervous, he removed the bottle of tequila and took himself down to the far end of the bar.

Kayla grinned. "You scared him."

"Good. Maybe it's time to shake people up a bit. I'm sick of everyone thinking they know who I am and what I need. I'm tired of being the girl next door."

Élise ran her fingers down the stem of her glass. "In that case you could go home right now, walk into Tyler's bedroom naked and help yourself to some of the between-the-sheets sort of fun."

"I haven't had anywhere near enough tequila for that, and anyway I've already embarrassed myself enough for one day." Brenna sipped the soda and pulled a face. "This doesn't make me feel better."

"You'll thank me tomorrow when you don't feel as if your head is being crushed by Thor's hammer."

"I'm going home to have an early night. That way I won't have to listen to the sounds of Tyler in the shower." Brenna slid off the bar stool and swayed. "Maybe I should have stuck to beer."

"No, you're fun after tequila." Kayla picked up her coat. "I'm buying you a crate of the stuff for Christmas. I'll walk you home."

"Thanks to you *home* is a few steps down the trail, and I can do that by myself." She dragged on her coat only to find her friends on either side of her, like book-ends. "What?"

Élise slid her arm through Brenna's. "We're walking you to the door."

"You're holding on to me because you'll fall otherwise."

Kayla smiled. "That sounds about right. Come on, tequila girl, let's get you home."

They crunched through the snow, Kayla sliding and grumbling, while Brenna wondered why she'd ever thought a drink with her friends might solve the problem.

Her head spun, her limbs felt shaky and she was scrabbling in her bag for her key when Tyler opened the door.

He was wearing a blue sweater pushed up to the elbows and a pair of jeans that made it obvious why her mother thought him dangerous. No woman in her right mind would look at him and see anything other than trouble.

He looked from her to her friends. "What have you done to her?"

Brenna growled. "Nothing. This might come as a shock to certain people, but I make my own decisions about how I live my life. Good night, girls. Thanks for the lift home." Disengaging herself from their grasp, she stepped forward while behind her, the girls melted tactfully away.

Keeping her eye on the lights of the hallway, she tried to walk past him but lost her balance and fell against his chest.

Strong hands closed around her shoulders, and she heard the breath hiss through his teeth. "Brenna, just—"

"There is not enough room in this doorway for two people." She was wedged against him, and she could feel the pressure of his thighs through her coat.

"No." He gritted his teeth. "There isn't."

"I think we might be stuck." She leaned her head against his chest. "Oh, *God,* you smell good." She felt his fingers tighten on her arms.

"Brenna—"

"If you are going to lecture me, don't. I have had

enough of being told what I should and shouldn't do. I am done with other people knowing what's good for me."

"I'm glad to hear it, but why don't you tell me all that inside so that we don't both get frostbite." He eased her inside and closed the door on the cold and the dark. "How much have you drunk?"

"Why? Are you going to lecture me on that, too?"

"No. But I've never heard you speak like this before."

"You're always telling me to be more assertive and speak my mind. This is what I look like when I speak my mind. I can drink what I like, I can work where I want to work, I can have sex with anyone I want to have sex with. I don't need public approval."

There was a brief silence.

A muscle flickered in his jaw, and then he released her.

"What you need," he drawled, "is coffee. I'll make some." He strolled into the kitchen, and she watched, her eyes glued to those strong, athletic legs.

"Ty, do you like the women you have sex with?"

There was a crash as a mug splintered on the floor, followed by uncensored male cursing. "What? What did you say?"

"I asked if you like them." She slid onto the chair and put her head in her hands, watching him. "Or is the only qualification needed to climb into your bed blond hair and big boobs?"

"What exactly did you drink tonight?"

"You have to answer my question before I answer yours. Hey—" she felt a rush of pride "—did you hear that? I was assertive. I stood my ground. I refused to roll over. Are you impressed?"

His jaw tightened. "The answer is yes, I have to like them. And there haven't been anywhere near as many as—"

"Tequila." She beamed at him. "I drank tequila. It was disgusting."

He scooped up the broken pieces of china and made coffee. "Maybe you should stick to beer next time."

"I'll drink what I feel like drinking. So you like them, but don't you ever want to see them again? I mean, you have sex and then that's it?"

He put a mug of black coffee down in front of her. "Why are you asking me this?"

"Why not?"

"My sex life isn't something we normally talk about."

"I'm done with *normal*. Who decides what's normal anyway? Let's push the boundaries. I want to talk about your sex life."

He sat down across from her. "If we're pushing the boundaries, you can start by telling me why you're going out with Josh."

"Uh, no—" she shook her head and then wished she hadn't because it made the dizziness worse "—first you have to answer my question."

There was a brief silence. "I don't want commitment, so yes, I try and pick women who feel the same way."

"Do you ever get it wrong?"

"Sometimes."

"Then they call you up and tell you they're in love with you?"

"I try not to let things get that far."

"So there hasn't been a single woman you've liked enough to want to spend time with when she has her clothes on?"

He stared at her across the table. She kept waiting for him to look away, but he didn't. The silence stretched on and on, but still he looked at her until her heart started to pound and her stomach felt squirmy. She was fairly sure what was going on in her body had nothing to do with the tequila.

"Ty? Are you going to answer?"

He stirred. "It's your turn."

"I can't remember what you asked me."

"Why are you dating Josh?"

"Isn't it obvious? He's hot. He's also strong, steady and reliable. He should be perfect for me."

"Should be?"

"Well, there is that tiny little drawback that I'm not in love with him, but most people don't let that bother them so hey—" she took a mouthful of coffee "—I'm not going to let it bother me, either. Sex without emotion. I can do that."

His jaw was firm. "No, you can't."

"Why not?"

"Because I know you. You'll hate yourself."

"Maybe I won't."

"You need to cancel that date."

"I have no intention of canceling that date."

He stood up suddenly, and the chair scraped on the floor. "You can't have sex with him, Bren."

"Are you telling me what I can and can't do?"

"I'm offering friendly advice."

"You don't look friendly. You look as if you want to kill someone."

"I don't want to see you hurt."

"Funny—no one wants to see me hurt, but they're the ones doing the hurting. If I want to have sex with Josh, then I will. And it will be my decision. But if you're worried about Jess, don't be. We can go back to his place." She slid off the chair. "I'm glad we had this conversation. I feel I know you better. I'm going to bed now."

"I'll help you upstairs."

"No need. I can manage." She walked to the stairs and paused. "Do me a favor, Ty?"

"What?"

"Don't take a shower tonight. I don't want to think of you naked on the other side of the wall."

SHE WOKE WHEN the alarm went off, feeling as if her head was trapped between two boulders. To make things worse she had a clear memory of everything that had happened the night before and all the things she'd said.

Oh, crap....

She didn't want to remember what she'd said.

After glugging down water and swallowing painkillers, she showered and made it to the mountain in time for her first lesson. The sun was blinding, the rays cutting like a blade through her pounding skull as she struggled through the morning.

"So as you complete the turn you need to extend, release, then plant your pole—" She was in the middle of a private lesson when her radio crackled. The slightest noise was agony and she winced. "Excuse me for one minute, Alison." It was Patrick, one of the newest instructors, asking where she was. "I'm at the top of Moody Moose." With a throbbing headache. She was willing to bet she was moodier than any moose.

She held the radio as far away from her ear as possible and listened as he outlined the problem. For a moment she forgot about the pain crushing her brain. "*What?* What are you doing on Black Bear?" She turned away and lowered her voice so that she couldn't be overheard. "It's one of the toughest runs in the resort. Why would you take a bunch of six-year-olds up there? They're babies!"

His voice crackled over the radio as he explained that one of the kids had gone the wrong way, and the others had followed. "They saw a blue sign and thought it was a blue run."

Brenna didn't waste time pointing out he should have had firmer control of them.

She glanced across the ridge, knowing it would take her less than five minutes to get to the top of the run where Patrick was trapped. "Stay where you are. I'm coming to help you."

Thankfully, Alison was a confident skier and together they traversed to the top of Black Bear.

"I don't see them, and I've never skied this run. It looks scary." Alison peered doubtfully down the slope and then looked back over her shoulder.

"They're out of sight." Brenna adjusted her gloves. "The top of Black Bear is deceptively gentle, so I'm guessing they bombed off without waiting and by the time they hit the steep section, it was too late to turn back. We're going to need to get them down the mountain somehow. I'm so sorry but I need to help Patrick, Alison."

"Of course you do! We'll reschedule. I'll call the Outdoor Center."

"Would you mind? I feel terrible, but I can't leave him to deal with this by himself."

"I'm here for another week, so it's not a problem. I'm going to take a different route down. Do you want me to call the ski patrol or something?"

Brenna considered the options and shook her head.

"We'll take them down one at a time. It will take a while, but that can't be helped."

"What can't be helped?" Tyler skied up behind her, his black ski suit hugging the muscular contours of his powerful frame.

If the Devil had ever decided to take up skiing he would have worn that suit, Brenna thought, noticing Alison's expression change.

"You're—oh, wow—I can't believe I've met you. I mean, I knew you lived around here but—"

"We have babies stuck on Black Bear." Trying not to think about all the things she'd said to him the night before, Brenna kept her eyes on the horizon.

"Is this a new policy? Challenge them young?"

"It's not funny, Tyler." Nothing seemed funny after tequila.

"Are they injured?"

"Not yet."

"Such an optimist." Calm, he bent and adjusted his ski boots. "So what's the plan?"

"It's too far to get them back up, so I'm going to have to ski down with them. And someone has to stay with the others, so I'll have to do it one at a time. It will take three runs. The whole of my lesson time with Alison."

"Hi, Alison." Tyler gave her a smile that could have melted snow, and Alison smiled back.

"Hi. I think you're amazing, by the way." Her face was scarlet. "That downhill run in Beaver Creek was off the scale. You skied like you'd broken out of jail or something."

Brenna gritted her teeth but Tyler didn't seem to notice, and if the reference to his past successes bothered him, he didn't show it. He was charming, charismatic and even gave Alison a couple of tips. By the time she skied away, she was wearing the biggest smile Brenna had ever seen.

"Aren't you going to follow her?" She told herself that the snap in her voice was the result of her headache, not jealousy. "I think you could get lucky. She's your type."

He shifted his weight on his skis and gave her a long look. "I'm going to help you rescue these kids. How many?"

"Four. Two boys, two girls." She felt small for having thought for a moment that he'd abandon them. Warmth spread through her. "Thanks."

"Are you feeling well enough to help?"

"Why wouldn't I be feeling well enough?"

"You don't have a headache?"

"Not a trace of one."

He gave a faint smile. "Right. So let's do this." He slid forward a short distance and without his body shadowing her, the sun blazed into her face. She didn't think she'd made a sound, but she must have because he turned his head. "Keep your goggles on," he advised, "that will help filter the sunlight."

"I don't have a problem with sunlight."

"Honey, that was a grown-up girl's drinking session, and you have a grown-up girl's hangover."

All warmth and good feeling faded. "I'd punch you, but I have children to rescue."

She skied past him, but not before she'd seen that he was laughing.

He caught up with her easily. "Do you remember anything about last night?"

"All of it."

"You were—"

"Shut up, Tyler."

He gave her a look that set her nerve endings tingling. "So here's the plan. You take one, Patrick can take one and I'll take two."

"What?"

"Kids. I'll take one under each arm."

"You can't do that."

"Why not? I thought you said they were babies?"

"Not *literally* babies."

"Let's take a look and see what we've got." Tyler glided past her and out of sight, leaving her with no choice but to follow.

Patrick, who was in his first season as an instructor, had the four kids huddled at the side of the run. Two of them were crying, one was building a snowman and the other was clearly desperate to ski Black Bear because Patrick had his hand locked in the back of the boy's jacket and was delivering a lecture on how important it was to listen, follow instructions and not ski off.

Brenna took one look at the determined expression on the boy's face and glanced at Tyler. "He reminds me of you," she muttered under her breath as she skied past him to join Patrick.

"I would have been at the bottom by now." Tyler sat down in the snow next to the boy who was crying. "Hey, there. What's up?"

The boy stared miserably at the vertical drop stretching below him. "T-too steep."

"Yeah, it's steep. Imagine how impressed the kids back home are when you tell them you skied Black Bear."

"Don't want to ski it. I'll fall—" he hiccuped "—or die."

"You are not going to fall or die. That's a promise."

The boy looked unconvinced. "Yeah, I will."

"No, you won't," Tyler said patiently, "because I'll be holding you. You can't fall unless I fall, and I'm not going to fall."

"You don't know that."

"I do know that. I always know when I'm going to fall, and it's not today. What's your name?"

"Richard."

Tyler leaned toward the little girl who was shivering with cold. "And what's your name?"

"Rosie."

"Pleased to meet you, Richard and Rosie. I'm Tyler. I can get you down this mountain, but I can't do it if you're crying because the noise messes with my concentration, and it's making my friend's headache worse. You need to do exactly what I say and if you do, you'll get a medal."

Richard looked interested. Sniffing, he scrubbed his hand over his nose. "A medal?"

"A medal. You can take it home and hang it on your door. I'll even take a picture of you wearing it." He leaned across and tugged up the zip on the little girl's jacket. "You need to keep that zipped, then you'll feel warmer. Are you ready?"

"Whatcha gonna do?"

"I'm going to carry you under my right arm."

"What about my sister?"

"She'll be under my left arm." Tyler stood up and stuck his poles deep into the snow at the side of the run. Then he stooped, unclipped their skis and jabbed them into the snow by his poles. "I'll come back and get those later."

"Why can't I keep my skis?"

"Because I don't want you poking me with them while I'm skiing down."

"I could carry them down," Patrick offered, and Tyler's gaze slid to the boy who had caused the situation.

"I don't think so," he drawled. "You're going to need both hands to handle him." He stooped and looked the boy in the eye. "You have to do everything Patrick tells you to do, exactly when he tells you to do it. Understood?"

The boy nodded, and Tyler stood still on his skis and let Patrick go first, presumably so that he would be in a position to intervene if necessary.

Brenna felt a lump in her throat.

Damn.

Just when she was totally mad at him, he did something like this.

He was a world-class skier; he griped at the thought of giving lessons to experienced skiers and yet here he was, a small child tucked under each arm and his eyes on the one trying to escape from Patrick. He could have been impatient or irritated, but instead he turned the whole thing into a fun game. He skied steadily, making the steep slope look like the easiest run in the resort. He was a man who could handle anything, and suddenly every emotion she felt seemed magnified.

Watching him, she felt as if her heart were being squeezed. The conversation with her mother had scraped her feelings so that she felt raw and exposed. Unprotected.

Living with him had deepened what she felt for him.

Seeing the way he was with Jess—

Brenna dragged her eyes away from him, wishing she could turn her feelings off or at least turn them down.

She told herself it was the tequila that was making her emotional.

"Are you ready?" She turned to the little girl who had been building the snowman, explained what she wanted her to do, and together they skied down, Brenna holding her all the way.

Tyler was waiting at the bottom, his helmet and goggles lying in the snow at his feet as he laughed and joked with waiting parents who didn't seem at all alarmed or angry that their children had come down one of the most difficult runs in the resort. And she didn't need to look far to find the reason for their unusually mellow acceptance.

The reason was standing right in front of her, all six foot three of him.

One of the mothers asked if they could take photos, and Brenna waited for Tyler to refuse, but again he surprised her, posing with each of the children in turn. At the insistence of one of the fathers, he pulled Brenna into the photo, too.

He looped his arm round her shoulder, dragged her against him and she pinned the obligatory smile on her face.

"Great to meet you." Richard's father shook Tyler's hand and then ruffled his son's hair. "That's one for the album. Thanks. And thanks to your girlfriend."

Brenna didn't dare look at Tyler.

"IT WOULDN'T TURN OFF with the key or the kill switch?" His phone wedged between his shoulder and his jaw, Tyler dumped two cans of tomatoes and a can of beans on top of the meat and turned up the heat.

The food looked unappetizing, and he had a feeling that nothing he did was going to improve the situation.

He jabbed at the mixture with a spoon and listened while Jackson outlined the problem. "I'll do you a deal—you come and fix dinner, and I'll fix the snowmobile. You're a better cook than I am."

Brenna walked into the kitchen, her hair wet from the shower. She was wearing a strappy top with a pair of yoga pants, and her feet were bare. Avoiding his gaze, she walked cautiously across his big open kitchen. Long legs. Bare feet.

Unfortunately, the lack of eye contact did nothing to ease the tension that now seemed to be a permanent part of their relationship.

It wasn't just living together that had caused the problem, it was the shift in the way they responded to each other.

When he'd encouraged her to speak her mind and be more assertive with people, he hadn't realized he would be one of those people.

It didn't matter whether it had been the tequila talking; she'd said things that couldn't be unsaid.

They'd talked about subjects neither of them had broached before.

Like sex.

Was she planning on having sex with Josh?

He felt something rip through him. An emotion he didn't recognize and had never felt before.

Jealousy.

He was never jealous. It was ironic that the first time he should experience jealousy would be with Brenna. He'd protected their friendship more carefully than anything else in his life apart from Jess. It shouldn't matter to him who she saw or what she did.

That wasn't the way their relationship worked, and it never would be.

Jackson was saying something from the phone but Tyler didn't hear him.

There was a roaring in his ears, and his brain was doing crazy things.

He wanted to flatten her to the wall and kiss her until she could no longer remember her own name, let alone think about Josh. He wanted to trail his mouth over her bare shoulder and lower. He wanted to rip that inadequate strappy top off her taut, mouthwateringly perfect body and feast on every part of her.

She dragged open the fridge and finally glanced at him, and maybe she saw something in his eyes she hadn't seen before because she froze. It made him think of a gazelle spotting a lion, afraid to move.

Given that he was on the verge of pouncing, it was an uncomfortable analogy.

She might have been safer with the lion.

He had no right to do this. No right to think thoughts he had no intention of following with actions.

Jackson's voice came again, sharper this time, and Tyler stirred. "What? Yeah, I'm still here." He watched as she reached into the fridge. She was fit and strong, slim and toned, and he knew the fact he was salivating had nothing to do with the meal he was cooking.

"Ty? Are you paying attention?" Jackson's voice came from the phone, irritated, and he forced himself to concentrate.

"Sort of." His voice was croaky, and he averted his eyes from the perfect dip and curve that was Brenna's waist and hips. What had she meant by that comment that he didn't notice her as a woman? Of course he noticed her. He was working so damn hard not to notice her, it was driving him crazy. "I'm here, unfortunately. I wish I wasn't because then I wouldn't be the one cooking dinner...." He listened to the predictable brotherly banter, his gaze sneaking back to linger on Brenna's smooth arms and the straight column of her spine. He'd seen her wearing less in the summer, but somehow this was different. "What? I don't think what I'm cooking has a name, but it looks as if something died in the pot. Hopefully, this concoction will ensure I never have to cook again. Élise is training Jess, so there's hope in my future. That's providing I have a future, which I may not have once I've taken a mouthful of this." He expected Brenna to leave, but instead she sat down at the table and curved her hands round the glass of juice she'd poured, listening.

Her skin was fresh and smooth, her hair the color of oak. She had the sort of face advertising agencies used to promote shampoos and wholesome soap.

Which made his thoughts all the more inappropriate.

She was his best friend.

And Josh was taking her to dinner.

He jammed the spoon in the pot, reasoning that no amount of savage stirring could ruin something that was already ruined. "Is onion supposed to be black? What?" He listened as Jackson spoke. "I'd rather fix the snowmobile than dinner, that's for sure."

"Jackson has a problem with one of the snowmobiles?" Brenna half whispered, half mouthed the words so she didn't interrupt his conversation. "I could go and help."

Was she looking for an excuse to escape?

He shook his head, even though he knew she was perfectly capable of fixing whatever was wrong. She knew her way around an engine as well as he did. "Do you see a black wire with a white stripe coming from the stator?" He shifted the phone so that he could talk and carry on stirring, not because he thought it would make any difference to the dinner, but because he couldn't reach out and grab Brenna with a spoon in his hand. "It's got a bullet-style connector and sometimes that gets knocked out— yeah, that's right. Did you have the air box off? Well, then, that's your problem. Without the wire attached, the sled won't die when you kill it."

He talked Jackson through the problem, and by the time he ended the call and put his phone down on the table, he was back in control. "I've made dinner. My advice? Order takeout."

"It smells—interesting." She stood up and walked across to the stove. "What is it?"

"Mexican. Or perhaps I should call it Mess-ican. It has beans and chili and some other stuff. Some of which burned. Blame Jackson. I was distracted. He called at the difficult part when I was frying."

She rested her hips against the counter. "The difficult part? Do you ever listen to yourself?"

Right now he couldn't hear a thing over his brain telling him to kiss her.

"I never listen to myself," he muttered, "because I have crazy ideas."

"Tyler, you rescued two kids and skied down a slope with one under each arm that ninety percent of the population wouldn't attempt with both their hands free. And you call this—" she glanced at the food "—difficult?"

"I'd rather ski that slope blindfold than cook dinner."

"It will be fine."

"You haven't tasted it yet."

"You're forgetting I'm not much of a cook, either. If

the way to a guy's heart is truly through his stomach, I'm doomed. Whatever you've made will be better than what I usually eat."

Was she interested in Josh's heart? Or other parts of him?

Tyler groped for his beer and took a big gulp. "So did you speak to Patrick about that incident with the kids?"

"Yes, but he was already freaked out enough without me laying it on. Thanks for helping out. I wanted to thank you yesterday, right after, but you dashed off and then we kept missing each other."

He'd worked really hard on making sure they kept missing each other. "Anytime."

"Listen—about the other night and the stuff I said—"

"Forget it." He glanced up with relief as Jess walked into the room. "Hi, sweetheart. You're late. Was the bus delayed?"

"Yes." Without looking at him, Jess made straight for the fridge, and Tyler was about to make a flippant comment about uncommunicative teenagers when he noticed her shoes.

"What happened to you?"

"Nothing happened to me."

For a moment he forgot about Brenna. "You're soaked through. You fall in a ditch or something?"

"It's slippery out there. I'm hoping tomorrow is another snow day." She poured milk into a glass, her hand shaking so much she sloshed milk onto the floor. "I ripped my jacket. I'll pay for a new one. Sorry."

"You don't have to pay. Since when do you buy your own clothes?"

"If I ruined something, Mom made me pay for it." She

drained the glass and topped it up. "She said if I paid for it, I'd learn to take care of my stuff better."

Tyler stared at her. "Yeah, well, accidents happen, and I don't expect you to pay for it. But I'd like to know how it got torn." Something about the way she held herself, the way she wasn't looking at him, told him there was more going on than she was telling him. "Did you—"

"Dad! Stop asking questions. I'm clumsy, that's all." Moody, scowling, she slammed the fridge door shut and then wrinkled her nose. "What's that *terrible* smell?"

"That terrible smell is what happens when you leave me to cook." Deciding that handling a teenage girl needed the skills of a bomb-disposal expert, he backed off. "It's ready whenever you're hungry."

"I don't think I'm hungry anymore." Jess walked across the kitchen and peered cautiously into the pan. "Have you tasted it?"

"Why would I want to do that? I made it. The rest is up to you." He threw the spoon down, strolled to the table and sprawled in a chair. He was about to put his feet on the table when he caught Jess's eye.

"You sit down, too, Brenna." She urged Brenna to the table. "Not this side because I'm going to be cooking and rushing around. Go around and sit next to Dad. I'll finish off dinner."

He didn't want Brenna sitting next to him.

He didn't want her anywhere near him, but apparently Brenna failed to notice that piece of blatant teenage manipulation because she did as Jess suggested.

"So how was school, Jess?"

Tyler wondered if she'd have more success than he had, but it seemed Jess wasn't eager to share details of her day with anyone.

"There was no skiing. Enough said." Jess stuck a spoon in the pot, tasted it cautiously and coughed until her eyes watered. "Dad! How much chili did you put in this?"

"I lost count. Blame your uncle Jackson. He was talking to me."

"It's not a good idea to lose count with chili." Jess guzzled water as if she'd been lost in the desert for a month while Luna nudged her leg hopefully. "You don't want this, trust me. It would blow your doggie brain." She rummaged in the cupboards, pulled out more tomatoes and puree and proceeded to add and adjust, tasting all the time.

"She ate your food, Ty, and she's still alive." Brenna reached across the table for the juice she'd poured. "It's a miracle."

The miracle was that he was managing to keep his hands to himself.

From this position he had a view straight down her top, and his gaze welded itself to the shallow dip between her smooth breasts. He saw creamy skin, a hint of lace and then lost focus.

He didn't breathe, didn't move, and when she sat down he sucked in air, feeling as if he'd been smacked in the gut by a heavy object.

Thanks to Jess, she was sitting so close he could see the flecks of green in her eyes and the freckles dusting her nose. He could smell that elusive scent that made him think of the long, slow days of summer.

And he could think of nothing but sex.

Why?

What the hell was wrong with him? Was it the memory

of the things she'd said under the influence of tequila, or was it simply that he was jealous of Josh?

He pushed his chair back, an involuntary movement designed to put distance between them. Keeping his eyes away from her shoulders and the smooth skin of her arms, he groped for his beer.

Across from them, Jess served the chili into bowls. "I've done my best, but it's probably still going to make you sweat."

He couldn't sweat any more than he was already.

It was having Brenna living here. Under his nose. Walking around in bare feet wearing nothing but a strappy top and clingy yoga pants.

And talking about sex.

He dug his fork into the chili, surprised by how good it tasted. "You're a genius, Jess."

The moody, sullen expression vanished and was replaced by a smile. "You made it. All I did was adjust it a little bit." She glanced at him and grinned. "Okay, I adjusted it a lot."

Somehow they made it through dinner, although he had no idea what they talked about.

Brenna had the sense not to mention school again and instead turned the conversation to skiing.

Still, Tyler could think of nothing but sex.

He ate quickly, decided against a second helping and swept his empty plate off the table. "Excuse me, ladies, I need to go take a cold shower." He stood up, banging against the table in his attempt not to look at Brenna.

"Now?" Judging from the look Jess gave him, he might as well have announced that he was taking up ballet.

"Yes, now. Cooking is sweaty work."

"Brenna and I are going to watch skiing. Will you join us?"

"Sorry, sweetheart, not tonight." Even the rush of guilt wasn't enough to make him give a different answer. "I have to help Uncle Jackson with that snowmobile."

Jess cleared the bowls. "*After* your shower?"

He opened his mouth but was unable to think of a single, logical explanation, mostly because there wasn't one. Logic had left the room along with self-restraint. "Last time I checked, a man was allowed to decide when to take a shower in his own house. Thanks for rescuing dinner. I'll see you later."

In the end, he abandoned the cold shower in favor of leaving the house as fast as possible. He grabbed his jacket, whistled to Ash and stepped out into the cold.

He walked along snow-covered trails toward the barn where they kept the snowmobiles and the rest of the outdoor equipment.

Jackson was lying on his back, fiddling with the snowmobile and using words that would have made his grandmother frown. Words that grew worse when Ash bounded over and landed on him.

"I thought you were training that stupid dog."

"It's a work in progress." Tyler strolled around the snowmobile. "So far there's not been much progress."

"You're not kidding." But he ruffled Ash's fur before he pushed him off. "So how was dinner?"

"I was cooking it, which should give you a clue. Fortunately, Jess came and rescued the food."

"That explains why you're alive. So if you're not here to tell me you've poisoned yourself and only have an hour to live, what are you doing here?" Jackson tested the snowmobile. "This machine is dead. I changed the plugs, but they're full of fuel when I take them out."

"Well, at least you know you're getting fuel, so that's not the problem. Sounds like the inlet needles are sticking to the carbs." Tyler pulled off his gloves and crouched down next to his brother.

For the next hour they worked together on the snowmobile, and then Kayla walked in holding two mugs of coffee. Maple, their miniature poodle, was at her feet.

"I thought you might—oh, hi, Tyler! I didn't know you were here."

Ash spotted Maple and bounded toward him.

"Sit!" Tyler bellowed, and Ash screeched to a halt, hesitated and then sprang again, but the brief delay had given Kayla a chance to put the mugs on the floor and scoop up Maple.

"Get that animal under control!"

"Believe it or not that is the under-control version." Tyler stood up and pushed Ash's rump to the floor. "*Sit* means your butt engages with the floor."

Ash wagged his tail, his gaze fixed on Maple.

"The dog wants to play." Jackson stood up and wiped his hands on a rag. "He's not going to hurt her."

"Maybe not intentionally, but Ash playing is enough to end Maple!" Kayla held the little dog close but Maple wriggled. "Do you have a death wish or something? I brought you coffee but most of it is on the floor now."

"So I see." Jackson leaned forward and kissed her slowly, taking his time.

Ash whined.

"Cover your eyes, buddy," Tyler muttered, "this is only the beginning."

Kayla eased away from Jackson. "How are you find-ing living with Brenna?"

Difficult.

And she was the one who had put him in this position.

Knowing that, he gave her the answer he knew she wouldn't want. "We've barely seen each other."

Predictably, Kayla's face fell. "Really?"

"We've been out doing our own thing. I was a bit worried she might be lonely so it's good to know she's seeing Josh."

"Seeing Josh?" Kayla's appalled expression made it clear she didn't know. "Since when has she been see-ing Josh?"

"How would I know? Her love life is her own busi-ness." He gave her a pointed look, and she had the grace to blush.

"Tyler—"

"The two of them have been friends a long time. Josh is a good man. I'm happy for her." He wasn't happy at all. And he wanted to savage Josh. "This thing is fixed so I should be getting back."

He picked up his gloves, whistled to Ash and left Kayla to stew.

CHAPTER TEN

"WATCH IT AGAIN." Curled up on the sofa next to Jess, Brenna pressed the remote. "Look at the timing of the pole plant. Do you see?" She played it again and then again, talking Jess through it, showing her how small changes could make a big difference to her technique and speed.

"Play one of Dad's winning downhill runs."

Brenna tried to think of an excuse. The last thing she wanted to do was watch Tyler in slow motion, but she couldn't think of a reason that wouldn't draw attention so she dutifully stood up. "Do you know where he keeps those DVDs?"

"They're stuffed into the back of the cupboard on your right."

Brenna tugged open the cupboard.

Five crystal globes sat on a shelf crammed between books, a few games and various DVDs. She picked one of them up reverentially. "This is where he keeps them?" It was obvious they'd been pushed there, rather than displayed, and yet they represented excellence in his sport.

"I warned you he was messed up about the whole thing. Most people would keep a World Cup trophy out where everyone can see it, not Dad. He hides them away. I guess he doesn't want to look at them. Never talks about it, either, even though it gives him serious bragging rights."

Brenna smoothed her hand over the surface of the coveted globe. Winning one would be a dream for most skiers. Tyler had five, two for winning the overall World Cup title, three of them for individual disciplines, in his case, the downhill. "For me, this means more than the Olympics. To win this you have to ski at a high standard consistently and across disciplines."

"Makes it all the more sad that he hides them away in the dark."

Brenna reached up and put one of the trophies on the shelf on display. "It looks nice here."

Jess shrank. "Oh, no—you can't do that."

"I'm doing it."

"Then *you* are the one taking responsibility for it, not me."

"I'll take responsibility. We'll start with one and see how it goes."

"Great idea. If you're still alive in the morning, you can put the second one out."

"He might not even notice. And here's the DVD you wanted to see." She pushed it into the slot and curled up on the sofa again, resigned to watching Tyler ski.

He gave an electrifying performance, hurtling full-tilt down the mountain, attacking the slope as if he was skiing for his life. It was one of the many reasons he drew crowds, thrilled by the excitement of watching him. He was a supreme athlete, breathtakingly gifted, which made the accident that had ended his career all the more brutal.

The fact that those five crystal globes were jammed into a cupboard behind a load of detritus confirmed exactly how much he was struggling with the loss.

This was the second winter he'd missed, but last year the O'Neil family had been so focused on saving Snow Crystal and learning how to move on after Michael's death, that there had been no time to dwell on Tyler's situation. And Tyler had found himself with a teenage daughter living with him, a change in his circumstances that must have had more impact than the possibility of losing the family home and business. This year was different. Snow Crystal was finally beginning to show signs of sustained recovery. Jess and Tyler were used to living together. He had more time to think about what he'd lost.

Should she talk to him? Give him a chance to confide in her?

Their relationship had changed, and she wasn't sure of the rules anymore.

She pressed the pause button. "Look at that. Right there. Everything is perfect. The angle of his skis, the weight—" She gave Jess something to focus on, rewound and played it again while she ran through the options in her head.

She could talk to him, but things had felt awkward between them since the day she'd moved into Lake House. Living under the same roof as him had somehow intensified everything, as if someone had shone a spotlight on her feelings.

And she knew he was finding it awkward, too.

He'd started avoiding her.

"You've had it on pause for about five minutes." Jess took the remote from her hand. "What are you looking at?"

Him. She was looking at him. At the determination in that jaw. At the ski suit molded to every contour of his hard, powerful body.

"Look at his position," she croaked, "look at the balance, look at the line he took and how close he is to the gate." Look at those shoulders, those thighs, the look of fierce concentration on that insanely handsome face.

And look at me make a complete fool of myself.

"I'll never be that good." Jess stared gloomily at the screen, and Brenna took the remote back from her.

"You could be. You have talent. All you need is practice."

"How can I practice when I'm stuck in miserable boring school all day?" There was despair in her voice, and Brenna remembered feeling the same way when she was Jess's age.

"Do you hate it?"

Jess slumped and nibbled the edge of a nail. "Every minute."

Brenna thought about the exchange earlier. The filthy shoes. The torn coat. "The lessons or the kids?"

"The lessons." Jess drew her knees up under her chin and stared at the image of her father frozen on the screen. "And the kids. They're totally lame."

Brenna sat still. "Do you want to talk about it?"

Jess gave a careless shrug that was supposed to indicate indifference but revealed how bad she was feeling. "Nothing to talk about. All the girls care about is their stupid hair and stupid boys. We have nothing in common."

"Are they giving you a hard time?"

"No more than usual."

Thinking about what *usual* had been for her, Brenna's insides knotted. "When did it start?"

Jess studied her nails. "Pretty much my first day at that school. It's never good being the new girl in town."

"But you're joining in. You were picked for the ski team!" The moment she said it, she wondered how she could have been so blind and stupid. "Oh."

Jess gave a short laugh. "Yeah, that's right. I've heard it all. How I was only picked because of my dad, how I'm crap, how I have no talent."

Brenna's stomach lurched. "Jess—"

"It's partly my fault because when I started at the school, I talked about him to anyone who would listen. I guess they wanted to make sure I knew my place—" She attacked another nail even though there wasn't much of anything left to attack. "Do you think that's why I got on the ski team? Because of Dad? Be honest."

"No. You're a gifted skier, Jess. You need more time on the mountain, that's true, but you have something that most people will never have even if they spend every minute of their lives practicing."

"So I'll keep telling myself they're wrong."

"Is anyone friendly?"

"A couple of the girls used to talk to me at the beginning, but they're worried about being in the firing line so now they ignore me, too. It's fine," she said a little too quickly, "I really don't care."

It was achingly familiar. "Is it mostly one person or a group?" Talking about it, remembering her own experience, made her feel sick. "Is there a ringleader?"

"Let's watch more skiing." Jess jumped to her feet and rummaged through Tyler's collection for another DVD. "Let's watch the one where he broke that bone in his foot. I want to know how he managed to get up and ski."

"He didn't know he'd broken anything. It was much later that they found a chip in the bone." Brenna sat, watching, wondering how to deal with this situation.

She could have left it. She could have moved on and not touched a subject that made her insides pitch. But she knew that wasn't going to help Jess. "Jess, honey, we can do something about this." She felt as if she were fifteen again. "You don't have to put up with it."

Jess stared at the screen. "I mean, I know it wasn't like a major accident or anything, not like his big one, but it still looked pretty bad. Most people wouldn't have skied down."

"Do your teachers know? Does anyone know?"

"No. And I don't want to tell them, all right?" Jess turned, her eyes fierce. "Otherwise, it will make it a hundred times worse. You have *no* idea. Parents think they can walk into school, demand it's fixed, and it will all be fine but it doesn't work that way."

"I know." Brenna's mouth was so dry she could hardly speak. "I know it doesn't work that way."

"Promise me you won't tell Dad."

"He knows something isn't right. You should talk to him about it. He could help."

"I don't need help. When he has a problem, he gets on with it. He doesn't talk about it all the time." She tucked her legs under her and stared at the image on the screen. "I'll handle it. I need to toughen up."

"No, you don't. It isn't about you. It's about them. Don't let them make you feel bad about yourself. That's what I did." It was painful to remember it, and Jess turned and looked at her.

"So what did you do?"

"Nothing," Brenna said simply. "I had no confidence. I let them strip that away from me, and I wish I hadn't."

Jess stared at her in disbelief. "You're like, *so* confident. I mean, you run this whole place, and you're the only person I know who can keep up with my dad on skis. You could have made the U.S. team."

"I'm confident on the mountain. About the stuff I know. Not about other things. I was hopeless with big groups of kids, I wasn't interested in any of the things the other girls were interested in. Hair, nails, dressing up, boys—" She blushed, because of course she had been interested in one boy in particular.

"That's how I feel."

"If you don't want to do anything different, I understand, because I felt that way. But maybe we could try and work this out together." She sat for a moment, remembering how lonely she'd felt when she was in school. "And you can talk to me. Sometimes it helps to talk."

Jess fiddled with her sock. "You won't tell my dad?"

"Not if you don't want me to. But you should think about telling him yourself. He really cares about you."

"Yeah, I know." Her cheeks were pink. "But you know Dad. I'm worried he'd care a little bit too much. He'd go stomping in there."

Brenna thought about the times he'd threatened to do exactly that when she was at school and knew that holding him back wouldn't be easy. "Maybe we can think of small things you could do. Like looking more confident or pretending you don't care."

"It wouldn't work."

"Maybe not, but it might be worth trying."

"Did you?"

"No. I tried to ignore it and struggled through each day, but I wish I hadn't. I wish I'd told them I deserved respect. That everyone deserves respect."

Jess curled her legs under her. "Did you have any friends?"

"Your dad." Brenna gave a half smile. "The moment I got out of school, I used to come up here and hang out with the O'Neils."

"Who was the person who was mean to you? Does she still live around here?"

Brenna stared at her, heart thudding. It was the one question she knew she could never answer. "No, she doesn't. I think we should focus on you—"

The sound of the front door opening made them both jump and the next minute Ash bounded into the room, trailing snow across the floor.

Relieved at the interruption, Brenna grabbed his collar and coaxed him to sit.

Tyler strode into the room, glowering like a caged beast. "He pulled away from me twice in the forest. He is out of control."

Jess was on her knees on the floor, arms around Ash as she cuddled him and kissed him. "You're a bad, bad boy. No one understands you."

"I understand him perfectly." Tyler shrugged out of his coat. "He's a thug."

"He's adorable."

"If that's your idea of adorable, I'm not looking forward to the day you start dating." He caught sight of the crystal globe on the shelf. "What is that doing there?"

Jess gave Brenna a look that shrieked *I told you so* and started a countdown. "Five, four, three, two, one—"

"I put it there." Brenna tried to head off the explosion. "You should be really proud of it. I can't bear that you keep them hidden away."

He didn't explode. Instead he stood still. His face could have been carved from stone, and she felt a sudden pang of guilt that she'd caused him more pain.

She waited for him to shout at her but instead he turned and strode out of the room, slamming the door behind him.

Jess sighed. "No wonder he's single."

IT FELT AS IF his whole life was unraveling. Things he'd had under control suddenly felt out of control. Emotions he tried to ignore were battering him from all sides.

Stepping out of the shower, he reached for a towel and then heard a tap on his bedroom door.

Knotting the towel around his waist, he strolled across the room and opened the door.

Brenna was standing there, and he saw guilt in her eyes in the brief moment before she looked away from his bare chest. "I didn't mean to make you mad. I'm sorry." She tripped over her words. "Actually, I'm not sorry. You shouldn't hide those awards, Tyler. They're part of you. They represent a huge achievement. You won them."

He wondered if she wore mascara or if her eyelashes were that thick and lush naturally. "I'm pleased you're speaking your mind, but why are you speaking it to the wall? We used to be able to look each other in the eyes."

"You're not wearing anything."

"I'm wearing a towel. If you're not ready to look at me when I'm wearing a towel, you are definitely not ready to have sex with Josh."

Her jaw dropped. "What does Josh have to do with this?"

Everything. Thinking of her with Josh was the reason he wasn't sleeping. "All I'm saying is that if you can't look a guy in the eyes when he's wearing a towel, you're not ready to have a night of emotionless sex."

"It won't be emotionless. I like Josh."

Tyler resisted the urge to punch a hole through the wall. "He is not the right guy for you."

"How do you know? Unlike you, I don't have a type."

"I don't have a type, either."

"Yes, you do. Why are we talking about this? I came up here to talk about the awards. You should put those crystal globes on display, Tyler. You won them!"

"I know I won them. I don't need to look at the stupid things every day to know I won them."

"But you're making it hard for Jess to learn to talk about things that hurt, because you don't do it yourself. You're teaching her to keep things bottled up, and that's not good."

Knocked off balance, Tyler stared at her. "Am I missing something here? What does me keeping those awards hidden away have to do with Jess?" He leaned against the door frame and saw her take a step backward. He remembered a time when they'd been comfortable with each other, but that time was long gone. It was like trying to dance when he didn't know the steps. "Brenna?"

"You need to encourage her to talk to you."

"Generally or about something specific? A few clues would help."

"There are plenty of clues, Tyler." She was still staring at the wall, and he felt a rush of frustration.

"Damn it, Bren, would you look at me when we're talking?"

"All I'm saying is that you need to foster an atmosphere of open communication, that's all."

Tyler gave a disbelieving laugh. "That sounds like something straight out of a self-help manual. And it loses impact coming from someone currently staring at the wall."

Color streaked down her cheeks. "I'm trying to help." She snapped the words, and he looked at her mouth, wondering how it had suddenly got so hard to be around her and not touch her.

"Open communication. I guess I can give that a try. How about we have a little open communication here, too, and you tell me the real reason you're dating Josh."

"Are you going to stop hiding those balls?"

Tyler tried not to smile and failed. "Anyone else would have thought twice before phrasing a question that particular way, but not you. This is why you're not ready for emotionless sex."

"Oh, stop it! For five minutes of your life you could stop thinking about sex." She sent him a furious look. "And put some clothes on! There's three feet of snow outside. You shouldn't be walking around naked."

He opened his mouth to point out that so far the snow hadn't entered his bedroom, but she'd walked off.

THE EVENING'S CONVERSATION stayed with him and the next morning, he decided to drop Jess at school himself instead of letting her take the bus.

She stared moodily ahead, not talking to him.

About at his limit with moods and unwilling to play twenty questions, Tyler took the direct approach. "What's up with you?"

"You were mean to Brenna!"

Genuinely astonished, Tyler glanced at her. "Mean? I'm never mean to Brenna."

"You were horrid. She put the crystal globe out on the shelf because she was so proud of you, and you gave her one of your cold looks."

Tyler, who hadn't known he had a "cold look" felt a flash of guilt. Was that why she'd been so angry with him? Had he hurt her feelings? "I didn't want it on the shelf."

"So wait until she's gone to bed and put it back in the cupboard again. Don't make her feel bad!"

Tyler opened his mouth to point out that looking at the globe made *him* feel bad and then closed it again. "If it makes you feel better, I'll apologize."

"I don't want you to apologize to make me feel better, Dad! You need to apologize because you're sorry."

"I'm sorry I upset Brenna. I'm not sorry I put that thing back in the cupboard."

"You won *that thing!* You beat everyone else down the mountain. Doesn't it make you proud? You should be boasting about it everywhere to anyone who will listen."

Tyler pulled up near the school. "I don't care what other people think."

"Why? I don't get it." Jess looked at him, puzzled and out of her depth.

"That wasn't why I raced. I know when I won and when I screwed up. I don't need globes or medals to remind me. I wanted to be fastest down that mountain. That was all."

The only sound in the car was his breathing.

"And you were. It's hard, isn't it?" Her voice was a whisper. "You always refuse to talk about it, but you hate that you can't race anymore."

Tyler opened his mouth to make light of it and then remembered what Brenna had said about open communication. "Yeah, I hate it." The words were dragged from him. "Especially on a day like today when it's snowing. It gnaws at my insides."

"I wish it hadn't happened."

He stared at the road, surprised to discover that his

throat felt scratchy. "Yeah, me, too, but there's no point wishing something hadn't happened if it already has. Waste of energy."

"That sounds *almost* like grown-up advice, Dad."

"Does this mean I'm getting good at this parenting thing?"

"You don't totally suck at it."

"Thanks. Feedback is important for improved performance." He glanced at her and found her looking at him.

"You've never talked about it before."

"Just to you, honey. Let's keep it between ourselves."

"Oh. S-sure, Dad." She was stammering, her cheeks pink with pride. "I want you to know you can talk to me anytime."

"Thanks, sweetheart." He wondered what it was about kids that turned a man from tough to tender in a single glance. "And you can talk to me, too."

Jess hunted for a grown-up response. "Life totally sucks sometimes."

Was that a reference to her life or his? Because he wasn't sure, he kept his response neutral. "It totally does. Things happen. Life happens. If you can't change it, you have to get on with it, but if there's something that can make it easier to handle, then you do it. Hey, listen to me." He winked at her. "That was more grown-up advice. I'm getting good at this. I'm pulling straight *A*s in parenting."

"And not looking at the trophies makes it easier for you?"

"Some."

Her eyes burned with love. "I'm going to lock them away where no one can ever find them. I'm going to put your gold medal in the trash."

The passion in her was disturbingly familiar. "No need to go that far."

"I've been wearing it." Her eyes were huge with guilt. "I made you feel worse."

"Having you around only ever makes me feel better. And you know what? I think you could have a medal of your own to hang round your neck someday."

"You're joking."

"I'm not joking. You've got something, Jess. We're going to work on that something together." He reached out to hug her and then remembered that probably wasn't cool and pulled back. "Sorry. Forgot we were outside the school. No hugging allowed."

"I don't care what any of them say. They're jealous because you're my dad." The way she said it confirmed his suspicion she was having trouble at school.

He struggled to access calm. "Do people give you a hard time over it?"

She opened her mouth to dismiss it and then changed her mind. "Sometimes. Kids are stupid, that's all. They'd all love to ski with you every day."

An ugly suspicion formed in his mind. "Jess, you came home in a mess yesterday—"

"I slipped on the ice. I have to go. Bye, Dad." She grabbed her bag, but he stopped her.

"Wait. I just talked to you. You should talk to me."

"I do."

But it was obvious to him she was holding something back. "Do you want to invite someone back this week-end? Sleepover? Because you can."

"No, thanks. I'm going to be skiing the whole time, and we still need to buy a tree. There's loads to do for Christmas. Talk about it later, Dad." She was out of the car before he could stop her, walking fast through the gates of the school, head down, not talking to anyone.

Tyler swore under his breath and fought the temptation to march in after her and demand to know what was going on. Because something was going on, he was sure of it.

He sat back in his seat, gripping the steering wheel tightly.

Was that why Brenna had been encouraging him to talk to her?

Did she know something she wasn't telling him?

Making a mental note to ask her, he drove back to Snow Crystal. A morning spent with a group of skiers with more money than skill did nothing to improve his mood, and by the time he collected Jess from school, his temper was wearing thin. It was snowing steadily, and there were no signs of it stopping. He wondered if Brenna and Josh might decide to postpone their date or even cancel altogether.

Jess walked out of school the way she'd walked into it, head down, avoiding eye contact, striding toward the bus. She would have walked straight past his car if he hadn't opened the window and called to her.

"Dad!" Startled, she glanced around her. "What are you doing here?"

"I had to go to the store for something," he lied, "so I thought I might as well pick you up."

He saw a group of mothers looking in his direction and realized he'd been blind to how having him as a father might have affected Jess. Did all these people spend their time looking him up on the internet? Were they reading the lies or, worse, feeding those lies to Jess?

She slid into the seat next to him and raked her hair away from her face.

"So how was today?" He'd read that parents weren't

supposed to subject kids to a barrage of questions, and he wondered how that was supposed to work. He wanted to pin her to the seat until she'd told him what was bothering her.

"Fine."

Tyler ground his teeth. "For the record, *fine* isn't an answer."

"I don't want to talk about it. I've been thinking about Christmas. If Brenna's going to be living with us, we should buy her a present. A big one. It needs to be a proper Christmas. She can't be the only one without a pile of presents under the tree and a stocking at the end of her bed."

Tyler, who didn't want to think about stockings or beds in relation to Brenna and was still trying to work out how to get something other than *fine* out of his daughter, nodded. "Sure. Whatever. No, wait a minute." He realized he hadn't done anything about Christmas gifts. "Who says there is going to be a *pile* of presents for you? Have you sent a letter to Santa?"

Jess slouched in her seat. "I stopped believing in Santa when I was six, Dad. And no one writes letters anymore."

"So?" Stuck behind a snowplow, he drummed his fingers on the wheel. "Send an email to the North Pole. Message him. Get him on Skype. Do whatever you teens do to communicate these days. The guy needs clues."

Jess laughed. "Skype with Santa. That sounds like something Kayla would dream up."

"It does."

"So you're basically telling me you don't know what to buy me."

"A few hints might be helpful. Do you really think I should buy something for Brenna? I never have before."

"She's living in our house. She's going to be waking

up with us on Christmas morning. It's going to be super awkward if we all have presents and she doesn't have anything to open."

He turned left at the sign that said Snow Crystal Resort and Spa. "So maybe she would like to write to Santa, too."

"He's going to be a busy guy." She leaned forward to look at the ski slopes. "The lift is still running. Can I squeeze in one run?"

"You have to do your assignment. What is it?"

"English. We're studying *Romeo and Juliet.* Kill me now."

"If your teachers think you should be studying it, then you should be studying it." He slowed as he approached a couple pulling two kids on a sledge. "I have no idea what to buy Brenna for Christmas."

"Do you know she was always given dolls and stuff for Christmas? She hated dolls. We should get her something she'd love. I'll think of something." She was out of the car before he could ask any more questions, leaving him to follow.

They walked into the house and were almost flattened by Ash and Luna. "You'd better take these two out for a quick walk."

"I'm going over to Grandma's later. They can come. Can I sleep over?"

"Sure." Tyler saw Brenna's coat hanging on the hook. "Are you eating with Grandma?"

"Yes, but I'll grab a snack because I want to get this stupid assignment done before I go."

He probably should have told her that the assignment wasn't stupid, but she was already gone, her bag swinging against her hip as she walked into the den, Luna at her heels.

He opened his mouth to remind her that the dogs weren't supposed to be in the den, and closed it again. With Jess occupied, this would be a good moment to talk to Brenna.

He took the stairs two at a time but heard the sound of the shower running and backed away again.

He was in the kitchen, contemplating the contents of the fridge with something close to gloom when she walked into the room.

Tyler almost swallowed his tongue.

Her dress was black and stretchy. Stretchy enough to sit snug and tight against every curve and dip. It was a dress designed for the woman with the perfect body.

And Brenna had the perfect body.

A body he'd made a point of ignoring until recently.

To make things worse, she'd added black stockings and a pair of shoes with heels that could have doubled as a lethal weapon.

If Jess had walked in dressed like that, he would have grounded her.

He slammed the fridge shut. "You're planning on going through with it, then?"

"Excuse me?"

"This thing tonight. You're going through with it."

"It's called a date, Tyler. And I'm not only planning on *going through with it,* I'm planning on enjoying it, too. Is that a problem?"

Yeah, it was a problem. Decking the chief of police was going to come with consequences. "The weather is bad tonight. Not the best night to be on the roads. You should cancel."

"Because of the weather? Josh grew up here, like you and I. He's driven in this weather since he got his license. If we stopped for the weather, we'd stop living."

"It takes extra concentration, that's all." And he was willing to bet Josh would be distracted. Who wouldn't be, with Brenna next to them? "Is that all you're planning on wearing? You might want to pick something a little warmer."

"This is the only dress I own, Tyler."

He wondered how quickly he could get another dress delivered. "You should definitely wear a sweater. You need to cover up."

"I don't have a sweater that's fancy enough."

"I'll call Kayla," he said desperately. "According to Jackson, she brought half of New York City with her when she moved. He's thinking of giving her a room especially for her clothes."

"I'll wear my coat. And Josh's car will be heated."

And she'd be in that car. With Josh. With those mile-long legs on display in those mile-high heels.

"You might be better in snow boots."

"Snow boots?" She looked at him as if he'd gone crazy.

"We had two feet of snow this weekend."

"But not in the restaurant, I hope."

"How are you going to get from the car to the restaurant?"

"I don't know, but I've been skiing Devil's Drop since I was six, so I think I can manage to walk up a path." Her eyes glinted with anger. "What is wrong with you?"

That was a question he couldn't answer. "I didn't have the best day." But nowhere near as bad as his evening was going to be. "Look, I was hoping we could talk about Jess. She said something today. Has she confided in you? Said something?"

"*Confided* generally means someone doesn't want you to disclose information."

"But this is Jess. If you knew something bad was happening, you'd tell me, right?"

Her eyes skidded from his. "You should be having this conversation with her, not me."

"I'm having it with you. She's my daughter, Brenna! She's vulnerable. If you know something, you should tell me." He broke off as the door opened and Jess barreled in with two thoroughly overexcited dogs.

"I decided to walk the dogs now instead, so I'm going to Grandma's and taking my English assignment with me." Freezing air and snow followed her into the house. "Can you give me a lift, Dad?"

Ash shook himself, sending snow flying, and then caught sight of Brenna and bounded toward her.

"Sit!" Tyler roared, and the dog skidded to a halt and plopped onto the floor with an offended whine.

"We're on our third lesson with Dana. He's trying so hard." Looking proud, Jess toed off her boots and then took her first proper look at Brenna. "Wow, you look *amazing*. Dad, you need to get changed. Wherever you're going, if she's wearing that, you can't wear jeans."

Tyler clenched his jaw. "We're not going anywhere."

"Brenna's dressed like that to watch TV?"

"No, Brenna is going out. She has a date with Josh."

"Josh?" Jess's jaw dropped. Her expression went from astonished to horrified. "*No way!* You can't do that."

Brenna shifted on those high heels. "Jess—"

"I mean, that isn't what—I wanted you to—" she shot an agonized look at her father "—why are you just standing there? *Say* something."

He didn't trust himself to say anything civilized so he focused on his daughter. "Let's go. I'll give you a lift to Grandma's."

"I can walk—"

"No, you can't. The weather is awful. Have a great evening, Brenna."

Jess planted her feet, more stubborn than the dogs. "Dad—"

"Move!"

"All *right!* Sorry for being alive." Sending him a sullen look, she jammed her feet back into her boots and stomped to the car, a vision of injured innocence.

It was a four-minute drive to his mother's house, and Jess used every second of those four minutes to tell him where he was going wrong in his life.

"Why are you letting her do this? She likes you, Dad!"

"Sure she does." Distracted, he drove too close to the side of the road. The snow was piled in deep mounds, and he felt the wheels spin. "That's why she's going out with Josh. Makes perfect sense."

"You are not allowed to do sarcasm. That's my role. I'm the teenager, you're the parent." Jess clenched her fists in exasperation. "You didn't see her the other night. We were watching you ski. She kept staring at the screen."

"If you were analyzing skiing then of course she was staring at the screen."

"That wasn't what she was doing. She had this look on her face. Sort of faraway. And now she's going out with Josh! Why are you letting this happen?"

"Last time I looked, I wasn't in charge of who Brenna dates." He turned the wheel to the left and steered the car skillfully out of the deeper snow. The surface was slick. Dangerous. "That is a whole lot of snow. We need to get this road cleared again."

"Stop changing the subject. Brenna isn't interested in Josh, Dad!"

"Then why is she going out with him? If you're such an expert, perhaps you can tell me that!"

"I don't know!" They were both yelling, and it struck him again how similar they were. It was like dealing with himself, and it wasn't a comfortable situation.

"In my experience a woman doesn't dress up in heels and a killer dress to date a guy she doesn't like."

"That's the only dress Brenna owns. It's not like she bought it specially or anything."

"How do you know that?"

"I was with her when she unpacked, remember? She is a jeans-and-ski-pants person."

"So why is she going on a suit-and-tie date with Josh if she isn't interested in him?" He almost laughed at himself. He was so messed up he was asking advice on women from his thirteen-year-old daughter.

Jess stuck her feet on the seat and then caught his eye and put them down again. "Probably because you never asked her out yourself, and she wants to have a life. She doesn't want to die old and withered without a sex life."

Tyler almost swerved across the road. "What do you know about—"

"Don't start, Dad. We are not going to have that conversation."

"Fine!"

"*Fine* isn't an answer."

He gritted his teeth as she threw his words back at him. "I see her all the time. Every damn day."

"You said *damn.* And seeing her around isn't the same as asking her out on a proper date and giving her a chance to dress up and look cute."

"Brenna doesn't need to dress up to look cute. She looks cute in jeans."

"Listen to yourself. *How* have you had so much success with girls? I don't get it." Jess bashed her head with her fist. "Dad, you need to *do* something. Go back there now and talk to her before Josh arrives."

Tyler pulled up outside his mother's house. "Look, I appreciate your interest in all this, but I can't have a relationship with Brenna just because you like her."

"You like her, too. You love her."

"I love her as a friend."

"Really? Then why have you been acting weird ever since she moved in? Why are you so angry she's going on a date with Josh? If you were really just her 'friend,' you'd be pleased for her."

Tyler opened his mouth and closed it again. He stared at the door of his mother's house, framed by tiny lights and winter greenery.

Christmas.

Family.

Brenna wanted all that, he knew she did.

"We don't want the same things."

"How do you know? Did you ever ask her?"

"I'm not good for women."

"Maybe it depends on the woman. And how you behave is your choice. You two are driving me crazy. 'For never was a story of more woe than this of Juliet and her Romeo.' Shakespeare had obviously never met you and Brenna." Jess opened the door and jumped out, dragging her bag with her. "See you tomorrow, Dad. Try not to be a jerk."

"Wait. Jess, I want to talk to you about—"

"Good night.. 'A thousand times good night.' That's

Shakespeare, although why Juliet says it a thousand times, I don't know. Probably because Romeo wasn't listening the first time. Men should wake up and pay attention."

The door slammed.

Tyler flinched.

So much for open communication.

Maybe Jess was right. Maybe he should go back and ask Brenna straight out why she was dating the chief of police.

She'd tell him she'd always had feelings for Josh, and that would be the end of it.

He drove back as fast as he dared and pulled up outside Lake House behind Josh's cruiser.

Relieved Jess wasn't still sitting next to him, he cursed fluently and then strode into his house.

The sound of laughter told him that whatever her reasons were for dating Josh, she wasn't under duress.

There hadn't been a trace of a smile on her face when he'd been talking to her earlier.

Tyler managed what he hoped was an approximation of a civil smile. "Josh! That weather must be keeping you busy." *But not busy enough,* he thought savagely, *because you're in my house with your hands on my—*

My what?

My woman?

Brenna wasn't his woman and never would be.

"Nothing we haven't handled before." Josh gave him an easy smile, and if he was aware of any tension in the atmosphere then he gave no sign of it. Out of uniform he looked younger, more relaxed.

Tyler guessed most women would find him handsome.

He knew plenty who were interested. Including Brenna, it would seem.

He glanced at her but for once found her impossible to read.

Josh was looking at her, too. "You look incredible."

"Really?" Her face brightened, and Tyler wished he'd been the one to pay her the compliment.

She did look incredible, something he'd been trying really hard not to notice.

"Can I get you that sweater, Bren?"

Josh reached out to help her with her coat. "She won't need it. Car's heated, and I have plenty of spare layers in case of emergencies. You might want to wear snow boots to walk to the car, though, Bren. Shame to ruin those pretty shoes. Unless you want me to carry you?"

Tyler seethed. "She's better off walking. You might slip. And if you have any problems with the roads, you can call me."

Josh looked at him steadily. "I'm pretty good at walking, and I think I can handle the roads, but thanks for the offer."

"If it's too much trouble to bring her home, call and I'll come and get her. Doesn't matter how late."

"When I take a woman on a date, I see her home."

A red mist formed across Tyler's vision. "She—"

"Tyler!" Brenna's eyes narrowed dangerously. "Don't let us hold you up. I'm sure you have things to do. Have a good evening."

A good evening? How the hell was he supposed to have a good evening, knowing she was with Josh?

He waited for the door to close and then groped his way to the den and reached for the whiskey bottle.

CHAPTER ELEVEN

"So we've been seen by at least three of the biggest gossips in the place," Josh said mildly, "which should ensure your mom knows you're telling the truth about dating other people." He broke off as a woman approached their table. "What can I do for you, Mrs. Cook?"

"Sorry to bother you when you're not on duty, Chief—" she nodded pointedly to Brenna "—I was wondering if you're going to be running that women's self-defense class again."

"You need to speak to Officer Marsh," Josh said easily. "He keeps a waiting list. He'll contact you when a new class is planned. Probably in the spring."

"And you don't think I'm too old to join?"

"No, ma'am." Josh gave her a warm smile that had Mrs. Cook beaming in return.

"Well, I'm sorry for disturbing you. You two have a nice evening now. And that dress is just perfect on you, Brenna. You look like a picture." She walked away, bumped into a table and Brenna grinned.

"Well, Chief. It seems you have yet another admirer. So you don't drug them or use handcuffs, you just smile at them?"

"If only it were that easy."

He was so patient, she thought. He had time for everyone. Tyler was unapologetically imperfect whereas

Josh was perfect for her in every way, and she was being ridiculous. She was turning into someone who thought the grass was greener on the other side.

If she carried on like this, she was going to die old and withered, regretting all the opportunities she'd missed and the things she hadn't done.

"Let's go back to your place and have sex." She blurted the words out and then gave a squeak of embarrassment. Oh, *God,* she shouldn't have said it like that. She should have flirted or at least been more subtle about it. She should have kissed him and let things take their course. When Élise talked about it, she made it sound so normal and natural, but Brenna had never felt less natural in her life.

Josh put his fork down slowly. "Now? Or do you want to wait until after dessert?"

She didn't know whether to laugh at herself or crawl under the table. "I didn't mean it to come out like that. I'm sorry—"

"For what?"

"For—oh, I'm so bad at this. *Why* do I have to be so bad at this? Everyone else finds it so easy, and I want to die on the spot." Mortified, she covered her face with her hands and then felt strong hands cover hers as Josh drew her fingers away from her eyes.

"If you die on the spot, you'd leave me with a whole lot of paperwork I don't need right now."

"You're mocking me."

"Honey, I'm not mocking you, and it's a hell of an offer but I think we probably need to talk about it some more." He shook his head as their waiter approached. "Not now. Thanks." He was firm, decisive and their waiter backed away, glancing nervously between the two of them.

Imagining how that conversation would go down in the village store, Brenna felt her face burn up. "Did he hear me? I'm going to have to move back to Europe. I can't believe I said that. I mean, I'd been thinking about it obviously, and—" She had no idea what to say or do, but Josh was smiling.

"I can't believe you said that, either. Want to tell me why?"

"I think moving in with Tyler has driven me crazy."

"You thought it was time to cure yourself of Tyler and that I might be the cure." The fact that he was so calm and reasonable made it worse.

"I'm so sorry."

"Don't be. I'm flattered you picked me."

"I do care about you."

"I know. I care about you, too, honey, which is why I'm still sitting here. If I weren't an officer of the law, I might be tempted to handcuff Tyler and leave him attached to a tree until he's had time to think through what he really wants." His tone was mild but there was flint in his eyes.

"It's not his fault." She put her head in her hands. "What is *wrong* with me? Other people have emotionless sex all the time."

"Thanks."

"Josh, I don't mean—"

"You can stop explaining. I've known you since you were four. There's only ever been one man for you."

"And he doesn't want me. And I have to stop this. I have to move on. I can't believe we're talking about this. I never talk about it." She leaned back in her chair, despairing, her emotions so close to the surface she couldn't hold them back. "What am I going to do, Josh?" And then she realized it wasn't fair to ask him, because he was in the same position as her. "I feel so bad, because I know you have feelings for me."

"But they're my feelings. I told you that already. Stop worrying about me, stop worrying about Tyler and start thinking about yourself. What do you want?"

She didn't even know anymore. "I need to be honest, but if I tell Tyler how I feel, he'll freak."

"Maybe he wouldn't. At least you'd know how things are. Isn't it best to be sure?"

She stared at her wineglass. "I'm scared of ruining everything."

"Scared?" Josh gave a faint smile. "Brenna Daniels, who once skied off the back of Baker's Ridge in a white-out? You're the bravest person I know."

"I'm not good at speaking up. Generally, I'd rather dig my head in the snow and hope that by the time it has melted, the problem will have gone away."

"This particular problem has been around for most of your life so I think it's fair to assume it's not going anywhere. Let's get out of here." Josh gestured to the waiter, and Brenna pulled out her purse.

"I'm paying. First I propositioned you, and then I whined all over you. You shouldn't have to pay on top of that."

"Give me a break, Brenna. If I don't pay, it will be all over town, and Ellen Kelly will never let me in the store again."

"In that case I'll give you cash when we're in the car."

"Then it will look as if you're bribing an officer of the law."

They argued, he paid and then drove her home in silence, through swirling snow and darkness.

When he finally pulled up outside Lake House, he kept the engine running. "I'll wait until you're safely inside."

"I had a really good time. And I'm really sorry about— well, you know. Basically everything." Feeling really awkward, she picked up her purse. "Do you want to come in for a coffee or something?" Oh, *God,* why had she said *or something?* Now it sounded as if she was propositioning him again, but Josh simply smiled.

"I think there's only so much Tyler can stand in one evening, and we've probably already pushed him past his limit."

Brenna sat, watching the snow drift past the windshield and melt away on the hood. "He doesn't think of me that way."

Josh breathed out slowly. "Brenna—" his voice was patient "—why do you think he was so angry when I came to pick you up?"

"He's protective, I know that." She stared at the snow-laden trees, remembering the fun they'd had playing in the forest. "I'm like his little sister."

"I have a little sister. I'm protective. Doesn't mean I want to strangle every guy she brings home." He turned his head, and his gaze locked on hers. "He cares about you, Bren. That business with Janet freaked him out, and he's backed off relationships ever since."

"I know. He was torn up over losing Jess."

"Which is crazy when you think about it because a man like him shouldn't have wanted to be saddled with a baby."

"He's a wonderful father, and he has always adored her." She leaped to his defense, and Josh sent her a look of exasperation.

"I'm starting to think I should lock the pair of you up overnight. Then you'd be forced to talk."

It rose inside her, that dangerous thing called hope. "No!" She tugged off her shoes and pushed her feet into her snow boots. "I'm not going to do that. I'm not going to imagine something that isn't there and want something I can't have. I don't want to live my life that way."

"Maybe it's time to tell him how you feel."

"And then what? He tells me he doesn't feel the same way and it's so awkward and embarrassing I have to leave my job? There is nowhere to go after a conversation like that. I wouldn't be able to look him in the eyes. Good night, Josh." She was out of the car before he could say anything else, her shoes dangling from her fingers. She jammed her key into the lock, relieved when he drove away but feeling guilty because he was a good friend, and she couldn't be what he wanted her to be.

Everyone was in love with the wrong person, she thought dully. It was like a stupid movie where the ending was like a giant car crash. The type of movie she hated.

Closing the door, she dropped her shoes on the floor, tugged off her boots and hung up her coat.

Tyler's jacket hung on the hook next to hers. She ran her hand over it, touched the fabric and then leaned in and buried her face in it.

"You're late." His voice came from behind her. "I was worried."

She jumped and turned, heart pounding, scrabbling for an explanation as to why she'd been nestling in his coat. "I—I lost my balance." *And fell with my nose in your coat.*

Oh, crap—

"Right." He gave her a strange look. "Did you have

a good time?" He stood in the doorway of the den, his powerful frame almost filling the space. His jaw was unshaven and his feet were bare. He looked strong, muscular and so handsome, it almost hurt to look at him.

Those brilliant blue eyes met hers. Her response to that look was so overpowering, she felt a flash of despair because she'd never felt a tenth of this sexual charge when she was with Josh.

"Yes, I had a good time."

"Are you seeing him again?"

This was the moment when she should say something. She could come straight out and say *Tyler, I have feelings for you and I'd like to know if you have feelings for me.*

She stood for a moment, balanced on the edge of a decision, afraid to take that step.

"I don't know. I need to go to bed." She needed to get away.

"Wait." His voice was soft. "Come and join me in the den. We could watch a movie or something."

He was suggesting they snuggle in the dark?

Why would he do that?

"I'm pretty tired."

"A quick coffee, then. In the kitchen."

Remembering what had happened the last time he made her coffee in the kitchen, she shook her head. "I really do need to get to bed." Her gaze collided briefly with his but it was enough to set her pulse racing.

Maybe he did feel something. Maybe this wasn't all one-sided.

He broke the tense silence. "I wanted to talk to you about Jess."

"Jess?" From riding high on hope, she crashed down to disappointment. So he didn't have a personal reason for wanting to spend time with her. It was about Jess. "What about her?"

"I suspect she's been having some trouble at school. She hinted that she'd talked to you about it."

"You should be talking to her, not me."

"If you know something, you shouldn't keep it from me."

There were so many things she was keeping from him, it hardly seemed to matter. "The best way to make sure a teenager never talks to you again is to break a confidence."

"So you do know something. Come on, Brenna, you have to tell me!"

Her head throbbed. Her heart ached. "I can't do this now, Tyler." She started to walk past him, but his hand closed over her arm.

"You don't seem like yourself." His eyes darkened dangerously. "Did Josh say something to upset you?"

"No. I had a lovely evening."

"Did you sleep with him?"

She froze. "That is none of your business."

"Tell me what happened." His grip tightened. "You're upset, and you weren't upset when you left."

"Nothing happened." And nothing was ever going to happen because she was in love with the wrong man.

"Are you serious about him?"

This was the moment. This was the moment when she should tell the truth and ask him how he felt.

"Why are you asking?"

There was a pounding silence. A moment in which she was aware of her breathing and his.

"Because I don't want him to hurt you. I care about you."

Hope, bruised and battered, struggled briefly back to life. "You do?"

"Of course. We've been friends forever."

Friends.

She stood for a moment, long enough to regain her balance and her sanity.

Honesty was one thing, but there was no point in asking a direct question when she already knew the answer.

"My love life is my business." She pulled away from him and walked toward the stairs, her vision misted by hot tears she refused to let fall. "Good night, Tyler."

CHAPTER TWELVE

TYLER SLAMMED THE front door and hung up his coat.

He waited to be assaulted by the dogs but instead was met by silence. There was no sign of Brenna or Jess.

He was wondering where they were when he heard a burst of laughter coming from the den. The door was closed, presumably to keep the dogs out.

Congratulating himself on finally having imposed rules and discipline on the household and relieved that whatever was bothering Jess at school didn't seem to be affecting her at home, Tyler walked across the hall and pushed open the door.

"Go away!" Jess screamed and stuffed something back in a bag as Ash sprang up, barking frantically.

Tyler raised his brows. "Always good to have a warm welcome at the end of the day."

"You can't come in here!" Jess pushed bags under the sofa. "It's Christmas, Dad. You have to knock on doors before you enter, not barge in."

"This is my house. I'm allowed to barge anywhere I want."

"Presents are supposed to be a secret! Wait there a minute." There was rustling and muttering and finally Jess mumbled, "You can come in now."

Accepting that grudging invitation, Tyler opened the door fully and saw Ash and Luna lying on either side of

Jess like bookends. "I thought we agreed to keep them out of the den and the living room."

"This is their favorite room."

"Funny, because it's my favorite room, too." He glanced at Brenna, thinking that she looked every bit as good in skinny jeans and a blue sweater as she did in that black dress.

"We weren't expecting you home yet, Dad. You said you had a late lesson."

"She canceled." His gaze flicked to the screen, and he saw an image of himself on the notorious *Hahnenkamm,* considered to be the most challenging course on the World Cup circuit. He remembered that particular run well. The light had been flat at the top, the visibility difficult. Three racers had fallen.

He turned away. "I assume you haven't eaten. I'll cook."

"I'll do it." Jess jumped up. "You hate cooking."

He hated it a whole lot less than he hated watching himself on TV.

"I'll cook steaks."

Ash whined and sprang to his feet, and Jess grinned. "I swear he knows that word."

"I'm prepared to cook for humans, but I draw the line at cooking for dogs." But Tyler stooped and made a fuss of Ash. "You are a bad boy."

"And you are an expert on *that* subject." Jess gave him a look. "By the way, I'm staying at Grandma's tonight."

"Again?"

"What can I say? She has a tree and her house is Christmassy. Ours is a Santa-free zone, and the fridge is empty again. At this rate, Christmas is going to pass us by."

Feeling a stab of guilt, Tyler raked his fingers through his hair. "I'll go to the store tomorrow. And we'll go and get a tree this weekend. We'll take the snowmobile."

"It's probably too late. They'll all be gone."

"Jess, we live in a forest."

"All the good ones will be gone."

She stalked past him toward the kitchen, and Tyler turned his gaze to Brenna, who was unusually quiet. "Am I missing something here?"

"She's excited about Christmas. We should decorate the house and get a tree. It's important." Without looking at him, she gathered up gift wrap, and he realized he still hadn't done anything about Christmas gifts.

"So if you were writing to Santa, what would be on your list? What do you want for Christmas?"

"I don't know. Nothing."

"There must be something." He pressed her. "What would you love more than anything in the world? What do you dream about?"

She sat still, a pair of scissors in her hands and a far-away look on her face.

Then she put the scissors down and finished tidying away the mess. "I can't think of anything."

"Yes, you can. There's something you want, I can tell." Whatever it was, he wanted to buy it for her. He wanted to give her something she really wanted and see her smile on Christmas morning.

"I'm not really a possessions person. You know that."

He did know that. What she loved more than anything was being outdoors. She loved being on her skis, enjoying the beauty of the mountains. The forest. But he couldn't see any way of giving her that as a gift. "Jess wants to decorate the house. Will you help?"

"Of course." She put the DVDs back on the shelf. "Do you have decorations?"

"Not many. Let's go to the kitchen and we can talk about it over dinner."

"I'm tired. I'm going to skip dinner and have an early night."

Tired? Tyler tried to remember what time she'd arrived home last night and whether that would have given her time to go back to Josh's house.

"Do you want me to bring you something up? I can heat soup."

"No, thanks. I'm going to have a long bath and then go to bed."

Distracted by a disturbing mental vision of Brenna naked in the bath, Tyler backed away and crashed into the door. "If you change your mind, shout."

SHE TOOK A long bath and then lay on the bed with a book on climbing, but instead of reading, she watched the snow settle on the forest, layer upon layer, piling up on branches and obscuring the winding trails around the lake. She heard Jess and Tyler leave to go to his mother's, and then heard him return alone.

She turned the light out and tried to sleep, but her stomach growled, protesting at her decision to skip supper.

Checking her phone, she saw it was midnight. She'd missed a text from Kayla asking if she was going to join them at the main house for "girls' breakfast." Realizing it was days since she'd spent any time with her friends, she was about to text back and then remembered Kayla's habit of never switching her phone off. The last thing she wanted to do was wake her and Jackson in the middle of the night.

She slid out of bed and stood for a moment, looking out the window. The snow gleamed, ghostly white. The frozen surface of the lake shimmered under the light of the moon.

Pulling on a sweater, she walked out of the bedroom and down the stairs to the beautiful living room with the huge glass windows that faced over the lake and the mountains.

She'd thought she could never love anywhere as much as Forest Lodge, but she'd been wrong. Lake House was perfect and Tyler, for all his apparent lack of interest in anything but skiing, had style.

The house was still and quiet, and she curled up on one of the deep, comfortable sofas and stared at the snow falling against the darkness of the night, thinking about Christmas. Thinking about the times she'd hovered near bunches of mistletoe, hopeful, thinking maybe, maybe this Christmas he'd finally kiss her.

He'd asked what she wanted as a gift, but she had everything she wanted except one thing.

Him.

She watched as the snow erased all traces of the day before. Animal tracks would be covered, branches coated in thick dollops of snow, the trails around Snow Crystal hidden under the heavy cloak of winter. This was how she loved it, smooth and untouched, before the snowplows came to clear the roads and tracks, before the sun coaxed the snow into submission.

Deciding that hot chocolate might help her sleep, she walked through to the kitchen and then noticed a flicker of light coming from Tyler's den.

Assuming someone had forgotten to turn off the TV, Brenna walked across and pushed the door open.

Tyler lay sprawled on the sofa.

Brenna was about to creep out again when she noticed what was on the screen. It was footage of the downhill race when he'd fallen.

It was the one recording she'd never been able to watch.

She'd been there. She'd lived through the actual event. It had been the worst moment of her life.

She wanted to turn away but was afraid to move in case she drew attention to herself, so she stood, forced to relive it. His name flashed up on the screen: Tyler O'Neil, USA. She saw him preparing to launch himself out of the start gate, and her heart started to pound. She wanted to tell him not to do it. To skip this race.

Growing up, she'd often thought that what Tyler did on the slopes was closer to flying than skiing, and he seemed to be flying now as he sailed out of the gate and straight into a tuck as he took the jump that claimed so many skiers. Not Tyler. If it hadn't been for the fact she knew what was coming, Brenna would have thought he was on his way to a faultless run.

He'd always claimed his aim was to get from the top to the bottom in the fastest time possible, and he made good on that claim, hurtling down the slope as if his skis were jet propelled.

Halfway down the course, Brenna held her breath because she knew this was the moment. She wanted to look away. She wanted to close her eyes because she knew what was coming, but she kept watching and for the first time saw the accident through the eyes of the camera. Saw the moment his body lifted into the air and tumbled, spinning, crashing until it seemed impossible anyone could survive it.

She didn't think she'd made a sound but she must have done because Tyler turned his head.

For a few moments he said nothing, and then he stirred.

"I didn't know you were there." His voice was rough at the edges, and she felt as if she was trespassing. Not on his territory, but on something far more personal. His private thoughts and feelings. He hadn't intended to share this part of him with another person. If he had, he wouldn't have waited until the dead of night to watch it alone in the dark.

"I'm sorry."

"Why are you sorry? And why the hell are you crying?"

Was she crying? She hadn't even known. Embarrassed, Brenna lifted her hand and scrubbed at her cheek with her palm, feeling the wetness of tears against her hand.

"I haven't watched it before." Her voice sounded clogged. "I couldn't. It was the worst moment of my life. I thought you were dead."

"It didn't feel too great from where I was, either." His flippant tone sent her over the edge.

"Why do you always dismiss it? I know you're hurting. You don't have to pretend and keep it all locked inside. Maybe it would help to talk about it."

"Nothing helps. I watch that damn footage over and over again trying to work out what happened that day. One moment I was on my way to winning, the next I was being lifted into a helicopter."

"You've watched it before?"

"Hundreds of times. In slow motion. It doesn't get any easier."

She sank down onto the sofa next to him. "I—I didn't know. I thought you never watched yourself."

"I watch this run." His tone was bleak, and she reached out and put her hand on his thigh. She felt solid muscle under her palm, felt that muscle flex and tense under her fingers. The atmosphere in the room shifted, and she started to move her hand away, but he covered it with his own, his fingers warm and strong as he held her hand there and took the comfort she offered.

This was new territory.

It was a topic neither of them had touched upon before, but their relationship no longer felt familiar. Everything had changed, and they both knew it. His confession. Her reaction.

The intimacy.

"Is it very hard for you?"

There was a brief pause, and his fingers tightened. "It's agony."

Although he never mentioned it, she knew from Sean that the cold made the pain worse. "Can I fetch you painkillers?"

"I wasn't talking about my leg. I've learned to live with that. The other, not so much." Still holding her hand, he stretched out his long legs and leaned back against the sofa with his eyes closed. "Pathetic, that's me."

She studied the strong lines of his face. "I don't think I've met anyone less deserving of that accusation than you. I'm sorry you're hurting." She knew words were inadequate, but she said them anyway. "I'm sorry this time of year is so hard for you. I wish I could do something. I wish I could fix it."

"It can't be fixed." And then he started to talk, telling her things he'd never told her, about how he struggled with calls from his teammates, how it felt to know they were still living that life, how they wanted him to fly over and join them in drinking sessions and how he couldn't face being on the fringe of something when he used to be in the center. He talked about regret, disappointment, frustration and she sat in the dark without interrupting, holding his hand tightly as he bared his feelings.

Finally, he leaned his head back and closed his eyes. "I can't believe I told you all that."

"I'm glad you did." Wondering if he realized he was still holding her hand, she eyed the whiskey bottle. "Does that help?"

"I'll let you know in an hour or two. Join me? I can fetch another glass."

"No need." She reached out with her free hand, sloshed some whiskey into his glass and raised it. "You were the best, Tyler O'Neil. But you're also a brilliant coach. You may not be able to compete yourself, but you can help others do it. Starting with Jess. Are you enjoying teaching her or is it hard seeing her do what you used to do?" She took a sip and coughed. "That might be worse than tequila."

He took the glass from her. "I'm enjoying teaching her, and I get a real buzz from seeing her improve. Doesn't mean I wouldn't give anything for a chance to win one more crystal globe."

"Why? All you'd do is push it to the back of the cupboard with the others."

He finished her drink. "I don't want to look at it." He thumped the glass down on the table. "I just want to win it."

It was a totally Tyler-like response. "Sometimes I don't understand you."

"You understand me perfectly. You're probably the only person who does." His voice was rough, and his grip on her hand was hard and sure. Then he turned his head, and his gaze collided with hers. "Don't cry. I hate seeing you cry."

The breath caught in her throat. "Whenever you hurt, I hurt. Whatever you feel, I feel. It's horrible, but I can't help it. I guess I've known you too long. It's as if we're connected."

He stared at her for a long moment. "I've spilled my guts, so now it's your turn. Tell me why you went on that date with Josh."

She stared down at his fingers threaded through hers. If she were going to tell him the truth, now would be the perfect time. "I did it to get my mother off my back. She was worried I wasn't dating. That I was fixated on someone else."

"And are you?"

Her heart pumped a little harder. "Maybe."

"So why not date that person instead of Josh?"

Her mouth dried. "He doesn't feel the same way."

There was a long pause. "Are you sure about that?"

He is never going to find you sexy.

Tugging her hand from his, she stood up. "It's late. I should go to bed." She took a step toward the door and then stopped.

She was doing it again.

Walking away whenever a conversation became difficult.

He'd been honest with her. He'd laid his feelings bare.

Maybe it was time for her to do the same. Maybe this once, she should be honest.

She hesitated, knowing that once she put the words out there, she couldn't take them back. "We've known each other a long time, Ty. We've talked about a lot of things over the years, but there's something I've never told you—" she turned, because if she was going to say the words, then she was going to do it while she was looking at him "—I—I have feelings for you."

His gaze was steady on hers. "What sorts of feelings?"

"Feelings I've tried to ignore. Feelings I probably shouldn't be having. Feelings—" *Oh, hell.* "I love you. I've been in love with you my whole life. I guess—you probably already know that."

Her confession hovered in the air between them.

For a long moment he said nothing, and then he stirred, and when he spoke his voice was husky. "I wasn't sure. You never said anything."

"You never talked about your accident. I guess tonight we talked about stuff neither of us normally talks about." She backed away, embarrassed. "It's fine. I know you don't feel the same way. I'm like one of the guys to you."

"One of the guys? Is that seriously what you think?" There was incredulity in his tone. "Hell, Bren, are you telling me you don't know how hard I've found it since you moved in?"

Her heart was pounding because there was something in his eyes she'd never seen before.

Something she'd waited her whole life to see.

And this time she wasn't imagining it.

This time it was real.

She tried to speak but her voice wouldn't work properly. She could hardly breathe. "You found it hard?"

"Let's put it like this—Josh and I may have had our differences over the years, but I've never wanted to kill him before the other night." He rose to his feet, and she took another step backward, afraid of what she'd unleashed. He was the most familiar thing in her life, but nothing about this situation felt familiar.

"I'm going back to bed before one of us says something we can't take back."

"Too late." He slid an arm around her waist, locking her against him while he used his free hand to stroke her hair back from her face. "Brenna." He spoke her name softly, and his tone was one she'd never heard before.

She stood, frozen by shock as his fingers trailed slowly over her face, tracing the line of her jaw, the curve of her cheek, as if he was seeing her for the first time. She felt the warmth of his hand through the thin fabric of her pajamas, the hardness and power of his thighs pressed against hers, and it felt incredible.

It felt like a dream.

She didn't want to breathe, didn't want to move in case she did something to break the spell, to spoil what was turning out to be the best moment of her life.

She felt his jaw brush against the top of her head, the warmth of his touch against her skin and she closed her eyes because it was so close, *so close,* to what she'd spent her whole life hoping for.

He cupped her face in his hands and dragged his thumbs over her cheeks. "Brenna—" he lowered his forehead to hers, holding her gaze "—do you know how I felt watching you go out with Josh?"

"How did you feel?" She whispered the words, mesmerized by the look in his eyes.

"Uncivilized." His voice was thickened. "I've known the guy since high school, and I wanted to flatten him."

"You were jealous?" It shouldn't have thrilled her but it did. She locked her hand in the front of his shirt. "That wasn't why I did it."

"I know."

"I thought you didn't— I mean, I assumed—"

"You assumed wrong."

She licked her lips. "You never noticed me. There were days when you didn't even look at me."

"Yeah, those were the days I worked extra hard." His eyes were on her mouth. "I noticed you. Every day. Turns out that when it's something that really matters, I have more control than I thought."

She lifted her hand and stroked his face, feeling the roughness of his jaw against her palm. "Why didn't you say something?"

"Because what we have is important. We've been friends for years. Ours is the only relationship I haven't messed up. I didn't want to risk what we have by confessing that all I wanted to do was have mind-blowing sex with you."

She was shaking. "I—I've never had mind-blowing sex."

His eyes darkened. "You're not—?"

"No!" She felt the heat flare in her cheeks. "I'm not used to talking about this."

"So you've had sex, but not mind-blowing sex?" His voice was rough, the words barely audible, and she saw his mouth curve into a slow smile. "Maybe it's time we did something about that."

She could feel the warmth of his breath against her mouth. His lips were close enough to tease but not touch, and she stood like a bird about to fly for the first time, exhilarated and terrified.

He was going to kiss her.

Finally, after waiting a lifetime, Tyler O'Neil was going to kiss her.

Bold, terrified he might change his mind, she rose on tiptoe and closed the gap, bringing her mouth to his.

A second's delay, a moment of heart-stopping hesitation, and then his mouth claimed hers, slowly at first and then with deep, sensual hunger. Raw, electrifying excitement rushed through her, and she moaned against his lips, opening her mouth as she felt the skilled slide of his tongue against hers.

Everything inside her melted, and she clung to his shoulders, grateful for the solid strength that kept them both upright.

She was impatient for more, and she'd thought he was, too, but he kept that side of him reined in as he kissed her slowly and thoroughly until sensation flooded every cell of her body. She closed her eyes, luxuriating in the skill of his mouth, knowing that nothing in her life before had felt as perfect and right as this.

His mouth slid over her jaw, down to her neck and fastened over a pulse beating at the base of her throat. The brush of his tongue brought a moan to her throat, and she tugged at his shirt, needing to touch him, needing to feel. He had the body of an athlete, supremely fit, honed from hours of hard physical exercise, and her seeking hands encountered hard male muscle and smooth skin.

He slid one hand behind her head and brought his mouth back to hers in a kiss that was hot and explicit. She felt him, hard and ready through the fabric of his jeans, and she could hardly breathe for wanting him.

Would it be here?

Now?

She breathed him in, tasted him, touched him and just when she was ready to do anything he asked of her, he eased his mouth away from hers.

His gaze was hooded, his expression unreadable, and then he scooped her up in his arms and carried her out of the den and up the stairs to his bedroom.

It was the only room in the house she hadn't seen. He lowered her to the floor next to the bed, which was positioned to take advantage of acres of glass. This time she wasn't interested in the view. Only the man.

Without shifting his gaze from hers, he slid her top over her head and then moved his hands down her body, peeling away clothing, his and hers until they were both naked. Curious, fascinated, she trailed her hands over his shoulders and down his arms, feeling the dip and swell of muscle under her fingers, exploring and discovering. She knew everything about him, but not this. This part of him had remained a secret to her. This was the only intimacy they hadn't shared in a lifetime of friendship.

Everything about him was strong, vital, virile, from the haze of dark hair over his chest to the smooth power of his shoulders. She leaned forward and pressed her mouth to his shoulder, sliding her hands over his abdomen and lower, feeling his muscles flex, hearing the change in his breathing as she closed her hand over the silken thickness of him.

"You're killing me," he groaned and then pulled her against the power of his body and into the heat of his kiss. "Brenna, Brenna—" He murmured her name over and over again, ran the tip of his tongue over her lower lip, explored every part of her mouth until she could hardly stand because this was Tyler, her Tyler, and he was kissing her as if the world was ending and this was their last moment together.

He lowered her to the bed in a fluid movement, so strong, so sure of himself as he eased over her, the muscles bunching in his arms as he supported his weight. And still he kissed her while his hand slid over her waist, her hip and down to her thigh, missing not a single part of her. And then his mouth followed, and she squirmed against the sheets, unable to stay still as he fastened his mouth over the tip of first one breast and then the other while his fingertips slid, stroked and explored with maddening skill. Sensation cascaded from all sides until she was dizzy with the thrill of it, drowning in thick, syrupy pleasure, consumed by savage sexual excitement.

She felt him part her, felt every slow, careful stroke of those clever fingers and then his mouth as he acquainted himself with every part of her body. Shyness was brief and quickly replaced by an urgency so sharp, she was almost driven mad by it. She shifted under him, dug her fingers into that smooth, hard flesh, and he eased his way back up her body until he was looking down into her eyes.

"Tyler, please—" She'd waited so long, *so long,* and she wanted it to be now.

"Are you sure?" He stroked his hand over her hair, her cheek, cupped her face so she couldn't hide from him, and she thrilled in the knowledge that his hand wasn't steady, that his control wasn't as absolute as it seemed.

"Are you seriously asking me that?" She slid her hand over his shoulder, behind the strong column of his neck, into his silky hair. "I've wanted you forever. It's always been you. Always." She watched, heart racing as he reached for a condom from the drawer by the side of his bed. Of course, she thought, after Janet he wouldn't want to take the risk.

"Look at me." His voice was a soft command, and she opened her eyes and met the blue blaze of his. Their legs were tangled; she felt the brush of rough hair against the sensitive flesh of her thigh and the solid weight of him as he lay, trapping her with the power of his body. And then he shifted position, and she felt the heat of him, the thickness and the hard pressure, and she knew there was no stopping, no turning back. This was it. It was finally going to happen, and it didn't seem real because in all her dreams it had been him, always him, *this man,* and finally her dreams were merging with reality.

"Tyler—" She breathed his name again, dizzy with anticipation, drugged by sensation so acute, she felt as if she'd explode with wanting.

Her hands moved down his back, over hard muscle and satin-smooth skin, exploring every contour of his body. She felt him lift her, felt heat and power and masculine thrust as he entered her slowly, carefully, giving her time to adjust, watching her the whole time, forever changing their relationship with every intimacy he stole. She didn't know she was holding her breath until he murmured, "Breathe, sweetheart," and then she snatched in air, holding his gaze as she felt the thickness and power of him stretching her, filling her. She knew he was holding back. She could see it in the glitter of his eyes and the streak of color on his cheekbones. It touched her that he'd be so careful, and she lifted her hand and touched his face, feeling the roughness of his jaw against the softness of her hand.

"Tyler—"

"You're beautiful." He murmured the words against her mouth. "I've never said that to you before, and I should have. You're so beautiful."

She knew she wasn't, but he made her believe it with the sincerity of his voice and the look in his eyes, and she knew she'd never feel as deeply connected to another person as she did right at that moment.

"I love you." The words slipped out of her as her feelings spilled over, her emotions too full to be contained. "I love you so much. I always have. My whole life."

"Bren." He groaned her name and slid his hand under her, thrusting deep, and she held still for a moment, feeling her body tighten around the thickness of him, and then he was moving with a raw, primitive rhythm that sent her excitement levels rocketing off the scale. Wrapping her legs around him, she lifted into each thrust, felt him adjust the angle to increase the pleasure. She cried out, unable to stop herself, and he lowered his mouth to hers, swallowing the sound, taking everything she was offering so freely. He was buried deep inside her, and she moaned again because something he was doing felt unbelievably good, and she felt the hot ripples of pleasure spread through her body. She heard the possessive purr that came from somewhere deep in his throat, heard him mutter something under his breath, and then her body tightened around his, drawing him to the same place until there was no holding back for either of them and they came together, the pleasure thick and intoxicating, flooding both of them until neither could breathe or move.

He dropped his head to her shoulder, fighting for breath, holding her tightly. Her arms stayed around him. She felt slick skin and strength, the steady thud of his heart and thought *dreams can come true*.

CHAPTER THIRTEEN

TYLER WOKE TO FIND her body curled against his.

He lay still, adjusting to the strange and unfamiliar experience of having a woman in his bed at Lake House. And not any woman.

Brenna.

His best friend. Except that what they shared could no longer be defined as friendship, could it? They were lovers. And he wasn't stupid enough to think that didn't change everything.

He'd done the one thing he's sworn he would never do.

I love you, Tyler.

Sweat broke out on his forehead, and he eased away from her, drenched in panic and regret. He had no doubt that those words had been heartfelt and genuine. He'd always known that about her, which was why he'd been careful to avoid this situation. He couldn't be what she wanted.

So what was he doing here?

The moment she'd said those words to him in the den, he should have walked out of the room.

He should have explained that he wasn't capable of giving her what she wanted.

Anything.

The only thing he shouldn't have done was take her to bed.

Had she noticed that he hadn't said it back?

What happened now?

Where did they go from here, and what would happen to the friendship they'd shared their whole lives?

This was his fault. He'd sat with her and spilled his guts, shared parts of himself he'd never shared with anyone before, and she'd done the same. For once in her life she'd spoken the truth, and that truth had snapped the strained leash on his self-control.

Unable to think clearly with her lying next to him, he slid out of bed and walked silently to the bathroom. Through the windows he could see the snow still falling, and it lay thick and deep over the trees and the forest trail. It showed all the signs of being a perfect powder day. Normally, he would have been hammering on her door, tempting her out before the rest of the world awoke but not this time.

Tyler ran his hand over his face.

He was afraid to wake her. Afraid to face what he'd done to their relationship.

He swore under his breath and stared at his reflection in the mirror. "You're an idiot."

"Why are you an idiot?"

He met Brenna's eyes in the mirror and saw her expression change from soft to wary.

She'd tugged on his blue shirt, and he found it endearing that she'd be shy with him, that she felt the need to cover herself after the intimacies they'd shared the night before. But it didn't surprise him, because he knew her and knew exactly how she'd react in any situation.

"Brenna." What was he supposed to say? This was new territory for him. He couldn't walk away. He couldn't pretend it hadn't happened.

He had to deal with it. Usually, he had no trouble speaking his mind, but right now, he didn't know his mind.

He turned, wishing he had Sean's smooth way with words or Jackson's natural diplomacy.

"You regret it, don't you?" Her voice was flat, her arms wrapped around herself, giving the comfort he should have been offering. "You're sorry, and you wish you could turn the clock back."

Did he wish that?

He didn't know, but the delay in answering condemned him.

There was a flash of pain in her eyes, and then she turned away. Tyler ran his hand over the back of his neck, out of his depth.

"Brenna, sweetheart, wait—"

"For what? For you to find a tactful way to tell me you made a mistake? Forget it." She grabbed her clothes from the floor and pulled them on, her movements ragged and uneven, her dark hair falling forward in a messy tumble. It didn't help to know he was the one responsible for that glorious disarray. *His fingers, his mouth, the movement of her body under his.*

He wanted to grab her, and he wanted to let her go.

He wanted to strip off that blue shirt and feel her naked under him again and at the same time, he didn't want to touch her.

Never in his life had he felt this conflicted. Until now, his liaisons with women had been short and brutally uncomplicated.

"Look, last night we talked about a lot of stuff. We were both saying things we'd never said before." He raked his fingers through his hair, feeling clumsy. "I value our friendship. I don't want to lose that." He saw her pause in the doorway. Saw her knuckles whiten as she gripped the door handle so tightly, it was a wonder she didn't wrench it from the wood. "We have a great relationship, and I don't want that to change."

Slowly, she released the door handle. Breathed.

"Everything has already changed."

And she walked out of the room without a backward glance.

WHY HAD SHE told him how she felt?

She wanted to rewind the clock and take it all back.

Brenna stumbled through the snow feeling the cold and the snow seep through her clothing. Somehow she reached Elizabeth's house and as she opened the door, she heard female laughter coming from the kitchen.

"So I said to him, 'you *have* to be kidding. There is no way I can get you an interview until—'" Kayla broke off as she saw Brenna. "Hi! You didn't answer my text so I wasn't sure if you were coming. I thought—crap, what's *wrong?*" She was on her feet in a moment and so was Elizabeth while Élise stood, her hand locked around the pan as she stared at Brenna's face.

"*Merde,* what happened?"

"Oh, your hands are freezing! Why aren't you wearing a coat! And gloves?" Elizabeth took her hands and rubbed them between her own. "There is more than a foot of new snow out there, and the paths aren't even cleared yet. Look at you—you're covered in it." She brushed it off gently and steered Brenna to a chair at the table. "Are you ill? Élise will make tea. It's gentler on the stomach than coffee."

Élise gave her a look. "I do not know how to make

good tea! I am not British. Kayla can make it." But she looked worried as she watched Brenna sit down. "*Merde, you are pâle comme un fantôme.*"

"She's what?" Kayla looked at her, confused, and Élise shrugged.

"Pale as a ghost."

"Then say 'pale as a ghost'!" Kayla spread her hands in exasperation. "I can't translate French this early in the morning."

"You can't translate French at any time of the day. You have no idea how exhausting it is to always be in someone else's language. I can never properly be me."

Brenna sat for a moment, numb with cold and misery, comforted by the normality of the interaction. These were her friends. And they cared. "I don't want tea, thanks. Is Jess here?"

"Snow day. She went across to check on Alice and Walter after all the snow we had in the night. Why didn't you wear a coat, dear? That's not like you." Elizabeth brushed more snow from her sweater, and Brenna shook her head.

"I—I wanted to get out of the house. I didn't think."

"Ah! So Tyler was being annoying. This explains everything, I think." Élise rolled her eyes, but Brenna didn't smile.

She couldn't talk about what had happened.

It was too private. Too personal.

"Élise, you are burning those pancakes." Calm, Elizabeth stood up, and Élise swore fluently in French and then English as she whipped the pan off the heat and glared at Kayla.

"This is all your fault."

"Of course it is. Everything is my fault." Kayla eyed

Brenna and then turned to Elizabeth. "You remember those photos you promised me? The ones of Tyler as a baby?"

"He would kill me if I handed those over."

"I won't use them without his permission, I promise."

Elizabeth opened her mouth and closed it again as understanding dawned. "Why don't I look for them right now? It might take me a while," she said vaguely. "I have no idea where they are. You girls enjoy your breakfast. Don't wait for me."

"I cannot believe I did that." Disgusted, Élise scraped the mess from the bottom of the pan and put it in the sink to soak. "If one of my staff was that careless, I would fire them."

"It amazes me that your staff loves you so much." Kayla sat down next to Brenna. "What's happened, Bren? Is it your mother?"

"No." Brenna shook her head. "It's nothing. I'm all right."

"Oh, please, you're talking to us, not a bunch of strangers. We can see you're not all right." Kayla reached out to rub her shoulder gently, and the kindness of the gesture tipped Brenna over the edge.

"I ruined it." She choked on the words. "I did what you all told me to do and spoke my mind, but it ruined everything, and I want to put the clock back but I know I can't and it's done now, but I've lost my best friend, and I don't know how I'll cope with that. Not being able to talk with him, laugh with him, ski together—" The enormity of it hit her, and suddenly she was crying so hard, she couldn't breathe, and she felt Kayla's arms come around her, felt herself hugged and soothed, but all that did was make her cry more. "It's over. For a moment I was the happiest I've ever been—" she hiccuped her way through the words "—and now I'm the most miserable I've ever been."

"I don't understand." Kayla stroked her hair and held her. "Why is it over?"

"Me, I am completely confused." Élise plopped into the chair next to her and squeezed Brenna's leg. "Explain."

"I told him how I felt. And then we had sex. I had sex with Tyler."

There was a brief pause, and she thought she felt Kayla punch the air but when she pulled away to rub the tears from her face, both girls were looking worried.

Élise pulled a face. "And was a bad thing because all your life you have wanted this moment and built it up in your head and it was a big disappointment, no?"

"What? No! It was incredible." Remembering brought more tears, and she dug in her pocket for a tissue and blew her nose. "It was the single most amazing night of my life. It was—oh, my God—*almost* worth blowing a whole friendship for." But not quite.

"Right," Kayla said slowly, "so why is this bad?"

"Because he woke up this morning and he said it was all a big mistake, he wished it hadn't happened and he wanted things to be the same as they were before."

Kayla sat back in her chair with a sigh. "Oh, Tyler, you fool."

"I will fillet him, yes?" Élise kept her hand on Brenna's leg. "I will serve him up medium-rare or well-done. Your choice. Then he will learn to be better at communicating."

"I don't want you to do anything." Brenna blew her

nose. "Or say anything. I don't want anyone knowing or talking about it. He can't help the way he feels."

Kayla pulled a face. "He's crazy about you, Bren."

"Obviously not." Brenna stuffed the mangled tissue up her sleeve. "I woke up this morning to an empty bed. He was in the bathroom having a panic attack. I saw it in his eyes."

Élise made a disparaging noise. "Men, they are such wimps."

"I told him I loved him." She blew her nose again. "I thought I'd try being honest and speaking my mind, and I'm so tired of trying to hide my feelings. And he seemed fine, it didn't change anything—but he didn't say it back. At the time—"

"At the time you were focused on the moment."

"Yes, but this morning—I saw it in his eyes."

"He is scared." Élise gave Brenna a brief hug and stood up. "He is terrified, and the terror it is making him stupid. This we can solve. He will calm down. So now you will stop crying and eat pancakes while we come up with a plan." She walked back around the table, turned the heat up under the pan and started again.

Brenna shook her head. "No plan. No more meddling. No more telling me to speak up. No more throwing us together." She glanced at Kayla, who blushed.

"I'm really sorry." She sounded contrite. "I didn't mean to hurt you, Bren. You were so unhappy, and I love you and wanted to fix it, and I thought if the two of you were together then maybe things might work out."

"Well, they didn't, and they won't, and now we don't even have our friendship anymore." She tried to control her breathing. "Whenever anything was bad in my life, when things were hard at school or at home, he was the one I turned to. He was my best friend. So who do I talk to now he's the problem?"

"You talk to us." Kayla touched her arm gently. "You have us."

"So you give up?" Élise poured the mixture into the pan and tilted it. "You are a strong, determined woman. This is not like you."

"It has nothing to do with strength or determination. I told him how I felt. I did that. And I wish I hadn't. I gambled and lost."

"You really believe he doesn't have feelings for you?"

Brenna thought about the night before. About his mouth, his touch, the way he'd looked at her, how gentle he'd been, how caring and tender.

"I think he has feelings. But you're right that those feelings terrify him. He hasn't been serious about a woman since Janet."

"He wasn't serious about Janet." Elizabeth walked back into the room. "I'm sorry, dear. I know you feel uncomfortable talking about this with me, but you shouldn't. You've been part of this family since you were a little girl. I love you as if you were my own."

Brenna's eyes filled again, and Kayla sniffed.

"Stop it, Elizabeth."

Elizabeth sat down in the chair vacated by Élise. "He didn't love Janet, you know he didn't. That wasn't how it was."

Brenna wondered if Elizabeth knew more about Janet than she was letting on. "But the whole thing freaked him out. Losing Jess. He felt like a failure for not being able to keep her, and it tore him in shreds, I know it did. He hasn't been seriously involved with a woman since."

"Ever." Elizabeth took the plate Élise handed her. "He

hasn't been seriously involved with a woman ever. And of course that is why it has taken him so long to finally admit how he feels about you."

"He hasn't admitted it."

"He finally shifted the nature of your relationship." Elizabeth was tactful in her phraseology. "And that is a step closer to admitting it. You need to be patient. Don't back off."

"There's nothing I can do. I saw his face."

"It is an insanely handsome face," Élise murmured, "but sometimes what goes on in the brain behind that face is screwed up. He is scared, *freaked out* as you say, so you must unfreak him."

Brenna looked at the pancake without seeing it. "How?"

Élise eyed Elizabeth, who gave a half smile. "Don't mind me, dear. If you have a suggestion, out with it."

"My suggestion is that you walk into his room wearing very sexy underwear and nothing else." Aware that they were all gaping at her, Élise shrugged. "You are not only a friend, you are a woman. Show him."

"I could never do that!"

"You had sex with your clothes on?"

Brenna felt her cheeks heat. "No, but—I'm not like you."

"Which is probably just as well or Tyler would be chopped to pieces by now," Kayla muttered. "I'm not sure Elizabeth should be listening to this."

Elizabeth stirred. "I happen to think it's an excellent plan. I will keep Jess for another night. She can help me stock the freezer for Christmas. She's turning out to be a natural chef. And talking of food—" Elizabeth leaned across, cut a slice of pancake and fed it to Brenna. "You need to keep your strength up, dear."

"Wait a minute!" Brenna almost choked. "For a start, I don't own any sexy underwear."

"Vraiment?" Élise looked appalled. "Not a single piece of silk or lace? Please tell me this is a terrible joke."

"No." Her face was burning, and she saw Élise glance at Kayla and then back at her.

"So instead be naked."

"He'll turn me down." The possibility of rejection made her shrink. "And then what?"

"You are no worse off."

"I don't think I can do that." Brenna shook her head. Despite what had happened the night before, Janet's words were still wedged in her brain. "If he doesn't want me, that's the end of it. I won't push myself on him. That isn't how I want our relationship to be. It's finished, and now we somehow have to get our friendship back to where it was." But what if they couldn't do that? What if it wasn't possible? "Can we talk about something else?"

"Of course. In fact, I have some news of my own," Elizabeth said casually, putting the fork down on the plate. "Tom has asked me to dinner, and I've said yes."

Kayla stopped with her fork poised in midair. "Tom? Tom who?"

Élise rolled her eyes. "You should try looking up from your phone occasionally. There is a whole world going on out here." She beamed at Elizabeth. "Me, I like Tom very much, and he grows the best tomatoes. He has good hands, I think, and I love a man with good hands. Sean, he is the same."

"Tomatoes?" Kayla's face cleared. "Oh, *that* Tom."

Brenna, relieved at the change of subject, sipped the

tea Élise put in front of her. Given that her friend was holding a hot pan, she decided not to tell her it was disgusting. "I love Tom. I've known him forever."

"He has been very patient." Elizabeth took a sip of tea, paused, swallowed and pulled a face. "I confess I didn't find it easy after Michael died. But Tom has been a good friend to me, and friendship is the best basis for any relationship, isn't it?"

"This is true," Élise said, "but you are never too old for good sex, as Alice is always telling us. And now you might as well pour away that tea because I can see you all exchanging looks and forcing it down. And next time ask me for coffee."

"GUESS WHAT?" JESS BOUNCED into the kitchen the following morning. "School is shut *again*. Snow day! Can we ski powder? Dad? Are you listening? Why are you staring out the window?"

Tyler stirred. "What are you doing here? I thought Grandma was dropping you at school."

"I just told you, snow day!" Jess frowned and dumped her bag on the floor. "What's wrong?"

Guilt mingled with thoughts that threatened to set his brain on fire.

He'd texted Brenna twice, and she hadn't answered.

He had no idea where she was.

"Nothing is wrong." Restless, Tyler grabbed his jacket. Maybe it would help to be out in the mountains. "Get dressed, we're going skiing."

Jess tugged on her boots. "Are we inviting Brenna?"

"She's teaching."

"Dad, what's going on?" Jess stepped in front of him,

forcing him to look at her. "Something has happened, hasn't it?"

"No. Get your coat." He was out of the door before she could ask any more questions.

They skied a few runs together, then Tyler coached her, making her do the same run over and over again, repeating turns until he was satisfied. And she didn't complain, not even when she caught an edge, fell and tumbled down the slope toward him.

She lay, winded, staring up at the sky. "I guess I messed that one up."

He stooped and hauled her to her feet, rescuing her skis. "Your weight was wrong on the inside ski. You're spraying snow, which means you're sliding not carving, but aside from that little lapse, you're doing good. Really good."

And Brenna was right. He was enjoying teaching her. Far more than he'd ever anticipated he would.

Jess emptied snow out of her gloves and scraped it from the front of her ski. "There's something I have to tell you."

"Go on."

"You'll think I'm a wimp."

"Tell me."

Jess shrugged and shifted her gaze to the top of the slope. "When I'm up there looking down, before I start, I'm scared."

"Of course you are." Tyler reached out and brushed snow from her jacket. "We all are."

Her eyes widened. "Even you?"

"Oh, yeah. You ask any racer, and he'll say the same. If he doesn't, he's lying. Most of us know how it feels to fall, and in that moment before you start when you're looking down the hill, you start to see the worst that could happen. And let's face it, when you're flying down at those speeds, it doesn't take much to make you crash— you hook an edge or take a wrong turn—" he shrugged, not wanting to dwell on the chilling options "—it's not that you don't feel fear, but you control it. And that takes discipline. What people don't realize is that it's not only a physical challenge out there, it's an emotional challenge."

"I thought maybe the fact that I'm scared might mean I can't do this."

"No. It's not feeling fear that's the problem, it's how you manage it. You can learn." He reached out and fastened her helmet. "You could do this. You have what it takes."

"Do you think one day I might even have my own crystal globe?"

"If you work hard, who knows? Do you want to?"

"Will you help me?"

He felt a rush of adrenaline and elation that he hadn't felt since his accident. He knew he could help, and he knew he'd enjoy doing it. "All the way."

"Then let's do it." Excitement burned in her eyes, and she knocked the snow from her boots and stamped her feet into her skis. "Let's take it from the top."

BRENNA FINISHED HER last lesson and drove back to Lake House. It had been a long day, and all she wanted was to relax in a deep bath and stare through the window at the snow falling.

What she didn't want was an embarrassing, uncomfortable moment with Tyler.

What was she supposed to say?

Forget it, Tyler. It was just one night. Plenty of people do it.

But she didn't. And he knew she didn't.

Let's pretend nothing has changed.

How could she say that when it was obvious to both of them that *everything* had changed?

She should never have said the *L* word.

Exasperated, and cringing with embarrassment, she was relieved to see no sign of his car. At least she could go straight to her room.

She opened the door, made a fuss of Ash and Luna and then saw the package lying on the floor with her name on it.

Luna whined and pressed her nose against Brenna's leg.

"I messed up, Luna." Brenna stroked her gently and then opened the package.

A flimsy wisp of black tulle and lace fell into her hand and she stared at it, and then at the note from her friends, in disbelief.

Maybe this is the day you have a date with destiny.
And it's best to be as pretty as possible for destiny.
Coco Chanel (with some tweaks from Élise and
Kayla xxxx)

"You *have* to be kidding me."

Luna whined, and she shook her head at the dog. "I cannot wear this. I can't."

She turned it over in her hands and then held it up.

She didn't need to try it on to know it was going to reveal far more than it covered.

She heard the slam of a car door and listened for the

sound of voices, but a quick glance through the window told her Tyler was on his own.

Without bothering to take off her coat, she sprinted upstairs to her bedroom and closed the door, the offending package still in her hand.

Heart pounding, she put the garment on the bed and checked the label.

French, of course. And expensive. Sheer, sexy and something she wouldn't wear in a million years.

Except—

Heart thumping, she took off her coat and hung it up, feeling as if the underwear was watching her, blaming her for being a coward.

Did Élise really wear that sort of thing? No wonder Sean was always walking around with a smile on his face.

What was to stop her doing the same thing?

From downstairs she heard a clash of pans in the kitchen and relaxed slightly. One thing she was sure of— there was no way Tyler would come looking for her. He was obviously as uncomfortable about the whole thing as she was.

After stripping off her clothes, she ran herself a deep bath and sank into the water.

She thought about the underwear lying on the bed.

It wouldn't hurt to try it on, would it? Then she could at least thank Élise and Kayla, tell them it was a lovely thought but that it hadn't fitted.

Leaving the comfort of the deep bubble bath, she wrapped herself in a towel and walked into the bedroom. The only light in the room came from the lamp next to the bed, and she dropped the towel and reached for the underwear. It felt soft and flimsy in her fingers, a whisper of wicked temptation.

Pulling it on, she turned to look at herself in the mirror. She'd never worn anything so light and delicate. It was like wearing nothing, and the tulle bra fitted her small frame perfectly.

She had a feeling Coco Chanel would have approved.

Piling the heavy mass of her hair on top of her head, she pouted and struck a pose and then shook her head.

She looked ridiculous.

If she walked into Tyler's room looking like this, he'd laugh. She could imagine his expression.

And then the door to her bedroom opened, and she didn't have to imagine his expression because he was standing in the doorway looking as if he'd been caught in the path of an avalanche. And there was no sign of laughter.

"Holy—"

"Tyler! What are you *doing* here? Get out!" She dropped her arms and tried to cover herself, then snatched the damp towel from the floor but it caught in her foot and she crashed down onto polished wood in a tangle of long limbs and black transparent underwear.

Dignity shredded, she lay sprawled at his feet thinking that when Coco Chanel had referred to *a date with destiny,* she hadn't anticipated that it would look anything like this. She felt as if she'd let the whole of womankind down.

Sorry, Coco.

She heard Tyler inhale and assumed it was because he'd never witnessed anything more clumsy or less provocative in his life.

"Are you all right?"

"No, I'm not all right! You're supposed to at least *knock* or something. Oh, my God, Tyler, just—*go!*" She felt the burn in her cheeks, and anger mingled with frustration, all aimed at herself. Élise or Christy would have given him a feline smile and beckoned him into the room. They wouldn't have fallen over and yelled at him.

"Are you hurt?" Instead of leaving, he hunkered down next to her so that those powerful shoulders were eye level.

"Yes. No." Her pride was hurt. Her confidence decimated. "What are you doing here?"

"I came to say— I wanted to—" His gaze dropped to the tulle bra. "Why are you wearing that? Where are you going?"

She could hardly tell him she was about to march into his bedroom and make an indecent proposition. He'd laugh at her, and she couldn't even blame him.

"I was getting dressed."

"Why?" His eyes darkened, his mouth unsmiling. "Are you going out with Josh again?"

"No!"

"Then why are you walking around dressed like something out of a bad boy's dream? Is that what you wear under your ski pants? If I'd known, I would have wiped out years ago."

And in that moment, hearing those words, she stopped feeling like a fraud and started to feel like a woman.

She'd already told the truth. How could more of the same truth make things worse?

"I was trying it on. Plucking up courage to walk into your room and proposition you."

His gaze lifted from the transparent bra, to her mouth, and then finally met her eyes.

"Excuse me?" His voice was husky, those eyes a

wicked blue under thick, dark lashes that sent his sex appeal rocketing off the scale.

"I don't agree with what you said last night." She thought of Elizabeth's words. "You wanted to put the clock back, to pretend it never happened, but we can't do that. We can't go back, Tyler, only forward. We're both a little freaked out by what happened, but it happened so now we have a choice." Her voice was firm. "And this is mine."

He was still, his breathing uneven.

She waited for him to say something, but he didn't.

Color seeped into her cheeks, a slow simmer of humiliation. Had she read him wrong? Was he about to tell her he wasn't interested? That last night had been the result of too much whiskey and honesty?

Her fragile confidence evaporated in the heat of the silence.

"All right, this is embarrassing." She pushed her hair away from her face with a shaky hand. "You need to go, Tyler. Right now."

"Go?" He seemed to be struggling to speak. "You went to all that effort to gain my attention, and now you want me to walk away?"

"Because you're obviously not interested!"

That statement was greeted by another lengthy silence. "Which part of what I'm doing makes you think I'm not interested?"

"The fact that you're not saying anything for a start."

"Honey, you're sprawled in front of me wearing pretty much nothing but an anxious look," he drawled. "I'm a man. We're simple creatures. My brain shut down the moment I saw what you were wearing. It's kind of hard for me to string a sentence together right now, so you need to be gentle with me." He rose to his feet and held out his hand.

Startled, she looked up at him. What she saw in his eyes made her stomach clench in a knot of savage sexual tension. His gaze burned hot, and there was nothing gentle about the expression on his face. He wasn't looking at her as if she was a friend. In fact, she didn't recognize this look at all. There was something in those brilliant blue eyes she'd never seen before, something that made her reach out her hand.

He pulled her to her feet and hard against him. She felt the thick ridge of his erection pressed against her, and then he was kissing her, and it was hot and crazy and nothing like the night before when he'd been so tender with her, so careful. This time his kiss was greedy, demanding, deeply erotic and unrestrained. He cupped her face in his hands, eased his mouth away from hers as if it was the hardest thing he'd ever done. "I'm afraid of hurting you." His voice was raw. "I'm so fucking afraid of hurting you."

"No. You won't. Don't stop. Please don't stop." The force of the excitement barreled into her, and she clutched at his shoulders, feeling the swell of male muscle through the fabric of his shirt. There was a vicious tightening low in her stomach, a rush of desire that turned her legs into useless objects, but it didn't matter because he lifted her and carried her to the bed, and any last reservations were blown away by the chemistry between them. She felt the warmth of his hands on her bare thighs, the brush of denim against her skin, and then he was kissing her again—first her mouth, then her neck. He sat her on the edge of the bed and knelt on the floor in front of her. The light from the lamp spilled onto his hair, glossy and

dark. There was a look in his eyes that made her catch
her breath, and she lifted her hands to unhook the bra,
but he caught her hands in his and dragged them down
to her sides.

"No way." He pressed his mouth to the pulse at the
base of her throat. She closed her eyes, felt the touch of
his lips and tongue as he moved down her body, exploring. The flimsy, transparent bra offered no protection at
all from his skilled assault, and as the tip of her breast
was drawn into the wet heat of his mouth, teased by the
relentless flick of his tongue, she gave a little moan, unable to hold it back, unable to hold anything back.

"Tyler—" She tugged at his shoulder but he ignored
her and moved lower, pushing her back on the bed with
the flat of his hand. He pushed her legs apart, and she
gave a gasp, squirming against the strength of his hands.
"What are you doing?"

"I'm moving forward, like you suggested." He spread
her thighs so that she lay in front of him exposed, vulnerable, the delicate wisp of fabric more promise than
protection.

His fingers slid along the edge of the silk, and she
raised her hips, squirming against the sheets, trying desperately to relieve the maddening ache building low in
her pelvis. He touched her everywhere except where she
needed to be touched, those long, clever fingers spinning
excitement with every stroke, tormenting her until she
couldn't take a full breath, couldn't bear the delicious
agony of the excitement, couldn't last another moment.

She gasped his name, begged him, but he simply
pushed her thighs wider with firm, determined hands,
covered her with his mouth, and she ceased to be capable of coherent thought because she was swallowed up

by sensation. The softness of silk, the slick probe of his tongue. She felt as if she were melting, coming apart, and then he peeled away the last of her protection, leaving her naked and at the mercy of his clever mouth and skilled fingers. She felt her body clamp down on his fingers and lifted her hips, but he withdrew gently and joined her on the bed.

She was close, so close, and she couldn't believe he'd stopped right then. It was cruel. It was—

"Tyler— I want— I need—" She moaned as she felt the brush of his body against hers, and then he drove into her with a single, smooth thrust that made her gasp.

"What do you need?" His voice was husky, his eyes so dark with passion, they were almost black, and he drove deeper still, so that for a moment they were joined so deeply, she couldn't breathe or move. "Tell me what you need, sweetheart."

She slid her hands down his back, stared into his eyes and fell deeper and deeper. "You already know."

And he lowered his mouth to hers and kissed her, giving her everything until all she could feel was masculine thickness, silk and intense heat. She clawed at his shoulders, dragged her fingers down his spine, closed her hands over his backside, but he kept up the same rhythm, driving into her again and again, deeper, harder, filling her until she felt her body begin to tighten and ripple around the power of his shaft.

He muttered something under his breath, and she knew he was trying to hold back, but she had long since lost control and her body fluttered, pulsed, quivered and tightened around his, and he groaned deep in his throat, a primitive animal sound as each spasm dragged him past the limits of his own control. He thrust deep, every movement intensifying her excitement, prolonging the moment of ecstasy.

Afterward she felt limp. Weak. There was sweat on his skin, and he dropped his forehead to hers, his breathing unsteady, their gazes locked.

She slid her fingers into his hair. "Don't tell me you're sorry or I will knock you unconscious."

"I'm not sorry." He murmured the words against her mouth, dragging his lips over hers, and then rolled onto his back, keeping her in his arms.

"And if you wake up tomorrow regretting it, I don't want to hear it."

"I may never wake up." His eyes were closed. "I think you may have killed me, but I don't want you to feel guilty about that. Just tell me one thing—where the hell did you buy that black, silky man trap?"

She smiled and pressed her mouth to his shoulder. "You didn't like it?"

"I was going to ask if it came in other colors." With a groan he dragged her hard against his body, and she curled around him.

The words *I love you* hovered on the edge of her tongue but this time she held them back, not daring to do anything that might upset this new balance, this new shift in their relationship.

Through the window she could see snow falling like confetti, and she smiled because the moment was perfect, and she wanted to hold on to it forever.

"I can't believe I'm in your bed."

"Technically this is your bed."

"Have you ever thought about doing this? Honestly?"

"All the time."

She thought of the party they'd had in the summer to

celebrate the opening of the Boathouse Café. "You hardly ever looked at me."

"I trained myself not to. I trained myself not to think of you that way. Our friendship was more important to me than a few nights of burning up the sheets."

That was what this was to him? A night of burning up the sheets?

She felt a thud of disappointment and then reminded herself that for Tyler, this was a big step.

He was here with her now. That was all that mattered.

"There's going to be powder tomorrow. Jess will have another snow day." She felt him relax and knew she'd been right to change the subject.

"We'll ski—" he tightened his hold on her "—and this time you don't have to climb out of the window."

"It was fun."

"It was." He stared up at the ceiling. "Tell me something about you I don't know."

"I never thought we'd end up here."

He turned to look at her. "No?"

Janet's words were embedded in her head. "Never thought you'd find me sexy."

"Seriously?" He gave a low laugh. "I always knew you'd be hot in bed."

"You did?"

"Of course. You're athletic, and you have a great body."

She glowed with pleasure. "What happens now?"

He stroked his hand over her hair. "I guess we're not going to need two bedrooms."

"I don't want to upset Jess."

There was a gleam in his eyes. "Why do you think Jess has been spending every night with my mother?"

Brenna blushed. "They're not subtle, are they?"

"Not even a little bit."

"Are you worried that our relationship has changed?"

"Not anymore. I've decided this relationship is perfect."

"You have?"

Smiling, he pulled her back into his arms. "Sure, because now as well as being friends, I can screw your brains out, which is a winning combination as far as I'm concerned."

CHAPTER FOURTEEN

IT SNOWED HEAVILY overnight and, as Brenna had predicted, schools were closed again.

"Snow day! Yay! This is awesome. I hope it snows every day until I'm eighteen." Jess virtually danced around the house, and Ash and Luna bounded after her, caught up in the excitement. "Can we go into the forest and choose a Christmas tree, Dad?"

Tyler, brain dead after a night of uninterrupted sex with Brenna, tried to rouse himself. "Yeah. I need coffee first, though."

Jess looked at him suspiciously. "You don't drink coffee."

"Well, today I'm drinking it." Wondering how he was going to manage to behave normally, he stuck his face in the fridge and kept it there as Brenna walked into the kitchen.

They'd agreed that for now they'd continue to be discreet when Jess was around, so they kept their distance when she wasn't staying with his mother.

"Hi, Jess." Brenna's voice was smooth and warm and he closed his eyes, wondering if he should drop ice down his pants.

"We're going to choose a Christmas tree today. Finally!" Jess grabbed cereal and tipped it into her bowl, scattering half of it across the table. "And then we're skiing. And maybe doing some Christmas shopping. Have you bought anything for Grandma yet, Dad?"

Deciding that frostbite was going to add to his problems, not solve them, Tyler withdrew his head from the fridge. "Not yet. I haven't bought anything for anyone."

Jess sighed. "Men."

"Excuse me." Tyler thumped the milk down on the table. "Do not make sexist remarks."

"Then don't behave in a stereotypical fashion!"

Tyler was about to answer when Brenna sat down across from Jess. She was wearing a soft fleece, and her hair fell, glossy and dark to her shoulders. Her cheeks were flushed, and she stole a look at him and gave a tiny smile that was just for him.

If Jess hadn't been sitting there, he would have abandoned all ideas of breakfast and used the kitchen table for another purpose.

"Coffee?" He forced the word past lips that wanted to be doing something other than talking and saw her blush.

"Yes, please." Her voice was low and he looked at her mouth, remembering everything they'd done to each other. Remembering how she'd looked wearing nothing but sheer black and an uncertain smile.

Crap.

"Let's get the Christmas tree." His voice sounded strangled. "It's a crisp, cold day." Cold was what he needed. Was it possible to have hot thoughts in freezing weather?

Turned out it was, especially when the reason for those hot thoughts was on the snowmobile in front of him.

Out here in the snowy forest, Brenna was in her element.

She drove her snowmobile faster than he did, and he could feel Jess jiggling behind him, her arms wrapped around his waist, holding on tightly as she urged him to go faster and catch her.

They drove through snow-covered blue-spruce woods, following the trail out of Snow Crystal deep into the forest. Once they were safely clear of the resort, Tyler increased speed, and Jess whooped encouragement, loving every minute.

He grinned inside his helmet, remembering the first time he'd done this with his father. He'd been four years old, and all he'd felt was excitement and exhilaration. It had quickly become his second favorite experience after skiing, and he'd spent several winters racing his brothers along the trails.

He could have found any number of potential Christmas trees closer to the resort, but Brenna was intent on making the most of the snow and the sparkling blue day, and she drove skillfully along the trails and pulled in at the chocolate shack.

"Oh, I love this place! Such a cool idea to come up here." Jess sprang off the back of Tyler's snowmobile and crunched through the deep snow to Brenna. "I'm riding with you on the way back. Dad is too slow."

"Yeah, that's me—slow." Tyler was struggling to keep his hands off Brenna. How had he managed to go so long without kissing her? Now he knew how she tasted, how that mouth felt, he wanted to spend every minute of every day kissing it.

Unsettled by that thought, he swung his leg over the snowmobile and removed his helmet.

When it came to relationships, he thought in terms of one day at a time. More often, it was one night at a time.

"Waffles and whipped hot chocolate," Brenna suggested, and she and Jess discussed the various options while they crunched through the snow toward the shack. A curl of smoke hovered above the chimney, and there were tables placed outside, positioned to take advantage of the weak winter sun and the beauty of the forest.

"It's a Narnia day," Jess said happily, tugging off her gloves and dropping them on the table. "Can I have one with everything please? Whipped cream, marshmallows, chocolate sprinkles—"

"Are you sure that's enough?" Tyler asked. "Brenna? Do you want whipped cream?" He glanced at her, intending to keep it brief, but it didn't turn out that way. His gaze meshed with hers. He saw color streak across her cheeks, and he knew that whatever she was thinking about, it wasn't hot chocolate.

"Sounds good." She dipped her head, and he wondered if anyone would think it odd if he stripped off his clothes and rolled in the snow.

"Right." He cleared his throat. "I guess I'm buying."

By the time Tyler returned with three mugs of hot chocolate, he had himself under control. He put the mugs down on the table, and Jess reached for a hot chocolate and poked at the cream with her spoon.

"So are you two going to carry on acting weird all Christmas or is this a one-time thing?"

"Acting weird?" Tyler picked the chair farthest from Brenna. "Weird how? I haven't even looked at Brenna."

"Exactly. Normally, you two talk about everything and anything, but today you're both jumpy. So have you guys had a fight or something?"

"No!" Brenna took her favorite blue hat out of her pocket and pulled it onto her head. "Definitely not. There's nothing wrong. You're imagining it."

Jess's eyes narrowed thoughtfully and then she grinned. "Oh, I get it. Wow."

Tyler's mouth tightened. "What do you get?"

"You two." Jess blew on her hot chocolate, a smug look on her face. "Don't worry about me. I can see you're dying to make out, and that's perfectly fine."

"Jess—"

"Dad, I'm not stupid." Jess sipped her hot chocolate. "And for the record, I'm totally cool with this."

Tyler inhaled deeply. "Sweetheart—"

"You do not have to explain," Jess said kindly. "I'm good with this whole thing so don't hold back on my account. I'm going to close my eyes, think about the tree I want and let you two do whatever it is you're trying so hard not to do."

Tyler glanced at Brenna.

She looked mortified, especially when she turned her head and saw Jess texting under the table. "What are you doing, honey?"

"I'm texting Grandma to tell her the good news."

Tyler cursed under his breath. "Jess, there is no good news."

"Believe me, you two finally getting it together is good news all round. I was worried it might end like Romeo and Juliet and believe me that would *not* have been good news." Jess pressed Send and finished her chocolate. "Right. Let's go and choose the Christmas tree."

BRENNA DELVED INTO the box for another decoration and handed it to Jess, who hung it on the tree they'd dragged back from the forest. Jess was talking nonstop about skiing, and Tyler answered every question patiently.

Brenna wondered how he could ever have worried about being a good father.

She watched as he reached to hang a decoration on a branch that was too high for Jess.

"I'd say we're done here. If we hang any more decorations, there will be no tree showing." He stepped back. "Switch on the lights, Jess."

She scrambled behind the tree, and Ash bounded after her, tail wagging and smacking into the low branches.

Tyler hauled him away, and Jess switched on the lights.

Brenna sat down on the sofa, and Jess came and sat next to her.

"Wow. What do you think, Brenna?"

"Great tree. It's beautiful."

It could have been difficult, but it wasn't. It wasn't awkward because she already loved Jess and even if nothing had happened with Tyler, she would still love Jess.

"Can we watch skiing together? All three of us?"

Knowing how hard that would be for Tyler, Brenna stood up. "Why don't you and I do that while your dad clears up here? I'll grab some drinks and nachos."

She saw the disappointment in Jess's eyes, but they walked into the den together, and Brenna picked a DVD.

They were sitting side by side on the sofa, Ash and Luna on the floor, when Tyler walked into the room.

He handed Brenna a bottle of beer and sat down next to her so all three of them were side by side on the sofa.

Jess looked first at Brenna and then at him. "You're going to watch with us?"

"If you want me to coach you then this is an important part of learning." Tyler stretched out his legs and lifted the beer to his lips. "Go on. Press Play."

His thigh brushed against Brenna's, and she felt the instant response of her body.

It might have been an accident except that the pressure continued, and she knew he was as aware of her as she was of him.

He kept his eyes fixed on the screen. "Watch him make the transition to the new edge—" he took the remote from Jess, paused and rewound the DVD "—did you see that? The end of that turn blends with the beginning of the next. He's pulling a tighter arc and cutting seconds off his time." He talked her through it, analyzing every turn, every movement, and Jess listened intently, asking endless questions about technique and his racing experience.

They'd been watching for over an hour when Jess's phone rang.

She dug it out of her pocket. "It's Mom. She hasn't called me for weeks."

Brenna felt the tension ripple through Tyler.

"You'd better answer it." He sounded calm. "No need to rush."

Jess glanced from her phone to the screen and back to her father. "You're not going anywhere?"

"No. I'll be right here when you're done talking."

Reassured, Jess slid out of the room, and Tyler leaned back against the sofa and closed his eyes.

"That woman is like a dark cloud waiting to rain on our sunny day."

Brenna curled up next to him and put her head on his shoulder. His arm closed around her, and he pulled her close, and they sat like that for a moment, staring at the frozen image on the screen.

"You're hurting."

"Only for Jess." His voice was deep and rough. "This is the first time Janet has picked up the phone in almost a month."

"Do you think it upsets her? She seems pretty settled to me."

"I think it unsettles her when her mother calls." Tyler pulled her closer and kissed the top of her head. "About tonight—"

"We can't. It wouldn't feel right with Jess in the house."

Tyler said something that would have earned him a stern look from his grandmother. "I was afraid you might say that. I may have to roll naked in the snow."

She laughed. "What made you decide to watch the skiing?"

"I couldn't stand the look of disappointment on her face when I said I wasn't joining you." He hesitated. "And I decided it was time. If I'm going to coach her, then I need to do this properly." He stared at the screen, and she slid her hand over his thigh.

"Is it hard?"

He turned his head, a wicked gleam in his eyes. "Oh, yeah—" He took her hand and moved it higher and she felt the thickness of his erection pressing through the fabric of his jeans.

"I didn't mean that!"

"I know you didn't, but I thought you should know anyway." He lowered his forehead to hers, laughing. "I love that you're so shy."

"I'm not shy! Easily embarrassed, maybe." Her mouth was close to his. "And I'm not used to being like this with you."

The laughter faded from his eyes. "You'll get used to it."

Would she? Or would this thing they had be over before it had really begun? Even in the hottest, most intense moments of their relationship, he'd been careful not to say the words she wanted to hear. "Was it difficult for you to watch the skiing?"

He lowered his head and kissed her slowly, taking his time. Then he eased back. "Not as difficult as I expected. Maybe because I'm watching for a purpose. Helping Jess."

"I think she has what it takes to make it big, Tyler."

"So do I." He broke off as Jess walked into the room, and Brenna leaped to the opposite end of the sofa.

"Everything all right?"

"I think so. I got to talk to Carly, not that she says much. Mostly babbling baby sounds. Then it was a whole load of awkward because Mom never wants to talk about skiing, which she hates, so instead of that she asks me about school, which I hate. I told her Brenna was living here. And by the way—" she glanced between them "—you don't have to stop making out because I'm in the room."

Tyler reached for his beer, relaxed, but Brenna's heart was thumping.

She forced herself to ask the question. "What did your mom say when you told her I was living here?"

"Nothing." Jess shrugged and so did Tyler.

"Don't worry about it," he drawled. "She couldn't wait to get away from me, so she's more likely to pity you than envy you. Sit down, Jess. Let's watch some more skiing."

But Brenna couldn't concentrate.

How could she, when she knew something they didn't?

For the first time in her life, she wondered if she'd been wrong not to tell Tyler the truth about her relationship with Janet.

She knew how much the woman loathed her.

Had the years diminished the animosity Janet had always felt toward her?

If not, there was trouble on the way.

A FEW DAYS LATER, Tyler was waxing skis, trying not to think about the time he'd had a whole tech team to do this very thing.

He picked up his phone and called the ski company who had sponsored him, talked about new developments and then ordered two new pairs of skis for Jess.

That was one Christmas present knocked off his list.

Unfortunately, there were plenty still to buy, including the most important one of all.

"I need to ask you a favor." Jackson strolled into the barn and watched as Tyler finished with the ski. "Could you take a small group into the woods later today? People are willing to pay a premium to lay tracks in untouched snow."

His mind still on Brenna, Tyler nodded. "What time?"

Jackson stared at him. "That's it? That's all you're going to say to me?"

"What else am I supposed to say?" He knew she didn't like possessions. She wasn't the type to fill her life with objects, so she wasn't going to appreciate a gift that gathered dust.

"Usually you say no. Then when I push you a bit harder, you scowl and ask how well they ski."

"I assume you've checked that." Maybe he could buy her ski gear. But she already had everything she needed.

"Are you sick?" Jackson strolled around him, eyeing him from every angle. "Drugged? Did you fall and bang your head? What the hell is wrong with you?"

"I said I'd take your skiers. Why does that mean there is something wrong?"

"Because you're not normally so amenable."

He tried to stop thinking about Brenna. "I've given up the fight."

"I saw Jess on the mountain with Brenna this morning. She has real talent."

"She's a natural." Tyler wiped his hands. "I'm going to train her."

Jackson leaned against the bench. "That's good to hear."

"She's good, and there is never any whining or moaning. If she falls, she's back on her feet again. I get a real kick out of seeing her improve." He lifted the ski, feeling the weight of it in his hand, realizing how much lighter he felt.

Jackson reached out and ran his finger down the edge. "She's going to need better skis."

"I've got that covered. Christmas." Tyler reached for his jacket. "Beats buying dolls and pink fluffy stuff. Brenna is harder to buy for."

"You're buying a gift for Brenna?"

"She's spending Christmas with us. Jess doesn't want her waking up on Christmas morning with nothing under the tree."

"Right." Jackson's gaze was steady. "So it's going well?"

"What?"

Jackson raised an eyebrow. "Your relationship with Brenna. You're more relaxed. Mellow. You're not snapping heads off bodies. You're saying yes to things you'd normally say no to, or at least argue about for an hour."

"Am I that bad?"

"Sometimes, especially during the World Cup, but it's hard for you. We all know that." Jackson looked at him expectantly. "So?"

"So nothing." Tyler put the ski down and decided it wouldn't hurt to be honest. "I'm taking this a day at a time. Trying not to screw it up."

"A day? Wow. That's a long-term relationship for you."

Tyler didn't rise to the bait. "Instead of enjoying my pain, you could give me advice."

"You're asking for my advice?" Jackson grinned. "This is a first. Give me a moment to savor the experience."

"You could offer up pearls of wisdom instead of gloating."

"I could, but where would be the fun in that?"

"I need help not to screw it up."

"Why would you screw it up?"

"Because I have every other time."

His brother eased upright. "You won't screw it up. If you do, Sean and I will kill you, slowly and painfully."

Tyler watched him walk away, envying Jackson's calm stability and the fact that he knew what he wanted.

He knew Brenna loved him, and the weight of responsibility was terrifying. It scared him more than any vertical drop he'd faced on the downhill circuit.

If this relationship went wrong he would hurt her badly, but what experience did he have in getting things right?

None.

He finished the skis, took a group of wealthy college kids for their first experience of powder and then went back to the house. Brenna had texted that she was planning to come back for an hour in the middle of her day.

He planned on surprising her.

With time to kill, he opened Jess's laptop that lay abandoned on the kitchen table and started searching for gifts.

What did Brenna like?

He scrolled restlessly through pictures of sweaters, boots, books, DVDs but nothing caught his attention.

Then he switched to a jeweler but he couldn't imagine Brenna having much use for dangling diamond earrings while she was skiing powder.

He could buy her skis, but she already had more than enough pairs along with several snowboards.

Pushing the laptop away, he sat back in the chair. He was useless at this. It wasn't that he didn't know what she liked, because he did, but nothing she liked could be wrapped up and stuffed under a Christmas tree.

Another hat?

No, because she loved her blue one. And he loved the way she looked in her blue one.

He was about to call his mother and ask if she had any ideas when he heard the doorbell.

Assuming Brenna had forgotten her key, he strode to the door and tugged it open, the smile ready on his face. "I thought I'd surprise you—" The words died in his mouth along with the smile when he saw who was standing there.

"That's funny," Janet said calmly, "because I thought I'd be the one doing the surprising."

Tyler gripped the door frame, knuckles white, emotions slamming into him from all sides. "What the hell are you doing here?" He hadn't seen her since the summer, on one of the rare occasions she'd come to see Jess.

"Nice welcome for the mother of your child." Janet glanced past him into the house. "Is she there?"

"No. She's skiing."

"Of course she is. Silly question given that she has your genes and was brainwashed as a toddler." Janet shrugged. "So I'll come in and wait."

"Wait for what? What are you doing here?"

"I've come to see my daughter."

"The one you kicked out last winter?" Tyler snarled the words. "The one you conveniently forget about for most of the year?"

"I didn't kick her out. She was going through a difficult phase." Her gaze shifted from his. "She was hard to handle."

"All the more reason to keep her close."

"Don't judge me, Tyler, when you had nothing at all to do with raising her."

"Your choice, not mine. And we've already said everything there is to say on that topic."

"She's been living with you a year, and suddenly you're an expert on parenting? Since when do you have any idea what a kid needs?"

"I'm not an expert—" his mouth felt as if he'd swallowed sand "—but I know kids should have stability. Someone they can depend on to always be there."

"When have you always been there for anyone? I doubt you can even spell commitment let alone practice it."

"I'm there for her. I would have had her from the beginning. I wanted that."

"Stop kidding yourself, Tyler." The smile vanished. "You were traveling the world with the ski team. It was like playing in a sweet shop. Do you think I didn't see the news coverage? You couldn't keep your pants zipped for five minutes. If you'd had Jess, would you seriously have been prepared to give all that up? Maybe I should have done that. Maybe I should have given her to you. That would have been a better punishment than keeping her from you."

"Punishment?" Five minutes with Janet, and he felt as if he wanted to scrub her off his skin. It was always the same.

"You got me pregnant, Tyler! Do you know what that did to my life? I had plans, too! Things I wanted to do."

"You kept Jess to punish me? What sort of a sick, twisted plan was that?"

"I should have let you take her and watched you try to juggle a toddler and a sex life. Think about it. A yelling baby, no sleep and no one to help out. That was my life."

"What about *her* life? Did you think of that?"

"I took her. I gave her a home. And all the time I was reading this stuff about you partying. Four women in a hot tub?"

He didn't bother telling her that particular story hadn't been true. He was too busy remembering how insecure Jess had been when she'd arrived. "She thinks she ruined your life. She thinks you blame her."

"She's right that having her ruined my life, but she's wrong to think I blame her. I don't. I blame you." Janet's eyes met his. "You should have used a condom."

"You shouldn't have walked into the barn naked."

Janet smiled. "You never did want to take responsibility for anything, did you?"

"I took responsibility for Jess," he growled, "and as for the other—you could have handed me a condom."

"So we're equally to blame. There is no difference between us."

"The difference is that I see Jess as the best thing that has happened in my life. You see her as a lifetime of payment for a childhood mistake."

"Yes, I do. I wanted a termination but my parents stopped me. Did you know that?"

"No." Tyler felt the blood drain out of his brain. He felt shaky. "I didn't."

"I don't know who they were more furious with, you

or me. We were never that close, not the way you were with your parents, but what we put them through ruined any chance I had of a good relationship with them. They didn't want to know me."

Tyler didn't point out that he'd put his own parents through the same thing. Nor did he tell her that there hadn't been a single day when he'd had reason to doubt their love or support.

For the first time in his life he saw how lonely it must have been for Janet and he felt a flicker of pity. "Are you staying with them now?"

"I'm staying in the village. And that's enough talking about old times. It's the future I'm interested in. We're both Jess's parents, and I want to talk about her, so can I come in?"

Tyler hesitated. Like it or not, she was Jess's mother. "If you upset her, I'll make sure you don't come near her again."

"I didn't see any of this macho, protective streak when I told you I was pregnant." Janet walked past him into the house, glancing around her. "Nice. I remember when this place was a dump. You've developed style over the years."

"I offered to marry you."

"That would have turned one mistake into two. You're not marriage material, Tyler."

Tyler held his temper. "You said you wanted to talk about Jess."

Janet wandered through to the living room and stared at the large Christmas tree. "I've never understood why anyone around here would want a tree in the house. This whole damn place is surrounded by trees, there's no getting away from them. There were days growing up when I wouldn't have cared if I'd never seen another tree in my life. How is Brenna? Jess says she's living here now." Her question caught him off guard.

He didn't trust her. Janet didn't make small talk, and she didn't speak without a purpose.

"It's a temporary arrangement."

"Of course, because nothing in your life is permanent, is it? Still, she must think she's died and gone to heaven. She has been in love with you since she was a little girl. Everyone knows that." Janet strolled into the center of the room and stared out the window while Tyler tried to work out her real reason for being here.

"The place is busy. She needed a place to stay."

"And there aren't a hundred other options?" She turned. "Brenna Daniels wants O'Neil after her name. It's what she's always wanted. She spent all her time with the three of you—virtually lived around here. Your family all but adopted her."

Tyler remembered what Jess had said about Janet being jealous of the O'Neils and wondered why he'd been so slow to see it himself.

"Her relationships are no concern of yours."

"They might be, if they affect Jess. If Brenna is involved with you again then it proves she has no self-respect or backbone." Her voice was venom, coated with a thin layer of sugar. "You already broke her heart once, and she's standing there and letting you do it all over again."

For safety's sake, Tyler kept the sofa between him and Janet. "She has more backbone than you will ever have."

Janet didn't move. "If she'd had backbone, she would have seduced you herself when she was eighteen. *She* would have been the one walking into that barn naked, but she didn't. Brenna Daniels doesn't have the first clue about seducing a man."

Tyler thought about the wisps of black and those long legs wrapped around his body. "I wouldn't be so sure about that."

"So you *are* sleeping with her."

"Who I am sleeping with is none of your damn business." He wondered why this conversation was all about Brenna when she'd said she wanted to talk about Jess.

"She is never going to keep a man like you satisfied."

Anger burned through him. "Get the hell out of my house. If Jess wants to see you, I'll let you know."

"She'll never hang on to you because she's not prepared to fight. She should have slapped my face for taking what she wanted so badly, but she didn't do that, either. She never said anything to me. Not one thing."

"Because she's gentle and kind." He gripped the back of the sofa, sickness rising inside him because suddenly he saw the truth, and the truth was so ugly he could hardly bring himself to look at it. "That day in the barn—it was never about me, or you—it was about Brenna. You weren't taking something you wanted. You were taking something she wanted."

If he'd hoped for a denial, he was disappointed.

"You thought it was because you were irresistible? Sure, you're hot in bed and nice to look at but like all the O'Neils, all you thought about was skiing, which is why Brenna fitted right in."

"You were jealous." How could he not have seen what was going on under his nose? "You did it to hurt her, because she was part of my family. She had something you didn't. So you broke her heart."

"No." Janet looked directly at him. "You did that, not

me. You broke her heart, Tyler. And it looks as if she's going to stand by and let you do it all over again."

He didn't trust himself to move so he stood there, hands clenched into fists by his side, his temper roaring in his ears as he watched her leave. She did it in her own sweet time, hips swinging and a smile on her lips.

Wherever the guilt lay, it was obvious she wasn't laying claim to any of it.

Pieces from the past fell into place, forming a hideous picture. Finally, he understood why Brenna had been so reluctant to tell him the name of the person who had made her school life a misery.

Janet Carpenter was the bully.

She'd done everything she could to make Brenna unhappy, and he'd unwittingly been part of it.

He closed his eyes, but all he saw was Brenna, her face pinched and white as she'd struggled into school each day. Finally, he had a name and a face for her tormentor. But he knew that whatever pain Janet had caused Brenna, it was nothing compared to what he himself had done.

He knew now that the reason Janet had pulled him into the Carpenters' barn that day had had nothing to do with sexual chemistry or even teenage lust. She'd wanted to hurt Brenna, and she'd used the weapon she'd known would cause the most damage.

Him.

He waited for the door to close behind her and just made it to the bathroom before he was violently ill.

CHAPTER FIFTEEN

BRENNA LET HERSELF into the house along with a flurry of snow. "It's freezing out there." Shivering, she kicked the door shut and peeled off her coat. "Tyler?"

She knew Jess was still out on the mountain with the rest of the ski team, so when she'd seen his car outside her heart had lifted. They could snatch some time together without worrying about anyone else.

She walked into the kitchen, made herself a coffee and sipped it while looking at the reflection of the sun on the snowy trees. The lake was frozen over, and she could see people skating at the far end.

Hearing the sound of a heavy, masculine tread, she turned with a smile on her face. "I was hoping you were here. What did you—" The words died on her lips as she saw his expression. "What's happened? Are you ill? Has something happened to Jess?"

"No." He leaned against the door frame as if his legs weren't able to hold him up without help.

"Then what?" She put her coffee down and walked across to him, a feeling of sick dread heavy in her stomach. "Are you hurt? Is it your mother?" She knew that only something happening to a member of his family was likely to affect him this way. "Has something happened to one of your brothers?"

He stared down at her, his eyes blank. "Why didn't

you tell me? Right from the start you should have told me, and then none of this would ever have happened."

She felt as if a yawning hole had appeared beneath her feet. "What should I have told you?"

"That Janet was the bully. It was Janet who made you so unhappy right through school."

He knew?

Brenna's legs started to shake. "How did you find out?"

"Answer my question. Why didn't you tell me?" He spoke through his teeth, right on the edge. *"Why?"*

She'd never seen him like this before. She backed away from him until her thighs were pressing against the kitchen table. "Because when I was with you, I forgot about it."

"You let her get away with it."

"That wasn't how it was." She scrabbled for the words that would help her explain. "She tainted the whole of my school life, I didn't want her tainting our friendship. I didn't want to let her do that. Can't you understand that? I didn't want to give her that power. That part of my life, the best part, was mine, and I didn't want her to touch it."

"But she did." His voice thickened. "And because I had no idea what she was doing to you, because you hadn't given me even the slightest clue and refused to give me a name whenever I asked you, I wasn't even suspicious. When Janet walked into the barn naked that day, I didn't even pause to wonder if there was a reason other than the obvious. I didn't stop to ask myself why she'd picked me."

The pain of it whipped across her skin. "You're blaming me for the fact you had sex with her?"

"No. The responsibility for that was all mine. But had I known how she was treating you, it would never have happened." His face was ghost-white. "It was nothing to do with me."

"So now your ego is bruised?"

"My ego is fine. This isn't about my ego, it's about you and all the things you didn't share with me. She did it to hurt you."

Brenna swallowed. "Yes."

"You knew?"

"When she discovered she was pregnant, she came to see me." Brenna closed her eyes, remembering how her mother had urged her to get out of bed, forced her to get dressed and face her tormentor. How she'd given her makeup to cleverly conceal the ravages of misery and pulled out a dress she'd bought that Brenna had never worn. The irony was that on that one occasion, Brenna had finally been the daughter her mother had always wanted.

She'd walked down the stairs on wobbly legs, wondering how she was going to do this, and then she'd felt her mother by her side, felt the strength that came from female solidarity.

"Congratulations." The word had been forced through her stiff lips, and Janet's eyes had narrowed, and it was obvious she wasn't sure if Brenna was congratulating her on the baby or on the fact she'd scored the winning move.

"Why did she come and see you?" Tyler's harsh question dragged her back into the real world.

"She wanted to make sure I knew. She apologized for hurting me, for the fact that you'd chosen her over me. And I wasn't feeling great," *sick, heartbroken, dying a thousand deaths of misery,* "but I could see she wasn't feeling great, either. And that made me feel worse, because she had what I'd always wanted, and it meant nothing to her."

Tyler closed his eyes and pressed his fingers to the bridge of his nose. "She told me today that she'd wanted a termination but her parents wouldn't allow it."

Brenna felt as if someone was squeezing her heart. "I'm so thankful for that."

He paced over to the window. "Why didn't you tell me later on? Maybe not before, but when the whole thing exploded, you could have told me."

"For what purpose? The whole situation was stressful enough for everyone without me adding in that extra pressure. And I wasn't really thinking about you. I was in agony."

He turned to look at her, his expression loaded with guilt. "Do you know the craziest thing about this whole situation? Yeah, it was all my fault—I was irresponsible and I thought with my libido and not my brain—but if I say I wish it had never happened then that means I'm saying I wish Jess had never happened, and that isn't how I feel."

"Of course it isn't."

"She's the best thing about this—" he swallowed "—and the worst thing is the fact that I hurt you."

"It's in the past, Tyler."

"Is it? Janet was in my house this morning. Like it or not, she's Jess's mother. She's always going to be part of my life."

"No, she isn't." A shaky voice came from the doorway, and they both turned.

Jess stood there, her face the color of a fresh fall of snow. "She was the bully. My *mom?* That's true?"

Brenna stood there, helpless, horrified, wondering how much she'd heard.

It was Tyler who spoke. "It seems that way. And I'm sorry you heard that, sweetheart."

"I'm not. I want to know—" visibly distressed, Jess dug her hands into her hair and then dropped them again, a look of revulsion on her face "—why would she do that? Why would anyone do that?"

It was a question she'd asked herself repeatedly. "I think she was unhappy," Brenna said quietly. "Things weren't great at home. And I think she genuinely liked your dad." It had taken her years to see that possibility through the twisted complexity of Janet's behavior.

"If you think that then you've never heard the stuff she says about him."

"I think she was hurt that he didn't share her feelings." She saw Tyler look at her, saw the shock in his eyes.

"I offered to marry her."

"But out of duty, not because you loved her. Because you thought it was the responsible thing to do. I think that was hard for her. She was lonely, scared and very unhappy."

Jess made a disgusted sound. "She made you unhappy. I can't believe she's my mother. She's a monster, and I hate her." She started to cry, great tearing sobs that ripped through her chest. "I wish she'd never had me. I wish I'd never been born."

Brenna was across the room in an instant, but Tyler was there first.

He hauled Jess into his arms, ignoring her attempts to push him away, holding her tightly, murmuring against her hair as she cried and sobbed. "I'm glad you were born. You're the best thing in my life. Always have been. We all love you. Gramps, Grams, Grandma, Uncle Jackson, Uncle Sean, Brenna—" he smoothed her hair "—so many people love you and care about you. And your mom loves you, too. I'm sure she does."

"No, she doesn't, and I *never* want to see her again. Never, ever—" Jess was crying so hard she couldn't speak. "Make that happen! I want you to get lawyers or whatever but promise me you'll make that happen. Dad?" She raised a blotchy face to his. "Do you promise?"

Tyler looked shaken. "I think we need to talk about this when you're calmer."

"I want you to promise!"

He took a deep breath and met Brenna's eyes over the top of her head. "I promise that if that's what you want when you've had time to think about it, then we'll make it happen."

"Why did she even come here?" Jess scrubbed at her face with the heel of her hand. "I haven't seen her, she never shows any interest in what I'm doing, she doesn't even *call* and then she shows up at the door. Did she bring Christmas presents or something?" She pulled away from Tyler and glanced between the two of them. "Well?"

"I'm not sure." His voice was rough. "If she did then she probably wants to give them to you in person."

"You're trying to make me feel better. But I still don't understand why she even came here." Jess broke off and her eyes filled with anguish as the truth dawned. "She came because I told her about Brenna. It's *my fault*. I told her Brenna was living here and how great that was and how much fun, and it must have made her angry and jealous."

"It's not your fault," Brenna said quickly, but Jess wasn't listening.

"She's married. She has another baby, and she still has to come rushing here when she thinks Brenna might be in a relationship with you. She can't have you, and she doesn't want anyone else to have you, either."

Tyler's face was pale. "She wanted to see you."

"Dad, I'm not six years old. If she'd wanted to see me, she would have called me and told me she was coming. We both know she isn't interested in me. She's told me that so many times I've stopped counting, so stop lying and covering for her."

"I'm not covering, but I think relationships are often complicated and messy things. That's why I've always avoided them."

Brenna felt as if she'd missed her footing and stepped off a cliff.

She told herself that his words weren't intended for her, that he was trying to comfort his daughter, but still it felt as if a dark cloud had suddenly appeared in the sky and cast a shadow over her happiness.

"I hate her, and I never want to see her again." Jess sprinted out of the room, and Tyler inhaled sharply.

"Jess!" He ran his hand through his hair and cursed under his breath. Then he glanced toward Brenna, visibly torn.

"Go." She wrapped her arms around herself, thinking only of Jess. "She needs you."

"I'm saying all the wrong things."

"That's not true. There's no right way of smoothing out a situation like this one. All you can do is be there and listen."

"What about you?"

"She's the one that matters right now."

"You and I have to talk." His gaze held hers, and she saw the uncertainty in his eyes.

"She is the priority. I can take care of myself."

And they had nothing left to talk about, she knew that.

The fact that he knew the truth about Janet didn't change the basic facts.

He didn't want a relationship for the long term.

He was never going to be able to get past that fear of commitment no matter how much she wanted him to.

She had no doubt that this latest crisis with Janet would fade, but the real problem wasn't Janet.

It was Tyler.

And no amount of talking was going to change that.

"She's asleep. Finally." Looking wiped out, Tyler sprawled on the sofa and closed his eyes. "What a day."

"You've been up there for hours. What were you talking about?"

"Everything. Her feelings. Janet. You."

"Me?"

"She finally talked about the kids who have been bothering her at school. Finding out that Janet was the one who bullied you seemed to unlock something. It all came tumbling out." He opened his eyes, blinking like someone who had walked out of darkness. "I've never felt so helpless. I wanted to drive down to the school and sort it out, but she doesn't want me to do anything, which puts me in an impossible position. If I ignore her wishes, I lose her trust. I won't risk that, but nor can I let this carry on." He was silent for a moment. "I hate it when she cries. It feels as if someone is twisting a knife in my gut."

"She was crying?" Brenna was on her feet, as stressed as he was. "Should I go up and check on her?"

"No. She wore herself out. She's asleep on Luna. I left the door open a crack in case she wakes again."

"You let the dogs in the bedroom?"

"If you're going to lecture me on consistency in parenting, save your breath. And it was only Luna. I banished Ash. I was worried he'd wake her up."

"I'm the last person to lecture anyone. I think you're doing a great job."

"Yeah?" His voice was loaded with self-derision. "If I'm doing such a great job, why do I have a kid upstairs who cried herself to sleep?"

"That has nothing to do with you."

"Yes, it does. First Janet and now the bullies. I'm the reason they're targeting her."

"Kids can always find a reason if they want one. Red hair. Glasses. Nerd. Tomboy." Brenna paced across the living room. The lights of the Christmas tree were reflected in the huge window, the festive cheer a cruel contrast to the emotions in the room.

"That was Janet's excuse?" His voice was rough. "She called you a tomboy?"

"We're not talking about me."

"So let's. Let's talk about you. It's a conversation that's long overdue. Come here." His voice was soft, and when she glanced across at him, her body heated as she saw the look in his eyes.

"I don't think that's a good idea."

"If you don't come here right now, I'll come and get you. Your choice."

"Jess might wake up."

"I know. I'm not suggesting Christmas tree sex. Just a hug. I need one even if you don't. Come and sit with me."

She did, and instantly felt better as he pulled her into

the protective circle of his arms. She snuggled against him, needing his strength. "I feel terrible for Jess."

"Don't. It was my fault she overheard. I should have been more careful."

"That wasn't what I meant. I can't believe Janet left her husband and baby at home and came here because she found out I'd moved in. It's been years."

"I want you to tell me about it, but not if it's going to make you feel worse. I've made enough women cry today."

"What do you want to know?"

He pushed her hair back from her face, his hand gentle. "When did it start?"

"I don't remember. Early on. She was older than me so I didn't see that much of her, but she used to wait for me after school. Once, she trapped me in the locker room to stop me meeting you. Eventually, a teacher came."

"They caught Janet?"

"No. She told them the lock had broken, and she was trying to rescue me. By then I was so late I thought you would have left, but you hadn't. You were still there. You teased me about staying late studying."

His arms tightened. "You should have told me."

"You would have said something to her, and that would have made it worse for me."

"I remember that day you came out of school with bruises." His voice was low. "How often did she hurt you?"

"Mostly it was psychological. She tried to undermine my confidence. I was *Boring Brenna* or *Brenna the Boy* because I didn't have big boobs. She went out of her way to make sure I knew I wasn't your type. 'Flat chest and brown hair isn't his thing. He'll ski with you but he will never, ever, want to have sex with you.' That's what she said."

"I will kill her." He spoke through gritted teeth. "Tell me you knew she was wrong."

"No, because I didn't. Not for years. I carried those words around in my head, and they changed the way I related to you, and the way I felt about myself. For ages I assumed I wasn't attractive at all. That no man would ever want to have sex with me."

He inhaled deeply. "Why didn't you tell me any of this?"

"That I didn't feel sexy? How was that conversation ever going to happen? We didn't talk about stuff like that. To borrow Jess's favorite expression, it would have been an avalanche of awkward. And to be honest, I liked the fact you treated me the same way as your brothers."

"I had no idea you felt that way. You were always so confident."

"On the slopes, yes. I was a good skier. I was good at a lot of things, but my confidence in myself was really low."

"I thought you were a bit shy. I should have known. You were my closest friend, Bren—"

"Yes, but I was in love with you. And I couldn't talk about it because I believed it." She heard him mutter something under his breath but carried on. "Maybe that's why I've never been good at the one-night-stand thing. I don't know. All I know is that it took me a while to get over that and realize that sexy means different things to different people."

"You're sexy, Bren." Tyler lowered his mouth to hers. "Anytime you want me to prove how sexy you are, say the word."

She lifted her hand to his face, exploring the rough texture of his jaw. "I think that's why she had sex with you that time. To prove she could."

"She came and found me. She knew where I'd be." He held her gaze. "Is it too late to say I'm sorry?"

"It's never too late, but in this case it's not necessary. You didn't owe me anything. You didn't know what was happening. We were friends, that was all." She leaned forward and kissed him. "What happens now? Where is Janet staying?"

"According to Jackson, a bed and breakfast in the village. And she's on her own."

"So she really did leave her husband and baby to come here simply because she heard I'd moved in with you?"

"Looks that way. I'd rather think she came here to see Jess."

"Do you think she'll come back?"

"I don't know. I have to assume she will because she hasn't seen Jess yet. I need to make sure I'm here when that happens. I feel as if I'm standing on top of a slope, knowing it's about to avalanche. And I can't do anything about it." He pulled her closer. "One thing I'm sure about, though. I don't want you to have to see Janet again."

"That's in the past."

"I don't think it's in the past for Janet."

The tiny lights on the Christmas tree sent a warm glow across the living room.

"Jess is the one we need to think about. Everything will settle down. This is difficult, but it will pass, and whatever happens with Janet, Jess knows she's loved and that she has you and the rest of your family. We can't let this spoil Christmas. If we do, then Janet wins."

"I'll take Jess to meet her on neutral ground."

"There's no need for that."

"Yes, there is. I can't stop her seeing Jess, but I don't want her anywhere near you."

"I can handle her."

"You didn't last time. You hate confrontation."

"I chose the path of least resistance. That was my choice. And if I could put the clock back, I'm not sure I'd do anything differently. And neither would you. You wouldn't change what happened because that would mean not having Jess."

"It's a mess."

"It's life. Life is messy. The bad comes along with the good, and you can't always separate them. Let's talk about something else. Have you bought Christmas presents for Jess yet?"

"Yes. I think she's going to be happy." He slid his fingers under her chin, lifted her face to his and kissed her. "I still have a few gifts to buy. I don't suppose you fancy writing a letter to Santa, do you?"

Despite the turmoil inside her, he made her smile. "I haven't done that since I was six years old."

"He'd appreciate some clues on what you want."

"I have everything I want."

It wasn't true, of course, but the only thing she really wanted, she couldn't have.

She wanted to tell him she loved him, but she was afraid of his reaction so she bit back the words and held them locked away deep inside, just as she had the truth about Janet.

CHAPTER SIXTEEN

BRENNA WAS IN THE kitchen making coffee the following morning when she heard a car pull up outside Lake House.

Tyler had left an hour earlier to take a group of guests to ski powder, and it was too soon for him to be back.

"Brenna!" Jess's voice came from upstairs, shrill with panic. "It's my mom! She's here! At the house!"

Her hand shaking, Brenna put the coffee mug down, walked to the hall and glanced out the window in time to see Janet stepping out of the car.

"What is she doing here?" Jess hovered on the stairs, panic all over her face. "I don't want to see her! I want her to go away. And you can't see her, either. Don't answer the door. We'll pretend we're not in. Can we do that? She hasn't seen us. We could hide under the bed or something. I tried phoning my dad but he isn't answering."

"He took that group into the glades as a favor to Jackson. There's no signal."

Which meant she was the only one standing between Jess and a difficult encounter with her mother.

You hate confrontation.

It couldn't be a coincidence that Janet was here. She'd picked a time when she knew Tyler would be out, presumably because she thought Brenna wouldn't put up a fight.

"Go back upstairs, Jess. I'll talk to her and arrange a time for her to come back when your dad is here."

This was one confrontation she was not going to avoid.

Jess looked appalled. "You can't do that. She made you so unhappy. You shouldn't have to speak to her."

"It was a long time ago, Jess. It's in the past."

"No, it isn't. She's here because she wants to upset you. She wants to ruin things between you and Dad, I'm sure of it."

Brenna was sure of it, too, and part of her wanted to do as Jess suggested and stay hidden away until she heard Janet's car drive away.

Her stomach roiled at the thought of coming face-to-face with Janet after so many years.

"Brenna?" Jess's voice was shaky. "Can we hide?"

Brenna turned her head and looked at Jess, saw misery and confusion and remembered the tears and her reddened eyes.

"No. We are not going to hide." Decision made, she pulled on a sweater. This time she didn't need a dress, makeup or her mother to help her stand up and do what was right. "If you don't want to come down, that's fine, sweetheart. I'll talk to her. You go back upstairs and stay with Luna."

"You can't see her by yourself! She was so mean to you."

"She won't be mean to me this time." Brenna walked toward the door, anger licking through her veins.

She stood for a moment, bracing herself to open it, and then she felt something nudge her leg and saw Ash looking up at her, his tail wagging.

"Hey—" She lowered her hand to the dog's soft fur and then opened the door.

For the first time in over a decade, she faced her tormentor. Her first shock was how normal the other woman
looked. Not a terrifying monster, but another human
being. She was older and a little heavier, but apart from
that, she didn't seem to have changed much outwardly.

"Hello, Janet."

Janet looked her over. "I came to see my daughter."

"It's not convenient." Brenna was studiously polite. "If
you call Tyler, he'll arrange a time that suits both of you."

Janet didn't budge. "You haven't changed at all."

Brenna thought of how she'd been back then and how
she was now. Maybe not on the outside, but on the inside
she knew she was different. "I'll tell him you called. He'll
be sorry he missed you."

"So finally you're living under the same roof as him.
It's what you always wanted."

"Drive carefully. The roads are icy." She started to
close the door, but Janet stopped her.

"He is never going to marry you, you know that, don't
you? He's never going to say 'I love you.'"

Ash pressed closer and Brenna put her hand on his
head. "Goodbye, Janet."

Keeping an eye on the dog, Janet took her hand off
the door. "You've been around all of his life, and I'm
willing to bet that not once in all those years has he ever
said those words. He isn't capable of it. You are wasting your time."

Even now, after so many years, Janet knew exactly
which words would hurt the most, and it was like a physical blow. Reeling from it, Brenna almost closed the door
but then remembered this wasn't about her, it was about
Jess.

Standing a little taller, she met Janet's gaze full on.

"What Tyler says to me is none of your business, and who he has a relationship with is none of your business, either. And my time is mine to waste in any way I see fit."

"So he hasn't said it." But instead of looking smug, Janet's eyes looked haunted. "Be careful he doesn't get you pregnant. Don't make the same mistake I did."

"Jess is a person, not a mistake. And you should be ashamed of yourself for saying those words to a child."

"It's the truth. Having her ruined my life."

"It didn't need to. There was help to be had if you'd asked for it."

Janet's bag slipped from her shoulder. "My parents wanted nothing to do with me."

"But the O'Neils were there. They would have helped. They wanted to, but you pushed them away, and you did it to hurt them because you knew how much they all wanted Jess."

"They wanted Jess, not me, and I couldn't stand to be tied to a man who didn't want me. You thought I had no feelings for him, but I loved him, too." Janet hauled the strap of her bag back onto her shoulder. "You were the one he spent all his time with. Every day after school you'd meet him and go off together. I saw you on weekends up on the mountain. Always together."

"You were jealous." Brenna's mouth was dry. It gave her no pleasure to have her suspicions confirmed. "That was why you hated me."

Janet's cheeks were streaked with color. "I gave him the one thing I knew you wouldn't, but afterward he got dressed in a hurry because he'd arranged to meet you. Do you know how that made me feel?"

Why hadn't it occurred to her sooner that the poisonous behavior might have had its roots in Janet's feelings for Tyler?

She'd been devastated, focused on her own survival.

She hadn't looked beneath the surface, and nothing on the surface had hinted at the presence of deep feelings.

She'd run away when she should have stood her ground.

"We can't change the way we behaved in the past, Janet, but we choose how to behave in the future. I don't know why you're here, but I hope it's because you care about Jess and want to see her. Otherwise, you have no business coming here and trying to unsettle a family."

"He's not your family. And no matter how much you kid yourself people can change, he is never going to. That's the difference between us. I see reality, and you live in a dream world."

"I was talking about Tyler and Jess," Brenna said, "and the difference between us is that I don't want him to change and never have. I love him for who he is, and my relationship with him is between me and him, no one else." She stopped because two broad-shouldered men appeared behind Janet.

"Janet?" Jackson's voice was hard, the expression on his face one that Brenna had never seen before in all the years she'd known him. "Get in your car and drive back to wherever you were staying last night. I'll make sure Tyler knows you were here."

Janet turned her head, glanced between Sean and Jackson and then turned back to Brenna. "I want to see my daughter."

Brenna heard a sound behind her, and then Jess stepped forward.

How much had she heard?

"I don't know why you're here, Mom." Jess stood close to Brenna. "You've told everyone I ruined your life, how having me was the worst thing that happened to you, how you wish I'd never been born. I wish you'd let me live here with him right from the start, but you didn't, and there was nothing I could do about that, but I'm older now, and I can make that decision for myself."

"No, you can't."

"Dad is going to make sure I stay here. He promised."

"I hate to disappoint you, but your father doesn't have much practice in keeping promises."

"He'll keep this one."

"And I'll help him keep it," Sean said pleasantly, pulling his phone out of his pocket and dialing a number. "In the meantime, I think this might be a good time to leave. I see our chief of police arriving, and rumor has it his life has been pretty boring lately. He might be glad of some entertainment."

"She was here and now she's gone?" White-faced, Elizabeth sank onto the chair and looked at her sons.

"Yeah, she's gone." Jackson looked up from his phone. "Sean has spoken to a lawyer friend. He's going to get it sorted out. Don't ask me the details."

"Don't ask me the details, either. My knowledge of law comes from watching a few episodes of *The Good Wife*." Sean yawned. "I fix broken legs."

Jackson looked at him. "It crossed my mind to put some business your way."

A ghost of a smile flickered across Sean's mouth. "Crossed my mind, too, but generally I'm better at fixing them than breaking them."

The door crashed open, and Tyler strode into the

kitchen without removing his boots. He had snow on
his shoulders, and his hair was wet. "What the hell has
been going on?" He saw Alice wince and gave her an
apologetic look. "Sorry, Grams. Janet was here? I didn't
know she was coming back or I'd have been here. I'm
guessing she knew that."

Jackson slid his phone back into his pocket. "I think
she chose her moment carefully."

"How did you know she was there?"

"Jess texted us both when she showed up at the door."

"She called and texted me, too, but I was up on the
mountain with no signal, and by the time I got her text it
was too late to help. Thanks for sorting Janet out."

"We didn't sort her out. Brenna did that."

"Brenna?"

"Yeah, Brenna. You don't ever want to make her mad,
I can tell you that." Sean gave a half smile. "You should
have seen her, standing on the doorstep, letting rip. It
was at least five minutes before either of them noticed
us. Even Ash looked nervous."

Tyler looked dazed. "*Brenna* let rip? But she never
said a word to Janet in the past."

"Then I'm guessing she'd been storing them up because she was throwing out plenty of words today. And
they were very well-chosen words, most of them relating
to the quality of Janet's parenting skills."

"Was she upset?"

"Janet? Not visibly, but she's a cold fish. Nothing upsets her."

"Not Janet—" Tyler frowned impatiently "—Brenna."

"Angry," Jackson said slowly. "She was angry. And
then Jess came down and said she didn't want to see Janet
anymore and that you'd promised to fix it."

Alice made a distressed sound but Tyler had his gaze fixed on his brother.

"And what did Janet say?"

"That you'd never kept a promise in your life."

A muscle flickered in Tyler's jaw. "So this lawyer friend of yours—" he looked at Sean "—can he fix it? Because if he can't, we need to find someone who can."

"I trust him. You can talk to him direct."

"I'll do that." Tyler unzipped his jacket, sending snow flying onto the floor. "Are they both back at the house?"

"No. I think Brenna took Jess skiing."

It made sense to him. Whenever life had been hard, Brenna took refuge outdoors. It was the place she went to heal and recover, and it was typical of her that she would have taken his daughter with her.

"I WISH I COULD ski like you." Jess watched as Brenna carved another turn to demonstrate her point.

"You're going to be better than me."

"Never."

"I mean it, Jess." Brenna leaned on her poles, staring into the distance. Jess gave her a worried look.

"Are you upset about what happened with my mom?"

Was she?

She tested her feelings, hunted for the sense of panic and misery that was never far from the surface when Janet's name was mentioned, but it had gone.

She'd faced something that terrified her and survived. Not only survived, she'd triumphed. She'd said what needed to be said and saying it had healed wounds she'd thought could never be healed. She felt different.

"Of course I was upset that she was there, but I think the two of us handled it."

"You were awesome. Do you really think she was in love with my dad?"

"I don't know. Actually, yes, I think she was. It would explain a lot." Brenna drew a pattern on the snow with her ski pole. "How do you feel about it all? Be honest with me."

"I want to stay here with Dad, and I'm terrified she might try and take me away to spite him."

"That isn't going to happen, Jess."

"Are you sure?" There was uncertainty in her eyes. "Because if she does I'll snowboard down the stairs every day until she lets me come home."

Home.

Snow Crystal.

Brenna glanced around her, breathing in the smell of winter. All around her the wide, smooth ski runs dissected the snowy forest like white satin ribbons tied around a beautifully wrapped gift.

"You have real talent. You're going to have to work hard, but you're going to do well."

"I'll work hard. And with both you and Dad training me, I will have improved by spring."

Would she still be here in the spring?

Janet was gone, but her words echoed in Brenna's head, refusing to be silenced.

He is never going to say "I love you."

It was probably the only thing she and Janet had ever agreed on, and she realized she had a decision to make.

It wasn't fair to anyone for her to carry on living here, existing on a diet of hope and nothing else.

"Do you know what I think? I think we should drive home via the store, buy every decoration Ellen Kelly has left on the shelf and turn Lake House into a grotto." She was relieved to see Jess smile.

"Dad would die. It almost killed him putting up a Christmas tree."

Brenna scooped up a handful of snow and threw it at Jess. "I think it's especially important to decorate his bedroom. With ribbons and garlands."

"And glitter. And maybe we could buy a small tree for his room." Jess scooped up snow and threw it back at Brenna, who ducked and skied fast down to the bottom of the mountain.

If this was going to be the last Christmas she spent with Tyler and Jess, she was going to make it a Christmas to remember.

TYLER OPENED THE DOOR to Lake House, fell over Jess's boots and was assaulted by both dogs.

Feeling as tense as he used to before a big race, he was relieved to hear laughter coming from the living room.

"No way. We can't." That was Jess. "Dad will kill us. Seriously. We'll have to move in with Grandma, or maybe even go to the North Pole and live with Santa."

Tyler smiled. Jess may be a teenager, but there were still moments when she was closer to being a child. Wondering what Brenna had done to make his daughter laugh on a day that must have been filled with stress and tension, he pushed open the door and stopped, his vision assaulted by what appeared to be a million tiny lights twisted around the beams and across the windows.

"What the—?"

"Is this straight?" Brenna was balanced precariously on top of a ladder, trying to fix another garland. "Is it the same height as the other one?" As she reached across, the ladder shifted, and Tyler crossed the room in two strides. "Come down." Steadying the ladder, he spoke between his teeth. "I'll do it."

"Don't be sexist. I'm quite capable of fixing lights and garlands."

"She is." Jess handed up another garland. "She's done all the others. Isn't it beautiful? We decided to make it extra Christmassy this year."

"So I see." Still holding the ladder tightly, Tyler scanned his living room. "It looks like a fairy grotto."

And, more to the point, his daughter looked happy.

If the meeting with her mother had unsettled her, there was no sign of it.

"Isn't it cool? Brenna bought every single decoration Ellen Kelly had in the store. Her eyes were almost popping out of her head."

Tyler looked up and met Brenna's gaze. "You hate clutter."

"This isn't clutter. It's Christmas." She secured the final garland and descended nimbly. "So what do you think?"

Tyler refrained from pointing out that with all the fairy lights and tinsel, there was a strong chance he'd need to wear his sunglasses indoors. "I think it's great."

"Santa needs to know which house to call at." Jess pushed a pair of toy antlers onto a long-suffering Luna. "There. She's my reindog. Where have you been, Dad? We were expecting you back hours ago."

Tyler stood for a moment, wishing he could postpone the conversation. He didn't want to be the one to ruin the happy moment. "I had a few things to do."

The laughter in Jess's face was replaced by anxiety. "You saw Mom?"

"Yes. We had a conversation. A conversation that was long overdue."

"Does she want me to go back with her?" Jess wrapped her arms around Luna. "She came here."

"I know. Uncle Jackson told me everything. I'm sorry I wasn't here for you."

"Brenna was awesome."

"She's always awesome." Ash sprang at him, and Tyler pushed him down, his gaze fixed on Brenna. "Thank you for what you did."

"I didn't do anything. Simply had a conversation that was also overdue."

Was it his imagination, or was there something different about her? She radiated a confidence that he normally only saw when they were out on the mountain, and she was smiling as she gathered up branches of mistletoe from a pile on the floor. "So how did the conversation go?"

"Better than I was expecting." He turned his attention back to Jess. "She doesn't want you to go back with her. That's all sorted. You're living here with us, and that isn't going to change. She's flying back tomorrow afternoon, but she has a gift for you, and she wants to give it to you in person. She wants to talk to you. I told her I'd ask you. If you'd rather not, that's not a problem. I'll fix it so you don't have to see her."

Jess stroked Luna's fur. "Why didn't she give it to me this morning?"

"I think she had a lot of things to work through in her head."

"And she's done that?"

"I think she's taken a step. Talking to Brenna gave her a few things to think about." He wondered what they'd said to each other. What truths had been exchanged that might explain the new, subdued Janet he'd talked to that afternoon?

"Where would we meet her?" Jess was looking worried. "Here at the house?"

"I thought somewhere public might be better. I suggested the café in town."

"Wouldn't people gossip?"

Tyler shrugged. "That's not our problem."

"I guess not." Jess kissed Luna on the head and took her time before answering. "Maybe we should see her. We could take Luna. She could wait outside. What do you think, Brenna?"

"I think you should do what feels right to you." Brenna was back on the ladder, this time hanging a large bunch of mistletoe over the kitchen door. "Don't be late for the ice party, though!"

"We won't. I'm so excited. Kayla has arranged to have a big ice sculpture in the shape of a moose as a joke because Dad's always teasing her." Jess slapped her hand over her mouth. "I wasn't supposed to tell you that!"

Tyler grabbed the ladder again. "I promise to look surprised."

"And there are going to be fireworks. And Dana is offering sled rides, and Élise is cooking amazing food then the next day is Christmas Eve and then Christmas Day! I can't wait! Have you finished your Christmas shopping, Dad?" Her gaze slid briefly to Brenna and back to him. "Because you really need to get it done."

And that, he thought, was his only remaining problem.

He had no idea what to buy Brenna.

CHAPTER SEVENTEEN

"WE'RE FULL! NO MORE room at the inn." Kayla danced in the snow outside the Outdoor Center and Élise rolled her eyes.

"Me, I do not understand why you are so happy. It means we will all be too busy to open our Christmas presents."

"It's fun. Tonight is going to be amazing. You should see the ice carving. Finally, I've met a moose that doesn't scare me."

"Where is it?"

"They're bringing it over later. I'm tempted to throw champagne over it and lick it off. We have a fire pit, delicious food and Dana is bringing a dog team over so we can offer short sled rides into the forest. Until I moved to Vermont I thought ice was best in a margarita, but I'm rethinking that. This ice party is going to be great. If it's a success, we'll do it every year."

Brenna checked her phone. She wondered how Tyler and Jess were getting on with Janet. "I've spoken to the ski patrol. They're going to do the torchlight descent before the fireworks start. I hope the weather holds for us. The tree is looking great."

Kayla glanced upward. The beautiful spruce twinkled with lights, and a carpet of new snow lay in deep folds around the base.

"Jackson and Tyler hauled it over here yesterday. We're trying to outdo Rockefeller Center."

"Rockefeller Center doesn't have the advantage of mountains and forest as a backdrop so I'd say you're winning." The cold air wrapped itself around her, and she pulled her hat out of her pocket. "I have to go. I still have things to do before tonight."

"Jess? Are you ready?" Tyler bellowed up the stairs and winced as Jess came thundering down, Ash and Luna at her heels. "You had the dogs in your bedroom again."

"I'm taking advantage of the fact you're worried about me." She reached up and hugged him. "Can they come to the ice party?"

"As long as you keep them on a leash. There will be children there."

"They're good with children!"

"They behave as if they're on drugs."

"Where is Brenna?"

"She's already there. The ski patrol is doing a torchlight descent."

They left the house and walked along the trail that led alongside the lake to the Outdoor Center. The snow lay deep, and the dogs pulled on the leash, following their natural instinct to run.

"They want to pull a sled. That's the next stage of their training. Dad, are you going to marry Brenna?"

"What?" Tyler stumbled and almost fell. "Where did that come from?"

"I wondered. Now that Mom is being so reasonable and all, there's no reason not to."

Panic spread through him like a virus. "No need to rush, Jess. These things take time."

"Dad, you've known Brenna for about twenty-five years, which is a little scary when you think about it. How much more time do you need?"

"*Scary* is the right word. I'm not great at this sort of thing. You know that."

"But you were the one who told me it's okay to feel scared. That the thing that mattered was controlling it."

They'd reached the edge of the path, and the stillness of the winter air was disturbed by shrieks of laughter and excitement.

Jess brightened. "I see Brenna! Come on." She sprinted across the snow, leaving him to follow.

The next few hours passed in a blur of winter celebration. Tourists and locals mingled together, enjoying the food and the spectacle. Dana was kept busy taking small groups for sled rides in the forest, and Élise and her team circulated with plates of warming snacks and jugs of hot mulled cider.

Brenna had disappeared, swallowed up by the crowd, and Tyler looked around in frustration, searching for her.

They hadn't had a moment alone since Janet's unexpected arrival.

Jess was back by his side, munching a slice of pizza when a girl appeared in front of her.

"Hi, Jess."

Jess paused with the pizza halfway to her mouth. "Hi, Molly." She said it cautiously, as if she wasn't sure if what was happening was real or not.

Her gaze skittered to Tyler and then away again.

He felt a knot of anxiety in his stomach because this was obviously one of her classmates.

Jess shifted awkwardly. "This is my dad."

"Hi, Mr. O'Neil. Are these your dogs?" Molly squatted down, giggling as Ash put both paws on her legs and tried to lick her face. Her hat ended up on the snow, closely followed by Molly.

"Ash! Down. Sit. Sorry." Jess was mortified. "I'm still teaching him manners. He's a slow learner. He's a Siberian husky, so really he wants to run the whole time. It's in the genes. I'm teaching him to pull a sled."

"He's gorgeous. I really want a turn on the sled but the line goes on forever." Molly picked herself up, brushed the snow from her jacket and ruffled Ash's fur.

"I'm taking Ash over there for some training after Christmas. You could come if you like. Dana might take us out if she isn't too busy." Jess said it casually, as if she wasn't bothered either way, and Tyler held his breath because he knew how bothered she was.

"Really? That would be wicked awesome. Thanks. Do you have my number?"

They swapped numbers, talked a bit about school and how anything that wasn't skiing was a total waste of a life and then Molly shrugged.

"Have you seen the ice sculpture? Want to come and take a look? You could bring your dogs."

Jess looked at her and then at Tyler, who nodded.

"Go ahead."

She smiled at him, and he smiled back because he understood. He, of all people, knew how important friendship was. How it felt to have someone you could trust.

He watched the two girls sprint across the snow, hair flying, the dogs bounding next to them.

Thinking of friendship made him think of Brenna, and this time when he searched the crowd he saw her, standing a little apart from everyone else as they waited for the fireworks.

He strolled across, resisting the urge to flatten her to the nearest tree and kiss her until she couldn't see straight. "This party is a success."

"Yes." Her cheeks were pink from the cold, and she had her hands wrapped around a cup of hot mulled cider. "Did I see Jess with a friend from school?"

"You did. Her name is Molly, and they've gone to take a closer look at the ice sculpture."

"I'm so pleased. Hopefully, that's a step in the right direction." She took a sip of her drink. "How was your meeting with Janet?"

"Good. I'm never quite sure what's going on in her head, but I've never known her to be so reasonable. Whatever you said to her must have made an impression."

"Maybe it was time for both of us to move on."

Something about the way she said that caught his attention.

He couldn't stop looking at her—at the sooty sweep of her eyelashes and those tiny freckles that dusted the bridge of her nose like the footprints of a butterfly. Her hair, dark and shiny like polished oak, peeped out from beneath her favorite blue hat. "I haven't had a chance to thank you for taking Jess skiing and for decorating the house. That was generous of you. I was expecting her to be stressed out, but the two of you were having fun."

"I enjoyed myself. I've never decorated for Christmas before."

The need to be alone with her overwhelmed his sense of duty to his family. "Let's go back to the house."

It was a moment before she answered, and when she did, her voice was so soft he could barely hear her. "I can't."

"Everyone is watching the fireworks, and Jess is with her friend. No one will miss us."

"That isn't why." She took a deep breath and turned to look at him, her gaze disturbingly direct. "I need to ask you something."

"Ask."

"Do you love me?"

Caught off guard, he almost bolted. "What sort of a question is that?"

"A straightforward one. I'm hoping you'll give me a straightforward answer."

Panic rippled through him. "I've known you my whole life. I have strong feelings for you. You're my best friend."

"I know we're friends. That's not what I'm asking. I'm asking if you love me. I want to know if you can say those words to me."

He looked over her shoulder, assessing the chances that one of his brothers might come and save him. It didn't look good. "I've never said those words. Not to anyone."

"I know, and I respect that you don't throw them around lightly, but that makes my question all the more important. And what I want to know—need to know—" she said it clearly so that there could be no mistake "—can you say them to me? Can you do that?"

He stared at her, feeling as if all the oxygen had been sucked from the air. "Brenna—"

"I need to know how you feel about me, and I need you to be honest. Whatever your answer is, I'll live with it. You're the one who encouraged me to speak up and say what I wanted. I'm doing it now." Her gaze didn't shift from his. "I want the truth. I deserve the truth."

All around them were sounds of the party. Children

laughing, adult conversation and then finally the explosion of fireworks complete with "oohs" and "ahhs" from the crowd. It was a time of celebration, the perfect moment for romance, for declarations of love, for promises.

Tyler looked down at her, into the face he'd looked at for most of his life. They'd grown up together, laughed together, fought, argued, made up and fought again.

And they'd made love in the moonlight, the snowy forest their only witness.

And still she looked at him, her gaze steady on his until his silence seemed louder than the shrieks of the crowd and the fireworks that exploded around them.

He saw a shimmer of something in her eyes in the second before she turned away.

"Thank you for not lying."

"No—wait—I care about you." It was desperately important that he convince her. "You're my best friend. My closest friend. I don't want to lose that."

"I don't want to lose that, either, but I can't be in a relationship that isn't even and balanced. I won't do that because I'd always be wanting more, and that isn't fair to either of us. I love you. I know it makes you uncomfortable to hear me say it, but not saying it is driving me crazy, and I can't live like that." She paused as more fireworks exploded in the sky above them. "I deserve more. I deserve a man who loves me the way I love him. And maybe I'm being stupid, and I won't ever meet that person, but better that than living in this emotional limbo wanting you to feel something you'll never feel."

Every person around the fire pit was staring up at the sky. Not him. He was looking at Brenna.

"What are you saying?"

"I'm saying that if this relationship isn't going anywhere, if you really don't want commitment, then it's time I moved on. It will be hard, but in the end it'll be the best thing for both of us."

"Move on? You mean leave?"

"Yes, I mean leave. You can't, because this is your home and your family needs you, so I'll need to find something else."

Once, when Tyler was fifteen, he'd been caught in an avalanche. He'd felt the slope give way beneath his feet and then he'd been tumbling, spinning, not knowing which way was up or whether he was ever going to see daylight again. He felt the same way now. "You can't do that. You can't leave."

"We'll give Jess the perfect Christmas and get through this and then I'm moving away. That will make it easier on both of us. I need to build a new life, Tyler, and I can't do that if I'm going to see you every day."

He tried to imagine a future that didn't have Brenna in it.

"No." He played the strongest card he had. "You love it here. Snow Crystal is your home as much as it is mine, and my family is your family."

"Don't do that. Don't try and stop me or talk me out of it. It isn't fair. I know this is hard on both of us—" her voice sounded choked "—but I need you to see it from my point of view. In all the years we've been friends, I've never asked anything of you, but I'm asking now."

"What are you asking?"

"I'm asking you to try and understand how I feel. I'm asking you to let me go." Her words were punctuated by a dramatic explosion of fireworks. "I need you to do that."

Without waiting for him to answer, she walked away from him, picking a route that led away from the crowd.

She slipped into the snowy forest with so little fuss it was unlikely anyone but him noticed her departure.

He watched until her blue hat was swallowed up by darkness, until he could no longer see her.

He felt numb with shock. Paralyzed by the brutal reality of her words.

I'm asking you to let me go.

"You look like someone stole the last beer from your fridge." Jackson was standing beside him, a couple of beers in his hand, his gaze fixed on the trail Brenna had taken back to Lake House. "You two had a fight?"

"No." A fight would have been easier. A fight could be fixed with an apology and make-up sex. This was far more serious.

"Do you want to talk about it?"

Tyler, who considered talking about his feelings to be one step up from wearing pink, shook his head. "Nothing to talk about."

Jackson gave him a beer and lifted his hand to a family who was waving to him from the other side of the fire pit. "She's in love with you, Ty."

Tyler ground his teeth. "I remember a time when the conversation around here involved other things apart from love."

"Yeah, we used to talk about debt and whether we'd lose the business. Those were fun times. I miss them."

Tyler rubbed his fingers over his forehead. "This isn't about what I want, it's about what Jess wants."

"Stop making excuses. You know Jess loves Brenna. There's no doubt about what Jess wants, and I'd say Brenna is pretty clear on what she wants, too. From where I'm standing, it seems as though you're the one who needs to make a decision." Jackson paused as more fireworks erupted above their heads. "Is it really so hard?"

"Yes, it's hard," Tyler snapped. "I'm scared of hurting Brenna."

"Why would you hurt her?"

"I'm not like you. You're the stable, strong, dependable one. I'm—" he ran his hand over his jaw "—I'm not. I've never had a long relationship."

"Not true. For a start, there is Jess."

"I don't mean that sort of relationship."

"The principles are the same. You've been there for Jess every step of the way."

"She's my daughter. I love her."

"You've been here for all of us, even if you complain all the time. So what's the problem?"

Tyler didn't smile. "I'm scared! There, I admit it. The whole idea of saying 'I love you' to a woman scares the crap out of me. I've never been in a relationship that's lasted longer than a month."

"You've been in a relationship with Brenna for most of your life, Ty. Think about that."

"That doesn't count. It's different. She's a friend."

"That's why it's different. It's not enough to want to bone a woman into next week. Eventually, you have to get dressed and have a conversation. Spend time together. And when that happens, it helps if the woman is someone you like." Jackson put his hand on Tyler's shoulder. "But if you really don't have those feelings, if you really don't love her and can't say those words, then you have to let her go. I can help her find a job in Europe. I'm not saying it won't be tough on her, but in the end she'll be fine. Brenna's the whole package. Sweet, sexy, loyal, loving—if she moves away and builds a new life, she'll find someone else eventually."

The thought of it made him want to double up.

Something that felt like panic rose inside him. "Do you want a black eye for Christmas?"

"No. I want you to see sense." Jackson gave him an exasperated look. "You've skied down slopes that the rest of us wouldn't touch, at speeds that most of us can't hit without the help of an engine and *this* is what scares you?"

"Skiing is different. I trust myself on the mountain."

"Right. So maybe it's time you trusted yourself when you're not on the mountain. Everyone is scared of something. Being scared doesn't matter. All that matters is whether you choose to let it influence your decisions." Jackson finished his beer. "Go home, Ty. Write your letter to Santa and ask him for the courage not to be your own worst enemy. And you'd better hope he delivers, or Brenna will be out of your life, and you'll be hell to live with."

CHAPTER EIGHTEEN

BRENNA ROSE BEFORE DAWN and did what she always did when she was upset. She went skiing.

She told herself there were other mountains, other men, but still she felt as if her heart were being crushed by a rock, and the misery clung to her like morning mist, refusing to lift. The sadness was smothering, but she knew she was doing the right thing.

Finally, she was moving forward.

She wasn't drifting or dreaming.

After her bumps-and-trees class, she drove to her parents' house, knowing there was one more conversation she needed to have before she could move on with her life.

Her father was out, and her mother took one look at her face and gave a sigh. "I don't even need to ask."

"Can I come in? There are things I need to say." She pulled off her boots, tired of formality, tired of holding back. She'd spoken her mind with Janet and Tyler, and now she intended to do the same with her mother.

Emotional cleansing, she thought. Exhausting but necessary.

They walked into the kitchen and sat at the table with the winter sun sending shafts of light through the window.

She found it harder to speak when she was sitting

down, so she stood. "I'm leaving Snow Crystal. I don't know where I'm going yet, but I'll be looking for a new job as soon as Christmas is over."

Her mother stood in the doorway, not moving. "I don't even need to ask why. I can see it in your face."

"Good. Because I'm tired of saying one thing and meaning another. I'm tired of hiding, pretending I don't have feelings when those feelings are so strong, there are days when I could burst with them. I love Tyler."

Her mother closed her eyes. "Oh, Brenna—"

"That's right, I love him, and he doesn't love me back." She managed to say it without her voice cracking. "And I have to stop wishing and wanting and start living my life, even though I can't imagine how I'm going to do that when he's the most important part of that life."

"I knew this would happen. I warned you."

"Yes, and I didn't listen. And that was my choice. I'm an adult, not a child."

"I didn't want you to make that mistake."

Brenna thought of the few days and nights when her life had been so perfect, it hadn't seemed real. "It doesn't feel like a mistake, but if it was then it was mine to make. And right now instead of blame and a whole bunch of *I told you so*'s I could do with a hug because I've lost my best friend and—oh, forget it—I don't expect you to understand. I didn't come here for sympathy." She covered her face with her hands, and the next moment she was pulled into her mother's arms and hugged as she hadn't been hugged since the last time Tyler had broken her heart.

"I do understand." Her mother stroked her hair. "I know what you're feeling, and you have no idea how much I wanted to spare you that, but it was like watching a train crash and not being able to do a thing about it. And if you think I blame you then you're wrong. How could I blame you? You're not the first member of this family to fall in love with an O'Neil and get burned."

Brenna pulled away. Her head throbbed, and her brain ached with thinking. "What are you talking about?"

"I grew up here, as you did." Her mother sank onto the stool, staring into the distance. "I met Michael when I was four years old."

"Michael?"

"Michael O'Neil."

"Tyler's dad?" Of all the things she'd expected her mother to say, it hadn't been that. "Oh, my God—"

"No! We never—" her mother shook her head "—it wasn't like that, but I wanted it to be. Oh, you have no idea how badly I wanted it to be. There wasn't a day I didn't dream of something happening between us, but to him it was only ever a friendship."

Brenna stared at her mother. Scanned the pretty dress and the neat heels. "I— You were in love with Michael?"

"We were friends. And we stayed friends until the day Elizabeth arrived to cook at Snow Crystal. Michael took one look at her, and he was gone. I saw it happen."

"Mom—"

"You can't help who you love, and I never had any doubt that Michael loved Elizabeth deeply, but that didn't stop the hurt or heal the pain caused by the fact that he didn't love me."

"I didn't know. Why didn't you tell me? It explains so much—explains why you've always hated the O'Neils."

"I never hated them. His family never knew about our friendship. I didn't ski or share any of their interests, but Michael and I were close. We talked. I knew he felt under pressure to take over the business. Maybe he found it easier to talk to me because I was an outsider. Because I didn't have that connection to Snow Crystal." Maura Daniels sat still, her hands frozen in her lap. "For a while after he met Elizabeth, I couldn't spend time near them because it reminded me of what I'd wanted and could never have. It took a while. A long while, but then I met your father and fell in love again. The old feelings faded, but by then I'd put too much distance between us to know how to bridge the gap with the O'Neils. And then you were born, and you bonded with Tyler from the first moment you met, and I saw it all happening again." There was pain in her mother's face. "Michael gave you your first skis. He was trying to mend fences, but I was worried that history was repeating itself, and I couldn't reach out. I regret that we didn't talk before he died. I regret so many things, but most of all I regret the mistakes I made with you. Instead of nurturing your talent, I tried to stop you skiing, tried to stop you spending so much time with them. But you climbed out of your window and went anyway. And maybe I was a little jealous because the O'Neils could give you something I never could. And when it came to Tyler, you were like glue. The two of you were stuck to each other the moment you laid eyes on one another."

"He's my best friend, Mom. He always has been."

"Yes." Her mother reached out and took her hand. "And I could kill him with my bare hands for making you hurt like this."

"He can't help his feelings. You said that yourself."

Her mother tightened her grip. "Are you still living in his house?"

Brenna nodded. "The resort is full, there's nowhere else to go."

"You could come here. You could sleep here."

"I can't." She thought about the tree, the presents, the house full of decorations. *Jess.* "Jess is excited about Christmas, and I'm not going to do anything to spoil that. Last year was hard for her. She hadn't been with Tyler for long, and things were tricky. I want this year to be perfect."

"She'll have to know eventually."

"I'll tell her after Christmas. Mom—" she swallowed "—I thought you didn't like the way I was. That I disappointed you."

"I was never disappointed, but I *was* scared. I felt your feelings as if they were my own. And because I'd had those feelings myself, I felt them all the more sharply."

"But you moved on. You met someone else."

"Eventually. And so will you."

"Will I?" She couldn't see any way that could happen. She'd given all of herself to Tyler. What was there left to give to another man? "What if I don't? What if I always feel this way?"

"You're determined. And strong. I saw it when you were a child and dragged yourself to school every day even though you hated every minute. I saw it when you faced Janet when she came here that morning, and I saw it when you went to work at Snow Crystal, loving Tyler and knowing he didn't feel the same way. Humans are resilient. You're hurting, but you'll carry on living, and the hurting will grow less over time. I'm proud of you, Brenna. I should have made sure you knew that. I should have accepted how you felt about Tyler instead of fighting against it. All that did was put distance between us. It stopped you knowing how much we love you."

Brenna stood, choked by emotion as she felt her mother's arms come around her. She stood stiff, holding everything back until holding back was no longer possible, and she closed her eyes and returned the hug. "I love you, too."

They stayed like that for a moment, and then Brenna pulled away. "I almost forgot, I have something for you. For Christmas." She delved into her bag and found the ceramic pot she'd bought at a craft fair in the summer. It was a sunny blue, and she'd thought it might add cheer during the cold winters she knew her mother loathed.

Her mother unwrapped it, and her expression softened as she turned it in her hands. "It's pretty, thank you. You always know what I like. If Christmas Day is difficult, you can always come over here." Then she smiled. "No pressure, but I want you to know you can."

IT SNOWED HEAVILY on Christmas Eve, and Tyler was finishing his preparations when Jess found him in the den.

"Dad, where have you been all day? I wanted you to ski with me."

"Tomorrow is Christmas Day. I had things to do." Things that had kept him awake most of the night and busy for all of the day. He stuffed packages under the sofa and Jess tried to peek.

"Is my present hidden under there?"

"It might be." It had taken him all day to put a plan together, but he thought he'd come up with a perfect Christmas for Jess. And as for what happened afterward—well, he wasn't going to think about that right now. He couldn't. "How was skiing?"

"The snow was awesome. I skied with Brenna again because we couldn't find you."

"We'll ski together tomorrow. I still have things to do, and I can't do them if you're hanging around watching me."

"Where have you been all day?"

"You told me to buy presents. I bought presents." Had he forgotten anything? He hoped not.

"Did you buy Brenna a present yet? There is still time to get to the store if you haven't. I can help you."

"I've got it covered."

"Are you sure?" She looked at him suspiciously. "What is it?"

"A present is supposed to be a surprise."

"Please tell me you haven't bought her something lame."

He thought about the gift he'd hidden away. "I hope it's not lame."

"But you don't know?" Jess looked worried. "Dad, you'd better tell me."

"I'm not telling you, and the stores are closed now so it's too late. If she doesn't like it then there is nothing I can do about it."

"It's not something for the kitchen, is it? Because women hate that."

"No."

"Something to do with the mountains?"

"In a way." He rose to his feet. "You have to stop with the questions now, Jess."

"I'm sorry, it's just that I want Christmas to be really special."

"I want that, too. Come here." He pulled her into his arms and hugged her. "You're awesome."

"That means you've forgotten to buy me a present."

"It doesn't mean that. I've bought you a present."

"Will I like it?"

"I don't know. I hope so. If not you can lodge a complaint with Santa."

CHAPTER NINETEEN

"HE'S BEEN!"

Brenna woke after a night of little sleep to find Jess at the door in her pajamas, a bulging red sack in her hand. Ash nosed his way past her and jumped onto the bed. Luna gave a whine, glanced at Jess and then followed.

Jess piled onto the bed with the dogs, and Tyler appeared in the doorway, yawning. His chest was bare, but he'd pulled on a pair of jeans.

It was the first time they'd seen each other since the night of the ice party, and Brenna glanced at him briefly, horrified by how awkward everything felt.

How were they going to get through the day?

He didn't appear to have had any more sleep than she had. Those blue eyes were tired, his jaw dark and unshaven.

It was killing both of them, her being here. She felt terrible. He felt terrible.

And she couldn't bear the thought of him feeling terrible.

It wasn't his fault that he couldn't feel the way she wanted him to feel.

For both their sakes, she needed to move on as fast as possible.

"Open your presents, Jess." She moved over in the

bed to make room and then wished she hadn't because Jess gestured to Tyler.

"You come and sit down, too, Dad."

His gaze briefly collided with Brenna's, and then he dutifully sat down on the end of the bed. "Those dogs shouldn't have been sleeping in your bed, Jess."

"They didn't. They slept downstairs all night, and I let them come up two minutes ago." Jess delved inside the sack and pulled out a package. She shook it and sniffed it. "I love guessing."

"The dogs were on your bed all night."

"You don't know that." She ripped off the paper, sneaked a look at him and sighed. "Oh, *fine,* so they were on my bed all night. How do you always know everything?"

"Because I am the head of the household."

"Ash is the head of the household. Do you check on me in the middle of the night or something?"

"Santa told me," Tyler drawled. "Damn dogs drove those reindeer crazy."

Despite the way she was feeling, Brenna smiled.

"Wow—" Jess pulled out a large chocolate bar. Ash whined hopefully, and she snatched it out of the way. "Naughty boy. Sit."

"He is sitting. On the bed." Shaking his head in despair, Tyler shifted position. "You could open your stocking downstairs, then we'd all be a bit more comfortable."

Without looking at Brenna, Tyler stood up. "I'm going downstairs to get breakfast started. Bring your sack down. There's more room down there and more presents under the tree."

He couldn't have made it clearer how he felt, Brenna thought.

He was obviously terrified she was going to say "I love you" again or, worse, ask him to say it.

And she wouldn't.

Not again.

His silence made his feelings clear, and now she had to think about herself.

Staying wasn't an option. It was agony for both of them.

She rescued Luna from underneath a piece of torn wrapping paper and pushed Ash off her feet. "Let's take it all downstairs."

She slid out of bed, thinking how only a couple of weeks ago she hadn't been able to imagine leaving Forest Lodge, but now she couldn't bear the thought of leaving Lake House.

Most of all she couldn't bear the thought of leaving Tyler and Jess.

Through the window she could see it was another perfect day, the snow dazzling white under a Mediterranean blue sky, as if nature was determined to mock her decision to leave.

Worried she'd give herself away, she kept her back to Jess as she pulled on ski pants and her favorite blue sweater.

"I smell bacon." Jess sniffed the air and sprang off the bed along with Ash. "Come on."

Ten minutes later they were sitting around the table eating bacon with waffles and maple syrup tapped from the trees around Snow Crystal.

Brenna didn't feel like talking, but fortunately Jess talked enough for everyone and then they moved into the living room and she started tugging presents from under the tree.

"Your main present is behind the sofa." Tyler stood with his hands tucked into his pockets, a smile on his face as he watched Jess scoot behind the sofa and gasp.

"Skis. Two pairs?" She lifted them, and her eyes went wide. "*Dad*. They're the best. Thanks. Wow. This is amazing." She smoothed her hand over them, studied them closely and put them down on the floor. "I want to go and try them out."

"Good idea. Let's do it now." Tyler stooped and picked up the skis while Jess gaped at him.

"Right now?"

"Yes, before the line for the lift builds up."

"But it's Christmas Day, and you haven't given Brenna her present yet."

"Later. Get your ski gear on. And don't forget your helmet." He strode out of the room and Jess followed.

"Dad, we can do that later. You need to give Brenna—"

"Close the door to the den. I don't want the dogs in there while we're gone."

"I can watch the dogs." Brenna handed Jess her gloves and helmet. "Have fun! Be safe."

Tyler tossed her jacket across the hall. "You're coming, too."

Was he that blind? That insensitive? She refused to believe he didn't feel the tension, as she did. Every moment she spent with him was agony. "Not this morning."

"Jess wants you there." He played the winning card, and she felt a rush of frustration.

Because the whole point of staying had been to give Jess the best Christmas possible, she couldn't find a reason to argue with that.

"For an hour, then."

She could survive one more hour.

They bundled into Tyler's car and drove the short distance to the ski lift.

Jess chatted the whole time, asking Tyler about the skis, what she should do differently, why he'd chosen those and not others, while Brenna sat quietly, watching the trees and the snow beneath her as the lift moved up the mountain.

Would this be the last time she did this?

Would there come a time when she and Tyler could be friends again and coming home didn't involve awkward moments? Or would she be like her mother, unable to bear the pain of seeing him with someone else?

They arrived at the top of the mountain, and Jess stamped her boots into her new skis.

"I love them. You lead the way, Dad."

Brenna was about to ski off and leave them together when Tyler caught her arm. "Stay close. Don't ski off."

He expected her to stay glued to him after she'd made her feelings plain? Was he really that heartless? "Tyler, I'm not—"

But she was talking to herself because he'd already glided away, with Jess close behind.

Left with no choice, Brenna followed, but instead of heading for one of the front runs that led down to the resort, he skied around the back of the gondola and down the small slope that led to their favorite mountain restaurant.

"Why are we skiing this way? You can't be hungry. We just ate breakfast." Jess stopped in a sudden shower of snow, and Brenna joined her.

"Tyler? What are we doing here?"

"I want to give you your gift."

"Here?"

"Yes." He jabbed his poles into the snow and pulled off his gloves. "I have something important to say, and I think—I hope—this is the right place to say it. The other night you asked me a question, and I wasn't ready to answer it."

It was the last thing she'd expected him to say.

Why was he bringing it up now, in front of Jess? "Can we talk about this later?"

"No. We're talking about it now."

"But Jess—"

"Jess should hear what I have to say. You asked if I loved you, if I could say those words to you and the answer is yes, I can." His voice shook. "I love you. I've loved you my whole life although it took a while for me to realize how much."

She stood, stunned, her breath clouding the freezing air as she tried to work out if she'd misheard.

She'd wanted to hear him say those words for so long, she couldn't allow herself to believe them. Hope was a roller coaster she was too scared to ride again.

"You love me like a sister."

"At the beginning, yes. But that changed a while ago."

Her heart was pounding. "I didn't think you felt that way. You panicked when I told you how I felt."

"Yes, I did, but before you judge me for that, you need to remember I've messed up every relationship I've ever had. The fact that I didn't want to mess this one up was a measure of how important you are to me. I've made so many mistakes—" he glanced at Jess "—and having you wasn't one of them, so don't misinterpret what I'm saying here."

Mouth closed, eyes wide, Jess simply shook her head, and Tyler turned back to Brenna.

"—so many mistakes in my relationships," he continued, "I didn't want to make another one. But after you walked away from me the other night, I knew the biggest mistake of all would be letting you go. I was afraid to be with you in case I hurt you, and the thought of hurting you scared me more than anything I've faced before, but then I realized that by letting you go, I was hurting you anyway. And I can't do it. I can't let you go. You're not only my best friend, you're the woman I love. I want to be with you, always."

"Tyler—"

"You've been by my side my whole life, through the worst and the best. When I had my accident, you were the one who sat in the hospital with me. When I couldn't see what the future held, you were the one who refused to give up on me, and you were the one who suggested I teach Jess. When I asked you what you wanted for Christmas, you told me there wasn't anything, and I was trying to think of the perfect gift that would show how much you mean to me. I hope I got it right." He tugged off his glove, reached into his jacket pocket and pulled out a small box wrapped in silver paper and tied with a bow the color of ice crystals. "Merry Christmas, Brenna."

Brenna stared at the box.

"Aren't you going to take it?" He held it out to her, and she noticed his hand wasn't quite steady.

And hers wasn't steady, either, because she was so afraid the gift wasn't going to be what she so badly wanted it to be.

She took it from him with fingers that shook as much as his and fumbled as she unwrapped it, afraid to be wrong. It could be earrings, or a charm—

She blinked as the diamond caught the sun, dazzling her. "Oh, Tyler—"

"Oh, my— *Dad?*" Jess covered her mouth with her hands. "That is the most awesome present *ever.*"

Brenna stared at the diamond and then at him, tears blurring her vision as he took her face in his hands and lowered his mouth to hers.

"I love you." He said the words against her mouth. "I always have, and I always will."

And finally, she allowed herself to believe it. "I love you, too. I always have, and I always will."

His fingers tightened on her face, and he leaned his forehead against hers, holding her gaze with his. "Enough to marry me?"

Her stomach dropped. Her heart flew. "Tyler—"

"I once asked you what you wanted, and you said these mountains. This life. It's what I want, too, but I want to share it with you. Say yes."

"Yes." She was laughing and crying at the same time. "Yes, yes, yes."

"Good. So let's do it right now."

She eased away from him, elated, thrilled and confused. "How can we do it right now?" And then she heard Jess gasp and turned her head to see what had caught the teenager's attention.

"Is that—*Grandma?*" Jess was staring at the snow-covered deck of the restaurant. "What is she doing up here? And Élise. I thought she was really busy in the restaurant today. And Uncle Jackson—Dad—" she turned to Tyler "—what is going on? Are we all having lunch?"

"No, that comes afterward." His gaze was fixed on Brenna, and she glanced from him to Elizabeth and then noticed Alice and Walter, wrapped up in layers to keep out the cold, and behind them Sean, Kayla and—

"Mom?" Startled, Brenna stepped forward. "What are you doing here?" And if seeing her mother was a surprise, it was nothing compared to the sight of her mother smiling at Tyler.

"I'm here in my official capacity."

"Official?" Brenna caught sight of her father standing next to Walter and only then did she notice that her mother was holding something in her hand. "What is that?"

"It's a marriage license. I thought about what your perfect wedding would be," Tyler said, "and I thought you'd want it to be in the mountains with snow, trees and family. You once told me that the things that are important to you are outside, not inside. Blue sky and fresh snow."

Brenna looked at him and then her mother. "You went to visit my parents?"

"Yesterday. After I told them how I felt and what I wanted to do, they stopped wanting to put dents in me. We talked for a long time and then we spoke to my family, trying to find a way to make this happen."

"Mom?" Brenna saw tears in her mother's eyes and then the smile.

"This is the first time I've been asked to bring a marriage license to the top of a mountain, but given the rest of your relationship has been conducted here, it seems right to do this part here, too. We're happy for you, Brenna. So happy."

Still dazed, Brenna turned back to Tyler. "You want to get married here?"

"Yes. If that's what you want."

She couldn't see properly through the tears. "I do,

but—what about clothes? Hair? I'm not even wearing makeup."

"You couldn't look more beautiful." With a rough exclamation, he took her face in his hands, but before he could kiss her she heard Kayla's voice.

"Wedding planner coming through, excuse me—"

With a soft curse Tyler released her. "You've worked hard enough to get us to this point, and now you're going to stop me?"

"Not stop, but delay long enough to make sure the bride is looking her best." Kayla whipped makeup out of her purse. "Hold still."

"She looks great." Tyler gritted his teeth. "This isn't necessary."

"You made her cry, Tyler, and it doesn't matter that they were happy tears—no woman wants to look like crap in her wedding photos." Kayla worked quickly, using concealer, a little blusher and a touch of lip gloss. "There. You are *so* pretty. Élise?"

"*Oui, j'arrive.* Take your jacket off, Brenna."

"I can't take my jacket off! I'll freeze!" And then Brenna noticed her friend was carrying a large bag. "What's in there?"

"Something to stop you freezing." Élise dug her hand into the bag and pulled out a white ski jacket with a soft faux fur hood. "We wanted you to have a white wedding. You have no idea how hard it was to find a white ski jacket on Christmas Eve."

Brenna started to laugh while Jess looked on, wide eyed.

"That jacket is *so* cool. Where did you find it?"

"New York." Kayla eyed Jackson, who rolled his eyes. "I don't want to know the details."

"Good. Because I'm not telling you. A girl needs some secrets. And talking of secrets—Sean?" Kayla beckoned, and Sean stepped forward, a small bunch of white roses in his hand.

"You don't want to know how far I had to drive to find these, either. You owe me big-time for this one." He slapped Tyler on the shoulder and bent to kiss Brenna. "You've been like a sister to me all my life. I'm happy you're going to make it official."

Brenna tugged one of the roses out of the bouquet and handed it to Jess. "Will you be my bridesmaid?"

Jess turned pink with pleasure. "I will. I mean I do." Everyone laughed, and Maura Daniels cleared her throat.

"Are you both going to sign this license? It was kind of Paul to agree to officiate, but I'm sure he's looking forward to enjoying Christmas lunch with his family, and I know Tyler has plans for you, Brenna, so let's get this done."

Plans?

Snug and warm inside her jacket, the roses in her hand, Brenna looked at Paul Hanlon, the local justice of the peace. She'd known him since she was a little girl, and she hadn't even noticed him standing there, hidden behind her father and Walter. "I've spoiled your Christmas Day."

"You've made my Christmas Day, Brenna." He stepped forward and faced the two of them, and after that everything blurred.

She remembered exchanging vows with Tyler, speaking words not from a piece of paper, but from her heart. She barely heard the words he said back to her because she was hypnotized by the look in his eyes, a look she'd waited her whole life to see.

And then he was sliding a ring onto her finger and kissing her as if he never intended to stop.

They were oblivious to their family, oblivious to everyone until Jess tugged at Tyler's shoulder.

"Dad. Enough. We're all getting frostbite."

"C'est vrai!" Élise nodded agreement. "Me, I love romance more than anyone but I am cooking Christmas lunch for half of Vermont so now I need to go, and I don't want to miss anything. Tonight we celebrate. There will be champagne."

"Better order plenty of it because we have lots to celebrate." Kayla was holding Jackson's hand. "Not just that Tyler has finally seen sense, but also that we're fully booked until March."

Tyler smiled against Brenna's mouth. "Good thing you're going to be living in Lake House."

"Come down to the house when you're ready." Elizabeth urged everyone back toward the lift. "Your parents are joining us for lunch. I've invited Tom, too."

A new phase, Brenna thought, as one by one they melted away, leaving her alone with Tyler.

"This is surreal. A few hours ago I was wondering how I was ever going to make it through today. It's gone from the worst day of my life to the best."

"The best hasn't happened yet. I saved that part until last. It snowed last night." He lifted the hood of her jacket to keep her warm, and there was a wicked look in his blue eyes. "I happen to know where we can find untracked powder."

"Now? The others are waiting for us."

"We'll join them for champagne later. It's our wedding day. We should spend it doing the things we love."

"Really? In that case—" Brenna locked her hand in the front of his jacket, and he gave a slow, sexy smile.

"Yeah, that, too."

They kissed until she wasn't sure her legs were capable of carrying her down the mountain, until she was dizzy with the excitement.

"You have to stop now." She spoke the words against his lips and felt him smile.

"I'm never going to stop, sweetheart. I'm going to be kissing you for the next sixty years."

"That would make you more than ninety."

"So? Gramps is still going to be kissing Grams when she's ninety. Probably at the kitchen table. You're an O'Neil now. You need to learn that displays of affection are mandatory at family gatherings to nauseate the opposition."

They skied down into the trees, through deep snow, and this time she led, skiing fast, challenging him as only she could, all the time aware of the unfamiliar weight of her ring inside her glove.

Brenna O'Neil.

She felt the warmth of the sun on her face and stopped in a glade because with a day of celebration ahead, she wanted this moment alone with him.

Tyler stopped next to her, sinking into the snow. "Something wrong?"

"Not anymore." She looked at the trees, cloaked in snow, dazzling in the sunlight. "We spent so much time here growing up, it's perfect to be here today. I can't believe you arranged all this. I can't believe you visited my parents."

"I needed a marriage license. And I needed your parents to know how I felt about you. I didn't want a lifetime of awkward duty visits. I needed to convince them I was serious. That I wasn't playing around."

"Knowing my mother, that must have taken some time."

He laughed. "Most of the morning and part of the afternoon. It helped when I showed her the ring."

"It's beautiful." She pulled off her glove and took another look at it, sparkling on her finger. "I didn't want to leave this place. I didn't want to leave you."

"I wouldn't have let you. We've been part of each other's lives for too long."

She turned her head and looked at the beauty of the snowy forest. "Somewhere around here is a tree with my name carved on it."

"There's a tree called Brenna Daniels?"

"Brenna O'Neil."

Something flickered in his eyes. "You carved that on a tree?"

"I was dreaming, and I wanted to see how it looked."

He lowered his head. "And how did it look?"

She wrapped her arms around his neck. "It looked perfect."

* * * * *

ACKNOWLEDGMENTS

THANKS, HUGS AND KISSES go to my talented editor Flo Nicoll who has worked with me on all three O'Neil Brothers books and sprinkled her own special brand of editorial magic over each story. Thanks also to Harlequin HQN in North America and Harlequin UK for all their hard work in putting this series into the hands of readers, and to my agent, Susan Ginsburg, for her invaluable advice and input.

Right from the start I knew how I wanted *Maybe This Christmas* to end. I'm indebted to Alison Kaiser, Town Clerk from Stowe, Vermont, for her guidance on the marriage license laws in the state of Vermont and for her patience in answering my many questions as I tried to find a way to make my dream ending a reality.

The process of writing this series has frequently slipped into family time, and without the endless support and encouragement from my husband and two sons I would have starved and been found buried under several months' worth of laundry. They are nothing short of brilliant (and I mean that even though they washed a red sock with my white shirt).

I owe the biggest debt of gratitude to my readers who continue to buy my books, thus ensuring I can continue with my dream job, writing them. Thank you. You're the best.

New York Times Bestselling Author

KRISTAN HIGGINS

Everyone loves Jack Holland, but Emmaline Neal *needs* him. Her ex-fiancé is getting married in Malibu and, obviously, she can't go to the wedding alone. In Manningsport, New York, tall, blond and gorgeous Jack Holland is practically a cottage industry when it comes to rescuing desperate women. He knows the drill, Em figures, so he won't get the wrong idea.

What *Jack* needs is an excuse to leave town. Ever since rescuing four teenagers from a car wreck, he's been hailed as a hero, and the attention is making him itchy, especially since his too-pretty ex-wife is back and angling for a reunion. He's always liked Emmaline. She needs a weekend date? No problem.

So when they wind up in bed together, Em chalks it up to red wine and chocolate cake, just one impulsive night not to be repeated. But Jack's pushing for more, and if she lets down her guard, either she'll get her heart crushed again, or discover that Jack's worth more than just dreaming about.

Available now wherever books are sold!

Be sure to connect with us at:

Harlequin.com/Newsletters
Facebook.com/HarlequinBooks
Twitter.com/HarlequinBooks

www.Harlequin.com

PHKH931

New York Times bestselling author

RAEANNE THAYNE

**welcomes you to Haven Point, a small town full of
big surprises that are both merry and bright.**

Nothing short of a miracle can restore Eliza Hayward's Christmas cheer. The job she pinned her dreams on has gone up in smoke—literally—and now she's stuck in an unfamiliar, if breathtaking, small town. Precariously close to being destitute, Eliza needs a hero, but she's not expecting one who almost runs her down with his car!

Rescuing Eliza is pure instinct for tech genius Aidan Caine. At first, putting the renovation of his lakeside guest lodge in Eliza's hands assuages his guilt—until he sees how quickly he could fall for her. Having focused solely on his business for years, he never knew what his life was missing before Eliza, but now he's willing to risk his heart on a yuletide romance that could lead to forever.

Available now wherever books are sold.

Be sure to connect with us at:

Harlequin.com/Newsletters
Facebook.com/HarlequinBooks
Twitter.com/HarlequinBooks

HARLEQUIN® HQN™
www.Harlequin.com

PHRAT907

There's nowhere better to spend the holidays than with *New York Times* bestselling author

SUSAN MALLERY

in the town of Fool's Gold, where love is always waiting to be unwrapped...

Noelle Perkins just got a second chance at life, and she intends to make the most of it in Fool's Gold, California. With business booming during the holiday rush, she is in desperate need of a little reinforcement...and it comes in the shape of gorgeous army doctor Gabriel Boylan. Gabriel's memories of Christmas are less than pleasant, but when fate hands you red-hot mistletoe kisses and love, only a fool could refuse....

Available now wherever books are sold!

Be sure to connect with us at:

Harlequin.com/Newsletters

Facebook.com/HarlequinBooks

Twitter.com/HarlequinBooks

www.Harlequin.com

PHSM899

BESTSELLING AUTHOR COLLECTION

CLASSIC ROMANCES IN COLLECTIBLE VOLUMES

#1 *New York Times* Bestselling Author

MAYA BANKS

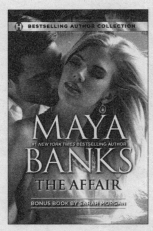

It was only supposed to be a vacation romance.
Passionate, exciting—and short-lived. But when Jewel Henley
arrived for her first day of work at a new job, she realized her exotic
lover was in fact Piers Anetakis, her boss. A boss who had a strict rule
about not getting involved with his employees…

THE AFFAIR

Available December 2014, wherever books are sold!

**Plus, enjoy the bonus story *One Night…Nine-Month Scandal*
by *USA TODAY* bestselling author Sarah Morgan, included in
this 2-in-1 volume!**

www.Harlequin.com

BAC1214

REQUEST YOUR
FREE BOOKS!

2 FREE NOVELS
FROM THE ROMANCE COLLECTION
PLUS 2 FREE GIFTS!

YES! Please send me 2 FREE novels from the Romance Collection and my 2 FREE gifts (gifts are worth about $10). After receiving them, if I don't wish to receive any more books, I can return the shipping statement marked "cancel." If I don't cancel, I will receive 4 brand-new novels every month and be billed just $6.24 per book in the U.S. or $6.74 per book in Canada. That's a savings of at least 22% off the cover price. It's quite a bargain! Shipping and handling is just 50¢ per book in the U.S. and 75¢ per book in Canada.* I understand that accepting the 2 free books and gifts places me under no obligation to buy anything. I can always return a shipment and cancel at any time. Even if I never buy another book, the two free books and gifts are mine to keep forever.

194/394 MDN F4XY

Name   (PLEASE PRINT)

Address   Apt. #

City   State/Prov.   Zip/Postal Code

Signature (if under 18, a parent or guardian must sign)

Mail to the **Harlequin® Reader Service:**
IN U.S.A.: P.O. Box 1867, Buffalo, NY 14240-1867
IN CANADA: P.O. Box 609, Fort Erie, Ontario L2A 5X3

Want to try two free books from another line?
Call 1-800-873-8635 or visit www.ReaderService.com.

* Terms and prices subject to change without notice. Prices do not include applicable taxes. Sales tax applicable in N.Y. Canadian residents will be charged applicable taxes. Offer not valid in Quebec. This offer is limited to one order per household. Not valid for current subscribers to the Romance Collection or the Romance/Suspense Collection. All orders subject to credit approval. Credit or debit balances in a customer's account(s) may be offset by any other outstanding balance owed by or to the customer. Please allow 4 to 6 weeks for delivery. Offer available while quantities last.

Your Privacy—The Harlequin® Reader Service is committed to protecting your privacy. Our Privacy Policy is available online at www.ReaderService.com or upon request from the Harlequin Reader Service.

We make a portion of our mailing list available to reputable third parties that offer products we believe may interest you. If you prefer that we not exchange your name with third parties, or if you wish to clarify or modify your communication preferences, please visit us at www.ReaderService.com/consumerschoice or write to us at Harlequin Reader Service Preference Service, P.O. Box 9062, Buffalo, NY 14269. Include your complete name and address.

ROM13R

New York Times bestselling author

NORA ROBERTS

brings you two classic stories about finding love in the most unlikely of places...

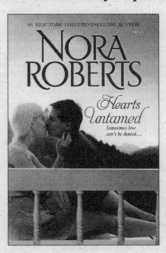

Available now wherever books are sold!

Be sure to connect with us at:

Harlequin.com/Newsletters
Facebook.com/HarlequinBooks
Twitter.com/HarlequinBooks

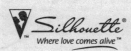

PSNR184